ANDERSON HARP

PINNACLE BOOKS
Kensington Publishing Corp.
www.kensingtonbooks.com

PINNACLE BOOKS are published by

Kensington Publishing Corp.
119 West 40th Street
New York, NY 10018

Map by Thom Hendrick

ISBN-13: 978-0-7860-3421-5
ISBN-10: 0-7860-3421-1

First printing: March 2014

10 9 8 7 6 5 4 3 2 1

Printed in the United States of America

First electronic edition: March 2014

ISBN-13: 978-0-7860-3422-2
ISBN-10: 0-7860-3422-X

To the first Marine I ever knew
and my memory of the night he returned from war
to come home to us.

And to every other member of our military
who has made the same journey.

The sword is ever suspended.
—VOLTAIRE

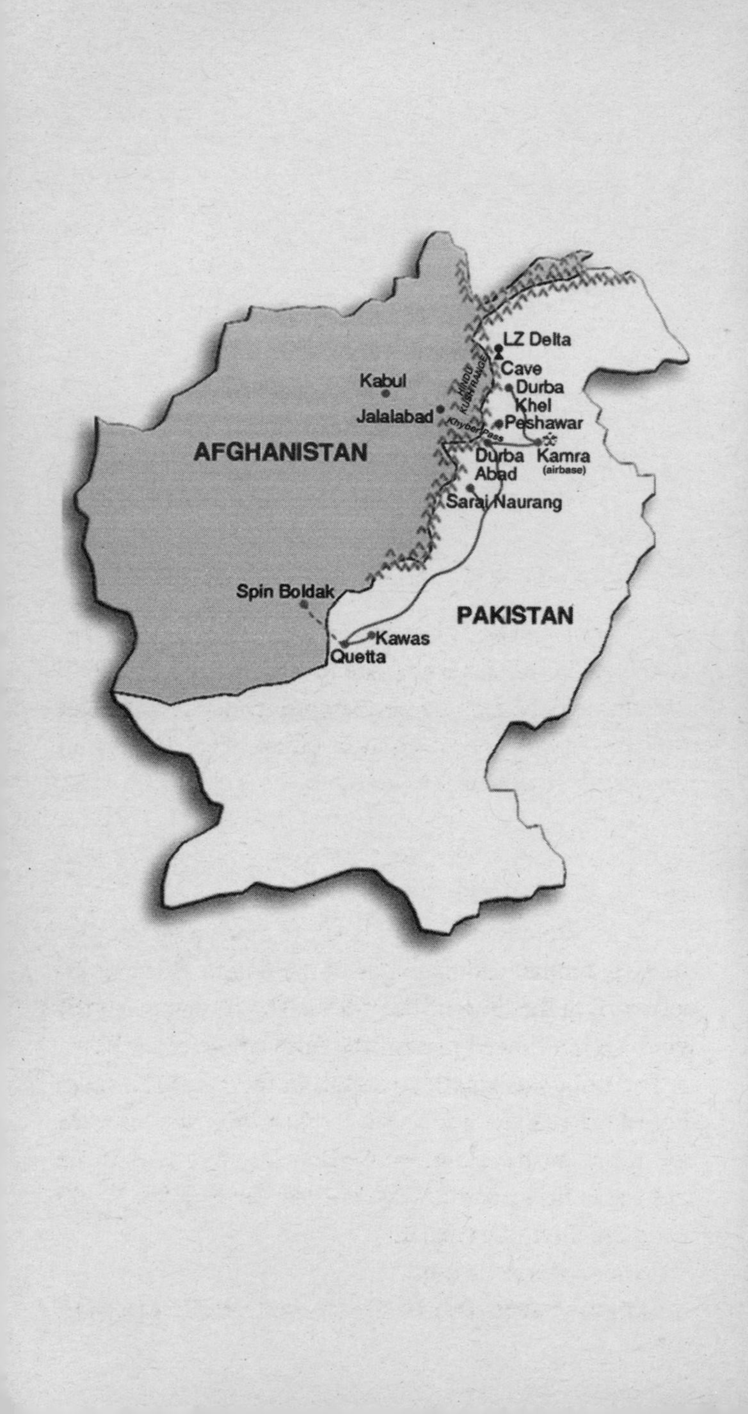
LZ Delta
Cave
Durba
Khel
Peshawar
Kamra
(airbase)
Kabul
Jalalabad
HINDU KUSH RANGE
Khyber Pass
AFGHANISTAN
Durba
Abad
Sarai Naurang
Spin Boldak
PAKISTAN
Kawas
Quetta

PROLOGUE

Fifty-three miles north by northeast of Navy Pier

The pilot gripped the yoke of the aircraft until her tiny, dark hands turned nearly white, choking off all circulation. The Cessna single-engine seaplane fought the wind as she kept it on its heading, south by southwest, just above the whitecaps churning below on Lake Michigan.

"*Allah Akbar*," she kept repeating to herself in a whisper. "*Allah Akbar*."

The floatplane was old, its white paint chipped particularly on the leading edges of the wings. She continued to fight the drag of the old Cessna Skylane and the wind, which flowed just off the nose of the aircraft.

The pilot was small; so small, in fact, that she sat in the pilot's seat on a cushion to raise her up. The seat belt hung on the floor, unused, as she had pulled the seat up as far as it would go so that her tiny feet could reach the aircraft's pedals.

"Allah, please be kind."

The other seats had been removed. White bricks of

explosives were stacked behind and around her. The Semtex had affected the weight of the aircraft, causing it to be even more sluggish in its movements. Her instrument panels featured empty holes where the transponder and other dials were once housed before being removed. All she had that remained was a compass.

The pilot pulled on the yoke as the airplane dipped in the wind. The two pontoons added even more drag, like a hand held out the window of a car by a child, flying no more than twenty feet above the white-foamed water. It was important for her to fly low, despite the driving snowstorm. The transponder's spot on the panel was empty for a reason. It was the transponder that marked the aircraft on radar.

The pilot looked at the map on her lap. A red circle noted the last marker she had just passed.

"South Haven Lighthouse." She spoke the words to herself. The words couldn't be heard. The engine spewed oil, its cylinders old, but it was bought cheaply, and meant for only one flight.

She did the calculations in her head. "Seventy-eight miles."

She was flying slowly. Very slowly. The weight and drag of the old pontoon plane heading nearly directly into the wind caused it to go no faster than a truck on a highway.

"A hundred and ten knots. At best, a hundred and ten," she told herself.

The aircraft would be at the pier in less than half an hour.

"Then I turn."

The pilot turned to the back, looked at the stacked bricks just behind her seat. Red wires led from a button on the yoke to the center of the block. It wasn't the plastic explosive that mattered. At best, that would leave a small crater. It was what was in the center of the blocks that mattered.

Death, she had long ago decided, would not be nearly so bad as her life. She tasted the salt of the tears as they rolled down her face and smiled.

She had been the child with the limp who still insisted on playing football with the boys. Americans called it soccer. In truth, it had been neither. They'd used a ball of tightly bound rags and socks held together by strips of plastic bags looped and knotted together like a web. The boys of Danish Abad had laughed at her, trying to keep up with her limp. After this, they would laugh no longer. . . .

"I will be remembered."

The Chechen had said it would be so. She smiled again. It was important to be remembered.

She lifted her head from the panel to the windshield, which had become coated with a light blue covering of ice and snow.

"Oh, shit!" she cried over the drone of the engine.

The shape of a ship suddenly emerged out of the white.

She dipped her right wing, pulling on the yoke, clinging to control of the aircraft as it slipped by the mass of black steel that had risen out of the white. It looked like a large, ore-carrying vessel, well over a thousand feet long. The rust of the ship and its dark ore cargo had been camouflaged by snow and ice, making the vessel nearly invisible.

In the flash of her eye, she saw a crew member running out of the bridge, waving at her. The deep sound of the horn seemed amplified by the cloud cover as it frantically repeated its warning. She felt the vibration from its sound through the aircraft's frame.

"Oh, Allah, I don't have much time."

The odd sight of her low-flying aircraft would surely be called in on the ship's radio.

The pilot pushed the throttle forward, increasing the pitch of the engine.

In ten minutes, it would be too late. As soon as she turned due west, just beyond the pier, it would only be a matter of seconds.

"Death over humiliation!" Her loud shout of what had become her personal motto belied her true state: the brink of utter exhaustion.

So much she had done. And in such a short time since it all began.

CHAPTER 1

United States Embassy, Doha, Qatar

"O'Donald."

Maggie O'Donald looked up from the e-mail that had just arrived from Riyadh. She'd long ago grown weary of how Pat barked her last name when he wanted to get her attention. It seemed childish.

"You see this?" Pat Stuart peered through the attic office window, a square of bulletproof glass no wider than a framed diploma. The light from outside had dimmed from the typical bright blazing Qatari sunshine to an ominous gray, giving Pat's face a cold pallor.

"You know what *simoon* means?" he asked.

She thought a moment.

"Devil's wind?" Maggie had been in Qatar as a CIA case officer for only a few months, her Arabic still lacking depth.

Pat shook his head. "A poison wind."

Translation notwithstanding, Maggie knew perfectly well what a *simoon* was: a violent windstorm from the west that could mean several days of choking, blowing dust. Winds could reach up to fifty miles an hour as sand and dust crept into every exposed corner, leaving a film of yellow, claylike particles in one's ears and hair and clothes. Even if you wore a surgical mask, you'd find grit in your mouth for days.

The last *simoon* had stripped the color from Maggie's new car, a titanium-green Taurus SEL that she had so proudly picked up at the import desk at the Doha docks only a month earlier. An industrial sandblaster couldn't have done a better job of reducing the vehicle to its primer coat. She'd felt literally sick when she saw it. But, right now, sandstorms posed the least of Maggie's worries.

She returned her focus to the hot e-mail. If it leaked, several would die, including, in all probability, the source. Even if it didn't leak, the survival rate would be low for anyone connected to it. She remembered that term from her training at Langley.

A low survival rate.

"This one's gonna be bad," Pat said, still focused on the coming storm.

Maggie shook her head, trying to focus on the emergency at hand. W. Patrick Stuart III loved to talk.

"You may have to cancel your little weekend in Kuwait," he added.

Maggie's occasional trips to Kuwait were off-limits, even to Pat. And he knew it.

Maggie had put up with her office roommate for more than three months now. In the first week she'd quickly learned that Pat was a true buttoned-down type, a man who wore medium starch in his blue-striped shirts even on a sweltering 103-degree Qatarian day. As the United States embassy's regional security officer, Pat considered the unrest in the Gulf an "opportunity." It certainly was the place to be for an advancing member of the diplomatic corps.

He'll probably do a few tours and then go to work for Exxon.

Maggie had also learned that Pat had a weekly habit of removing everything from his desk and polishing it with a bottle of furniture wax he kept in a lower drawer. The pencils were all lined up in a row, always on the left. Only number twos. A white writing pad on the right. She accused him of being a Prussian, everything kept strictly in order.

And that's not bad, she thought, *if that is what he really wants.*

As for Margaret Elizabeth O'Donald, since her days at Stanford she had been the polar opposite of Pat Stuart, always the one with her desk piled too high. Copies of *Jane's* on weapons and shipping were shuffled with satellite imagery and intelligence memos across her desk. *Jane's* was a spy's bible. The encyclopedia of weapons and war machines contained the specifics on every killing machine ever made. And Maggie took great pride in knowing exactly where each copy lay, along with the scattered photos and documents. She also knew the mess drove Stuart crazy.

Maggie's desk had one other unique feature. In the corner stood a very small photo frame with no photo in it. The bright gold frame, no bigger than a passport, surrounded only a blank, white mat background. Odd as it might look to a visitor, Maggie knew which photograph belonged there—a picture of her lover and herself on an ivy-covered path leading into Battery Kemble

Park in northwest D.C. It had become their traditional meeting place. They had put both of their careers at risk simply by having the photo taken. Maggie could never let Pat or any of her other colleagues see it. Instead, Pat, along with each and every visitor, was left to view the empty picture frame . . . and wonder.

Pat's wife had come the closest to divining its meaning. In fact, Maggie had overheard her describe Maggie as a "distraction" for her husband when Maggie first arrived in Qatar. Pat's wife never spoke to Maggie directly and, for her first week on the job, she hadn't spoken to her husband much either. Pat had attributed his wife's behavior to her pregnancy and the accompanying mood swings she seemed to have. That was not true. Maggie knew that it scared her to death that her husband spent days in the close quarters of a small office with a young, attractive woman.

Since childhood, Maggie had been slender and olive-skinned. When she visited her grandfather's cattle farm, they had called her an *abolengo*, after the land-rich elite descended from the first Spanish to arrive in Colombia. All this, along with her deep green eyes, she had gotten from her mother.

From her father, a lifelong career diplomat, Maggie had inherited only his strong-willed stubbornness and Irish name. O'Donald was not her true birth name. Her birth certificate said Mary Louise O'Neil. Like O'Donald, it was Irish, but like all at the Agency she had an acquired name, and the name she was known as was Margaret O'Donald. She had used O'Donald so long that sometimes she had forgotten that it was not her name at birth. Since the death of her parents, she seldom visited the thought of her birth name. She didn't forget, however, her father's Irish will. She was known to be intractable, but despite her stubbornness, she had inherited a very bright mind. And hopefully, she thought, the judgment needed to handle this e-mail from Riyadh.

I can't forward this just yet.

It would eventually be classified as "top secret: for the eyes of only those who needed to know." She felt the thumping beat of her heart. The chess game had risen to a new level.

Lately, she'd come to suspect that she was being fed information for some purpose beyond what she could immediately see. Over the course of only six months in the field, three of them in the Gulf, she had developed a top-level source in the House of Saud. It all seemed too easy, especially now.

The light in the room began to change yet again. Maggie looked up to see Pat's face darkening in the gloom. A wall of opaque light approached the urban sprawl of Doha, its movement visible now. Sandstorms came that quickly in Qatar.

"It's gonna shut this little city down," Pat sighed from the window. "Hey, I've got something to show you."

Maggie looked up from her desk.

"You remember the reception at the Radisson."

She nodded. "The one for the alumni of Michigan."

"Right." He walked over to her desk with his cell phone. "I took a photo of the Michigan people as they left. I caught this in the background."

A group of people dressed in tuxes and evening gowns were crowded together next to a Mercedes limo.

She looked. "So?"

"Look in the background."

A tall figure was standing next to a small white car.

"And?"

"Something about him struck me."

"Like what?"

"Like he was looking at me." He paused. "Or you."

"You know the drill."

He was the security officer for the station.

"I'm going to send it in and let them run it." Pat walked back to the window, his mind back on the approaching dust storm. It was getting darker.

Still undecided about the e-mail, Maggie rose and crossed the small room. She would say nothing of the e-mail, nor would she forward it to Langley. Not yet. If it turned out to be false, her next assignment might be Guam.

She took a peek through the office's other window. The thick, green-tinted, bulletproof Plexiglas offered only a limited view of the embassy's courtyard and, beyond, the soccer field. The field, she'd learned, had been intended not so much for sport as for its alternate role if the need arose—a helicopter landing zone.

"Is your car in the garage?" Pat asked.

"Oh, yeah." She wouldn't make that mistake again. "After last time—"

A flash of brilliant light came through both windows, and an explosion followed that rocked the building like a sonic boom. It sounded more like a deafening thud than a crack, as if the winds had muffled the sound in some strange way. Book, magazines, and files tumbled to the floor as the bomb's concussion wave passed through the building.

Pat lurched back to the window. “What the hell was that?”

Maggie ran over to the window on his side of the embassy and peered over his shoulder. The sandstorm continued to rage outside.

“They must have used the storm to camouflage the attack,” she said as alarms began to sound throughout the building. The red light from the staircase just outside the door began to flash continuously.

“God, it may not be over.”

“You get the door,” Maggie barked to Pat, who strode across the room and swung the vault door closed. It could be closed and locked from both sides. Pat turned the wheel, spinning the locks.

Maggie ran to her desk. In an instant she inserted a USB flash drive, which asked for a password. She typed in the only one that she knew he would think of. Then she hit the Delete System button on her computer. As if a flashbulb exploded, the screen on her computer went blank. Next, she pulled away the backing of her empty picture frame and slid the small flash drive inside. Putting the mat and backing back in place, she took the .40-caliber Glock from her drawer and joined Pat back at his window. He glanced at her, then the gun.

In the year she had been posted with the Agency, she had never taken out the Glock. She didn’t need the practice. Maggie’s grandfather had taught her to shoot pistols from a very early age on his ranch.

“It must have been a smaller bomb to blow the fence,” he said loudly over the blare of the alarm.

“If that’s true, the next one will come at us right out of that storm,” Maggie shouted back.

Pat turned and stepped toward his desk. Maggie saw him reach for the small photo of his family.

A movement out of the corner of her eye brought her back to the window. Two figures ran across the courtyard, each with a weapon of some kind. The sound of random firing from a machine gun carried from the soccer field on the north side of the embassy compound.

Maggie watched a cement truck emerge out of the darkness and head directly for the embassy's main building. It seemed impossible, but the boy driving the truck seemed barely able to peek over the steering wheel.

"Oh, God."

The flash blinded her like a direct glimpse of the sun. And then everything went pitch-black.

CHAPTER 2

7,553 miles west of Doha

William Parker awoke to a lightless, frigid bedroom, the green glow of his digital clock the only thing visible.

Damn.

As always, his internal clock had awakened him at three in the morning. He clenched his fist, once, twice, and then a third time. The flexing was a habit, often unconscious, that he had developed during therapy to restore function to his scarred right shoulder.

Parker sighed and pulled back the covers, standing up in the chill air. It was that time of year, the changing of the seasons, between air-conditioning and heat. Not that the heat would come on any time soon. He preferred a cold house. The clock, though . . . the clock was hers. Parker didn't need one. Combat had taught him sleep was a luxury, not a necessity. His experiences in North Korea and Iraq had trained him to sleep for only a couple of hours at a time. Even the bed was a comfort he had never gotten accustomed to.

Parker made his way through the dim light, down the stairs, across the wide space of the lodge's main room to the kitchen. He could smell the faint, oaky scent of burned wood from the fireplace. He closed his eyes as he swung the refrigerator door open. Intentionally blinded by his shut eyes, he felt for a bottle of water on the second shelf. She insisted on Dasani.

As the fridge door closed, he opened his eyes while looking away, but the last flash of light from the refrigerator passed through the kitchen, across the main room and through the large windows and doors that framed the stone fireplace. In the instant that it occurred, Parker sensed a stranger outside.

He moved along the wall, again in the darkness, keeping something solid to his back. Another habit of combat.

Always keep the unknown in front of you.

He reached the corner of the room near the glass door on the far right of the fireplace. Others might have reached for the Glock in the drawer by the kitchen's back door, but the pistol would be the least of any intruder's worries.

The grassy knoll behind the lodge was draped in the darkness of a quarter moon. Most, looking out through the door, would be barely able to make out the shapes of the rocks or the tree line beyond the edge of the small field. Here, though, darkness wasn't Parker's enemy.

Something moved.

A hidden motion detector triggered a light. And like a flashbulb, it froze a deer standing in the center of the field. Her large eyes stared directly into the light. The green reflection from her retinas glowed with an almost chemical color. The condensation from her breath left a wisp of a cloud around her nostrils. Except for the faint sign of breath, the doe was motionless, as if a wax model of a living creature.

Parker smiled.

The doe stood her ground for what seemed to be an eternity, not moving a muscle, frozen, and then, as if comprehending a danger, she darted off into the darkness. Her white tail flashed in the light.

Parker's smile vanished.

He, too, sensed something.

CHAPTER 3

Doha

The concussion wave from the blast shattered windows for several city blocks. The crater on the edge of the building quickly filled with water as the main to the embassy was sheared in the blast. It was an odd sight of smoke, blowing dust, and water spraying up from the pipe.

As the winds began to die down with the passing of the storm, the smell of burned rubber, wood, and human remains overwhelmed the rescue crew searching through the pile of debris for survivors.

The soccer field now served as the landing zone it was intended to be. Marine CH-46 and CH-53 helicopters landed in wave after wave, and soon the smoldering ruins were an armed camp with men in black jackets stenciled with FBI combing the wreckage. The teams were on the grounds before the last of the wounded had been pulled out from under the timbers and shattered blocks and bricks.

Later, the regional security analysts concluded that

the attack was a failed attempt on the ambassador's life. They were wrong.

The actual target had been caught under the torn wreckage of the building, her legs pinned under a fallen steel roof beam. The rescuers raced to jack up the beam and pull the limp body out from under the weight of the debris.

Locked within Maggie O'Donald's unconscious mind was the password.

"Air Force Six-Niner hold."

The bulky C-17 Globemaster's brakes squealed as the medevac aircraft stopped on the taxiway of the Al Udeid Air Base just outside of Doha.

"Six-Niner holding." Colonel Danny Prevatt looked over to his copilot with impatience.

"What now? Don't they realize we need to get these folks out of here?"

Danny Prevatt knew that several of the wounded were on the verge of their mortality. It was an unusual record for his trade, but Prevatt had never lost a life on a mission. He attributed it to speed, skill, and mostly luck. As always, he planned to climb fast and catch the best winds.

The only good news for the bombing victims was that the aircraft had been at Al Udeid refueling when it had gotten the word. Every asset had been only minutes away. And Air Force 69 knew what it was doing. Danny and this crew had flown well over a hundred medevacs out of Iraq without a loss. But time remained the critical factor.

God, what a base. From his vantage point in the

pilot's seat atop the C-17, Danny could see out over the fifteen-thousand-foot runway and, across from the runway, the new hangars and aircraft bunkers of Al Udeid. It was one of the newest military airfields in the Gulf.

During his last stopover at Al Udeid, Prevatt had asked another pilot, "Why Qatar?"

"Well, beyond its central location in the Gulf . . ."

Qatar had not been known to most of the world until after September 11. The small country jutted out into the central Gulf. Surrounded by Saudi Arabia to the south and west, UAE to the southeast, and, across the Gulf, Bahrain, Kuwait, Iraq, and Iran, for centuries it was a crossroads for merchants. Its markets were full of Persian rugs, some more than a century old, smuggled out of northern Iran, and brass handcrafted urns and pots. Each rug reflected the mystical story of its respective village in maps of bright colors, designs, and shapes. The pots were shaped by hand with thousands of blows from a hammer that turned the metal.

"In 1939," the pilot had explained to Prevatt, "Sheikh Thani bin Mohamed let engineers dig for oil. They didn't find one oil field but three. Stacked on top of each other. Any one of 'em would've made this Bedouin tribe a bunch of billionaires. But then, below those three, they found the mother lode."

"Some super oil field?" Prevatt asked.

The pilot had shaken his head. "The largest natural gas field in the world. Trillions, and just when the rest of the world was starting to perfect LNG technology. Liquefied natural gas. They cool the stuff down so that they can ship more of it and send it off to Europe for all of those energy-efficient cars."

Now, thirty or forty years later, all that wealth stood visibly on the skyline of Doha.

Still, it was just another assignment to Prevatt. He loved to fly and sighed at the mere thought of his next assignment: A desk job, which to a pilot was akin to a diagnosis of cancer. At least this one would be in the Afghanistan theater. As air officer to the combined task force, he would control the air support for all of the units in theater. If he couldn't fly, at least he would be in combat. It was a cruelty of advancing rank. Colonels could not fly as often as captains. He would be grounded by his rank and he resented it.

Just as he now resented waiting on the runway. For what?

Prevatt looked up to see another aircraft on final approach in the distance.

"Air Force Six-Niner, hold for a passenger."

His copilot stared at him. "What the hell is this?"

Prevatt scratched his head. "I think it's that same executive bird that was going into Kuwait last night."

He had heard the call sign as the two aircraft crossed the North Atlantic on parallel paths the night before.

As he spoke, a Gulfstream jet landed before them with full flaps extended. As the wheels settled on the surface, the massive jet's engines went into reverse, causing the aircraft to stop like a hesitant motorist with a last-minute light change. Smoke from the wheels puffed up underneath the aircraft. The pilot wasn't wasting any time. The plane turned to taxi off the active runway and, as it did, the bold markings of blue, white, and silver, reading UNITED STATES OF AMERICA, flashed by the C-17. It was one of the executive fleet aircrafts and Prevatt watched as it pulled up on the side of the medevac aircraft, stopped, and, as its door opened, two armed men carrying M4 automatic rifles ran down the stairs to the tarmac. Both stood at the wingtip of the jet as another man, dressed much like a corporate attorney, disembarked and approached the C-17.

"I know that man," Prevatt said.

His copilot peered over the pilot's seat, craning to see the three men on the ground.

"Yep, it's the damn deputy director of the Central Intelligence Agency himself," said Prevatt as he turned to the flight chief behind him. "Go unbutton the door for our guest."

The CIA deputy director climbed from the blazing hot tarmac into the dark, chilly cave body of the C-17, losing his vision for a brief moment. The flight chief took him by his arm and led him and his bodyguards over to three web seats in the bay of the aircraft.

"Strap in, sir. We are ready to roll." The flight chief pulled their seat belts out and handed them to the passengers.

As Deputy Director Robert Tranthan fumbled with the seat belt, his senses began to adjust to the dark, the antiseptic smell, and the quiet. The jet rolled forward and the engines began to spin up in a high-pitched roar, until he felt the aircraft tilt sharply upward. As it tilted and his eyes were adjusting, he realized the bay was crammed, wall-to-wall, with the beds of the injured, the IVs swinging with the motion of the aircraft. Some were lying on gurneys, their heads wrapped in white gauze stained bright red.

"Sir, I'm the physician in charge of this flight." A lanky, thin man in a desert brown flight suit stood over Tranthan. His stethoscope hung loosely around his neck. He seemed to be a look-alike of Jimmy Stewart and had the same easy, soft voice.

"Robert Tranthan." They shook hands. "We diverted from Kuwait City when we heard about the bombing. How many do you have on board?"

"Thirty-six wounded."

Tranthan was concerned only about one in particular, but he could not allow himself to be so direct.

"How badly?"

"I am told that the cement truck had about two tons of explosives in it. It left a crater twenty feet deep. Six are reported missing, with no trace that they ever even existed." The flight surgeon spoke in his low, somber voice, barely audible over the hum of the engines.

"How about the ambassador?"

"He wasn't even in the embassy at the time."

"Do you know who the six missing are?"

"Two Marine guards, three locals, and the security officer."

Maggie had mentioned Pat Stuart to Tranthan on several occasions. In fact, she had even joked that Tranthan must have put her with Stuart, a married man with a pregnant wife, so that Pat could act as her watchdog.

"What happened to the security officer?"

"He apparently stepped directly into the bomb blast. Nothing was left."

"What about the woman that worked in his office? Our representative at the embassy, Ms. O'Donald?"

"A concussion, but that isn't the worst of it. A beam of the building collapsed onto her legs. It took them over an hour to get her out of there. If the blood loss isn't too great, she might make it."

"God." Tranthan rested his head in his hands. His first sight of her had been those long legs walking down a stairway at Langley. He felt sick. She would not have been in Qatar but for him. It was supposed to be a safe place. The relationship risked both his marriage and career. He had weighed the decision carefully. She had to be placed out of sight. He just didn't anticipate how good she would become in her new job. Maggie was coming up with intelligence that no one had even a hint of.

"Where is she?"

"Follow me." The doctor led him back down the row of injured to the last gurney. She looked so small and helpless. Two small tents covered her legs and a bandage covered most of her head.

"Maggie," he whispered into her ear. As he leaned over, he saw the shimmer of the gold necklace and locket that he had given her prior to her leaving.

"Maggie," he whispered again, but she didn't react to his voice.

He touched her on her shoulder. She turned upon being touched, and he looked directly into her dazed eyes.

"Hey," Maggie mumbled under the morphine.

"Hey, you, Maggie E." Tranthan didn't really know what to say. He could only use his nickname for her. Her body was virtually covered except for those green eyes. Blood-tinged gauze wrapped around her head.

She seemed slow to react to his words, as if, in addition to all the other damage, the blast had deafened her.

"Hey," she said again. He could see the confusion in her face. "We need to pull it."

"Pull what, Maggie?"

"Pull it out."

"Pull what out?"

"Yes, that's what we need to do. Pull it out." She kept repeating it in a low, soft mumble. It was as if she knew what to do but had no idea how to do it. *Pull it . . .* He had no idea what she was talking about. Perhaps the severe head injury had torn apart her memory.

"Where's Pat?"

He could barely hear her voice.

"He may be in the back," he lied.

"His phone . . ." Then her eyes closed as she drifted back into a deep morphine sleep.

"Hey, Maggie E, don't try to talk. Just take it easy." Tranthan spoke the words encouragingly, but he felt desperate, powerless. He slumped next to her until sleep found him as well.

Tranthan stayed by the side of her gurney throughout the long night. And it was near the end of that night that he made a decision. Both his career and his life had been nothing but safe moves, but now he wanted to hurt someone very badly.

After the C-17 landed and Maggie was installed in the trauma unit in Landstuhl, Tranthan's Gulfstream returned to Washington. He could not be seen with her at the hospital. He knew she would understand.

"There was an operation two years ago called Nemesis." Tranthan leaned over his desk back at Langley, speaking in a low voice to the man across from him, Brigadier General Ben Arnault of the United States Marine Corps.

"I don't recall that one," said Arnault.

Tranthan expected this. Those who knew of the Nemesis operation could be counted on the fingers of one hand. One of those lived at Number One Observatory Circle.

"A man named Scott was involved," said Tranthan. "I know him. He used to be pretty good."

"Yes, sir," said Arnault patiently.

Tranthan liked his young general. Arnault came to work at 4:00 A.M., seven days a week, and rarely left until well after dark. He was always at his desk, just outside Tranthan's office, except for two workouts a day, which were runs or swims while the boss was either at lunch or away from Langley. He also felt comfortable being assisted by a military man. Tranthan himself had left the army after twenty years of service. He could have become a flag officer like Ben Arnault. Tranthan was fluent in both Farsi and Russian, he had a master's in psychology, and he was married to the oldest daughter of the senior senator from Pennsylvania. His ticket had all the necessary punches. But after the wedding he had been offered a mid-level appointment to Langley and left his army career behind. It had been the right decision. Langley represented the chance to play in a different game, at a different level. It had an edge. It had opportunity. It gave a young, ambitious climber the chance to gain a lot of IOUs. And he knew he would be good at it. But still, deep inside, Tranthan was aware that he'd always be that army major. And if he were honest with himself, he got a charge out of having a flag officer at his beck and call.

"Oh, Ben. Before I forget . . . The security officer in Doha may have had something on his phone."

"Yes, sir."

"Can we check that out?"

"Done."

"Good. Now, as I was saying . . . Nemesis involved the insertion of a freelance agent into North Korea. A missile engineer was working on a project that would have given them an intercontinental ballistic missile that was going to take out our Pacific GPS satellites."

"Was he a North Korean?" Arnault asked, eyebrows raised.

"No. In fact, he was a Marine."

"Korean American?"

"No. Anglo as you and me. Someone they brought out of the reserves."

"Really? Why—"

"Have you ever heard of Cardinal Mezzofanti?" asked Tranthan.

"Yes, sir," Arnault said. "Learned about him at Monterey."

Arnault also spoke Russian after being sent to DLIFLC for a year. The Defense Language Institute in Monterey was a special opportunity for any young officer.

"Spoke thirty or more languages, right?"

Tranthan nodded. "Not only spoke them, but spoke them with the exact inflections and dialect of someone who'd spoken them all his life. He'd hear the language once, and that's it: he'd be perfectly fluent."

"So this Marine was a—" began Arnault.

"*Is*, Ben. He's a Mezzofanti—Korean, Arabic, you name it. I need to get to him immediately."

"Yes, sir. How, sir?"

"Start with Scott, the guy who ran Nemesis. He can get to the man we need. Get *him*, and we can get somewhere with this bombing. I want to know who was behind it." Tranthan looked his aide directly in the eyes. "I want to know who hurt Maggie."

CHAPTER 4

South of Atlanta, Georgia

The pickup truck turned off the paved highway onto the dirt road, plunging into the absolute darkness of the predawn countryside. Although the leaves of fall had started turning to orange and yellow, the trees still managed to blanket out any hint of the quarter moon. A cold front had dropped the temperature down.

"How far now?" Michael Hendley had come straight from the graveyard shift of the credit card–processing company. He should have been exhausted. He leaned back in the seat, put his Red Wing hunting boots up on the dashboard, and pulled his John Deere cap down.

"Get your damn boots off my truck."

Mike Hendley smiled and dropped his feet. His cousin's Silverado had cost him a year's worth of pay in brush guards, running boards, and winches alone. A gentle level of harassment was common between the cousins, and it went both ways.

Not only was Hendley not feeling the expected fatigue, but also he hadn't been this charged up in months. Unlike his father, Hendley used his past military experience with computers to become "white-collar labor," as he liked to call it. He made sure that the machines kept churning throughout the night as they received data from credit card users around the world, but he was still caged in a cubicle with walls he could touch with extended fingertips. It paid well and, as with his cousin, it kept him in fairly new trucks, but the clock moved slowly on the graveyard shift. Deer hunting season, however, woke him up. Even the remote promise of a record buck turned the adrenaline on. Sleep was a low priority this time of year.

"Almost there," said the cousin, referring to the end of the road, not their final destination. After parking the truck, they'd hike at least another three miles.

Mike knew that his cousin wouldn't have even told him about this hunt except that a hike out of the woods with a two-hundred-pound trophy buck would have been too much for one man.

He also guessed that wherever they were going, they would be trespassing. But it really didn't matter. A trophy deer with a point score over 170 was a five-figure deer. A hunting show had paid $25,000 just to display a record Boone and Crockett buck last year at its show. In Mike's world, $25,000 would buy a new four-wheeler, a Winchester with a scope, and a letter from the tax man six months later reminding him of the government's share.

At the end of the road it was so dark that Hendley only sensed his cousin's presence by the sound of his movement as he came around the truck.

"We bringing the deer stands?" Mike asked. The hunter, to pull himself up into a tree to gain elevation and a clear line of sight, used the camouflaged aluminum cage with a seat.

"No, this place is sweeter than that. Just wait and see."

The cousin turned on his small LED light, which only illuminated the trail directly in front of him. Mike followed closely behind except for the occasional limb that slapped him in the face. With their rifles slung over their shoulders, the pair cut deeper into the woods, their breath billowing up in the light as it bobbed up and down on the trail.

The cousin stopped at the top of a hill, fully out of breath, and shined his light on the metal sign that said POSTED—NO TRESPASSING. He turned off the flashlight for a brief moment. They stood still while their eyes readjusted to the dark. What were the chances anyone was nearby? Even in the deep woods of Georgia, it was rare to not see a light well off in the distance or hear a truck grinding through gears on some highway. Here, they both stood in absolute darkness and silence.

The hunters followed the ridgeline as it skirted around a small, deep valley below. Again, they began to climb up, over an outcrop of rock that led to a ledge. After passing through a stand of hundred-year-old pine trees, they had come to a forest of hardwood trees, oak and hickory, which now stood below them. Hendley knew that the oak and hickories would pull in the deer. The shelter of the hardwoods and the constant supply of acorns created the perfect chemistry for a record-setting buck.

"This is sweet."

"You haven't seen anything yet." The cousin lay down on the grassy ledge.

The grass soaked Mike instantly as he lay prone with his rifle. The damp, chilling wet grass from the early morning dew quickly passed through his sweat-shirt, but the excitement of the hunt overcame any discomfort.

They lay side by side in complete silence. He could only hear his heartbeat as both hunters waited for the sun to rise. Their vantage point well above the valley robbed the deer of one of its primary defenses: smell. They knew, as the sun began to turn the darkness into a pink-and-orange-tinted gray, that the first hour was critical. It was then that the big buck would move, searching for food. They could not budge during that critical time, as the slightest hint of their movement or even a faint whiff of their scent would cause the game to dart back into the deep woods. One mistake and the day would be a waste.

The cousin saw the buck first. He tapped Mike on his arm and pointed. It came out of a thicket well to the left of the field. It was a full buck, with a huge rack, eighteen separate points that he could count from this distance. The deer had to have survived several years to have gained that size and shape. Boone and Crockett dimensions, easy.

The deer moved slowly, stopping often to search and scan the surroundings. His head turned like a natural radar. Without the deer's movement, it would have been virtually invisible. But the movement was to the hunter's benefit. It gave the animal away.

"Biggest I ever seen," Mike whispered.

The cousin shushed him with a gesture, then pulled the front stock of the Remington 700 rifle under his forearm, steadying the weapon on the brace of his elbow. The Leupold scope amplified the dawn's light, allowing him to see much farther than the human eye. The deer moved again, only a short step. It was a long shot, but with a calm hand he could make it.

Mike watched as his cousin drew in a breath. Slowly, the shooter would let it out and squeeze. Then—

Click.

The sound of a safety being released on a weapon. A rifle. Every hunter ever born knew what it meant. But it wasn't his cousin's rifle and it wasn't Mike's. The sound had come from behind them.

They both lowered their rifles.

"What are you doing?" The cousin was pissed.

"That wasn't me."

"Fellows, you need to slowly pull back the bolts." The voice came from behind and above them. Close. Very close.

Mike turned to see the oak tree above the ledge. He couldn't make out anything. His eyes followed the shape of the tree from its gnarled, barked base up to the first branches. Still, nothing. The voice was too close for it to be from farther away.

His cousin was still pissed. Without looking the cousin called back, "You ain't got no right to tell us what to do. We got the landowner's permission."

Mike waited for the man's response.

"I *am* the landowner. Now turn around and get up."

Mike turned over on his side, and as he did, the sleeve of his hunting shirt pulled up just enough to reveal a part of a tattoo on his forearm, an anchor and a globe.

"Where'd you serve?" the man said. His voice came from somewhere near the base of the tree, but Mike still couldn't see him.

"Artillery at the Twelfth Marines," Mike said proudly.

"Who was the Twenty-fourth MEU commander?"

Was it Mike's imagination, or had the voice warmed a degree or two?

"Colonel Jordan."

"Bucky Jordan?"

"Yes, sir. That's what they called him."

The voice paused for a moment. "You two come back another day. Same exact place. Just one day. If that buck comes on this field, you can take him. But only once. And only one deer. Agreed?"

"Yes, sir," said the cousin.

Hendley repeated it. "Yes, *sir*."

William Parker stepped away from the oak, dressed head-to-toe in the camouflage that perfectly matched the hardwood tree. The coat, gloves, hat, and pants all bore the same camouflage pattern, making him indistinguishable from the same shape and colors of the bark and limbs. He remembered the tag. It quoted Webster: *Incapable of being apprehended by the mind or the senses*. It was 5.11 Tactical gear, named for the difficulty of a mountain climb. Like the gear's namesake, Parker had undertaken a 5.11d climb once. It had been called the Unfinished Symphony, a brutal two-day trek. But the 5.11 gear had handled it. And he could tell now by the confusion in the young man's eyes that their camouflage worked equally well.

Parker smiled as he shouldered his Woodsmaster

rifle, a boyhood gift from his father. He hoped he hadn't scared the pair more than necessary. It wasn't so much that they had trespassed, invading his lonely, quiet perch above the field. No, it was the intrusion into this particular time of day, the only hour that seemed lately to offer Parker the brief, few minutes that he could sleep. The morning twilight worked like a powerful drug, enabling his mind to stop and body to rest. And all the better when he did it outdoors.

It was ironic that now, in his currently quiet life, that Parker felt more sleepless than ever before. It seemed as if life had suddenly become *too* simple. He no longer worked as a district attorney, galvanized by his duty to the murder victim's family or the challenge of beating his opponent. He no longer had to worry about cross-examining the drug dealer's alibi witness or the toxicologist from the University of Chicago. He no longer had to worry about picking the right jury or pleasing the temperamental judge.

Instead, Parker's world had become a condition of continual boredom. The Korean mission had brought reward money, tons of it, and with the millions of dollars came the ability to buy the land that his father had only dreamed about. But Korea had also cost him the D.A.'s job. He simply could not go off for several months on a secret mission and still be the district attorney. He had no interest in representing criminal defendants, and he didn't have the patience to learn how to be a civil lawyer. So as a consequence, he had too much time on his hands. His life had become ordinary, and he couldn't stand it.

Most days he headed out as early as three in the morning. The woods were a friend. But this day's opportunity for rest had passed. The sun was climbing high already, revealing a brilliantly clear and perfectly cloudless blue sky. A singular streak of white cut across like a chalk line over a light blue blackboard. The contrails of a passenger jet pointed to the east. Parker saw a flash of light bounce off the aircraft as the morning sun's reflection aligned itself briefly with the steel skin of the airplane and Parker on the ground. He thought of the passengers in another airplane.

God.

The thought made him sick.

Pan Am Flight 103 had only been in the air a short time when, over Scotland, the bomb had torn through its forward cargo hold. Seats 3A and 3B were held by the Parkers, coming back from a rare pre-Christmas holiday trip to London. Their son was finishing up exams in college. Only hours before, Parker's mother had called him from Gatwick. It was one of those "too little said" conversations that he would regret for the remainder of his life. It was only a few hours after that conversation that he had heard the news bulletin. It was one of those moments that he remembered exactly where he was, exactly what he was doing, and exactly the bitter chill of the day.

The explosion in the thin air at thirty-one thousand feet immediately sucked out several of the passengers, whom the experts later theorized were instantly pulled into the engines that continued to spin at full speed and were shredded by the turbines and then effectively cremated by the jet blast. His mother must have been one of them. There was no trace that she ever even existed. The woman who held him close, who stayed up with him when he was sick, who stood much shorter when she reached up to hug him, was gone.

Parker began the hike back to his cabin, in the opposite direction of the hunters, to the west side of his land. The cabin—more of a lodge situated on a small plateau—looked out over the river on the far west border. A dark blue Toyota Camry, newly parked, awaited his arrival. The car was familiar, but this was an unusual time for her to come here. She'd left for work hours ago and should not have been home until dark.

Parker came in the back door and set down the rifle, its chamber clear. Clark's shoes were next to the door. She was in the kitchen fiddling with the coffeemaker, a stainless-steel machine that ground up the beans. He couldn't have cared less, but she liked it.

"What's going on?"

Clark looked up with those deep green eyes, but her face was etched with concern. "Someone from the Agency is looking for you."

CHAPTER 5

The cabin

Clark Ashby poured a cup of coffee into her travel mug and held it with both hands. It was an unusual hour to see each other. Normally she'd have been rushing to the courthouse for work. But this day was different.

"Who was it?" William asked, standing across the kitchen from her.

"Scott." She waited for him to respond, then looked away.

"Don't you have a trial?" he said at last, rather clumsily changing the subject.

Clark held him with her gaze. "When the judge told me a Mr. Scott had left a message about you, I had someone else cover for me."

"How about a run?" William was trying to change the subject again. He gave her a small smile. "It's perfect weather for the trail."

She sighed and put the coffee mug on the kitchen counter. "All right. Let's go."

Clark hadn't been a runner until she met William Parker, but she had always had a runner's body type. Or so she'd learned. For months they had been training for her first marathon, enduring the ten-mile cross-country run that they called the trail. At first, the idea of a marathon had struck her as simply being insane. Clark hadn't run a mile since her Alpha Chi Omega sorority charity functions at Vandy, and that had been more of a walk. Strolling a few miles for cancer was not a marathon. Twenty-six miles seemed unimaginable.

She was already dressed for the run in her shorts, bright orange T-shirt, and New Balance shoes. He made her wear orange. It was the only protection against another trespassing hunter willing to shoot at anything that moved. But the slim running outfit showed a suntanned, freckled, tight, fit shape. Clark had cut her hair for the heat of the summer into a short, angled bob and wore a baseball cap during the runs. Despite the change of weather, she kept it short. Clark could tell from the way William looked at her that he liked it.

"It'll take a second." William bounced up the stairs to the bedroom to change.

Damn. She felt angry, mostly with herself. She assumed and expected too much. William could be distant at the best of times. She'd clearly broached the return of Mr. Scott the wrong way, shutting down any chance of him openly discussing Scott's return. But, Clark wondered, how could she have done it differently?

"You're too slow," she yelled up to him from the bottom of the wide-slat pine stairs. William had built the stairway himself from dark, aged heart-of-pine logs taken from a house close to the riverbank. The old cabin that was scrapped for its parts had stood there, over the river, for well over a hundred years. The logs were seasoned with time and showed black knotholes that curled in the wood as if Van Gogh had painted them on.

"What's the hurry?" he called back. "You're not going back to work, are you?"

"No, it's just getting hot." The day had warmed up quickly. If the New York Marathon ended up taking place on an unseasonably warm day, Clark would be ready for it. Training during the south Georgia summer had drained her, literally, requiring an infusion of water by the gallon. She carried her bottles everywhere.

Finally William joined her, and they still had a head start on the building heat of the day. Even with the chill of the Canadian clipper that had blown through, the days would warm up quickly. They would be soaked in their sweat in only a matter of minutes. And even though it was daylight, the mountain trail would descend into several forested valleys that were still in near complete darkness. So they began slowly, sticking to the roadway for a few miles as the sunlight would continue to illuminate the forest. By the time they reached the end of the gravel road, they could see the entrance to the trail. She would feel the temperature drop when they turned into the dark, well-canopied trail. It wound down the river for several more miles. The land covered well over three thousand acres and stretched west and south along the Chattahoochee River. As usual, William led, but she stayed right in his draft.

The trail wasn't easy. The river valley had a small run of hills that paralleled it to the east. An occasional deep ravine cut through the hills, down toward the river, causing the trail to take a sharp cut down and a stair-like climb back up on the other side. It was the perfect training ground to develop the endurance needed in the marathon. The hills would push the heartbeat up, and then a short downhill would let it briefly recover before the strain of another hill pushed it up again.

And lately he would cut her no slack. In the beginning, she knew he was impatient as she strained to even keep up with his slowed-down pace. But she had also begun to run at the courthouse, on the lunch breaks from the trials, and slowly she'd built up her strength and endurance.

The trail cut through the forest following a creek that fed into the main river. Several of the rocks were worn smooth on this section of the path, which had been a part of the main trail of the Creek nation traveling to the west. Once he'd stopped after a rainstorm, picked up a flat, milky white, well-chiseled, triangular-shaped rock, and handed it to her.

"An ax head cut from chert."

She'd felt an edge that could slice through a sheet of paper.

"It's probably been sitting there for a thousand years."

The ground around their feet had been littered with sharp-edged rocks, both big and small. As she focused her eyes, she saw fragmented shapes of clay shards from broken pottery left there from some Indian village hundreds of years ago. Clark picked one up and held it in her hand. A perfectly straight line, with a row of dots and curls, marked what was once the curvature of a small clay pot. The hand that crafted it had been dust for centuries.

Eventually, the runs became a way for them to communicate better with each other, a side benefit, along with the endorphins, that came with marathon training. They had been carrying out this regimen together since early March. All summer, as the miles built up, they had stuck to a rigid training plan. Over the last two months they had built the training pattern up to two workouts a day. Now, in the final weeks, both were in top form. The long Sunday runs involved two laps of the trail, which pushed the mileage well above twenty miles. She was ready for the race.

The New York Marathon was meant to be special. It was her first. He would run it with her and help push through the wall at twenty miles. When she had doubts, he would push her on.

Would have, she corrected herself. For with Scott's call came the very good chance that William would not be available to run the marathon with her.

"You know if I do what Scott wants," Parker said, "I can't tell you anything about it. Not who, or where, or when. Nothing."

It was almost as if he'd been reading her thoughts.

"Yes." She knew what it all meant. And she didn't want him to go. But his insomnia, his restlessness, and his recurring nightmares provided a compelling counterargument. Clearly, William was not cut out for the quiet life, which must have felt like premature retirement to him. If taking on some other military or intelligence mission meant he'd be happier, then it would be hard to convince him to decline it. In truth, Clark had been expecting such a telephone call for some time.

"Can you trust Scott?"

"Probably not."

"Oh." She looked away, wondering if she should have ignored the call. She had been the only feasible way of contacting William Parker. His cabin lay far off the beaten path and had no phone, computer, or fax. To call Scott back, in fact, William would have to use her cell phone.

"What exactly did he say to you?"

"Just that he needed to talk to you as soon as possible. It concerned your past."

William stopped running and turned to face her in the path. "My past?"

She nodded.

"Exactly how did he say it involved my past?"

Clark took a breath, then said what William must have expected—or feared:

"He said it was about Lockerbie."

CHAPTER 6

South of Quetta, Pakistan, near the Afghanistan border

The two pickup trucks bounced wildly over the potholed road, leaving a cloud of dust as they crossed the plateau. Both were packed with turbaned, bearded men carrying AK-47 rifles. Occasionally, the lead truck would veer off what little was left of the paved road and cross the open desert, thus avoiding sandstorm drifts, some as high as the cab of a truck, that blocked the main route.

Finally, they entered through a mountain pass into a small, enclosed valley. The valley was surrounded by a range of jagged, chocolate-brown mountains with steep walls that cut down to its floor. On the far end of the valley, a village of mud and stone huts tucked up against the mountain ridge. As they got closer to the outskirts of the village, they came to a patchwork of small apple orchards.

The valley lay so deep among the steep mountain walls that any eyes in the sky could only view the village when directly overhead. The American drones were limited in number. They had to cover much of both Afghanistan and the western border; consequently, they flew farther to the north. Satellites were a bigger concern. The people on the ground now knew the flight path and timing of such space-borne surveillance craft. When one of the birds was set to fly over, everything below would become quiet. The farmers would tend their apple orchards. The children would play and smoke would come from the fire pits. The truck-mounted weapons were pulled under the thatched roof huts. They knew the game.

The lead truck turned off the main road, cutting through a small orchard, the driver haphazardly avoiding the branches of the trees at breakneck speed. His passengers swung with the truck as it cut first to the left and then to the right, ultimately sliding to a stop in front of a small, stacked-stone house tucked up against a wall of rock at the far western edge of the valley.

A short, pudgy man, dressed in a white-collared shirt and Western-style brown slacks, stepped out from the passenger seat of the truck. Despite his young age, Masood Akram, barely in his thirties, had a round face and large belly that pushed his white shirt out over his belt. The people of this tribe all looked hungry, had sunken eyes, and showed ribs when they removed their woolen shirts. One look told them that Akram was from the West.

There he is.

The reason Masood had withstood nearly thirty-six hours in cramped economy seats.

"Yousef!"

A man turned, hearing his name, and stopped playing with his two children for a second. Then one of the toddlers climbed on the father's back, giggling loudly, as the father yelled out a false protest and then collapsed as if overcome by a stronger force.

This is the man who will change the history of Islam. Masood waited patiently for Yousef to turn his attention to him.

The guards in the truck jumped out and formed a semicircle, facing out toward the orchard as Yousef al-Qadi stood to greet his younger visitor.

"*As sala'amu alaikum,*" Masood said to Yousef.

Yousef al-Qadi was much more than just the senior member of the pair. The rail-thin, bearded man with a bony face and mournful eyes was even much more than a leader of the jihad. Yousef had set forth a goal that eclipsed even the greatest aspirations of al-Qaeda. It was this goal that had brought the younger visitor halfway around the world to meet Yousef al-Qadi.

"*Walaikum as sala'am,*" responded Yousef, who turned to his two children, kissed them on their foreheads, and instructed them to go inside to their mother.

"Your children are growing up quickly."

Yousef al-Qadi smiled at the compliment. "You have come a long way. I have some tea and sweet biscuits for you."

He pointed to an opening in a stone gate to the side of the mud-walled house that led to a small garden, where a trellis, covered with a twisted, thick grapevine, provided some shade and protection. A stacked-stone wall surrounded the garden, and the smell of juniper followed a faint breeze up from the far side of the valley. They sat across from each other on two stone benches as a woman brought a silver tray with small, blue Dresden china cups of tea and a plate of honey-soaked biscuits. The tray and china seemed strangely out of place in these bare surroundings.

"Tell me, how is your charity work?" Yousef spoke softly through the gray-streaked beard.

"Fine, very fine."

Masood had first heard of Yousef al-Qadi as a young college student in RU-MSA, the Rutgers University Muslim Student Association. The other students spoke of the mythical man who'd graduated from Harvard Business School as bright, serious, and often intense. He also had become the man who would create a new state of Islam out of the wilderness of western Pakistan, Afghanistan, and some of Iran—the old kingdom.

As always, Yousef wore the dress of a Pashtun, the common brown, rough weave of a farmer. Masood knew that Yousef's dress belied his lineage. Yousef was a sayyid, the son of a descendant ten generations removed from the Prophet's daughter, and the son of the Muslim Brotherhood. But he had also been the only son of his father's third wife, the daughter of a gardener, who as a child of fifteen was married to the owner of the garden. She was a frail child and had died giving birth to her son.

Being the grandson of a gardener, Yousef received little respect from the other wives and children. Growing up that way, Yousef's self-respect had come to depend upon the respect of others. Masood understood this, for he'd had a similar childhood.

Yousef's father would often beat the child with bamboo, as it was the father's role to be the strict, often brutal disciplinarian. In many families, the mother would be there to console the child. Masood's own father had disciplined him with a stick, but Masood could always turn to his kind mother for relief. For Yousef, however, there had been no consolation.

But the father did give Yousef al-Qadi something Masood did not receive. Oil. Whether the father had guilt or not, he gave his third wife's son the El Haba oil field that would pump crude for generations. Although Saudi Aramco operated the field, 27 percent of its revenue would go to Yousef and Yousef's children and grandchildren for more than a hundred years.

Yousef's large brown eyes stared intently, his arms crossed in judgment, making Masood feel suddenly unprepared. Masood had witnessed his mentor's rage more than once. Once, when Masood had failed to follow his master's specific instructions and held a stock position too long, Yousef told him that they would discuss it when he next made the trip to Afghanistan. Nothing else was said. But when he arrived, Yousef's voice soon had Masood literally trembling in fear. But Yousef had every right to such anger. Like Muhammad, Yousef had rejected the rewards of this world. His half brothers and sisters flew their Gulfstreams from Riyadh to Gstaad. But the master believed the Koran spoke of a different way of living. It required a humble life. And it required that infidels be sought out and a great slaughter be made. The respect Yousef lacked as a child would be gained as a man. And Masood would follow this man on his jihad.

"Your plan has been tremendously successful," said Masood. "We are in three markets that are returning well over twenty percent, even in a recession."

Yousef had built the business model himself and

was very proud of it. "*Alhamdulillah,*" he said, praising Allah.

"They were not as successful in Doha." Masood changed the subject to the bombing.

"Yes."

Masood saw a glimmer of the fire in his master's eyes. It may have been a mistake to raise the subject.

Yousef knew much more than his response indicated. He changed the subject. "We need to remain as liquid as possible at all times."

"Yes, sir."

Masood had also attended college in the United States. Ironically, many of the Ivy League schools had trained the best of the leadership. Masood, born in Cairo, was raised in East Orange, New Jersey. From an Egyptian family of limited means, he was only able to attend Rutgers because of a full scholarship from the Islamic Scholarship Program. At the mosque, he was quickly recognized for his bright mind, and after graduating from Rutgers, he was selected from several applicants to be the executive assistant to the head of BMI, Inc., an Islamic investment firm based in New Jersey.

Masood had quickly earned a reputation as a trusted manager. His short, portly frame disarmed many. He would always smile, his round face and bright eyes indicating shyness, humility. Yes, Masood was disarming, though he'd never be able to hide anything from Yousef.

A young boy, barely as high as the stone wall that surrounded the garden, ran up and jumped on Yousef's lap.

"Patoo!"

Yousef's voice was stern, but he gently picked up the child and raised him up to where he could almost touch the trellis and then dropped him to the ground like a brakeless elevator, stopping only at the last moment.

"Go to your mother." Yousef patted the child on his backside in a mock manner of punishment.

Patoo ran away, knowing not to push his father too far.

"What is the next market?"

"As you know, we are finishing up in Baltimore," said Masood. "Perhaps some commercial property in the South?"

"Atlanta. On the north side of the city. Anything near its Georgia 400 highway will turn a profit. We can concentrate on selling locations to drugstores. Properties with high traffic counts."

The world had become much smaller. Although Yousef was hiding in the near-lawless mountains of Pakistan, a guest of the Sherani clan of the Pashtun tribe, he knew the real estate market of Atlanta in detail.

Masood, listening intently, nodded.

"They will continue to have growth," Yousef said. "With our ability to leverage on the land in a high-traffic-count area, anything will be a profit."

"Yes, sir."

"We will have another private offering of stock. The stock will be issued to IIRO." IIRO, known more formally as the International Islamic Relief Organization, had been established by the royal assent of Saudi Arabia's ruling family. IIRO provided millions upon millions in relief to Islamic families devastated by the tsunami and various flood and earthquake disasters that had followed around the world. It also provided the source of funding for other projects. The profits would make their way back to Yousef.

"There is someone I want you to meet." Yousef signaled with his hand to the guards in the front of the stone house.

As Masood turned, a man with a sparse red beard and a deep scar across his cheek, jaw, and neck approached. The beard accentuated the path of the scar, which looked like a chalky white streak cutting through the red. His looks were out of place among the Pashtun mountain men. Although built like a brute with wide shoulders and thick hands, he had an orange-freckled complexion.

"This is Abu, my brother and compatriot. Abu Umarov, a Chechen."

"*As sala'amu alaikum.*" Masood spoke first.

"*Walaikum as sala'am.*" Abu's light blue eyes bored a hole in Masood's mind.

Good God. This man made Masood more uncomfortable than Yousef did.

Abu swung his AK-47 off his shoulder to shake Masood's hand.

"Umarov is a true Muslim warrior," Yousef said proudly. "He fought the Russians in Chechnya and the dogs in Bosnia. He was a lieutenant under Delić. Now he kills Americans and Jews."

Masood nodded in appreciation.

"He is my second-in-command. Do you know why?"

Masood stood there in silence.

"His loyalty is absolute!" Yousef's voice rose as he spoke. "My Chechen!"

Abu Umarov smiled slightly at that.

"In Grozny, he was a construction engineer. He built buildings. Buildings that last."

"Not like the Americans," Masood put in.

"Then Tsentoroi came and all of Umarov's family, his wife, his children, his mother and father, were shot like dogs on the street."

Masood watched Umarov's face and saw not the slightest change in his expression.

This man is cold.

"Umarov once served with Sabri al-Banna." Yousef said it as if Abu Umarov had been a veteran of some great war. "Look at this!"

Yousef grabbed Umarov's arm and pulled it up in the air like a referee's final verdict in the ring. At the same time, he pulled Umarov's shirtsleeve down, revealing a tattoo.

Masood had to look at it twice to understand.

"It's a swan?"

"Yes," said Umarov. "Hell yes."

"I don't understand."

"You don't know what that means?" asked Yousef.

He explained that any man who carried the black swan and had fought with Sabri al-Banna was a man to be feared. Sabri al-Banna, a son of a wealthy Palestinian farmer, was also known by his more famous name: Abu Nidal. As Nidal hated the Jew who took over his father's orange orchards, Umarov hated the Russian. They both made their enemies bleed.

"There is something else." Yousef suddenly shifted the conversation again, avoiding the question altogether. "Do you still have the New York box?"

"Yes, of course." They had maintained one address, a P.O. box in a small Brooklyn post office under a unique alias. Only Masood kept the key.

"You will receive something in a few days. The instructions will be clear."

Masood nodded.

Yousef seemed to stare into space as he spoke.

"The plan has several steps."

"I understand." Masood didn't always understand, but he knew enough not to say more.

Yousef looked up into the pale blue, cloudless sky as he spoke. "Masood, if you are not staying the night, it is time that you returned." He pointed up as he spoke, meaning that the U.S. spy satellite would soon be crossing over the valley in its orbit.

Masood looked at his watch. "Yes, brother."

"Someone in Riyadh is trying to point the CIA in our direction. It is my understanding that the CIA woman in Doha has now been transferred to Walter Reed Hospital." Yousef spoke with his hands as much as his voice.

Yousef glanced at Umarov when he spoke. Both knew more than they were saying.

"We need to find her source."

And with that, for the first and last time in their meeting, Yousef smiled.

CHAPTER 7

Hartsfield–Jackson International Airport, Atlanta

The baggage claim area felt like a ghost town. The last flight out of Washington had put him into Atlanta well after midnight. Even one of the busiest airports in the world would go into a lull during the midnight hours.

I'm beat, Scott thought, checking the time again on his watch. The black illuminated dial of his Rolex Submariner showed 12:50 A.M. It had been a long week.

But I am *back in,* he reminded himself. *And on my terms.* For a moment he felt like a schoolboy who just caught the smile from that girl in his math class. A grin crossed his well-worn face.

The thought of that schoolboy brought him back to a different world. He didn't have a girl in his math class. Not at Godolphin House. The old proctor would have had a heart attack if he thought a girl was anywhere near Eton College's Godolphin House. He never learned to like that old man, who'd taken the stick to him on more than one occasion. Eton College raised the elite of Great Britain, and all were taught to be reserved. The private boarding school had raised kings since 1440.

The Americans think they know the British, but they have no *idea.*

"Mr. Scott?"

James Fordon Scott turned around to see a hulk of a man approaching.

That actor in The Green Mile. *What was his name? Duncan?* While Scott was tall and lanky, this man looked like a wall. He would easily have towered over any linebacker on an American football team.

"It's Stidham. Sergeant Shane Stidham. You got a checked bag, sir?"

Mentally, Scott filed through the bios of Parker's original ANGLICO team. Shane Stidham had been awarded two Bronze Stars and a Purple Heart for his service in Iraq. If Parker meant to send a message, he'd picked a fine messenger.

"No checked bag." Scott had given up on checking bags after September 11. The hassle became too great in public transportation. He slung the overnight bag over his shoulder. "Just this," he said. "Where's your colonel?"

"He's waiting for you on the other side of the airport. Follow me."

It had taken Scott several days to find a lead on William Parker. First, though, he had flown to Qatar to meet the FBI team. The hole in the ground in Doha was much deeper than he had even imagined from the photographs. The body count had gone up since the original report. Six more didn't survive their head injuries, bringing the total death toll to twelve. He remembered the smell.

"Semtex?" Scott had asked the bomb team.

"Yes, sir, but not with the usual tracers." The FBI's bomb expert was holding a test tube with a brownish material inside. "This is probably Czech Semtex. A Chechen from Grozny was connected to a purchase recently of a ton of this stuff."

Scott knew the Chechen well: Abu Umarov. He also had a good guess as to who Umarov was working for.

As for Parker, after Korea, he seemed to have disappeared. Fortunately, Scott had remembered the woman who was with him at the end. A court reporter. He'd left several messages with the clerk of the court, only to learn quickly that the courthouse staff was a close family. Finally, he caught an assistant clerk who apparently didn't know better. She gave Scott the cell phone number for Clark Ashby. And then, all he could do was plead with Parker's lover to have Parker call him, if she knew where he was. He'd heard the reluctance in her voice, but somehow it had worked.

"Can't I take that bag?" boomed Stidham's bass voice. He seemed frustrated by Scott's slow pace.

"Thanks, but no. I'm fine. What do you mean he's on the other side?"

Instead of answering, Stidham ignored the question and continued walking. Scott could tell that Stidham rationed his words carefully. He had a slight stutter and he was no doubt conscious of his voice's uniquely low-octave tone.

Finally they stepped outside, across an empty street

and into a parking lot. This part of the airport also seemed as quiet as a cemetery at one in the morning.

The bitter cold air surprised Scott a little. This must be an exceptionally cold night in Atlanta. A layer of frost covered the windshields of cars that had been there for some time. As he walked, Scott mentally picked out the few cars that had clear windshields. He knew that those, only three cars out of fifty or more, had just recently been parked there. It was an absent-minded habit of observing and deducing that kept him alive in the spy business all these years.

Stidham headed toward a black Jeep Cherokee with a clear windshield. He clicked his remote, and the lights of the Jeep flashed with that obnoxious beep.

"Hop in."

Scott threw his bag into the backseat. The Jeep was meticulously clean. It had a unique smell he couldn't quite place in his mind. The leather seat had a slippery feel to it.

Armor All. That's the scent.

The Jeep had a customized interior with an in-dash panel that glowed in the dark when Stidham turned on the ignition. Scott could tell why Parker chose this man to pick him up. He was absolutely dependable. No one would care for a machine the way that this one did and not be.

"What are you listening to?" Scott knew that all conversations eventually led to insight, intelligence, and information. He pointed to the iPod hooked into the dash panel. Scott knew that as long as you took more than you gave, you gained something.

"Davis, Coleman, some Ellington, a little Basie, and Puente."

"Puente? *El Rey*."

"El what?"

"The king. *El Rey del Timbal*. You need to get *Night Beat*."

"Yeah, that's on there. He had energy."

Now Scott had a point of commonality. From a discussion of Ornette Coleman, they would move to family, or friends, or food, or, eventually, Parker. Scott had played the game a long time.

They headed out of the parking lot. The Jeep headed north, as if going downtown, flying through the turns and curves. But instead of taking the exit, Stidham turned onto the cargo road that circled the airport.

"Hard trip, sir?" Shane Stidham gave his guest a little more respect.

"Your friend was hard to find."

"Maybe with good reason."

Scott thought this was a good opportunity. Despite working with Parker on the Korean mission, he still didn't have a feel for the man.

"How long have you known him?"

"We go back to Desert Storm. The gunny and I were on his ANGLICO team."

Scott knew the history well. Parker's air and naval gunfire team was trained to call in fighters dropping thousand-pound bombs or artillery-lobbing shells on Iraqi National Guard troops. In complete overcast, with the bombers high above the solid ceiling of clouds, the ANGLICO team would mark the unexpected target with a laser beam or call in its location. In the Battle of al-Kafji, Parker's team destroyed over ninety Iraqi tanks, trucks, and APCs. They unleashed hot steel that tore through hundreds of the elite of Saddam Hussein. The Iraqi soldiers, panicked, would huddle together in a group. They knew the main Marine force remained miles away, yet somehow the bombs were dropping with complete accuracy. As those elite units concentrated together, the forward observers on the team called in the strike.

"Is your man tough enough?" Scott asked.

"For what, sir?"

"For another Korea."

"Yes, sir, he can handle it." Shane paused a moment. "How well do *you* know Colonel Parker?"

Scott chuckled. "Not as well as you."

" 'He is terrible in his onset and prompt in his decision,' " intoned Stidham.

"Sun Tzu?"

"Yes, sir, sure is."

Scott turned his gaze out to the line of jumbo jets, parked in a row, waiting for their turn in the maintenance hangar. Up ahead, he saw an illuminated sign that said ATLANTIC AVIATION.

Stidham turned into the gate at the FBO. Scott knew a fixed base operation, or FBO, was the private airplane's parking lot and gas station. A twin-engine turboprop sat at the end of a line of private jets, its engines running. The door was open in the back with a stairway down. Stidham wove through the line of aircraft and pulled up next to the airplane's stairway.

"There you go, sir." He pointed to the twin.

Scott opened the Jeep's door, and as he did, the high-pitched engines and the blowing wind filled the Jeep with dust and a deafening noise. The blast of frigid wind drove down his neck. Scott took his bag, ran over to the aircraft, and climbed aboard.

"Pull the door closed, Mr. Scott. Make sure you lock it."

The voice came from the plane's only other occupant. The pilot turned as he spoke.

"Come on up here and have a seat." Parker pointed to the copilot's seat next to his. "Strap yourself in, Mr. Scott."

The Cessna twin moved forward as Scott, somewhat confused, climbed into the copilot's seat. It was a tight squeeze. With little midnight traffic, the airplane was on the active runway in less than a minute. As it became airborne, Parker tilted it upward in a sharp, turning climb, passing over the terminal and parking lot where Scott had just been. The two engines' loud hum drowned out any chance for much talk. With the aircraft climbing into a bank of clouds, obscuring all visibility, Parker pointed to a headset. The airplane rocked back and forth and would occasionally drop for a brief second as an invisible air pocket dropped it like a descending elevator.

Scott could hear other pilots as they talked to each other and some "control center." Even this late, the radio conversation sounded like an auctioneer controlling a fast-paced bidding war. He wasn't a pilot, but he could read a compass and saw that they were heading south. The lights of the small airplane gave a glow to the clouds, and with the hum of the engines, Scott could barely keep his eyes open. He wanted to talk, but the exhaustion of the long week weighed heavily on his eyes. The cabin was warm, and the engines continued to hum at a near-deafening pitch. The twin turboprop was not like a jet engine–powered aircraft, where the thrust and sound were well behind the cabin.

It seemed like an instant had passed before he felt a nudge. He looked down at the low glow of his Rolex and saw it was nearly 3:00 A.M. He could feel pressure in his ears as the airplane descended. Through the clouds, Scott could barely make out the tip of the wing, which gave him this odd sensation they were actually flying upside down. He looked over to Will, who adjusted the throttle of the engines like an accountant on his adding machine and settled back into the seat.

"Don't go to sleep on me again, Mr. Scott. We're getting ready to land."

Scott leaned forward and glanced out his window just as the airplane broke through the bottom of the clouds. As far as he could see, the land below was a dark, lightless forest for miles. It was hard to get a sense of depth, but as the airplane got closer to the ground, he could make out several hills to his left.

Suddenly, the lights of a runway directly ahead of him appeared through the total darkness. He heard a mechanical thump—the landing gear lowering—and saw three bright green lights, in a triangle, flash on the panel in front of him. The airplane gently swung back and forth as Parker continued to correct its path toward the landing.

As they neared the ground, the engines spun down, and just as Scott felt the nose tilt upward, he heard the rear wheels strike the runway.

They taxied up to a small hangar, its fluorescent lights nearly blinding him. As he stepped out onto the pavement, Scott could tell that this was the only hangar on the one-strip runway. Parker had his own airport somewhere well south of Atlanta.

"Come with me. We'll go up to the cabin." Parker

unlocked the aircraft door and let down the steps as he led Scott out of the aircraft. A black pickup truck with oversized mud tires waited next to the hangar.

"Jump in," said Parker.

Wearily, Scott climbed up into the raised cab.

The road circled around the airfield and climbed up a wooded ridgeline. After a short time, Scott could see the airfield in the valley below, which suddenly became dark as some kind of timer shut down the lights. They traveled on in silence, perhaps because of the late hour, up the paved road into the dark.

On top of the rise, they came to an opening in the woods and a brightly lit, stacked-stone and timber house, like one would see on the slopes of Aspen or Vail. Scott got the sense that it was positioned on top of the small mountain.

"I say, you have damned fine tastes in hideouts."

Parker smiled and led Scott through the door and into a room framed by exposed chestnut and oak beams and with a stone fireplace that climbed up to the ceiling. This was far from a cabin, with its antiques, Persian rugs, and well-aged landscape paintings. A fire lit the room and had apparently been well tended, despite the late hour.

"Anything to drink?"

"Scotch, straight up. No ice."

"Your British is showing. How about Dalmore Thirty?" Parker lifted a clear glass bottle.

"Yes, please."

Parker handed him the Scotch-filled glass and pointed to two leather chairs near the fireplace. As Scott sat down, he could feel the heat of the fire on the left side of his leg. The smell of wood seemed to add to the taste of the Scotch. He swirled the amber liquid in the crystal glass, treating it as if it were a rare, delicate wine.

Parker, still as steeled and muscular as when they'd first met, looked comfortable in his element. Although it neared dawn, he showed no sense of fatigue, his blue eyes gazing at Scott with intensity.

"Now, why are you here?"

"Would it matter to say I need your help?" Scott asked. It would not have been an understatement to say it was a plea. They had let him back in because of the Korean operation and only because of that. Scott had been a minor actor in that play, but he didn't understate his role to them.

James Scott had spent his life on the adrenaline edge of this spy business, not because he was particularly smart or sly or skillful. Years ago he'd seen more opportunity, after Oxford and several tours in MI6 at Vauxhall Cross, with the Central Intelligence Agency than his own country's spy service. He knew that most of the intelligence world involved the seduction of people's weaknesses—the adulterer caught with another woman, the closet gay, or the embezzler. But he liked the action of the occasional operation, which seemed to be fewer and farther between. Americans seem to have more of an inclination for fieldwork. The Korean operation had been too loose, surprised too many in the Agency, and had almost buried him. Until it succeeded. The Agency had to pay millions to Parker in reward money and the budget wonks had screamed bloody murder. But few operations *ever* had been the success that Korea was. Parker had stopped a very bad situation in its tracks in North Korea. For much less than the cost of the several Tomahawk cruise missiles it would have taken, Parker had put the Korean missile program back a decade. And unlike the cruise missiles, Parker left no trail indicating where he'd come from. The mission left no fingerprints.

"Who?"

A simple question. William Parker's single word asked who the target was, who was involved, who was so important that they would resurrect a retired operative and send him to find a Marine who'd been officially discharged from the service.

"Maybe the better question is, why?" Scott said. "A very close friend of a very important person was seriously hurt." Again he paused. "Very badly hurt in an explosion at an embassy in the Persian Gulf." Scott thought a moment, as he took another sip. *Hell, the Scotch, the fatigue . . . I may be saying too much.*

"People get hurt all the time in this new world. Why should it really matter, to me or you?"

Scott wasn't surprised by Parker's bluntness. Parker really had no reason after Korea to trust him. But Parker wasn't going to do this mission for Scott no matter what he said. William Parker accepted a mission for his own reasons.

This mission would not be an easy sell, but as he looked around the room, he felt certain that Parker would buy it. The great room was perfectly furnished with the finest art, rich leather chairs, and sterling silver lamps with white silk shades. There was even a single freshly cut red rose in a crystal vase. However, there was not one photograph—not a single photo of family and friends, no pictures of children on swings, or aged, kindly parents. For Scott, this confirmed his initial hunch: He had William Parker.

"Have you ever heard of an Iranian operation called Operation Intekam?" Scott took another sip of the Dalmore.

"No." Not a complete truth. Something about the word struck a chord in Parker. *Intekam?* He let the word play in his mind as he turned the glass in his hand.

"There is a Saudi named Yousef al-Qadi. He didn't seem very important. He had plenty of money and got out of Harvard with a MBA back in the mid-eighties. But he kept a low profile. Until recently."

"Why now?" William Parker watched his guest lean back in the thick leather chair. He could see the fatigue in Scott's eyes.

"His name keeps coming up. We think he is making his move."

"Move?"

"Yes."

"To what?"

"We don't know, exactly. In a word, jihad. At some time, fanatics like him always make their move. A desire to be remembered, to be revered—who in the hell knows? We do know that he is charismatic, egotistical, absolutely ruthless, and fully capable of anything. He's the next generation."

"Sounds right for the part."

"But this guy's got ambitions that make others look like pikers."

Parker shook his head in acknowledgment as he swallowed the Scotch. It had a smoky flavor with a sharp, stinging feel as it went down his throat. Parker was more a bottled-water man than a Scotch drinker. He preferred the high from the physical exhaustion of running ten miles to a drink.

"And he has a particularly hard Muslim from Grozny who's known to do his dirty work."

"That probably describes several."

"Yes."

Scott moved his glass in front of his body. His eyes wandered to the ceiling.

"Intekam and Yousef are connected. We didn't discover the Intekam operation until some time after the bombing." Scott moved his hand to his cheek, stroking it several times, his eyes moving up and to the right. "And we didn't know of Yousef's involvement until much later."

Parker waited for Scott to continue.

"Intekam was Lockerbie."

"The CIA didn't know of Intekam until later?" Parker asked the question with a specific purpose.

"Did we know of Intekam until later?" Scott repeated the question. "No, absolutely not."

A lie. Parker knew the liar checklist from his days as a prosecutor. There were other signs. Scott's hands were turned down. Parker looked directly at his eyes. Scott looked away, again up and to the right. His body language was stiff. He repeated the question and got the same response. Scott hit every box on the liar's checklist. His body language was absolutely clear.

"So what's the point?"

"Yousef is on the path to be much more in the Muslim world. He is protected by the Pashtun tribes in the mountains of Pakistan. The Sherani clan treat him like a sheik. No." Scott hesitated. "Even more. He could have a man's child executed in front of him with a point of the finger."

"So what's the threat? He seems another tyrant quietly killing his people on the other side of the earth."

"He wants to kill more than just those in the Sherani clan he doesn't like. Some time ago this man, in the shadows in a videotape on the Internet, started talking of a new state of Islam."

"Where?"

"Good question. On the lands of the Ghaznavid Empire. Ghaznavid stretched from western Iran, across Afghanistan, and into most of Pakistan."

"Okay . . ." Parker's response was more of a question than an acknowledgment.

"Even more important is why. He wants to establish a totalistic Islamic state."

"The Ghaznavid Empire was over a thousand years ago."

"Yes."

"It was known for butchering the babies of its enemies. But he has one sizable problem."

"I know what you're going to say."

"Central Command is in his way." Parker had to give Yousef credit for dreaming big. Much of the military force of the United States lay in the center of his planned kingdom.

"Don't think he is a fool," Scott said. "He is bright and persuasive. And extremely well financed. He makes bin Laden look like a child."

"Shit." Parker rubbed his shoulder. "What would it take for him to pull this off?"

"A horrific event that breaks the will of the American people."

Scott paused.

"Do you want to meet him?"

"Yousef?"

"Yes, the man who put the bomb on Pan Am Flight 103. Would you like to meet the man who murdered your father and mother?"

Parker said nothing. Scott was being obnoxious in his directness. He stared into the fire as the wood popped with the occasional flare-up. The ember bounced against the screen and flew back into the fire. Listening to Scott, he had to wonder whether he was the ember or the fire.

"We'll talk in the morning."

Scott slept well past sunrise, which was unusual for him. He was nearing his fortieth birthday but felt closer to fifty as he rubbed his face with both hands while sitting on the edge of the bed. He had not slept for more than five hours at a time in the last decade. As he dressed, he slipped on his Rolex, looking at his watch. It was well past 9:00 A.M.

The bedroom was connected to a small library that was just off the great room where the night before he and Parker had drinks by the fireplace. Scott heard the rattling sound of someone in the kitchen on the other end of the lodge. The previous night he thought he had heard the same noise of someone in the kitchen, out of sight. The smell of fresh, brewing coffee was mixed with the smoky residue of the fireplace.

Scott paused as he stepped from the bedroom into the library. It was more of a small office than a library, with a table desk, a leather chair where the arms were well worn, down to the yellow leather under the stain, and across from the desk another smaller table with a chessboard. The marbled men on the board were paused mid-game. He recognized the opening move. The knight had been moved before the bishop.

On the center of the desk was a small blue-and-yellow Chinese ceramic bowl with a gold-leaf trim around its edge. It was full of medals. Scott picked up one of the medals, each having long, brightly colored ribbons. This one was pewter and engraved with Boston Athletic Association and the Boston Marathon. Next to the bowl, on the center of the desk, was a gold pocket watch linked to a thin chain. Scott, without thinking, picked it up. The chain had a fob on the end. A Phi Beta Kappa key etched on the back with "Columbia University, Class of 1959."

Obviously not Parker's. *Perhaps his father's,* Scott thought. He knew that both of Parker's parents had been killed by the terrorist bomb that took down Pan Am Flight 103 over Scotland. William Parker knew what terrorism was well before September 11.

Scott absentmindedly looked up at the other titles in the shelves behind the desk. *The Peloponnesian War, The Decline and Fall of the Roman Empire, The Encyclopedia of Military History,* and *John Paul Jones.*

Gibbon . . . Scott remembered from his days at Godolphin House who was the greatest fan of Gibbon's *The Decline and Fall of the Roman Empire*: Winston Churchill. Churchill relied upon Gibbon for his sense of phrases and credited Gibbon with teaching him the perfect English language.

In the shelf below stood *Songs of America* and *Existence.*

"A soldier who reads poetry," Scott remarked to himself. He turned and stepped out into the great room. In the bright light of day, he realized that the large windows that flanked both sides of the stacked-stone fireplace were actually glass doors that led out onto a broad slate patio. It was a crisp, brilliantly clear day. He saw the back of a man sitting in one of the chairs.

"Good morning."

"Well, hello, Mr. Scott." Parker took a sip from his cup of coffee. The bright sunlight had already warmed the day to the point that Parker was dressed in a long-sleeved shirt with the sleeves rolled up.

"Good God!" Scott exclaimed as he took in the view. The porch led down to a grassy knoll, brown from the early winter chill, and beyond to a cliff looking out over a broad valley forested with pointed pine trees, oaks, and hardwoods. Below, a river cut through the valley, and off to the north he saw, well in the distance, the tall stacks of a mill of some kind. The stacks produced a streak of bright white smoke, stretching across the cloudless blue sky.

"What river is that?" Scott said.

"The Chattahoochee."

"I've got no bloody idea where I am."

"Good." Parker smiled. "Would you like coffee? Or tea?"

"Neither," Scott said.

"What is it you want me to do?" Parker pointed to a mahogany porch chair across from his.

"That's rather direct of you."

Parker smiled again. "District attorneys make their living on direct."

Scott nodded. "We have an idea as to how to get close to a key player. And I have been given license to conduct an operation that could cause serious harm to a network of very bad people. But, you must have credibility to get close."

Parker knew what he meant when he said *close*. Close, as in getting near the enemy, behind their lines, and all of this alone. It could even involve *being* the enemy.

"Credibility to get close." Parker laughed. "That may be the understatement of the year. So you think you have a way of getting to this target and doing him damage?"

"There is a newspaper in London called *Al-Quds Al-Arabi*. We know it's followed by thousands upon thousands of Muslims in the Mideast. Several organizations follow it so as to monitor the Muslim community in Europe." Scott squinted in the sunlight.

"So, what are you suggesting?"

"You are multilingual. You pick up languages with incredible ease."

"I'm still lost."

"There is a journalist named Sadik Zabara. He has a following in his home country of Bosnia. Mr. Zabara was recently offered a job at *Al-Quds*. Publicly he has rather radical leanings and tends to attract those with similar views."

William Parker instantly saw the genius in the plan. "A Bosnian Muslim. A Caucasian as radical as any extremist."

"Exactly," Scott said.

"You said publicly . . . meaning that privately he thinks something else?"

"Yes." Scott didn't explain.

"And you're fishing for a big fish with this bait."

"And the big fish is nibbling. Zabara starts work at his new job in only a few days, and already he has been invited to a meeting with Yousef al-Qadi."

"Why? Why so soon? And why would Yousef al-Qadi want the attention?" Parker leaned up in his chair.

"Radicals such as al-Qadi have never shied away from news coverage. Before September 11, bin Laden sought out ABC and NBC and every major American network. After 9/11 they have gone to more protected sources but have nevertheless continued to use the media."

Scott had a way of staring at you as the conversation became more intense.

"Now that bin Laden is dead, a vacuum has been created. Someone will fill it."

"Yes."

"The media is a weapon. It's complicated. Men like al-Qadi want to gain a following in the Muslim world. Their jihads only succeed when they have a following. But many of the countries are controlled by governments that have no intention of letting men like al-Qadi be any part of the news. So they use a back door. *Al-Quds* or CNN International gets to the same people."

"That explains why their acts are so violent."

"Exactly. It's all about PR. They want to get on CNN. But to be on CNN, terrorists have to blow other stories off the front page."

"So why al-Qadi and why now? And why should he trust Zabara to meet him?"

"Actually, Yousef was instrumental in getting Zabara his job."

"Now I really don't understand."

"This asset has been buried for some time. It's killing MI6 that we've asked for him. Zabara has been writing articles for years saying that the time of bin Laden has passed. That there is a new warrior needed to lead the jihad."

"Enter Yousef al-Qadi." Parker sensed the multilayered plot. "So he gets this journalist the job at a paper with a much bigger distribution to provide his own new media platform."

"Exactly. And the time has come. Zabara has received an invitation to visit Yousef on Yousef's home turf. There, from deep in the Hindu Kush, he's to conduct an extensive interview with our man."

"When?"

"Soon. Very soon. But no date's been set. The problem is that once the date is set, we won't have a minute to spare."

"But what then? And how long?"

"We have a commitment for virtually unlimited funds and time. There will only be one person above me: the deputy director of the CIA. No one else. His aide is out of the loop. His staff, their wives, are all out. No one knows. Period."

Very much like the Korean mission, thought Parker. Including the fact that there would be no rescue wagon if things went south.

"So Zabara gets put in storage somewhere."

"Yes, MI6 puts him in a safe place before he even gets off the airplane in London."

"And you're suggesting I become Mr. Zabara?"

"Yes."

"So I get the invite and fly around the world. Let's say I pass muster. Then what? A GBU in the right place?" A reference to the laser-guided Mk-84 bomb, which carried over two thousand pounds of explosives. The explosion would crater a football field.

"Possibly. A botch job. A quick and dirty. Maybe a bullet to the rear of the skull with something small slipped in."

"Hmm. I'm not sure of that." Parker had killed men in combat and knew his share of death. But this was not James Bond. One doesn't fly in, shoot a man in his head, and then take the next international flight out of the Sherani clan's local airport. No, this would take something far more sophisticated.

"Don't forget that we have both Yousef and his Muslim from Grozny to reckon with. You would need to get both of them. And their tribe is more than just two. If you don't get them all, they'll be gone. A chased fox only goes deeper into the woods and then pops out somewhere else to hunt again." Parker looked down at his coffee. "The fox needs to have a reason to be pulled out of his den. A strong reason."

Scott nodded, both agreeing to the point and acknowledging that they had no simple solution.

"There is one way to pull the fox out." Parker looked across the distant trees as he spoke his thoughts.

"Short of assassinating the president of the United States, we have license to do whatever it takes."

"You know my ANGLICO team."

"Yes."

There was no point in being coy. Parker would assume that Scott would remember the team from Korea and, if not, would have at least researched Parker's contacts.

"One of them was Hernandez."

"Staff Sergeant Enrico Hernandez."

"Yes. He's with the Centers for Disease Control now. Works on their security team."

"He mentioned to me a doctor there named Stewart. I think his name is Paul Stewart. I would need to start by talking to Dr. Stewart."

"When?" Fire had appeared in Scott's eyes. If he wasn't already seeing the direction of Parker's idea, he was at least energized by the fact that Parker was hatching a plan.

"Now."

Scott nodded. "One more reminder, Colonel Parker, of the stakes involved. If Yousef wants to make a name for himself, it will take something very violent."

"Yes," said Parker. "I can only imagine."

CHAPTER 8

Lake Sidney Lanier, Georgia

William Parker tried to hold the steering wheel steady on the road while he glanced at the iPhone in his hand. He would look down at the electronic map loaded on the iPhone, then glance up at the roadway and then again down to the map. Each time he glanced down, the rental car tended to pull to the left and the center line. The occasional pickup truck coming in the opposite direction laid on the horn as he wandered closer to the paint.

This is stupid. He knew better as a pilot. Lesser distractions had caused many an airman to plow into the ground.

Waldrip Road. He knew the turn was somewhere to the left. He had seen it from the air as he flew over the western portion of the lake. There it was. Parker took the turn.

Can't be more than a few miles to this house.

He'd reached the western side of Lake Sidney

Lanier. Lake Lanier sat an hour's drive northeast of Atlanta, just west of Gainesville, and squarely in the path of the tidal wave of people moving from Detroit to Atlanta. Property on the lake, if you could find it, went for millions.

In a few miles the turn would be to the right. He glanced down at the iPhone again. Up ahead, a street sign stuck out from the bushes with a visible lean to the right.

Martin Terrace. His next turn. Parker saw a driveway to his right and the lake beyond as he crept down the single lane that twisted through pine trees. Another house lay ahead.

MONCRIEF PAINT COMPANY.

Finally. The sign hung on a tree below another that advertised Lake Lanier Construction. Parker turned onto the gravel driveway and saw an old beaten truck with a tailgate that looked broken and a slew of empty five-gallon buckets tied together in the bed. The side of the truck also showed MONCRIEF PAINT COMPANY and, below it, PAINT CONTRACTOR. And below that, in smaller but perfectly neat type: GUNNERY SERGEANT—USMCR (RETIRED).

The Cape Cod house was in its final stages of construction. The copper gutters and shake shingles gave it that distinctive look of an expensive cottage, as if pulled up and dropped down from a lake in the White Mountains, but the front yard was still a wide mess of red clay dirt. Deep tire tracks puddled full with water showed the recent rains. Black plastic tubes from the sprinkler system stuck out of the dirt in a regular pattern across the yard. It was only a few weeks away from the final touches, landscaping, and plantings that would take the house from this rough stage to something ready for *Architectural Digest*.

As he neared the front door, Parker heard a fast, loud voice engaged in a conversation with another, similarly energetic voice. Parker smiled and swung the door open quietly, as if sneaking into his parents' house well past midnight. He could have called out to Moncrief, but catching him by surprise would be worth it.

"Goddamn it, the prince was right!"

The sound of a hotly contested debate came from the small living space just to the right of the front door. There, a man, maybe a hand's width at most under six feet, spread cream-colored paint on the walls. He was solid, with broad, muscular shoulders that reminded one of a charging bull or linebacker. His shoulders tapered down to a tight waist, giving him a dogged, self-assured bearing. A high-and-tight haircut helped frame the head with a new Yankees baseball cap squarely on top. His garb looked far from spotless—white paint overalls splotched with a variety of colors—but the Yankees hat was spotless. It might have just been issued by the team uniform manager.

"Yeah, well, the Astros were fools," he replied.

Parker looked around the room and smiled, realizing there was only one voice in this conversation. Yes, maybe two minds, but only one voice. He decided to watch and listen for a while.

"In the sixth round."

Kevin Moncrief actually sounded angry with himself, painting all the while. Parker quietly pulled up the sleeves to his blue denim shirt and leaned against the wall in the hallway, enjoying the show.

"The kid was drawing pictures of pinstripes in Mrs. Padley's class! Hell, Newhouser knew what he had. Soft hands. A feel for the game. A natural. A pure, goddamn natural."

Parker tried not to laugh, listening to this high-strung conversation between Kevin Moncrief and his good friend, Kevin Moncrief.

"An American League MVP drives three and a half hours to see a kid play, and then the front office tells him to go to hell." He kept rolling paint as he continued to talk, his attention focused fully forward the entire time with no clue that anyone else had joined him in the room.

Moncrief's debate was over the rejection of Hal Newhouser's advice to the Houston Astros to sign a kid from Michigan named Derek Jeter. Newhouser told management that this skinny teenager would be the anchor of a winning Major League club. They signed a no-name instead. The teenager went on to have five World Series rings locked up in his safe-deposit box. Newhouser, the man who was always perfectly dressed, quit baseball for good after his advice was rejected.

"Newhouser should have been a Marine." He sighed and then paused for a split second. "Colonel?" he said suddenly, never once looking back. "Your fancy denim shirt has some Sherwin-Williams Copper Harbor on it now."

Should have known. Parker checked his shoulder, only to find a streak of yellow-orange paint. *Oh, well.* It was worth it.

"Gunny Ndee." Moncrief's nickname explained much. Only three men on the planet had license to call him by that name. A biker once overheard it being used in a bar in San Diego. He thought it was funny. He made the mistake of expressing that fact. The biker didn't even get the final syllable out, trying to repeat the word, before he was unconscious on the floor in a pool of blood. Moncrief was one-eighth Chiricahua Apache on his father's side. Although Apache was the name that their enemies gave them, the warriors called themselves *Ndee.* And there had been no more determined warriors on earth than the Ndees. The tribe, when necessary, could strike their tents and move—warriors, squaws, barefoot children, the crippled and ill—more than a hundred and fifty miles without stopping and without hesitating once for a drink or rest. Moncrief had that same relentless, strong-willed, pit bull mind-set. And like an Apache warrior, Kevin Moncrief had a sense of perception, especially on the battlefield, that had become legendary in the brotherhood of the few good men.

"What are you doing here, boss?" Moncrief finally turned toward Parker.

"I need your help."

Moncrief stopped, laid the roller on top of the screen on the bucket of paint, wiped the paint off his hands, pulled back the Yankees hat, checked it again to make sure that not a drop of paint was on it, put it back with a tilt on his head, pulled out a wrapped, short stub of a Gloria Cubana cigar, unwrapped it, stuck it in the corner of his smiling mouth, and said, "Let's get out of this overpriced dollhouse."

The lake was still recuperating from the nearly decade-long drought. The bleached rocks and raw, exposed shoreline showed the drought's success. But really, two thieves were involved in the crime. Mother Nature took what water it could, and the growing city of Atlanta used the rest. At last, in recent months, the rains had returned.

"They're hoping that by the time they move in, it will still be a lake house." Moncrief smiled as he spoke and pointed out over the lake, making reference to the receding waterline. They pulled up two chairs. "How's the shoulder?"

"Fine. Do you still have a contact in DIA?" Parker asked. The Defense Intelligence Agency had been a good source for Moncrief for years.

"Yes, I actually do."

Parker nodded. It wouldn't have surprised him to learn that Kevin Moncrief took a break from painting every so often to help out his friends from the past.

"I need to find out everything I can on Operation Intekam."

"I've heard of that." Moncrief pulled out his cigar and absentmindedly smelled it as he spoke. He looked up and for a moment stared at Parker. "It was the Iranian operation after the *Vincennes* shot down the Iranian passenger jet. Some thought it was linked to the Pan Am flight."

"Exactly. *Intekam* is Farsi for 'an equal and just revenge.' They lost two hundred and ninety innocent people, and they were determined to get an eye for an eye." Parker knew that the USS *Vincennes* had given Iran Air Flight 655 no chance, misreading the commercial aircraft as an inbound fighter. The SM-2MR surface-to-air missile tore through the Airbus 300, ripping the wings from the airplane. At that altitude, death was instantaneous.

"I need to know if a man named Yousef al-Qadi is

connected to Intekam and, more importantly, whether Intekam is connected to Lockerbie."

Moncrief smiled and took out a pad of paper and pen to write the name. "Do I smell a mission coming on?"

"Perhaps."

"I'm in." The gunny looked like a kid on Christmas Eve.

"There is something else I need to know," Parker said. "What was the CIA's connection to all of this?"

Moncrief raised his eyebrows. "You think the big boys were in on that?"

"I'm not sure. Something doesn't feel right. How quickly can you find out about this?"

"How much time do we have?"

"A matter of days, maybe less."

"I always work well under pressure." Moncrief took out his cigar and smiled his best broad, toothy smile. "We'll use our backdoor e-mail."

No sooner had Parker landed back at the lodge than his computer showed an e-mail from Moncrief. They had a special scramble program that Moncrief had lifted from his friends in the IDF. He'd modified the program to use words from the Apache language as keys. It could be broken, like all crypto programs, but it would take some very big computers working on it for several days and by then the operation would be over.

When will you be available? The e-mail came from "Quo-Qui," a name that Moncrief used often.

Anytime, Parker shot back. *Did you find out anything?*

Mossad has someone in western Europe who confirms that the Semtex used on 103 was a part of a shipment bought with monies raised by a certain financial whiz kid trained at Harvard.

Parker stared at the lines of text for some time. That one line made up his mind. Parker was now in on this mission. It didn't matter if the CIA were lying.

How about Intekam?

Yes, that too. Can you do a VTC in the morning?

Yes.

Good. 0600 will be noon in Paris.

CHAPTER 9

South of Atlanta

Parker checked the computer at 5:58 A.M. Two more minutes until Moncrief contacted him. If there was one thing he knew about the gunnery sergeant, it was that he'd never be late.

Bing. The computer chimed at exactly 6:00 A.M.

Two faces came in on a split screen. One was Moncrief. The other was a man, seemingly in his mid-fifties, wearing modern, stainless metal glasses with small rectangular lenses. He wore a wool turtleneck that was black and in sharp contrast to his milky-white complexion. If Parker had to guess, he would imagine the man was sitting behind his computer in a flat somewhere on the outskirts of Paris.

"This is my friend Ludwig." Moncrief had seemingly the same cigar in his mouth from the day before. Parker suppressed a chuckle. Only Moncrief would be chewing on a cigar at six in the morning. "We served together when I was attached to the IDF several years ago."

"Hello."

"I understand from my friend Moncrief that you have an interest in Yousef al-Qadi." The man on the split screen spoke English with a Dutch accent.

"Yes, indeed. What can you tell me?"

"Several years ago we intercepted a telephone call between Mohtashemi-Pur and an unknown person."

"I know that name. But I can't place it." Parker said.

"Mohtashemi-Pur was the interior minister in Tehran. He was talking to this unknown person about the transfer of some eleven million dollars to an Ahmed Jibril." Ludwig spoke in a clear, methodical voice without referring to any documents. It struck Parker that Ludwig must be a very good spy. A good spy always knew the details—and how to present them.

"I know that name as well. Ahmed Jibril." Parker had attended the trial of the Lockerbie conspirators. The evidence included several intelligence reports.

"Yes, the head of the PFLP-GC. The Popular Front for the Liberation of Palestine."

"Can you connect the dots for me?"

"Yes. After the transfer of the funds, the Libyan PFLP-GC purchased some seven hundred pounds of Semtex from a corporation named Omnipol. It was the same Semtex that was in the Toshiba radio that brought down Pan Am Flight 103."

"I see." Parker leaned forward in his chair. His body became tense as he heard the words being spoken.

"Also, Ali Muhammad al-Megrahi was a member of the PFLP-GC."

That was one name that Parker didn't have to struggle to remember. In the trial that followed the downing of Pan Am 103, he saw the little man sitting in the dock. He looked like a college student with long, curly hair and ink-dark eyes framed by similar colored eyebrows. Unlike a college student, however, he hadn't a speck of kindness in him. Like some few men, al-Megrahi surely had no mother and must have been born to the fate of an orphan, for if he had a mother he would have some capacity to comprehend the true brutality of his acts. Parker studied him for days. A few years in prison and then he was set free. It took the cancer years to catch up to him. Some thought that with the death of his protector, Mu'ammar Gadhafi, an overdose of morphine had done what the Scots had not been willing to do. He had received what 270 souls had not. A simple death.

Parker raised a hand to interrupt. "Do you have any idea why al-Megrahi was released?"

Moncrief cut in. "Skip, you don't want to know." He wiped his hands with a stained white rag.

"We believe it was part of a play being made by certain Western forces, but the intelligence can only a play guessing game at this point." Ludwig seemed to enjoy being indirect.

"Translate *Western forces* for me?"

"Well, the best person to ask may be Mr. Scott."

Parker lost patience with the extent to which Ludwig would avoid directly answering the question.

"So the CIA wanted al-Megrahi out."

"Yes."

"What about this Omnipol?"

"That's the interesting part." Ludwig's eyes shifted around as if he was looking to make sure the room was clear.

"Yeah, you gotta hear this," Moncrief chimed in on the video conference.

"Omnipol is a Czech company based in Prague. It is one of the world's largest suppliers of arms. It is, by far, the largest supplier of Semtex, and the Semtex they supplied had a certain chemical trace to it. But that's not the important part."

"Okay?" Parker prompted.

"We believe it is owned by Yousef's cousin, Ali bin Saleem, who is the secretary of the council that will select the next king of Saudi Arabia."

CHAPTER 10

The village of Kawas, east of Quetta, Pakistan

The night before the meeting, the village had been in an uproar. The brothers of the woman named Medi had suspected for several weeks that she was meeting her lover in his two-roomed home, tucked well into a wash in the hills just outside the village of Kawas in western Pakistan. Medi, of the Mahmoond tribe, was barely out of her teens, and stupid. Both her brothers had warned her repeatedly.

A neighbor who lived up the trail had heard moaning as he passed the mud stucco and thatched-roof hut just after sunset. A man from the village representing the elders went there the following morning and found the walls covered in sprays of blood—the floors as well. He stepped into a puddle of black, congealed blood, which stuck to his shoes like molasses. Flies swarmed around the room, occasionally landing on his cheek, even as he brushed them aside. The bodies had been pummeled with bricks found nearby, covered in the same sticky blood. Both of her brothers owned up to the crime. No arrests followed.

Yousef had heard of the incident. He knew better than anyone that their cultural laws ran deep. A sister or daughter who committed adultery was stoned to death. He was concerned, though, that it drew attention to the village and threatened to compromise the meeting place.

"Are we late?" He looked at his watch again while the truck, jumping back and forth like a porch swing, slammed into another pothole. The road was meant more for the mule-pulled carts than for a four-wheeled vehicle.

"No," said the driver, his hands gripping the wheel so tight his knuckles turned white against his dark skin. The truck slowed for a pack of ragged, emaciated dogs that had gathered at a crossroad, then followed the other road up into a gulch. No more than a stone's throw away, he saw men gathered in their black-and-white-checkered turbans, smoking their cigarettes. Apparently, this was the road that led up to the murders.

The Americans have a better chance of breathing life back into those two dead bodies, Yousef thought, *than of changing these people.*

The death of some young man or woman as a martyr in a suicide bombing was insignificant. And with the monies given to the martyrs' families, the supply was endless and unstoppable.

He thought of the two bodies with the blank stare of death, their heads deformed by the beatings. He thought of the fragments of broken bricks embedded in her forehead. Her round, brown eyes fixed in an eternal stare.

"Hate," he muttered. Hate was the limitless raw energy fueling this Muslim nuclear reactor. Hatred combined with deep, pitiful poverty. A simple breach of culture or tradition, or even an inappropriate word, could set off waves of hatred which, in this part of the world, transformed swiftly into violent action.

The truck pulled into a three-walled hut just outside the village. The thatched roof would hide the vehicle from the UAVs and satellites that were constantly patrolling the skies of western Pakistan.

From the hut they would walk the remaining miles. The road quickly became steeper and was cut in two by several washouts that a man could stand in up to his knees. A wind brought up a choking cloud of dust that hung in the air, causing Yousef to cover his face with his turban.

After several miles they climbed up the final hill and crossed over into another valley, which had an orchard of short, stumpy apple trees. The twisted brown trees with their canopy of green leaves stood in stark contrast to the rocky hillsides on both sides. A ditch of a stream cut through the grove, the obvious source of the water that kept the trees green. There, near the end of the row of trees, was another mud-brick house. Several guards with AK-47s stood watch in front of the hut.

"*As sala'amu alaikum,*" Yousef yelled to the party as he approached.

"*Walaikum as sala'am,*" the oldest guard said with a wave of his rifle, knowing Yousef both by sight and reputation.

He pointed to a path near the side of the hut and Yousef followed, traveling down a short hill to a tent beneath the trees. Its walls were rolled up, as the staggering heat of the day would have made a closed tent unbearably hot. The fabric of the tent was a strange, thin material that had a metal reflection to the bottom side.

Yousef reached up and touched the material. It felt like paper-thin copper, no thicker than a sheet of aluminum foil.

"It protects us from the infidels' eyes." The older guard was pointing to the sky.

There, seated on several rugs, their legs crossed like Boy Scouts at a campfire, were three men, one of whom he recognized. The other two were strangers.

"*As sala'amu alaikum,*" Yousef said again.

"*Walaikum as sala'am,*" said the older, gray-bearded, thick-spectacled man as he pushed up his glasses on his round nose. He was a cousin to a cousin of the House of Saud. A physician by training, he was considered a reliable messenger whom the elders respected. The doctor smiled at Yousef like a mentor at his student. He had known Yousef since he was a toddler.

These meetings were very rare. It had been several years since Yousef and the doctor had been together in one spot, their last having taken place in Paris. Although this meeting was much closer to the danger of the American troops and more recently the Pakistan Army's intrusions into the region, the valley near Quetta was considered safe. The Sherani clan of the Pashtun tribe took great pride in protecting their guests. From the time of Muhammad, it had remained a basic tenet that one must receive into his tent the guest and protect him. Yousef remembered from his youth the tale of Bu Zaid. A hero of the Bani Hillal tribe, Bu Zaid slaughtered his last camel so as to provide food for his guests. With the loss of his last camel, he would starve, his family would starve, but his guest would be cared for. And so it was written.

"Yousef, I want you to meet these two brothers, Malik Mahmud and Mohagher Iqbal."

Yousef had heard of both men. Mahmud was a leader of a Muslim group called the Free Aceh Movement. It was known in Malaysia as GAM. GAM's small force was dedicated to establishing a Muslim state in Aceh, a province of Indonesia. More important, the guerilla army was feared by the world because they were at the chokehold of the western Pacific called the Strait of Malacca. The large vessels would pass within easy reach of the armed marauders. More than sixty thousand ships passed through the strait every year.

Iqbal was a leader of the Moro Islamic Liberation Front, a group that was better run than Mahmud's crowd. Thanks to the Front, there were certain areas in the southern Philippines where the Philippine army would refuse to go. The soldiers knew that Iqbal's soldiers often beheaded their prisoners, always an effective strategy.

Yousef had been told to expect two strangers at the meeting. He guessed the purpose.

"Have a seat, brother." The doctor sat at one end of the rug and dominated the meeting. The doctor was and always had been—even back to the war with the Russians several decades ago—the voice of the movement.

Yousef sat at his side, legs folded, with pillows on each side. "Our assets now exceed six billion in Saudi riyals. We have more than thirty sources that are indirect and, of course, several that are direct in funding the mujahideen fighters," he told the doctor.

The doctor nodded. "What are we able to pay the martyrs' families at this time?"

"At least one hundred thousand riyals," said Yousef. "The Al-Aqsa Fund has had the direct support of the Saudi royal family, and has provided at least half of those monies. Other generous donators, such as the bin Laden family, have provided the remainder."

He updated them on the Atlanta strategy he'd recommended to Masood.

The doctor nodded again. "You will receive additional funds, which will be allocated for the direct benefit of our brothers here from the Philippines and Indonesia. It has been decided that we must help make our Muslim family stronger, worldwide." The doctor was suggesting a worldwide, coordinated, and well-financed Muslim movement.

"I have a condition." Yousef unfolded one of his legs as he spoke.

"Brother?" The doctor turned his ear toward the younger man. He had lost much of his hearing, due to old age and having been too close a witness to several wars.

"I will not give money to anyone who has not shared blood with me. They needed to fight with us."

"What do you suggest?"

"These men need to serve with our brothers in the TTP."

The Pakistani Taliban had been the host and protector of Yousef since the Soviet army had been their enemy.

"I agree." The doctor didn't hesitate.

Yousef knew neither of the guests would not object. It would bring them honor to fight beside their brothers and sisters against the Americans. It would also build a lifelong loyalty, as well as create a broader net for his followers.

"You have been successful in both growing the funding and keeping it discreet. You will be given one hundred million dollars for each of these two groups as a principal investment, and with your past record of growth, you will be able to provide funding for their efforts for years to come."

The plan was simple. Yousef was to become the stockbroker for worldwide terrorism. The two guests smiled at Yousef.

"Brother," Iqbal said. "We understand that you have gotten over a ten percent return the last five years, even in these economic times."

Yousef shrugged and nodded.

"We are grateful for your support, brother."

Iqbal seemed to be one of those men who was easily misjudged. He didn't need degrees of higher education. Yousef could immediately tell why his men followed him. Iqbal was bright and articulate.

"Yousef, let me talk to you privately for a moment. My brothers, if I may ask you to step outside." The doctor was getting old, and it was more and more an inconvenience for him to rise up off the carpeted floor of the tent. Yousef knew that the guests would not mind. For the last several years, they had lived off the land, saving every round, taking weapons from the dead of the soldiers sent out to hunt them down. Now, they would have funding to buy new weapons.

When only the doctor and Yousef remained in the tent, Yousef spoke first.

"We have the cell," he said in a low voice. He did not feel comfortable discussing the details, even around their trusted guests. "One from Danish Abad had been chosen and is learning now."

"And?"

"My Chechen has made a trip to America."

"This is the one that found out about the woman in Doha?"

"Yes." Yousef whispered. Only three men could have the common knowledge of all and the doctor needed to know the least. "I know the Americans' weakness. I have found a hole in their defense." Yousef pointed to the space in front of him, as if there was an imaginary map of the United States.

"And?" The doctor let his eagerness show in his expression.

It had always struck Yousef as odd that a brilliant man such as the doctor, who had been trained by the best in medicine in both Egypt and the United States, would be so comfortable with a project that would kill thousands. "This will be devastating. It will break the back of their will."

"Good."

"They will pull back from our world. They will retreat in shame."

The Americans had withdrawn some, but no one believed that they would ever truly leave Afghanistan. Their president had promised it, but it was a lie. Yousef's plan needed everyone to leave.

"And with that withdrawal you will soon have your state," the doctor said.

"Allah's will!"

"No, this will be Yousef's will."

Yousef smiled at the compliment.

"The one from Danish Abad was chosen at birth. We will rename her village in her honor."

"You will activate the cell once you have what you need?"

"Yes, from this." Yousef held up a cell phone. It was not the one that would be used, but a similar twenty-dollar cell phone would initiate the mission that would be remembered by every person on the planet. It was remarkably simple. Yousef would use a Motorola V180 with a special Pakistani SIM card and only one number in it. It would be activated only once—and used only once. He would dial a number, put in the text code, and press Send.

"Good. And Allah will protect you."

"Yes."

"Allah and our brothers, the Sherani!" the doctor said.

"Yousef, you have been a good warrior." The doctor sounded like the father that Yousef had always wanted but never had.

"Yes."

"God understands."

"This jihad will be remembered." Yousef was no different than the many other warriors. He began this journey because of a loss.

"I remember seeing you at that store in Riyadh. What was it?"

"Lamsa."

"Yes, you were buying her an *abaya*." The black floor-length *abaya* was made of silk. "Was it her first?"

"Probably, yes." Yousef thought the doctor was asking too many questions. It didn't really matter now.

"Sira, that was her name, wasn't it?"

"Yes." Yousef decided to break off the conversation. "When will I see you again?"

"She couldn't have been more than twelve, maybe thirteen."

The doctor didn't take the hint.

His niece was only twelve when she died. She was not supposed to have been on Iran Air Flight 655. She was returning from a visit to her mother's family. She was only a child, meant to be safe while being raised in Riyadh.

"This will probably be our last meeting, brother." The doctor sighed.

"I understand." From here, God would take Yousef down a different path. He would be alone. His family would live even more of a nomadic life than they had lived until now. They would constantly be on the move. No one would be trusted.

But that was the future. He still had much to do in the present.

CHAPTER 11

The Atlantic Aviation Fixed Base Operation, Hartsfield–Jackson Airport

William Parker saw Scott standing next to the door to the flight line, nervously looking at his Rolex.

Someone like Scott being nervous. . . .

Parker didn't like it. No one could afford to be nervous in this business.

Parker continued to watch for a second as Scott stared at the giant jets as they taxied by the FBO. An Air France Boeing 777 rolled by. As it did, Parker could see over Scott's shoulder the pilot going through the final takeoff checklist, reaching up and flipping switches. The gigantic wings, full of fuel, passed above them as the aircraft moved by.

"Mr. Scott."

Scott turned around to see Parker standing in front of him.

"It's good to see you."

"Let's step outside." Parker pointed to the door to the flight line.

As the two stepped outside, the roar of the Air France jet engines was deafening. The engines threw up a hot wind that blew past them.

"So, are you in?" Scott couldn't disguise his impatience.

Parker could read the tension in his voice. No doubt Scott was already imagining trying to talk the British into the backup plan, one they wouldn't like. A UAV would try to follow the real Zabara to the meeting in the mountains of Pakistan, and then, at just the right moment, a Hellfire missile would be dropped from a high-altitude jet out of sight to those on the ground. MI5 would lose a valuable asset, and all who knew Zabara would become suspect to the jihadists. Still, it would probably be a fair trade-off, but they'd vastly prefer the Parker plan.

"Yes," Parker said at last.

"Good. We're a bit struck for time."

Parker nodded. "But we are going to do it the different way I suggested before."

Another jet, this time a much smaller, triple-engine jet, colored in plain white, taxied by and, with it, another roar of the engines. Again, the engines kicked up a blast of hot wind and the smell of kerosene followed. The roar of the engines, however annoying, would also make it impossible for anyone to overhear the conversation.

"I need to meet with Dr. Stewart as soon as possible."

"The meeting with the CDC has been set up for now. They're already waiting for you."

"Good. Are you getting an idea of what this involves?"

"Given your interest in the CDC, I would surmise that you will carry a very bad bug into the camp and release it, and as a consequence Mr. Yousef will become sick and quickly die."

"Right. Or, failing that, it should flush your target out into the open. If Yousef gets sick and has a doctor near him, he'll likely be told that the only thing that can save him will be very special antibiotics at a high-end hospital. That should limit the number of places he could run to. Meanwhile, if the bug works quickly enough, or if the doctor misdiagnoses him, he dies in his camp." Parker paused. "Along with hundreds or thousands of others, if you don't mobilize shipments of vaccine and antibiotics into the region quickly enough."

"We'll take care of that," Scott said. "But what about you? Being that close to a germ like that?"

"You're right. I'll need the right antibiotics available. Having them there will be your job, Mr. Scott. I will need the right team there, very nearby, so that I can reach them quickly."

"We can do that. Like I said, our resources are unlimited."

"About my team . . ."

"Yes?"

"I want my gunny on it."

"You mean Moncrief?"

Parker nodded.

"Done. Now we need to get you to London and have you become Zabara as soon as possible. As soon as we have you in place, we will figure how to get you together with your team."

"What about *your* team, Mr. Scott?"

Quickly, Scott explained that he'd spent the last twenty-four hours putting the various pieces in place. First, he'd established a command center in London, near where Parker would be living. An ops center would be created at a nearby British air base, where the support team would assemble and be trained. And they'd already started planning for a command center in the eastern mountains of Afghanistan. This one would have to be mobile, able to move at the last moment, as they learned where exactly "Sadik Zabara" was going to meet Yousef.

"Make sure you include the best infectious-disease physician you can get," Parker said. "And I'll need him near the meeting point."

Scott nodded. "Now the bad news."

Parker smiled, waiting.

Scott returned the grin, obviously relieved to see that Parker, like any good operative, had assumed that there would be bad news.

"It's about the time frame."

"Tell me," said Parker.

"Sadik Zabara finally got his summons from Yousef. They're to meet in ten days."

CHAPTER 12

Centers for Disease Control and Prevention, Atlanta

"Hello, Mr. Jones."

William Parker turned from the wall of framed diplomas when he heard the voice behind him. Dr. Paul Stewart's voice held more than a faint hint of sarcasm when he spoke the words *Mr. Jones*.

"Hello, Doctor." Parker extended a hand, but the doctor took a seat without shaking hands.

Yeah, he doesn't like this at all. Clearly the scientist assumed this visit, ordered from above, was not for the benefit of either Dr. Paul Stewart or the American public.

Dr. Stewart was an older Buddy Holly look-alike, complete with out-of-date black-rimmed glasses and gelled hair. His plaid shirt and khaki trousers, both wrinkled, with worn Rockport shoes showed that he cared more about what was growing in his petri dish that day than what others thought about his appearance.

"You would think they could come up with something better than *Jones*." Parker offered a conciliatory smile as he said the words.

"Yes."

He sighed inwardly at the tone of Stewart's one word.

"Sometimes it may save someone's life to not know too much, Dr. Stewart."

"Yeah, right. You've made your point." The doctor held up his hands, as if in submission. "I understand from our director that I am to help you in any way possible. In fact, she was emphatic in saying that you have free license to ask anything."

Parker had heard from Hernandez that this man was well respected by the others at CDC. Dr. Stewart had one particular interest that had caused Parker to ask for him.

"I appreciate that," Parker said. "Let me ask you about Neisseria meningitidis."

Stewart leaned back in his chair, for the first time showing some comfort with the situation. This, Parker knew, was because Steward was the world's leading expert on meningococcal disease, a deadly, vicious process of infection in the fluid that surrounded a person's spinal cord and brain, the effects of which were particularly cruel. Those victims who did not die often suffered brain damage that was permanently debilitating. And those who did not suffer brain damage frequently lost limbs, fingers, and toes. A lucky patient would only be deaf for life. And this would be only after a quick and aggressive treatment from several powerful antibiotics. The body had to be flooded with the drugs for someone to stand any chance. But it had to be the right cocktail. Several bugs could cause the infection, some viral and some bacterial, but the nastiest was the Neisseria bug.

"Okay," said Stewart, "what exactly do you need to know?"

"Can it be contagious?"

Stewart chuckled. "Very much so."

"Can it be contagious even to those who have lived in the meningitis belt?"

"You are well read, Mr. Jones."

The layperson rarely knew of the meningitis belt. Parker had done his homework. A zone that crossed over the countries of mid-Africa from Gambia on the west coast to Ethiopia on the east coast, it suffered epidemic outbreaks of meningitis every so often. Both central Africa and certain islands in the Pacific would have rampant outbreaks of the disease. Many thought that if one survived living in the meningitis belt without catching the disease, the immune system would be particularly well equipped.

Dr. Stewart stood. "Come with me. I want to show you something."

Parker followed Stewart out of the office, down the hall, and across to a single elevator that was marked with several signs that warned of limited access. Security cameras were on each corner of the lobby surrounding the elevator. Stewart flashed his pass at a magnetic reader and led Parker onto the elevator. He pushed the button for the sixth floor.

"Have you ever been in a bio lab, Mr. Jones?"

"No, sir."

Parker noticed that Stewart had dropped the sarcasm. He imagined that he had been judged as not being one of those insufferable visitors from the Pentagon or the CIA who didn't seem to have the capacity to respect Stewart or his work.

"Well, in that case, you're going to start right at the top."

Paul Stewart was not remarking on the elevator trip. As the doors opened on the sixth floor, Parker was confronted with two armed guards behind a Plexiglas security stand. Again, several red signs warned of limited access. Another sign warned of restricted access to Biosafety Level 4. Parker had read enough to know this was the maximum-security biological laboratory. The very worst bugs were kept in Biosafety Level 4.

Stewart signed in with the guards as they gave the unrecognized guest a stern look.

"This is Mr. Jones. Putting aside his unusual name, he has direct authorization."

"Doc, if you don't mind, we would like to call on that."

The man stood immobile and stone-faced. He was clearly not an ordinary security guard. At a glance, Parker could tell that the man had been trained to kill and knew how to do so without conscious thought. His pay would be at the highest level possible of any security guard in the United States. No doubt he'd passed endless evaluations, background checks, psych testing, and training before he stood his first day's watch.

"Certainly."

Parker didn't mind. If it were easy for a Mr. Jones to get in a Biosafety Level 4 lab, it would be easy for others. This security was appreciated.

The guard made a call, then gave the thumbs-up. "Okay, Dr. Stewart." A vault-like door clicked and swung open, allowing the two to walk onto the biological lab floor. It was far simpler than Parker had expected. At the end of the hallway they passed through a door that led to a small room with lockers.

"We will now climb into a level-four suit," Stewart said.

The outfit was straight from a *Star Trek* movie, with an oversized hood and a thick, greenish-blue padded material that was not particularly light. It seemed to add twenty or thirty pounds to Parker as he walked around the change room. Stewart strapped tape around their wrists and ankles. They stepped from the locker room to another, with multiple showerheads and a hose coupling for each of the suits. He felt the rush of cool air as Stewart helped connect the hose.

"Can you hear me?"

"Yes." Parker was surprised how well he could hear Stewart when he spoke.

"The shower will come on shortly. It will spray the suit with a disinfectant that should, we pray, kill anything. Hopefully, you don't have any leaks in your suit." This was the first bit of humor that Parker had heard from the scientist. "One more pressure test and we are done."

Again, Parker felt air coming in to the suit.

They entered the laboratory through the vault-like door. It was far smaller than Parker had imagined. There were several glass cases with gloved portals, and inside he saw trays of seemingly harmless vials of different colored liquids. The thick Plexiglas window had a frost coating inside the cabinet.

"You see this one over here?" Stewart pointed to a small, pink vial that had some marking on it Parker could barely make out. "Ebola. That vial could wipe out New York City," Stewart said in a flat, matter-of-fact manner. "Twelve million easy."

It had not made an impression upon Parker until he stared down on the small, seemingly harmless container of pink liquid. The laboratory contained vial after vial of liquids, each with the same lethality. As he glanced across the room, he realized that the bacteria and viruses in that one room could devastate much of the planet's population.

"Here's your friend." Stewart stuck his hands into the glove portals and lifted a smaller, bluish liquid vial. It was marked with a numeric code. "Neisseria."

"Dr. Stewart, let me ask you a question."

"Go ahead."

"A hypothetical." He paused. "A specific, highly contagious bacteria that could be combated by the rarest of antibiotics. The carrier need be infected, highly contagious for a period of time, but curable. And the bacteria must be able to infect even those who have lived in the meningitis belt and may have developed their own immunity. Would that be Neisseria?"

Stewart hesitated, as if wondering whether he should even answer the question. As a scientist, he would have one opinion. As a physician, another.

"We found a particularly virulent form of bacteria that seems to have the contagious qualities of serogroup A." He walked over to a round stainless-steel container while he spoke. He lifted a thick, vault-like lid and as he did a white frozen vapor came out. Inside, he pulled out a much smaller vial, marked with several numbers. It too contained a pale blue liquid that seemed so incapable of causing harm.

"We call this NM-13. It came from a small village called Xudun somewhere in northern Somolia. A person infected with this would be highly contagious for a twelve- to thirty-six-hour period. It is actually indeigenous to this one place in the meningitis belt. With the right stuff at exactly the right time, it can be nonlethal. And thus, not even classified as a biological weapon. But without some very specific antibiotics, he would suffer a horrible and nearly unimaginable death thereafter."

"Survivors?"

"Odds are very, very few. Probably the black plague descendants."

"I don't understand?" Parker kept looking at the pale blue liquid.

"A very few that are the great, great grandchildren of the survivors of the plague seem to have a super defense mechanism, but they would have to be from eastern Europe. Otherwise, no." Stewart paused as if he were an accountant tallying up the numbers. "No survivors."

"How would it be transmitted?"

"Saliva. A cough, a sneeze, a shared glass."

"And what of the carrier?"

Parker could tell that Stewart felt uncomfortable with the questions. The physician was tugging at his conscience. He was committed to do no harm. Parker imagined that Stewart sensed where this was going and who the carrier was, and he didn't like the choices this conversation was giving him.

"I don't recommend this, Mr. Jones. The period of incubation could be much shorter and the damage irreversible. I would not recommend that any human being knowingly be exposed to this beast."

"But with the right battery of antibiotics, do you have a probability of stopping it?"

"Yes, you probably have a seventy to eighty percent chance of stopping it if you pour on exactly the right antibiotics within six to eight hours of the infection."

"Thanks, Doctor." Parker paused for a moment. "Let me ask another question, if I may."

"Sure."

"Have you ever been to Afghanistan?"

"No."

Parker smiled. If his life depended upon the right antibiotics at the right time, then Dr. Stewart would be making his first trip to Afghanistan soon. His screams of protest might be heard all the way up to the bio lab, but the director would remind him that a paragraph buried deep in his contract stated that in times of a national emergency he was commissioned as an officer in the Army medical corps. More important, she would stress that the call came directly from the highest authority.

Oblivious to the reason for the question and the smile, Stewart offered a last warning:

"You need to understand that although NM-13 has a seventy to eighty percent chance of being stopped, it also has a twenty to thirty percent chance that nothing will work." Stewart's tone became somber. He stood directly in front of Parker, so as to allow no escape, and looked him directly in the eyes. "Once that packet is open and you feel it in your hand, you have, at the outside, twelve hours before you started with a headache that you wish you could find a gun to blow your brains out with, then your neck will feel like it had been welded in place, and then you die limb by limb, piece by piece."

CHAPTER 13

The cabin

As with most days, William Parker rose and left the lodge well before dawn.

Unlike other days, however, this time he wasn't coming back. Nor was he packing for a normal trip. In fact, in his top dresser drawer he left his watch, wallet, and all of his other personal possessions.

This should be interesting, Parker thought as he drove away from the darkened lodge. The thought of some state trooper stopping him and his explaining that he didn't have a lick of identification amused him as he descended the mountain.

Clark has Stidham's number.

Comforting as far as her safety went, though no emotional consolation for either of them. He thought of her, still in bed, pretending to be asleep, and he began to regret his decision. They hadn't said anything about it the night before. She didn't want him to go, but she also knew it would be a mistake to do anything but let him complete the mission.

Parker shook his head and reminded himself it was too late to rethink the situation. No, all that mattered now was that if Clark needed help, Shane Stidham would move heaven and earth to assist her.

Parker pulled his truck out onto the highway, heading north. A deep ache began to throb in his shoulder. He squeezed his fist, again, and then a third time.

Rain.

Like all wounded, Parker knew when the barometer was dropping.

North to Atlanta. Leave the truck there in long-term parking. He laughed. *Maybe very long-term.*

Parker didn't want anything that could be trailed back to the lodge. A flight with his twin airplane might leave a record on the several Internet sites that tracked the movement of aircraft. From Atlanta, Scott would have a Gulfstream waiting at the FBO.

No trace, no trail.

Every move involved some level of risk. Parker knew that. It didn't bother him. William Parker wasn't a fearful man.

He rubbed his face and the stubble of his new, growing beard with one hand as he drove past the Chevron station in Cusseta. Pickups had stopped at each of the pumps, coughing up clouds of exhaust in the cold, predawn morning. Several had trailers with four-wheelers, all heading toward the woods, all trying to get to their deer stands well before the first light.

And Sadik Zabara? Parker thought as he headed north.

Where is he?

CHAPTER 14

Terminal 1, International Arrivals, Heathrow Airport, London

Ali Sitwa continuously played with his short beard, unconsciously twisting the hair as he stood, waiting, under the arrow sign. The meeting point was Heathrow's arrow sign, which was just beyond the customs release gate. Everyone knew of the arrow sign, and if by chance one didn't, the crowd of waiting people just beyond the gate made for an unmistakable signal.

Sadik Zabara was a stranger to Sitwa. But he, like everyone who worked at his London newspaper, was familiar with Zabara's reputation. Zabara had survived the worst of the ethnic cleansing of the Bosnian war, becoming a Muslim legend. His posts to the *Oslobođenje* newspaper recorded three years of the brutal bloodshed, during which time Muslims were dragged out into the streets on a daily basis, begging for their lives, only to be knifed or shot or raped by the drunken Serbian death squads. Zabara and his wife managed to escape the purges in the attic above a neighbor's shop, like a modern-day Anne Frank, living on cold *kupus* and *grah*. His host, a Serbian farmer who couldn't stomach the death squads, became, like few in mankind's history, a hero who protected a fugitive family from its predators. It was truly a miracle that the Muslim journalist had survived.

Al-Quds Al-Arabi had become the media lifeblood of hundreds of thousands of Muslims in Great Britain. Readers as far away as Scotland and western Europe followed the paper's daily report of Muslim affairs. Zabara would extend *Al-Arabi*'s already broad reach, perhaps dramatically.

A lanky man accompanied by a woman carrying a toddler on her hip pushed their luggage cart through the arrivals door. There could be no mistaking Zabara, though he appeared taller than Sitwa had expected. More expected was the poorly cut sandy hair, tight to the extreme on the sides and long and wavy on the top, and the stubble of several days' growth. Zabara's outfit—an off-green plaid shirt and brown trousers—appeared well worn and looked like the garb of someone who lived day-to-day in a poor country.

Sitwa had been told that Zabara was a pale Caucasian. This had come as a surprise. It was Mansoor's own prejudice to assume that a Muslim must be darker-skinned. At least he was able to recognize that prejudice and let it only be a passing thought. But it wasn't only the skin tone that raised Sitwa's eyebrows. As Zabara came closer, he looked much more fit than the newsman had expected.

The wife, however, had the look of a once-attractive woman who had lived through too many years of war and nights of fear. The baby girl, with her round face and large brown eyes, hung closely. But she didn't resemble either the mother who held her or the father who stood nearby. Her red, curly hair, in fact, seemed quite her own. Nor did she match their relatively advanced age.

Sitwa looked more closely at Zabara's wife. She was well-proportioned for a woman in her mid-forties, although her shape was well camouflaged by an oversized orange-and-blue coat that looked like a decade-old ski jacket. Where it hung open, Sitwa could see a rather slim waist. She carried two stuffed plastic shopping bags marked with the name of some store in Sarajevo, and he pushed a cart that carried three bulging suitcases that were well worn and frayed on the edges. Stacked on top of the suitcases were two rolled-up prayer rugs tied tightly with hemp.

"*As sala'amu alaikum, Sadik Zabara.*" Much shorter than his newly arrived employee, Sitwa looked up into Sadik's light blue eyes.

"*Walaikum as sala'am.*"

The two men briefly hugged as Zabara's wife looked on. She seemed sad, and her eyes were flat and distant.

"You must be Mr. Sitwa of *Al-Arabi*?"

"Yes, I am, and welcome to Great Britain. We are all excited about having you on at the paper." For now, both Sitwa and Zabara spoke broken, heavily accented English.

It had surprised Sitwa when his usually cautious editor had suggested hiring the Bosnian journalist. Sitwa's boss was a man who always chose the safe route, eschewing stories about jihad for the tame lifestyle articles that pleased advertisers. One day, though, when an argument over the paper's vision heated up with his editorial board, the editor told everyone to submit a list with three names on it.

"You think there is a problem here. So you give me names and we will see."

Several had put Sadik Zabara on their lists—a bold gesture indeed, since Zabara was well known for editorials that announced the end of the bin Laden era and called out for a new leader of the jihad.

The greatest shock of all had come when Sitwa's editor had told him to contact Zabara with an offer of employment.

Zabara smiled broadly and put his hand on Sitwa's arm. "I am honored to be here and write for *Al-Arabi*."

The baby started to fuss, then cry.

Zabara's wife comforted her. "*Otac, otac, otac* . . ."

The child kept crying.

"Such a young child." *For middle-aged parents,* Sitwa was thinking.

"Ah." Zabara smiled. "She is our niece. The daughter of my wife's younger sister."

Sitwa didn't need to ask. The child's mother would not have let her daughter go abroad with her aunt and uncle if she were still alive. In all likelihood, both of the child's parents had been lost.

"*Otac* . . . What word is that?" Sitwa asked.

"Oh, it is just a child's word." Zabara rubbed his hand on the child's head as the mother tried to silence her. Suddenly Zabara grimaced and clenched his fist; once, twice, and then a third time.

"Is your arm all right?

"Oh, yes. No problem. Too many hours on airplanes."

"I have a car waiting. We have a flat for you on Spruce Hills in Walthamstow, just off of Forest Street. It's near Walthamstow Central Station. Very easy to get around."

For centuries, the East End of London was the first stop for migrating people moving into Great Britain. It was near the docks. New immigrants would get off the boat and immediately settle in the nearest neighborhood. But the Olympics changed the city. Where tenants had once lived at arm's length, now there were large plazas and stadiums. Now the new immigrants wandered farther in from the river, huddling in neighborhoods of similar others. For Bosnian Muslims it became Walthamstow. It had become a haven for the growing Muslim population of London.

"Is it near the paper?"

"No. The paper is, unfortunately, on the other side of the city. But your flat is on a main road and within a short walk of the Victoria Line. The paper is just a few blocks from the Ravenscourt Park tube. Once you get the hang of it, you will be fine."

Zabara smiled as he pushed the cart through the doors and followed Sitwa, who carried on the conversation while talking over his shoulder.

"Besides, there is a restaurant just a block away from your flat that serves *begove corba*." Sitwa wasn't from Sarajevo and knew about the lamb stew only from what he was told, but he wanted Zabara to become comfortable with his new life.

"Really?" Zabara glanced at his wife.

Sitwa saw the ghost of a smile flit across her face.

"Yes, indeed. The restaurant is called Jehzh Café."

"I am sorry about our flights," Zabara said. "We

were delayed almost a day in Vienna. Apparently, Lufthansa had made an error with our tickets."

Sitwa had wondered why the trip had taken so long. He had expected Zabara the day before.

"It still is difficult coming out of Sarajevo," Zabara continued.

His wife followed, quietly whispering to the little girl.

Perhaps her English is not very good, Sitwa thought as they cut across the roadway to the pickup point. He began frantically waving his arm.

"There is our driver."

He pointed to an old Volvo station wagon parked at the curb. Upon seeing Sitwa, the driver jumped out and opened up the hatch.

"It is good to have you at *Al-Arabi,* brother." Sitwa lifted the first bag into the car. Like the others, it was heavy. It had to be. It, and the few others, contained all of this family's possessions. "And I must say . . . we are particularly excited about the invitation you have received."

Zabara nodded thoughtfully. "Indeed."

CHAPTER 15

Walter Reed National Military Medical Center, Bethesda, Maryland

The neurosurgery critical-care ward at Walter Reed Bethesda remained filled to capacity, as it had since the first IED injuries began to arrive in 2003. Head trauma had left countless soldiers in deep comas, the breathing machines continuously beating to a constant rhythm of inhale and exhale.

"WRNMMC?" Robert Tranthan smiled as he mumbled to himself. "Only the military could reduce Walter Reed's merger with Bethesda to WRNMMC."

Tranthan had never been to the Walter Reed National Military Medical Center before, but the neurosurgery floor quickly gave him a sense of the weight of the war. Most of the patients were young men with expressionless faces, shaved heads with long, horrific, Frankenstein-like scars over their skulls. A few were young women. The face of war had changed, IEDs being entirely nondiscriminatory.

"Excuse me?" he asked a doctor in the hall.

"Yes?" The neurosurgeon looked understandably impatient. She was on the twelfth hour of a fourteen-hour shift.

"I am trying to find out the status of a patient."

"Are you a member of the family?"

"No, but perhaps you can tell me where the doctor is?"

Dr. Reynolds's eyes narrowed. "What do you need?"

Tranthan could have summoned the rear admiral in charge to come out on the floor to help him. But one thing the deputy director of the Central Intelligence Agency didn't need was to make this unplanned, unannounced visit to Walter Reed Bethesda become a public event.

Tranthan took his voice down a notch. "I'm sorry. Perhaps I said something I shouldn't have. I am told that a young lady who worked for me was up here. She was injured in a blast in Qatar."

Instant recognition sparked in the doctor's eye. "Oh. Yes. She's in room 604."

"Might I ask about her condition?"

"You know about the amputations of her legs. She has a traumatic brain injury with a loss of memory from the concussion caused by the blast."

"You're the doctor?"

"I am the resident neurosurgeon. Dr. Anne Reynolds." She held out her hand, in a very indifferent way, while tucking a chart under her arm. Clearly, to her the patient mattered far more than a "VIP" visitor.

"Thank you, Doctor. I'm Robert Tranthan." Tranthan paused, not wanting to identify himself further. He shook her hand. "You say she had memory loss."

"Yes, very common with traumatic brain injury. When she was first evaluated, they gave her a GCS score of six. Her Rancho is level five, but that may be very generous."

"Forgive my ignorance. What do those tests mean?"

"Initially, we judge the severity of the brain injury by the Glasgow Coma Scale. Just with fourteen out of fifteen, she could have significant memory loss. She was a six."

"Good God."

"The Rancho Los Amigos Scale judges her present status."

"So what is level five?" Tranthan had known it was bad, but he felt physically sick as the doctor explained.

"Our fives wander. They float in and out of conversations. Sometimes, briefly, you can get their attention, but their memories are all over the place." The doctor was looking over Tranthan's shoulder, only partially engaged in the conversation.

"Will she get her memory back?"

"I couldn't predict that." Dr. Reynolds reached over to the rack of charts and pulled another one from its slip. "She just came in. Her memory is spotty but somewhat recovered for her life before the explosion, but at best only up to a few months before the injury. She's a blank slate about what happened. My guess is that she will get some of her memory back, but never all of it."

An unexpected note of compassion entered Dr. Reynold's tone as she took in Tranthan's expression, which must have been pitiable.

"The truth is, we really don't know. Some folks surprise us. Anything could happen."

Tranthan stared down at the chart. In bold letters, it said *Margaret Elizabeth O'Donald*. Until now, he had forgotten what her middle name was.

"Like I said, she's in 604." The doctor was already moving away.

"Thanks," Tranthan said absently, then moved to follow Reynolds. "Excuse me, Doctor. If there is any change, please let me know."

He handed Reynolds the business card of the deputy director of the Central Intelligence Agency.

She was the only patient in room 604 and seemed to be in a deep sleep—the machines continuously beeping in sync with her heartbeat. The room's window looked out across a courtyard, and the sunlight, through the open shades, illuminated her incredibly small figure in the bed. Small tents formed the shape of her legs that were no longer there. She looked pale and whiter than he ever remembered seeing her. He had always loved that natural tan she seemed to have inherited, with the striking black eyebrows and long, curling hair. But the black eyebrows now stood out against her pale white complexion.

He pulled up the chair and sat down next to her. The chair bumped the bed as he pulled it up alongside, and the slight bump caused her to wince and grimace in pain. She opened her eyes and smiled.

"Hey, you," she said in a near whisper.

"Hey."

"Is my car all right?"

He was confused by the question.

"Your car?"

"I just got it yesterday."

"You must be Robert." A nurse spoke from behind him.

Tranthan turned around as a woman with a clip-board and floral-printed scrubs in orange and black came into the room. A stethoscope hung around her neck. Her hair was cut short and gray with traces of black.

Tranthan stared at her.

"I am Nurse Cook. Billie Cook. Her nurse assigned to her care."

"Ah, yes, I know who you are." Tranthan had specifically approved her assignment. Billie Cook was a veteran staffer at the hospital and had a top-secret clearance. She had been told on day one that Maggie O'Donald worked for the Agency. A patient with a head injury who had worked in the intelligence field could mumble something to the wrong person. She had to be watched and those with access had to be limited.

"I appreciate your helping her."

"She's a good patient, behaves herself, and doesn't get too wild."

Maggie smiled.

"What is this about her car?"

"She believes that she was in a bad car wreck. This happens a lot with our patients that have suffered a concussion and memory loss."

Tranthan pulled his chair back as the nurse slid past and began taking Maggie's blood pressure and pulse. Cook reminded him of his fourth-grade teacher. Her mannerisms were both stern and compassionate.

"She's come a long way. It's good for her to have a visitor."

He knew what that meant. She had no family nearby.

Maggie's father had died while she was at Stanford, and her mother had come down with fatal ovarian cancer soon after. She was gone only a few months after the diagnosis. Maggie cried on Tranthan's shoulder when the call came. Now, there was no one.

Tranthan looked at his watch. It wasn't that he was pressed with some more important engagement; it was a nervous reaction and inability to know how to handle the situation. The woman he had fallen in love with was no more.

"Could I ask a favor?" he asked Billie Cook.

"Sure."

"I need to speak with Maggie alone for a second. It's about her work."

Cook nodded curtly. "Okay, but you'll need to keep it short. She still doesn't have a lot of energy."

"Certainly."

Cook slid the door closed to the room. Since it was intensive care, each room was more like a glass-encased cubicle than a typical hospital room.

"Maggie. Do you remember what you were working on?"

"Sure, sure I do."

"Riyadh—your source? You never said who your source was or what you had found."

Maggie had protected her source. No one would know who the source was. It had taken months to develop that trust. Any hint that others knew and the source would be forever gone.

"I know it. I'm sure I know it."

"Maggie, Patrick, your security officer?"

"Yes, how is Pat?"

"He's okay," Tranthan lied. "There was a picture on

his cell phone." It was a miracle that the chip in the phone had retained anything retrievable. The phone, like Patrick, had been scattered in small pieces in the bomb's crater.

"A man was in a photo from a University of Michigan party."

"Yes, I remember. Pat asked about him."

"He's a Chechen named Umarov. Did you know him?"

"No, I don't think so."

"Maggie, it's important. Things are rolling. We need confirmation. Who was your source? Who was on the inside in Saudi Arabia? How did you contact him? How do we contact him?"

He didn't add that the Chechen would, at this moment, be looking for this person as well.

"I know it. Just let me think a minute."

"We know it was probably one of the members of the royal family."

"I know it." Her face was twisted, in a confused look. "I'm sure I do."

Tranthan heard the slide of the door behind him.

"Sorry. Like I said, not too much." Cook smiled but was firm in her comment.

Tranthan stood reluctantly and tried to smile. "Bye for now, Maggie. I'll check on you again in a couple of days. Nurse, please call me, day or night." He handed her a card as he had with the neurosurgeon.

Tranthan walked out of the front entrance of WRNMMC, down the stairs to his waiting black executive Tahoe. The driver hopped out of the SUV as soon as he saw Tranthan coming, cut around to the side, and opened the door.

"Thanks."

The driver had been the deputy's assigned driver for two years now but Tranthan, if pressed, could barely remember his name. Prior to that, the driver had worked for the Agency for nearly twenty years after a short enlistment with the army. He could shoot straight and drive, if need be, like a NASCAR driver.

"Back to Langley."

"Yes, sir."

The black Tahoe pulled out of WRNMMC and turned right, heading north.

"Something is going on." Robert Tranthan stared out at the joggers as they ran past the entranceway to Bethesda. "Something bad."

CHAPTER 16

Lake Rotorua, New Zealand

"This is not typical." The instructor in his blue flight suit stood under the covered porch of the cabin. It was a constant rain. On any other day, the porch would have had an unobstructed view of the crystal blue waters of Lake Rotorua. The volcanic mountains that surrounded the lake framed the view like the Grand Tetons.

A class of only three flight students sat in their chairs holding on their laps the three-ring binders of flight instructions. Their faces did not reflect a wealth of experience.

"So who do we have here? It's a nice class size. We can learn much from each other." He was right. They always wanted more students but three and the instructor fit perfectly into the aircraft. "We have one from Darwin?"

A man of thirty looked up from his seat leaned up against the post of the porch.

"You are training for a hunting guide service."

"That's right," he said with a smile, his Australian accent thick.

"And one from Sydney?"

"Yes, sir." This kid seemed barely old enough to drive. He looked no more than fifteen, but in reality, he had logged the most flight hours.

"And a young lady."

She nodded, clearly determined to be silent and quiet.

"You are training to fly for one of the oil companies?"

"Yes, sir."

"Well, welcome to the Lake. You will learn that our bird drags like hell and is unforgiving. If you sneeze on a landing or takeoff, you will flip head over heel until you are sausage."

He paused for a second.

"But the float plane can take you to places no one else can go, and no one will ever know you are there."

CHAPTER 17

London

Parker pulled up the collar of his coat to block the drizzle from the late fall storm. It was another wet day, and he found London in late fall depressing. At least he had a new Barbour rain jacket suited to the climate. He wouldn't wear a cap, and his long hair and new beard were damp from the continuous drizzle. So he stood there, in the dark and rain and cold at nearly three in the morning, waiting for a bus that should soon be arriving carrying a certain man.

He was exhausted. His trip had grown lengthy long before his arrival in London. On a C-37 Gulfstream to Germany he boned up with the language instructor from Monterey on the subtleties of Bosnian and Arab languages. The Agency jet was set up more like a small office, from end to end, with documentation, clothing, haircuts, inoculations, cultural training, and everything else that could be crammed in. He'd had no time or room for sleeping. Fortunately, after meeting the real

Zabara in Germany, Parker was able to get one hard, solid hour of sleep on the flight to England.

I must be crazy.

Parker rarely had self-doubt. He had learned some time ago that doubt can never be a benefit to anything. But in only a few days he had gone from private citizen to deep-cover agent.

If it weren't important, I wouldn't be here . . .

The reason for the mission obliterated any doubt: Everything the Agency knew, everything that they told him about Yousef al-Qadi, only confirmed what he suspected. Not only had he helped kill Parker's parents, he would also kill many thousands more if not stopped.

A fire-engine-red double-decker bus pulled around the corner, and Parker climbed onto its rear, heading directly toward the stairway to the second deck. A man with a baseball hat stood on the first step, blocking the stairs with his weightlifter's body. Parker measured well over six feet, but the stranger towered above him. The guard had a crew cut below his cap, clearly a member of the military. Parker took a step toward the stairway and the stranger put his hand across the landing and grabbed the railing on the other side.

Parker glanced around to see that the few remaining passengers were sitting up front near the driver. It was a slow day and, being mid-morning, the passenger traffic had slowed down considerably. He leaned over to the man.

"Scott."

The oversized stranger immediately pulled his arm away from the railing.

Parker climbed the curved stairs up to the second

deck. It was empty except for one man sitting near the front reading the *London Times*.

Scott laid down the newspaper when the bearded man came up and sat down in the seat across from him

"Well, William, it's good to see that you made it."

"Thanks."

"Our unit has put together several articles for you. They should keep the hook baited." With the help of MI6, Parker was to publish a quick series of fiery op-ed pieces supposedly penned by Sadik Zabara. Britain's own Scotland Yard had not been told the truth, that "Zabara" was in fact a deep plant, for fear of a potential leak. Consequently, Parker, aka Zabara, was already being listed by several domestic law-enforcement agencies as a danger. His initial comparison of Al Qaeda to the American Revolutionary heroes had already stung his host country twice while rapidly making him into a folk hero for the extremist Muslim community in Great Britain.

"The e-mail from Yousef came."

"Yes."

"I'm supposed to be in Peshawar by noon on November seventh."

Scott blinked. "What else?"

"Nothing. It simply said that if I wanted to meet a great leader I was to be at the Khyber bazaar at noon."

"That's it?"

"I imagine Yousef has not survived this long without being cautious."

"This is a new PDA," Scott changed the subject abruptly, handing Parker what looked like a BlackBerry cell phone. Unlike a BlackBerry, however, it had no logos on it. "It wasn't ready for you earlier."

"Okay."

"It's a Sectéra Edge. It can handle top-secret, and if you lose your password, it becomes a four-ounce brick. No one can get into it."

"An Edge? That's poetic." Parker was leery of having his life depend upon any technology, let alone a cell phone, but he wasn't planning on using it much anyway.

"It has your new articles attached to the e-mail in it." Scott knew that Parker could retype the stories, adding his touches that identified his style, and submit them to the editor.

"Watch this." Scott held up the phone. "It's Bosnian." The initial screen showed a bold blue-and-white Telekom Srpske logo. "You have to go through two windows and a password to get into the inner phone."

Parker took the phone and scanned through the initial screens.

"What about my backup?" Parker asked, referring to Afghanistan.

"We've got your support team ready."

"Moncrief has to be on it."

Scott nodded.

"And I need to meet the leader of the team."

"Okay."

"How's the missus?" Scott asked wryly, referring to Zabara's wife and her niece, who were living with him.

Parker was not amused. "At night she comforts her niece, who still cries for her parents." Parker had spent hours already listening to Zabara's wife rocking the child in her arms and singing to her softly in their Bosnian language. It was not pleasant.

"Well, once they get through this, they get their golden ticket."

"What do you mean?"

"All three of them will be relocated to the U.S., get new names, and be made American citizens."

Parker had assumed as much. Still, he was amazed at what the wife was putting her niece and self through. Zabara was being kept well out of sight, probably at some remote location in Scotland.

"Scott, I need you to do something."

Scott shrugged.

"A favor."

"What is it?"

Parker knew he had Scott over a barrel. The entire mission depended upon this one man. At this point, any request could be made.

"I need you to get me somewhere by tomorrow night at the latest." Parker handed him an address written on a piece of paper.

"Are you serious?"

"Yes, very."

Scott stood as the bus approached its next stop.

"This is where I get off. The password for your phone is x-ray, alpha, niner, question mark, five, percent." Scott spelled it out so there would be no doubt.

"What is that supposed to mean?"

"Nothing. It's just what the techs say is a reliable password. Take care that you don't forget it. I'll e-mail you about your request."

Parker watched as Scott—clearly not happy about Parker's special request—and his bodyguard crossed over Green Street and hailed a taxi. He activated the telephone and typed in the password. A Microsoft Windows operating system opened. Parker selected the e-mail application and saw only one, from Scott.

"Whatever you need." It had, as an attachment, two new stories.

Parker turned it off and slipped it into one of the inner pockets of the Barbour coat. It was getting colder. *Might even see some snow.* That's when it occurred to him. He was the same city where his parents had spent their last night. It had snowed then as well.

Yeah, he thought, *This is worth it.*

CHAPTER 18

Riyadh, Saudi Arabia

Yousef al-Qadi had not been to the capital of Saudi Arabia in nearly a decade. He had not been home. He had not been allowed home. The House of Saud had made it clear that he was not welcome. And then, suddenly, he had been summoned.

ArRiyadh, he thought as he looked out over the early morning skyline as the Gulfstream jet circled for landing. The fresh air of the morning seemed to amplify the sparkle of silver-tinted glass, steel, and aluminum and the giant palm trees that surrounded the buildings. The city had a population of barely a million when he'd last left.

It began as an oasis, a garden surrounded by the wasteland of the desert. Now Riyadh had grown to more than six million. As his airplane tilted in its turn, the sun flashed off the tall buildings of glass and steel, which spread out across the skyline. Riyadh had been kind to the inspirations and unlimited budgets of young architects. The Al Faisaliah Tower's point stood out just beyond the airfield. It appeared more like the point of some gigantic spaceship ready for launch into the stratosphere. Again, across the city and beyond the King Fahd Highway, the bright Markaz Al-Mamlakah skyscraper seemed to confirm that the students of I. M. Pei had been given the city as a playground. The glimmering metallic tower dominated the skyline, rising over a thousand feet from the desert floor.

As a member of the Muslim Brotherhood, Yousef was a descendant of the House of Saud. Unlike bin Laden, although born in Riyadh as well, Yousef was not the son of a Yemeni immigrant. In that regard, Yousef's banishment had been more painful.

It had taken the death of bin Laden for Yousef to be summoned back home; and even so, his return would be brief, only for one specific meeting with the secretary of the Bay'ah Council. Politics were divided in his homeland. Some were happy about bin Laden's death. Others thought of Yousef as necessary and needed. He was the new bin Laden. But even his supporters worried about how far he was willing to go. Yousef wanted a new pure Muslim state shaped out of the wilderness. It was an unpredictable event.

The Royal Saudi jet landed and taxied up to the general aviation terminal, where it parked in line with nearly a dozen other Gulfstreams, Boeing business jets, and Boeing 767s built as exclusive private aircrafts. A white GMC Yukon with two security escort vehicles were waiting as the jet pulled up. One of the escort Humvees was topless with a machine gun and gunner in the back. The vehicles cut across the city on the multilaned King Fahd Highway, flying at breakneck speed as they cut from lane to lane. The highway was tiered with four lanes above and four lanes below. Yousef looked up as the drivers of the cars in the lanes above stared down when they heard the sirens. The city was far more tense than the city he knew as a child. It seemed on edge.

The security escorts peeled off as the Yukon entered the grounds of the palace of the secretary. As a member of the Bay'ah Council, the secretary was one of the most powerful men on earth. In 2006, by royal decree, King Abdullah had carved into stone the creation of a new Bay'ah Council, a council with virtually unlimited power. It would choose the next ruler of the kingdom, who would control well over 25 percent of the world's oil. And the Council not only chose the next king. It would also determine who would never be king.

The kingdom had struggled for years after a stroke had incapacitated the former crown prince. On several occasions, the power struggle almost erupted into bloodshed. The sons of the House of Saud realized that the incapacitation caused as much risk to the stability of Saudi Arabia as any war. Much depended now on the Council's judgment, wisdom, and speed.

"*As sala'amu alaikum,*" the secretary greeted Yousef at the entrance, below a high arch of white stone and a stained-glass ceiling. Waterfalls on both sides of the entrance gave a backdrop of sound that was almost deafening. To the desert, it was a commodity far rarer than oil.

"*Walaikum as sala'am.*"

Yousef knew the secretary from their days at elementary school many decades ago. Now they were both middle-aged men. The secretary, however, was dressed in one of his bespoke suits. Gieves & Hawkes provided a private tailor from Savile Row to visit him regularly twice a year. His face was full and round, unlike his distant cousin's bony face, and his beard neatly trimmed. He had the sweet smell of Grafton, a London gentlemen's aftershave, along with tobacco.

Yousef, relegated to playing the poor country cousin, smiled to himself at the thought of their respective, starkly separate worlds.

"Come with me, Cousin."

Yousef knew the secretary was being generous in calling him *cousin*. He could have called him *brother*, as in the Muslim faith, but it would have had less of a meaning than *cousin*. He led him through the hallway, across a vast room with red and gold carpets and Louis XV–styled, gold-trimmed settee sofas and chairs, to a sitting area that looked out over a garden that extended for hundreds of meters.

Yousef felt no pangs of envy as he absorbed the surroundings. Yes, all the comforts of the modern world were available if he simply chose another way. But he had chosen his path years ago and his mind was clear. Muhammad had lived a simple life. And so would Yousef.

"Congratulations on your being named secretary." Yousef suspected that his cousin knew how much he despised him.

"Yes, it is a great honor, but there are always complications."

"I heard." Yousef knew that despite the fact that the thirty-five members of the Bay'ah Council were all brothers and sons of brothers, the stakes were too high for politics not to play a part. Thirty-five sons and grandsons of Abdullah bin Abdul Aziz were given the power to select the next ruler from a list of three provided by their king. They also had the power to reject the choices. Without doubt, the one selected would be a son of Aziz. It stood to be a battle of epic proportions. And the battlefield was starting to take shape.

The play to become king required the utmost balancing act of interests. Like the selection of the next pope by the Vatican Council, the early candidates polarized the votes and rarely succeeded. Now, with the death of bin Laden, the princes that supported moving the world by violence had been left without an antagonist.

"I was saddened," said Yousef, "by the cowardly attack in Pakistan."

The secretary nodded.

"Do not wonder, Cousin. When the day ends and the sun sets, a new Muslim state will rise to vanquish the infidels."

Yousef watched the secretary for his reaction. He knew perfectly well that the secretary and those on the Council considered Yousef a dangerous weapon, capable of doing far more harm than good, as far as they were concerned. Rumor had said for some time that Yousef was bent upon being the father of a new Muslim state to be carved out of the western provinces of Pakistan and eastern Afghanistan. Many believed that a new state would begin a rallying call for fundamentalism in the Muslim faith. It would serve as the anchor. It would be a challenge to the constantly Westward-leaning House of Saud. If it hadn't seemed such a ridiculous long shot, Yousef knew, the House of Saud would have acted overtly against him, not simply banished him from the country. But his dream of forming a fundamentalist

Muslim state was considered, at best, a long-shot lottery ticket. Now, with the constant strikes on the al-Qaeda leadership, a vacuum had opened up.

"You are an ambitious man," said the secretary at last, showing no emotional reaction whatsoever.

"You have said that before."

It was not meant to be a compliment.

"No one has ever doubted you, Yousef." The secretary stood up, signaling the end of the meeting. He signaled for his servant with the wave of his hand. "Oh, by the way, Saudi Aramco informs me that it is best that we reduce our production."

"Yes?"

"The production of El Haba will need to be tightened."

Yousef frowned at the thought of his family's income being reduced, especially as a childishly punitive measure.

"I'm afraid that we all must sacrifice some, my cousin."

Yousef bit his tongue and nodded. The message had been sent and there was no point in quarreling about it now.

The secretary turned to face Yousef squarely. "Our stability here relies upon the stability of the American market."

So that was it? Yousef had been summoned to receive a warning against reacting too severely to the attacks on the al Queda leadership—against carrying out *any* major, anti-American operation before the Council had finished its byzantine maneuvering and named a successor?

"I understand." Yousef acknowledged the warning without agreeing in any way. "Are we finished?"

"While you are here, you must go by your father's home."

"There is nothing there for me."

"My brother, Riyadh will always be your home. Do not turn your back on it."

CHAPTER 19

Al-Quds Al-Arabi newspaper, King Street, London

The glare of the afternoon sun made the young receptionist's computer screen nearly impossible to read. She sighed and rose to adjust the blinds. Her *abayah* and pashmina shawl met the traditional requirements of the Muslim newspaper but, in direct sunlight, felt almost unbearably hot. As she stepped to the second-floor window, she noticed a man standing across the street, looking up at the newspaper office. The unwavering attention struck the receptionist as unusual because the building was nondescript, especially for the shops and stores of King Street, and had no signage whatsoever. Most would not have even known that the Muslim newspaper was located there but for a speakerphone at the street entrance that had the tiny words *Al-Arabi* taped to it. But the man kept staring at the second-floor windows and, in turn, at the receptionist as she lowered the blind.

"What's he up to?" She spoke to the other woman who shared the front office.

"Who?"

"There's a man across the street."

Together they peeked around the shades. The man continued to watch, standing there in his strange, black-and-white striped sweater hat pulled down over his ears, long black beard, and zipped, collared jacket. He paused only to look down at a map he was holding, and then resumed his watch over the newspaper's building.

Both women were on edge, like all who worked at *Al-Arabi,* and with good reason. The newspaper itself was always on edge. It wasn't under the threat of any radical Muslim or jihadist. On the contrary, many thought of the paper as the voice of the radical and fundamentalist Muslim community. But such popularity bred unhealthy obsessions, plus opposition from extremists from other camps. Not to mention the attention of numerous government agencies.

"He's coming." The first secretary spoke the words as the man folded the map, placed it in his coat pocket, and then started to cross the hectic street toward the building.

"Should we call the guard?"

The guard was the oversized, overweight man who always wore the same suit, one too small, and was kept by the newspaper to provide security around the clock. He had to turn his shoulders to walk down the narrow stairs of the second-floor flat. But at the moment he was in the back, taking one of his notorious naps. He was effective in providing an imposing wall between the workers and any unwanted visitor, but generally he had little to do. He was there more to appease the women who were constantly on edge.

"Hello." A voice crackled over the speaker. The traffic noise often made it barely audible.

"Can I help you?" The first secretary spoke into the box with hesitation.

"Yes, I looking for Zabara." The man seemed to struggle over the English words. "Sadik Zabara."

"Come up."

The other receptionist gave her a shocked glare of displeasure at the invitation. They both stood behind the first desk as they heard the door swing open and heavy steps coming up the stairway.

Close up, the visitor's skin shone a milky white. His black beard and dark curly eyebrows gave the impression of a Rasputin. He had unforgettable eyes. One was brown and the other green.

"Yes." The man worked hard to choose his words, then resorted to what he'd said before. "I looking for Zabara. Sadik Zabara."

"May I ask why you would want to talk with Mr. Zabara?" In his very short time at the paper, Zabara had earned the respect of both women. In the international language of the sexes, he was tall and attractive. He also seemed very determined. So far he'd worked late, very late, and he always smiled at the receptionists as if he appreciated what they did to help produce the weekly paper.

"Zabara a friend of my friend."

"And who are you?"

"We both from Sarajevo."

"Oh, you are from Bosnia?"

"Bosnia, yes."

"And your name?"

"Knez. Jovan Knez."

"Knees?"

"I write for you." Knez took a pad from the desk and wrote out *Jovan Knez*. He wrote down the telephone number to the small hotel where he was staying. "Please tell him it involves General Delić. I am a *Crni Labudovi*. A black swan."

"A black swan?"

"Yes. He will know." Knez pulled up his sleeve to show the tattoo of a small black swan with the words *crni labudovi* in script underneath.

"And that is *labudovi*?" The first secretary wrote down on the note *laboodovey*. It was wrong but close enough.

"Yes, yes."

The man turned and headed down the stairs. Both women turned to the window, following the stranger as he crossed over and headed down King Street, toward the Hammersmith tube station.

He didn't know it, but William Parker had only missed the stranger by an instant. As he walked out of the entrance from the tube station, the man passed him walking in. They exchanged glances, but neither recognized the other. For the time being, it kept one of them alive.

"Mr. Zabara." The secretary waved at Parker as he came up the stairs to the newspaper. They knew his step, as he would always take two to three steps at a time.

"Yes?"

"Mr. Zabara, a man came to see you."

William Parker gave the first girl a brief look, a look of confusion.

"Who?"

"He left this note." The note was a yellow Post-it. In pen, it said *Jovan Knez*—Delić. And in a different handwriting, the word *laboodovey.* One word stood out: Delić.

"Thank you." Parker put the note in the pocket of his Barbour jacket, turned around, and yelled over his shoulder. "I'm going to get some coffee. Can I get you two something?"

"No, thank you." They both spoke over the other's words.

He smiled and walked back out to the street, crossing over through the traffic to the small coffee shop near the other train station, Ravenscourt Park, which lay just across the street from the Hammersmith tube. He preferred the smaller station, as the coffee shop afforded him a wide view of the street and the much busier Hammersmith tube station across the street. Any pedestrian traffic using the London subway would more likely come from the Hammersmith station, and anyone heading to the newspaper's office would most likely pass through the Hammersmith tube entrance. He paid for a cup of Colombian coffee, with low-fat cream, took a table in the back, near the window, pulling his chair up against the wall, and sat so that no one was behind him. He pulled out the PDA and entered the password.

William Parker sent a simple e-mail to Scott. *Jovan Knez? Delić? Laboodovey?* Parker had a good idea of what he was going to get on Delić. Rasim Delić had commanded the ARBiH—the Bosnian Army—his Muslim troops famously slaughtering bound Serbian prisoners of war. Delić had also led smaller death squads called *Crni Labudovi*. The Black Swans. Delić had been prosecuted as a war criminal, been sentenced to jail, but died of a heart attack in Sarajevo while awaiting the outcome of his appeal. Most of his Black Swans had never been apprehended or identified.

Parker sipped the coffee, waiting for a reply. It didn't take long.

Knez: junior officer of Delić
Rasim Delić: Convicted war crimes criminal, now deceased
Crni Labudovi: Black Swans, Jihadist killers
Believed to be funded by Saudi CP via your friend
Beware.

A Saudi crown prince. Parker looked at the reply. *Your friend.* So Yousef did more than just kill Americans. Christians of all types were fair game. Parker needed to visit with someone very quickly.

He tossed the still-hot coffee in the trash can near the door to the small shop, pulled up the collar to his coat, and cut across the traffic to the Hammersmith tube station.

In the shadow of the pillar in front of the city hall across the street, a man watched.

It took some time for Parker to cross back over the city to the neighborhood of Walthamstow. It didn't matter how long he was away. The newspaper would have to wait. Parker had an article in his PDA that was ready to be downloaded, so it wouldn't affect his output. Far more important, he had to get to Zabara's wife.

The flat was on the second floor, a walk-up, with only two bedrooms, each of which was no bigger than the queen-sized beds in them. She would be there with the child. There was really no other place for them to go.

The brick had been painted over and had started to peel back, showing the red clay color under the felt green covering. Tall, cracked, paned windows showed the sheets that were being used for drapery on the second floor. The wood of the windows was painted in a darker green, but that was peeling away as well. The front door was in a stoop. Parker stopped, swept the street with his eyes, and pulled out the key.

"Zdravo!" he yelled up the stairs. She wouldn't expect him this time of day. She didn't go out. Her late sister's child was her life, and these few rooms in this flat were now her entire world.

"Zdravo! Zdravo!"

"Yes. What is it?" She put her hand up to her mouth. "Amirah." She whispered the name. It was clear that the child must still be sleeping. "You just left. Why are you here?"

"I need to talk to you." He took two stairs at a time. They were wood, without carpet, a dark wood worn to a polish by years and years of steps. He figured the building survived the blitz, if not more. It creaked like the old lady it was.

"Yes, what?" Her tone serious. She was always serious. Some people never had the luxury of acting any other way.

"There was a man who came to the newspaper."

"Who?"

"Jovan Knez?"

"Yes, I have heard of him. He was an officer in the *Crni Labudovi*."

"Did Sadik know him?" His mind raced ahead: Would the mission be derailed in the first few days?

"He knew of him, but no. He spoke of Knez and the other Black Swans always in the third person like in *they*, or *them*."

Of course. She was here because Zabara was *not* a Black Swan. He and his wife long ago had their fill of the Black Swans and their tactics. In fact, Zabara had begun cooperating with MI6 because he'd dreamed of leaving such violence behind.

"Okay. Good. I need your help."

"Yes, I know."

CHAPTER 20

Rotorua City, New Zealand

"Hello?"

The international cell phone only had a few minutes on it. She was to call the given number exactly at midnight. She would never know who was on the other end.

"Yes."

"I was to call."

"Yes, how is the training?"

"It is fine," she lied. It had been five days of hell. The Cessna 206 floatplane pulled hard to the right adjusting for the turn of the propeller. It had scared her far more than expected. The landings on the blue waters had to be just right. It was a volcanic lake, deep, with aqua green borders that followed the shoreline. An airplane that flipped over and sunk would be down a thousand feet before they could guess it was even missing.

"Does the land agree with you?"

"It smells."

"What?"

"It smells like rotten eggs." She was young, and this world was far from Danish Abad. At night, she slept on the floor in the bathroom. The carpeted floor felt—and smelled—too strange. To bathe, she filled the small trashcan with water and squatted in the tub as she wiped herself. A shower was too foreign. She hated this place.

"You will soon be with your brothers."

"I have this dream." Now that she had gained the skill of flying the airplane she saw the mission in her mind's eye every night. "It was snowing. I did not know snow." In New Zealand she first saw the white peaks and on one flight they flew up into the mountains and through a snowstorm. "Not until I came here."

"Yes." The voice was brief and distant.

"You will be proud of me."

"Yes, Allah be great."

There was silence. The wording on even this phone call needed to be considered. He said nothing. With the silence, she knew the error.

"You leave Sunday." The voice was very businesslike. Almost cold. It was not like when she left Pakistan. She left Danish Abad being hailed as a heroine.

"An electronic ticket has been set. Air New Zealand Flight AC6105." He didn't go into further details. She had been trained to know that was all that was needed.

The phone went dead. She pulled the chip out, tossed the phone into a nearby trash bin behind her motel, and broke the chip into three small pieces. The fragments would be tossed, each separately, onto the side of the road miles apart.

Air New Zealand Flight AC6105 would connect to Air Canada.

CHAPTER 21

South Audley Street, London

The London taxicab's horn blared as it swerved, just missing William Parker as he crossed over from Green Park. Parker cut across several more lanes of traffic, weaving through the cars, and walked into an alleyway behind Old Park Lane. At the end of the alleyway he kept up his pace, turned the corner, cut through a vegetable market with an old woman wrapped in a shawl standing guard over a table of pumpkins and gourds, stopped, looked behind, and then entered an adjacent street.

Parker stopped at the corner, stepping into the doorway of a flat to avoid the chilly blast of wind before staring across several more lanes of traffic. Calmly, he walked out, slowly, steadily, crossing over South Audley Street to the building on the other side. The front doors to the ornate Victorian structure faced directly to the corner of the block, and above the doors in gold a lion and unicorn held up the crown and standard. The Royal Warrant of the Queen showed the store was on the approved list. Below the warrant and above the doors, the store's name, James Purdey & Sons, was engraved into white marble.

As Parker walked through the doors, both floor attendants looked up. The older one, the one with wavy, pure white hair and a face that had spent most of his life taking hunters north, in the sun on the moors of Scotland hunting grouse, smiled a wide, toothy smile. His eyes, however, squinted in just such a way as to show a degree of doubt. The customer was dressed in a fairly new clover green jacket, but otherwise he looked very common. His pants were baggy and well worn, and his shoes—more like boots, although black—were scuffed so badly as to show cuts into the gray leather below. His early growth beard was starting to show curls; above, a crushed chocolate-brown felt hat pulled down to his ears.

"Can I help you, sir?" The white-haired clerk said the words pleasantly, but the tone was doubtful.

Purdey's sold some of the best shotguns in the world, and Parker looked nothing like their typical customer. The walls were lined with cabinets stacked deep with blue and black steel shotguns in glass cases, engraved with gold and silver pigeons in flight, and outfitted with marbled glossy stocks of walnut and burl. The small white tags on the trigger housing showed prices of 85,000 and 92,000. Some showed 110,000. All of the numbers meant British pound sterling. Above the cases, mounted antelope, stags, and boars looked down.

Parker picked up one of the shotguns. It was an over-under with two barrels riding one on top of the other. It felt light in his hands. He pulled it up into his shoulder and aimed down the line of the weapon. He stroked the stock with his hand, feeling the glass-like finish over the burl wood, his slight smile a show of appreciation for a craftsman's work of art.

He turned to the clerk. "I'm looking for the Long Room."

"Oh, yes, sir. Please come this way." The clerk took the shotgun back and put it in the cabinet. He talked as he led Parker. "That one is a favorite. It's a twenty-bore, with rose and scroll engraving, done by Martin Smith."

"Very nice." William Parker knew that the 20-bore Purdey would be bought and used and then handed down to generations of sons, followed by their sons. It would kill with perfect accuracy thousands of doves and quail in its life. It would age and be seasoned and smell faintly of burned gunpowder, spending most of its life in some rustic country cabin.

"Eighty thousand pounds, that one." He led Parker down a hall, to a door on the back corner of the store, twisted the handle, and swung it open for the guest who stepped in. The long room's central space was occupied by a long, red felt table, with the walls of the room adorned with paintings and photographs of the great Purdey men and their royal customers over the centuries.

"Well, here he is!" Sitting at the end of the table was none other than Gunnery Sergeant Kevin Moncrief.

"Gunny." William Parker walked over and gave him a bear of a handshake.

"Charlie, this is my friend Colonel William Parker."

The clerk stuck his hand out. "It's a pleasure, sir. A friend of the gunny's is always welcome."

"Charlie is related to the Purdeys somehow, but what he is known for is his career as a Royal Marine Commando. He's a retired WO-1."

"I'm impressed. But how did you get to know this troublemaker?" Parker pointed to Moncrief.

"He's one of our best customers."

"No!"

"Oh, ye of little faith," tut-tutted Moncrief with a smirk.

"With your new sportster, how many in your collection, Gunny?" asked Charlie. "Six?"

"Well, I have a Holland and a Rigby." Moncrief was naming some of the best shotguns in the world.

"Yes, we must count those, mustn't we?" Charlie humorously acknowledged the competitive brands.

"Charlie, we need to talk. Can you give us a second?"

"Absolutely, the long room is yours for as long as you need it."

"And let us know if you see anyone."

"Our security system covers two blocks. We saw the colonel from the alleyway on." Charlie closed the door as he left. Besides making shotguns, discretion was another Purdey skill.

Parker pulled up the seat at the corner of the table. "Good friends to have, I'd say."

"Charlie's been a pal for years. The room is one of the most protected rooms in downtown London. And there is no chance that the wrong type will wander into this store. Hell, they probably have fifty million in inventory in this little building alone."

"Does Scott know you're here yet?"

"No, he thinks I'm coming in tonight."

"Good. I need you. But remember: Both Yousef and Scott will be shadowing me. No phone calls, no e-mails, nothing that we can't assume isn't being read or listened to."

"How'd you do getting here?"

"Switched the tube six times in six different directions. If they followed me here, they are very good."

Moncrief laughed.

"What more do we know on Yousef?"

"Well, he's a first-class bastard. That's one thing. He'd throw his four-year-old under the bus if it helped the cause. The Semtex I told you about had a chemical marker that tracks directly from a Czech factory. The chemical gave the explosive a unique smell that could be easily detected by the dogs. It's called DMDNB."

"So what does that do for us?"

"We know that the explosives in Lockerbie and in Doha had the same tracer. Both were part of the original sale of seven hundred pounds that went through Libya. And both bombings were arranged and financed by Yousef. Oh, one other thing: the same tracer showed up in UTA Flight 772."

"UTA 772?"

"A passenger jet blown out of the sky in Africa to get back at the French. And my source found something else."

"The guy we spoke with?"

"Sorry, Colonel, yes."

"The Mossad source?"

"Yeah."

"What else?"

"There's a theory that the CIA *let* the Samsonite containing the Semtex onto 103. Witnesses said it passed through customs that day without anyone even lifting a finger to inspect it."

Parker sunk down into the leather chair.

"Why?"

"They thought they were running a tag on a heroin cell. Pure dope from Afghanistan being used in New York to raise bucks for the jihad."

Parker didn't want to believe that his own country shared culpability in the death of his parents. But it made sense. No one would ever admit it, though. It would remain buried deeper than the Mariana Trench.

"MI6 was working with the Agency at the time."

"I'd say they had to be. Flight 103 coming out Heathrow." This was the one fact that didn't cause Parker much surprise.

"And guess who was assigned to Heathrow out of MI6 at that time?" Instead of his usual smug look, Moncrief looked dead serious.

"Who?"

"One James Scott."

Parker shook his head in disgust. Nothing surprised him anymore. But it wasn't like he had trusted Scott implicitly to begin with. This served as an important reminder, though, that the only people Parker could trust were Moncrief and his own team.

"I am going to be off the net tonight." Parker switched the subject. *Off the net* meant he was going somewhere beyond communication, somewhere off the communications net.

Moncrief gave him a puzzled look.

"It's nothing." Parker didn't want to tell Moncrief the details. "You go ahead and check in with Scott like you just came in."

"Yeah. Will do."

Parker nodded, stood, and clapped Moncrief on the shoulder. "And let's keep our 'partner' in front of us at all times."

As they left the room, Parker's phone vibrated in his pocket. He entered the pass code and scanned down to the text. It was labeled *P-Message*. The P stood for "plasma." The identifier meant the message was hot, very hot. At six thousand degrees Celsius, plasma was hotter than the sun and, as a consequence, it was their flag for the most important of messages.

"What's up?" asked Moncrief.

"Speak of the devil," said Parker, reading the message. He shook his head, then handed it to Moncrief.

FYEO: FYI . . . 411 RE: MOSSAD. PRW . . .
URGNT . . . MEET AEAP/SCOTT

Moncrief raised his eyebrows and whistled long and low.

The text meant that it was a *for your eyes only*, a 411 message, regarding the Mossad: *People are watching, you are target, meet as early as possible, Scott.*

Evidently the Mossad had just initiated surveillance on Sadik Zabara, whom they no doubt considered part of a hostile new cell in Britain.

In all likelihood, this had been part of Scott's plan from the beginning. After all, there would be no better way of establishing Zabara's credentials for Yousef's people than by having the Mossad declare him a hostile target. The Mossad would serve as the perfect reverse character reference. Unfortunately for Parker, the Mossad would be swallowing the Zabara identity in earnest—one more lethal pitfall for Parker to avoid on a daily basis, as his situation grew ever more fragile.

CHAPTER 22

The new headquarters building,
Central Intelligence Agency, Langley, Virginia

The earpiece was the only visible clue. Otherwise, the guard looked like a well-suited stockbroker who might have played football in college. On second thought, given the scar under his lip, make that a rugby player.

"Gentlemen, may I bother you for your identification?"

"Yeah, no problem." FBI Agent Tom Pope flashed his credentials and badge. The agent with him did the same.

"Need a little more than that, sir." The guard still held his hand out. "This is Langley. You can understand."

Pope handed over his badge. Rarely in his career had he needed to visit CIA headquarters, but he knew the protocol. It wasn't his favorite place to visit.

The guard led them across the entrance hall to a side door where, inside, the clerk scanned the identification credentials, cross-checked them with the database, and smiled as she handed them visitor passes.

"Follow me, fellows."

The guard led them back into the main hall, with its curved roof and far walls of glass. Tom Pope moved a little slower than the others, forcing the guard to slow down as well. The casual observer would notice only the slightest limp. Since Pope had a touch of gray in his hair, one might assume his age caused him walk that way. They would be wrong.

Pope was an unusual agent in today's FBI. But for the waiver, he would have never been allowed into the Federal Bureau of Investigation. Prior to the Bureau, he had flown an attack Cobra helicopter for the Marines into Grenada. On that mission, a Russian ZU-23 shell tore through his leg. He kept the resulting Silver Star and Purple Heart medals in the bottom of a footlocker somewhere in his attic. Most days, he had more pressing things to think about than his military past, and today was no exception.

The brilliant sunlight of the early fall day bounced off the white linoleum floor, making the entrance almost unbearably bright. The trees in the garden beyond the glass wall had turned to bright, warm fall oranges and reds. They crossed over to the old headquarters building and the deputy director's office.

"The deputy director is waiting for you." The officer opened the door to an oak-paneled conference room lined with gold-framed photographs of the deputy director and leaders of intelligence agencies from around the world. The background of each of the photographs gave telltale hints, with some showing palm trees, others Bavarian ski chalets buried in deep snow. They looked like frames from a James Bond movie, and the tale they told was far from the truth.

The side door swung open.

"Hello, gentlemen, I am Robert Tranthan."

"Mr. Deputy Director, I am Agent Pope. Tom Pope. And this is Special Agent Garland Sebeck."

"I know of you, Mr. Pope. You were instrumental in stopping the North Korean agent several years ago."

"I was involved in that. Yes, sir." Tom didn't think of that case as being the best definition of his career, but he was certainly known for hunting down the North Korean agent who had crisscrossed the globe, killing scientists.

"If you don't mind, Agent Pope, the general counsel's office wanted to be here. Someone should be here shortly."

"No problem." Pope leaned back in his chair. He didn't want to show a threatening posture. It wasn't really the intent of the meeting.

The other door to the conference room swung open, and an attractive woman carrying a black leather writing portfolio came into the room.

"Gentlemen, excuse me for being the last one here. I'm with the counsel's office."

The men stood and welcomed her, introducing themselves.

"We're sensitive around here about making notes."

"I promise to keep it to a minimum." Pope's response was pleasant but firm.

"Okay, gentlemen, but I have a hell of a lot of things going on right now," said Tranthan. "What can we do for you?"

"Mr. Tranthan, there is a Chechen by the name of Umarov."

"Yes, we know of Abu Umarov."

"We had a call."

"A call?"

"Intercepted. He was on a flight leaving from LaGuardia. He spoke of an 'Operations officer' from Doha."

"And your question is . . . ?" asked Tranthan, his expression indicating nothing.

"Would that be your officer?

The question had two meanings.

"It could be Maggie O'Donald." Tranthan hesitated. "You know where she is."

"Yes, sir."

The greater implication, the one that worried Robert Tranthan was the use of "your" Maggie O'Donald.

"He disappeared after his airplane landed."

"Where was he going to?"

"Chicago."

CHAPTER 23

Spin Boldak, Afghanistan, near the Pakistan border

The town of Spin Boldak stood just beyond the border on the flat plain that extended from south Afghanistan into western Pakistan. By truck, it wasn't much more than seventy miles from Spin Boldak to Quetta, across the border. The main highway that passed through the center of the small town provided the only southern access to the country. With the many forces occupying southern Afghanistan, the highway continued to be busy with trucks bringing cargo loads of gasoline, engine parts, building materials, and much more. The convoy-created dust cloud drew a continuous line across the open desert.

On the north side of Spin Boldak, a ridge jutted up from the desert floor. At the one end of the ridge near the north side of the town, a square, mud-brick fort stood watch, as it had since the nineteenth century.

Abu Umarov scanned the walls of the fort with his binoculars. He noticed the antennas that stood beyond the parapets. They marked the French battalion. Its tanks and armored carriers were behind the walls. He counted the number of guards from left to right. It would be dark soon, and the French would be out of play. Except for the occasional patrol, the French didn't wander beyond the walls of the fort when the sun went down. And he would know the instant a patrol left the fort. On the horizon, the brown fog of dust crept up the valley. The setting sun would bring a breeze from the south, hastening its arrival. Soon visibility would be severely limited.

The Americans' unmanned aerial vehicles would be committed to the north. They were deadly, but Umarov had timed this well. A movement of his fellow soldiers to the north, above the Khyber Pass, would attract the Americans and their UAVs. Even the Americans had a limit to their assets.

Yousef had picked out the target after his return from Riyadh. The trip was important, Yousef had told Umarov. But Umarov doubted it. And Yousef had seen the doubt in his face.

Umarov didn't like the idea that his leader would go home when summoned. But he had kept his counsel, not daring to question Yousef aloud.

Even so, Yousef had decided to explain. "Never forget: there are more princes than the secretary. We will need the House of Saud to be divided when we move. We need voices that will approve of our new state. They must know we are serious."

The explanation had satisfied Umarov. Yousef's vision was clear. He knew his path. He knew that when word passed in Riyadh that Yousef had been home and had met with the secretary, others would return his e-mails and send money. Just the meeting would cause a stir.

But Umarov didn't like the trips this close to the operation. Chicago wasn't needed. He knew the target. Fortunately, he convinced Yousef to stay far away from the cell and Canada.

Secrecy didn't matter. Not for this operation. He would rot in Guantanamo for a decade before they got anything out of him. And by then, this would all be over.

"Is it time?" The boy stayed low, below the rocks, touching Umarov's boot from behind to get his attention.

"No. Go back." The Chechen didn't respect the boy. He was no more than fourteen and was here for the money. The kid would fire his rifle and run. Umarov knew that the boy would be killed, but more important, he might get Umarov killed as well. He wasn't a Chechen, not a true warrior.

"There he is." Umarov saw the truck sitting next to the house on the far end of Spin Boldak. It was a white Nissan with oversized tires and a roll bar behind the cab. It was too new to be owned by just anyone from Spin Boldak. It had been paid for with drug money. It was owned by the son of Abaidullah.

The trucks that left Afghanistan, after dropping off their cargo, brought back another cargo on their return. And Abaidullah ensured that they were safe on their trip when they passed through Spin Boldak and crossed the lawless land back into Pakistan. But Abaidullah had become too brave. He enjoyed a new pastime. He enjoyed killing the soldiers of the Taliban. After one horrific firefight, Abaidullah had the bodies piled up in a dump truck and taken to the border. There, just into Pakistan, the bodies were dumped in a pile, just like gravel or even worse, garbage, on the side of the two-lane highway. The stench had dogged drivers for days.

"Boy." Umarov slowly signaled with his hand below the rocks.

The boy looked up at the Chechen. The fourteen-year-old had an odd face, tanned and dark, but with clover-colored green eyes. He wore his brown fleece *pakol* pulled down around his ears. A powderlike dust caked his face and the *pakol*. His hands looked like hands of an old man, nails caked with dirt, used for any task and never cleaned.

"Yes, *Chaac neen*?" It took some time for them to learn to say the word. It didn't sound right.

"Come here."

The boy slid up in the hillside of the ravine they were hiding in, slowly moving his head up to its edge.

"There will be dogs. You hear them?"

The sun was beginning to set, and as it did, barking dogs began to howl in the distance. The sweltering heat had kept them hiding in ditches and ravines and in boxes discarded on the side of the highway, anything that provided some protection from the brutal sun.

"Yes."

Umarov was close to the boy. Even in the lowering light, he could see the boy's eyes were glassy. Heroin abuse was commonplace now. They would inject it just before the fight. It made them bulletproof. It also made them foolish.

"Take the dead dog. The one we brought. Move slow. Put it in that ravine to the side there." Umarov pointed to a cut, short of the rocks, to the far right of their position. The boy would cut the dog's belly so that the last of its blood would gush out onto the dry earth, attracting the other dogs. The arsenic would kill off the scavenging pack in minutes and the valley would become quiet.

Umarov watched as the boy moved from rock to rock, dragging the carcass by its leg. In daylight, the boy would have revealed their position. He would have been killed by either Umarov or the French. But the light was low and Umarov could hear the clanking of pots from the French compound. The sound of music accompanied the laughter as well. He knew the French. They were good fighters, tough, cold, but they loved to eat. The Americans would eat their combat meals packaged in plastic, but the French would prepare meals with bread and wine.

The dogs saw the boy cutting across the ravines and began to follow. Umarov then saw the boy slip back up the ravine. Fortunately, by then, the pack had picked up the smell of the blood and followed the trail to the carcass. Soon they would be dead.

Umarov checked the blade he carried on the side of his calf. He had lost count of the men who felt the razor steel pull across their throats. Several were boys, Russian boys, some younger than the boy with the dog.

"Let's go." He signaled to the five men down below him in the ravine. They all had the same glassy eyes. Umarov noticed two needles lying on a rock next to the men.

The Chechen didn't say much on these missions. He wouldn't, but more important, he didn't need to. He had trained them over the last several months. They would move slowly, in coordination, aware of where the others were at all times. They worked their way down the ravine, past piles of sagebrush, slowly moving down to the house with the white truck. They weren't there just to kill the man.

Two of the fighters moved to the side of the white truck, looking in, seeing the keys, and signaling back to Umarov. It was what he had hoped for. No one in the village would dare steal the truck of the son of the chief of the Afghan Guard. It made the plan possible.

Umarov was here to do the killing. The others would ensure that no one came up the alleyway or to the other side.

Umarov pulled the door open to the house behind the truck, hearing the music of Ali Omar on the radio. In the past, music had been banned.

The son of Abaidullah lay asleep on the couch.

"Don't say a word." Umarov pulled the boy's head up by his hair as he slid the blade underneath his chin. Umarov could feel the boy's body jerk as he awoke from his sleep to feel the steel cutting into the flesh of his neck.

"Come with me." He dragged the boy, struggling to keep up with the blade holding his head in place under Umarov's arm. Outside, one of the other fighters taped the boy's hands behind him. He was dragged into the bed of his truck as another of the killers taped the boy's feet and then his mouth and eyes.

Umarov slipped in behind the steering wheel and quietly started up the engine. He pulled the truck out from in between the houses, into the alleyway, and turned down the road. The other men jumped into the bed of the truck. He drove it in the dark, without the lights, going between the buildings, while the others in the back held down their victim. Even if someone saw the truck, they would recognize it and let it pass. The white Nissan of the son of the commander would never be stopped.

Several miles out of Spin Boldak, heading back to the east in the direction of Pakistan, the truck pulled off the highway and changed directions to the north. The rocky trail cut through the ridgeline and eventually led to a ravine that was wider and farther than the others. Near the end of the ravine, a truck trail cut up through the mountains heading east, farther into Pakistan. After several miles, curving through the pass, they came upon a cave that was cut out of the limestone. It was more of an overhang than a true cave, but it served its purpose.

Umarov pulled the boy out of the truck by his hair.

"Wait a moment!" A man came out of the cave. It was Yousef.

Umarov nodded to his leader.

"Go and get the cameraman," Yousef barked to one of their younger soldiers.

"I have it, brother." A small, thin boy, still a teenager but with the face of a man, came from within the cave with a video camera in a clear plastic bag.

Yousef took the camera from the bag, blew away any remaining dust, and set it up on a tripod.

"All right, I am getting ready to film. So pull up your scarves."

Each of the men pulled their scarves up, wrapping them around so as to only let their eyes be seen through a small slit.

"Pull that worthless piece of dog into the light." Yousef pointed to some gas lamps that stood well within the cave.

The teenager sobbed, but his cries were muffled by the layers of tape wrapped around his face. Umarov and the others dragged him to a rock no larger than a coffee table. And there they began to beat him mercilessly while the camera taped.

Finally, after they had beaten the boy to a near pulp, Yousef held up his hand.

"How much is left on the camera?"

"Ten minutes at the most," said the teenaged soldier.

"Umarov, show them what Nidal taught you."

"Is there enough light?" Umarov knew that this could only be done once.

"Yes, pull the light closer. Pull it near the hole." Just beyond the boy, a shallow grave had been dug into the soft floor of the cave. The hole wasn't any deeper than the waistline of a man standing in it.

"First, I want to say something."

Umarov had to hand it to Yousef. He was bold. Abaidullah would see this tape and swear to pursue his son's killer to the ends of the earth. But Yousef knew that. And he knew that the killing would galvanize the men of the Taliban behind him. The sons of the men in the pile beside the road would pledge themselves to Yousef's cause, speaking Yousef's name with reverence. And they would die to defend him. It was the first of many steps on his part to consolidate his power, solidify his following. The tribes of Afghanistan would be either behind Yousef or the Americans. Those behind the Americans would die.

Yousef spoke to the camera. "To the men of

Abaidullah, I say: He could not protect his son. Why do you believe he can protect you? Or your children? Do not take up arms against us."

Yousef spoke the words coolly, without passion. Again, Umarov admired his style.

"Okay." He pointed to the hole.

Umarov was off camera, but before he came into view he pulled his scarf up over his face. His *pakol* was pulled down, and his black scarf was pulled up tightly so that only his eyes were visible. It didn't matter. Even now, everyone had heard of the Chechen. He was much bigger than the others. He stood out.

Umarov pulled the boy into the full view of the camera and cut the tape off his mouth and eyes. Again, he pulled the boy up by his hair, still whimpering and sobbing, so that the camera could focus in on the face. Bloodied and swollen as his face was, no one would doubt that this was the son of Abaidullah. Umarov dragged the kid into the hole and then pulled a piece of plastic pipe out of his rear pocket. He would do this just like he saw Nidal do it to the man that Nidal called a traitor. With his boot on the boy's chest, he pushed the tube into the boy's mouth. The camera picked up the sound of the gurgling.

"Begin."

Umarov stepped out of the hole as the soldiers buried the boy alive. Shortly, only the tube stuck up from the pile of dirt.

"Abaidullah, you son of a dog," Yousef cursed on the camera as he began to pour water, in small amounts, down the pipe. "Come here." Yousef signaled to the cameraman to come closer. The camera panned in closer to the hole, focusing on it as Yousef poured water down the pipe. He didn't put much, only enough that in desperation the boy would swallow the water and dirt as quickly as he could. Gasping in the black hole, with the dirt crushing down on his chest, trying to breathe through the hole while the swallows of water stopped.

"Abaidullah, this is your fate as well." Yousef let his voice grow more intense. The glow in his eyes made him seem possessed. He pulled out a small pistol and fired down the pipe. He kept firing the pistol into the tube. He pulled the trigger until, finally, the weapon only clicked.

The camera light went black.

Umarov smiled. Abaidullah would remember the face of Yousef until the last breath passed. So would many others. In fact, with the release of the video, the entire world would know what Yousef al-Qadi looked like.

CHAPTER 24

New York City

The Verrazano Bridge would be the worst of it. Thousands of runners, pushing and shoving, like salmon making their way upstream. Later, as they moved through Brooklyn, the runners would spread out, making one continuous stream that would last for hours.

Despite the crush, Clark felt the adrenaline as she moved outside, crossing the bridge. On the far outside lane she could glimpse north, seeing the boats on the East River. The weather was meant for marathoners. A chill had descended on the northeast that caused her teeth to chatter just before the gun went off. She knew that her body would warm up fast as the sun began to burn off the chill, but she would be miles into the race before heat became a problem.

Clark felt a breeze cutting up the East River. Helicopters covering the New York Marathon zoomed over the bridge. She felt energized; happy, even. Happier than she had felt since Parker had left.

Boston had no effect. The runners were a sea of red,

white, and blue. There seemed to be more energy than a nuclear reactor's core. They were not to be deterred.

It surprised Clark that she had the energy even to let her mind wander. Parker would have wanted her to concentrate on the race, not him.

God, he has really trained me for this. She was holding a solid pace, already starting to pass other runners. Clark could feel lightness in her stride.

She passed the ten-mile mark.

I need to keep the liquids. William had reminded her that early on the energy would feel limitless. The adrenaline would be pumping. This was her first marathon and the lack of humidity in the north would energize her even more.

Clark cut over to the water station at mile twelve and forced herself to slow and grab a cup. Again, at the end of the tables, she grabbed a Gatorade and a Power Gel. She drank as much of the liquid as she could force down.

I feel so alive! She laughed at herself. *I sound like a commercial.* The others in the courthouse had made fun of her for weeks now. The general consensus was that she'd collapse after mile ten. She laughed at that thought as the fifteen-mile marker passed by.

I'm over halfway. A little thirsty, but nothing bad. Clark was even maintaining the same pace. She looked at her watch. 7:45-minute miles. *That can't be right, 7:45?* She was ahead of her targets. And this was mile sixteen.

Clark realized that two of the runners had kept the same pace with her now as they neared the eighteenth mile. They were slightly ahead of her when she came across the Verrazano. It looked like a father and son, a gray-haired man with a runner's body but legs white as a newborn child. He obviously had trained in the far north, where the cold rarely let one run without his sweatpants. The son, in his early twenties, inherited more from his mother than his father. He almost appeared to be Cajun, with a dark complexion. At first they chatted as they ran, but as they crossed the Queensboro Bridge, they became increasingly quiet.

"You still with us?" the son asked Clark as they passed by milepost eighteen.

"Oh, yeah." She still had the energy to smile. "Are you slowing down?"

"Don't make me laugh, it hurts too much." He smiled at her, but you could see the beginnings of it being a forced smile.

William had warned her of the gap between milepost twenty and twenty-five. It would be there that she'd be truly tested. Clark started to pull apart from the others as she passed the sign *20*. Now she was passing fewer runners. Runners would occasionally pass her. It was here that she'd have to reach deep. It wouldn't be easy.

Dad would be there. Standing at the side. Smiling with that ridiculous pipe stuck out of the side of his mouth. Her legs were burning now. Somehow, some way, she was still passing a few other runners. Some looked desperate, soaked in sweat. Now her mouth was dry, like she had swallowed a cup of dust, and her lungs began to burn.

Just don't ever let the thought of giving up get into your brain. Not for one second. William had said that repeatedly, again and again, when the runs had gotten longer. *Don't stop. Don't let the word* stop *exist.*

The Madison Avenue Bridge was coming. Now, the

legs would feel even the slightest incline. It would burn as she came up the bridge's elevation, but she would be back in Manhattan for the final time. Clark tried to keep her head up as she passed through the bridge, looking at the people cheering, pushing, and prodding her on. They were generous. She could feel their energy.

A man stood next to the bridge abutment on the Manhattan side. She glanced at him, but when she looked up again he was gone.

No, it can't be. God, I'm losing it.

It was then that the pain began to worsen. Her pace was slowing down now as she crossed into Central Park. The trees were such a change. It reminded her of the runs on their hill trail.

I'm going to make it. She was getting close.

Marker twenty-five was just ahead, with water and ice, but Clark knew now she was in the danger zone. A stop, even for a split second, for a cup of ice-cold water or Powerade could result in her stopping for good. Like an ocean liner that comes to rest, the force of energy required to move again could be unattainable.

No, Clark Ashby would not stop. Never. One foot would move in front of the other. Now it took too much effort to look up. She stared at the pavement in a continuous trance, watching her feet, in a trance, moving forward one at a time, one after another.

It was then that she heard the noise. A band was playing and thousands of people were yelling. The crowds on both sides were now layers and layers deep. Little children held signs for their mothers or fathers. No, stopping now was not an option.

God, I am *going to make it!*

Clark barely noticed the finish. It was the broad stripe on the ground and the sudden stopping of movement. In a moment, the people that had surrounded her for hours now had come to a stop. A stranger wrapped her in a silver thermal blanket. Another gave her a frozen Gatorade. She inhaled it, took another, and tried to slow it down to sips.

Clark walked toward the trees. The salt on her skin felt like a dry powder. She needed some grass and something to lean up against. She knew that if she lay down, it might be hours before she would ever get up, but who cared? Clark Ashby had finished a marathon! The New York Marathon! She was a marathoner! She would go to parties years from now. The conversation would wander around, and then she would work it in. *Yes, I ran New York*. Her dad would be beaming.

She slid down at the trunk of an oak, feeling the cold, damp grass under her butt. It was a mistake. Her body would become glued to the ground. Her sweats were in a basket somewhere on the other side of the finish line. They would have to wait. Clark wasn't moving for anything.

A man with a Yankees cap pulled down, sunglasses, and a new beard sat down next to her on the grass. Clark pulled back from the stranger who suddenly appeared in her space and then looked up.

"Hey. I'm proud of you."

Clark couldn't get out any words.

"William?" Tears suddenly flooded her eyes. The exhaustion, the pain, and then this.

"Can you walk?"

She would be stiff, especially by making the mistake of sitting down. The muscles quickly froze up after hours of constant motion.

"I think so. The hotel is just across the park." Despite the pain, Clark was now riding an endorphin high. She felt euphoric. William had come!

"We'll get you to a hot shower. I'll get your sweats." He smiled at her, kissed her on the forehead, and then looked into her eyes. "Your arms full, and your hair wet . . . I was neither living nor dead, and I knew nothing, looking into the heart of light . . ."

"Who's that?"

"T. S. Eliot."

"You remembered that one just for me, didn't you?"

"Especially the wet hair part."

She laughed, then winced.

"Oh, my God, I'm too tired to laugh!"

Her running mate had made New York after all.

If it weren't for the other runners crowded into the lobby of the Carlyle, the two would have been an odd sight. Only on the weekend of the New York Marathon. Even the rich, the famous, and the well known could enter the hotel dressed in Gore-Tex and Nikes.

They were in the elevator alone.

"You'll like the room," William said.

She nodded, resting her head on his chest. They'd made the reservation months ago. She had stayed at the Carlyle once as a child on a trip with her father. Her memory was of a palace with crystal chandeliers and fresh-cut flowers in crystal vases. She remembered the starched hand towels and the sweet soap.

"Clark, I don't have long."

The smile left her face. "How did you get here?"

"I had the most expensive seat in transatlantic travel." The F/A-18 jet fighter flew the Atlantic in half the time of a commercial jet. Scott hadn't liked having to put in the request.

The elevator opened and they walked slowly toward their room.

"I only have a few hours."

"Okay."

"You remember Mack Dennson at the sheriff's office?"

"The one who had the baby last year."

"Yes." He handed her a piece of paper. "You've got Stidham, but it could take him an hour or more to get to you. Just in case you need someone quicker who can also call in the cavalry, I want you to have Mack's number. Put this in your cell. Put it as the first listing. He knows your number, and if he sees it, he will come. He owes me."

"What's wrong?"

"Nothing. I just found out that this may go all the way back to Pan Am."

"Oh, God."

"It's okay. It's going to be fine. But like I said, we live out in the middle of nowhere. It could even take Dennson half an hour or more to get there. If it comes to that, you get out of there any way you can, you hear?"

She nodded.

"Good." He opened the door to the room. "These men don't play."

CHAPTER 25

Danish Abad, Peshawar, Pakistan

The side streets of Danish Abad were packed with barefoot children chasing each other, hardly noticing the men who walked down the alley near the canal. A stream of water no wider than the length of a man's arm, the canal drizzled through a ditch cut between the mud-brick houses stacked tightly together one upon the other.

The orphans who lived in Danish Abad knew that the canal was a necessity. A stranger would not be able to bear the overwhelming stench from it, and many of the locals would hold their hands over their nose to force themselves to breathe through their mouths as they passed by. Everything that the poor had no use for was dumped into the canal. Carcasses of dead dogs, punctured plastic jugs, and torn trash bags lined the banks. Rats were the only creatures that seemed to flourish there. They poured out of the pipes that constantly dripped green liquid into the countless tiny tributaries that fed the canal.

Most times of year the canal seemed to be an unfortunate trash dump, but it had a purpose. In the desert, once in several years, a colossal storm would come, and with it days and days of rains. The monsoon would turn the creek and canal into a raging wall of water. In a matter of minutes, the stream would turn into a torrent that poured over the banks and ripped through the mud-brick walls, sucking the orphans of the city into it. Without the canal, everyone and everything in Danish Abad would be pulled into the churning brown water.

The men in the alley had been here many times before, and they were being led through the maze of alleyways by a friend who had lived his entire life in the place. He had never left Danish Abad of his own choosing, and he'd returned a hero after his sole departure.

The Pakistani Taliban controlled Danish Abad. It was described as being lawless, but it was far from lawless. The Taliban set the rules. Those who disobeyed the Taliban's laws suffered greatly. Only the week before, two men disobeyed the directions of Zulfiqar Mehsud, the leader of the Taliban in Danish Abad. Their real crime was that they hid some of their profits from burglaries on the other, more affluent side of the city. But they were accused of being spies for the West. The charge was convenient and their sentence simple. Their heads were cut from their bodies with dull knives as their screams turned to gasps and pleas, then gurgles, and finally silence. They didn't die bravely. They died like the desperate men they were.

Yousef knew that the man who led them through the alley could be trusted. More important, he knew the village could be trusted. Especially since the release of the video. Now, even the urchin children and simple thieves, from orphans who lived in the culvert to back-street pickpockets, knew to say nothing to outsiders about Yousef's arrival in Danish Abad. The law of the Taliban in Danish Abad now mandated that Yousef al-Qadi be protected at all costs.

Yousef and Umarov took the stairs on the side of the house to the second floor. The meeting would be short. They would never meet in the same place twice. The room had no furniture to speak of. Several of the men had laptop computers. They had their prayer rugs, they would remove their sandals, and then when the call came, they would turn to Mecca and pray. Then they would sit with their legs folded and plot and plan. It was an odd clash of old and new, prayer rugs inherited from grandfathers and wireless notebooks. It was in a room like this that the World Trade Center attack had been planned.

On the wall was a map. A black marker boxed in several provinces of eastern Iran, Afghanistan, and some of the western provinces of Pakistan. A thin thread of tribal cooperation and shared Muslim beliefs formed this state. It looked like an early colonial map of the United States. On the side of the map, a chart listed the governors and structure of each of the subterranean governments that ruled within this federation.

Yousef now stood in front of the map. "The true and perfect state. From this we will build a Muslim world."

Yousef was not the only one in the room who believed, but he was, among the men, uniquely on edge. They had driven through the night and he had not slept now in more than twenty-four hours. The trip to Riyadh only added to the exhaustion. At least Danish Abad gave him refuge from the constant threat of Predator strikes when they were near the border.

I will sleep tonight.

"Samullah?" Yousef was speaking to Samullah Ullah, the man who had guided them through the spiderweb of alleyways. He was an officer of the Taliban. He was also a lieutenant of Al Jihad. If asked, he would say he worked with the IIRO, a charity worker helping the orphans of Danish Abad, keeping them away from the canal during the rains.

Samullah could be trusted for another important reason. He had a particular hatred for the Americans after spending five years in Guantanamo. Eventually they had released him, convinced that he only wanted to return to his simple farmer's life. Again, they were wrong. He had kept his Koran from Guantanamo. The children of Danish Abad revered it, touching it like the holy relic they believed it to be.

Samullah was an asset for yet another reason. Guantanamo gave him a particular understanding of how the Americans thought.

"Tell us what you see."

Samullah nodded. "The word is traveling. The tribes of the north have heard of your war with Abaidullah. They have heard of Spin Boldak."

"Allah be praised."

Yousef turned to Umarov. "It's time we brought the battle back to American soil." He rubbed his hands over his face in a prayer like motion. "The limp daughter of Danish Abad will change the world."

Umarov knew when to say nothing.

"Samullah, your sister will serve us well." Yousef paused. "This is good." He smiled, suddenly reversing his thinking. "This is very good."

Umarov gave him a quizzical look, but still didn't say anything.

"Attacks on Islam. Dissent in the Saudi Council as anger grows against America. True believers everywhere are looking for someone to carry the battle flag. And, lo and behold, a London journalist is coming to meet with us in only a few days."

Samullah and Umarov relaxed visibly, suddenly grasping what Yousef envisioned.

"We will have opportunity out of this chaos." Yousef smiled at his map. "It has been a thousand years since Mahmud of Ghazni built his Islamic empire on these grounds." Yousef took a black marker and outlined a new country that extended from the south of Iran, across Afghanistan, and into western Pakistan. "His empire was on these same lands. It was of the true faith."

The other men in the room stirred, clearly feeling the elation, seeing the possibility grow before their eyes.

"As Mahmud the Great did a thousand years ago, on the foundation of the Koran, we will commence a battle cry that will cause all the tribes to unite. A holy war with a purpose!"

The men murmured in agreement, smiles widening all around the room.

"But first we must spread the word."

Loud cheers now, from all in attendance.

"A holy fighter will rise, one who'll rid your lands

of the unbelievers. A *mujahid* to rid the land of unbelievers and expand the faith."

The men repeated his words, and then cried them again in a chant.

And Sadik Zabara will be the one to introduce the world to the new mujahid.

CHAPTER 26

Riyadh

"An inopportune time." The secretary finished his cigarette, the last of the pack of Marlboro Gold Touch, as he thought of Yousef. He stared at the empty pack before crushing it in his hand. As he inhaled, he twisted the gold signet ring on his little finger, stopped, removed the cigarette, and crushed it in the Rolls's ash-tray.

A nasty habit. He had picked it up as a teenager at the private school his father sent him to in Lebanon. The stretch Phantom's windows were tinted extra dark, so as to ensure that no one would see him smoking. In Riyadh, it was forbidden. No one would question his smoking, but there would be talk. It was better to smoke behind the tinted windows.

"What time is the meeting?"

"Ten, sir."

"And what time is it?" The secretary never wore a watch.

"Quarter 'til."

The secretary extended his open hand to his assistant, which meant only one thing: He needed another pack of the Marlboro Golds. They were flown in from London by the case so as to ensure that none were purchased on the open market. He didn't need an imam preaching his name from the pulpit.

The Rolls-Royce pulled up to the gate of the Al-Yamamah Palace. The guards came to attention, saluting, as the car passed. He lit another cigarette with his gold lighter, knowing that he had time to inhale only once or twice.

He was fully aware of the irony of his smoking habit. *The Americans will kill me. One way or the other.* He didn't care.

The guard opened the door to the automobile. A billow of smoke escaped, but no matter. The guards always looked away.

The gold doors to the palace were framed above in palm leaves, also made of gold. The gold's glint reflected off the milky white marble floors. The man the secretary was expecting to meet was waiting for him just inside.

"Al-Waleed!"

"Cousin!"

"Let us talk."

The secretary led the way for his cousin, Prince Al-Waleed bin Talai bin Abdul Aziz al-Saud. Al-Waleed was his younger cousin and also one of the richest of the princes of the House of Saud. He was wealthy for a good reason. Al-Waleed enjoyed the powerful backing of the secretary.

"I understand you have received your newest airplane. Tell me about it, Al-Waleed."

The secretary already knew that the Airbus 380 had cost more than four hundred million. The largest aircraft in the world had been modified for bedrooms, movie theaters, and gourmet kitchens. The master bedroom was equipped with a Jacuzzi. The baggage hold was being modified so as to carry three Rolls-Royces.

"It will be magnificent," Al-Waleed admitted.

"I understand that the Jacuzzi was a particular problem?"

"Yes, the American FAA had a problem with it."

"And we need the American FAA?"

"Otherwise, they will give us difficulty landing in New York."

"How is Prince Khalid?"

Khalid was a member of Bay'ah Council, but he didn't act like it. His frequenting of the bars of London and Moscow was well known. The problem was that they were not simply bars. The back rooms would hold young Russian girls, innocent and barely out of their teens. Khalid had become a liability and an embarrassment, but he was still one of the thirty-five votes. Every vote mattered.

Enough preliminaries. The secretary had not come to discuss jet-borne Jacuzzis or perverted cousins. He had much bigger issues on his mind. He liked Al-Waleed for one important reason. The cousin never tried to play the game of politics within the House of Saud. Instead, he'd become a vehicle for family members to invest in other world economies, to pull dollars out of Saudi Arabia in order to diversify their wealth.

Saudi Arabia remained on a dangerous course and everyone in the House of Saud knew it. The birth rate predicted a population increase to forty million within a decade. Only seven thousand of those millions were members of the House of Saud. Add to that the state's ever-decreasing oil resources and you had a rather grim outlook, long term. *Instability* scarcely began to describe it.

"What is your opinion of Yousef?" the secretary asked, well aware that Al-Waleed and others knew that he'd helped create Yousef.

"He is getting bolder."

The secretary pulled his chair up close to his cousin. The smell of perfume and cigarettes exuded from Al-Waleed.

"What is the sense of the vote?"

"For many," said Al-Waleed, "Yousef is an asset."

"Yes, yes, I know."

The secretary felt torn, debating the pros and cons of his connection with Yousef. The secretary's contact with Maggie O'Donald in Doha had a purpose. She was his escape hatch, his plan B. If Yousef became uncontrollable, the CIA would take care of the problem. At the same time, his connection with Yousef was buying him some important votes. But the message had become garbled. Now Maggie lay near death in the United States. Her mind and memory were reported to be confused. If she made the wrong comment at the wrong time to the wrong people, the consequences would be devastating.

"You walk the fence." Al-Waleed hesitated. "But, despite many of our cousins' rantings and ravings about the Americans, our world would be very different without them."

"I need you to do me a favor."

"Of course."

"You will buy my interests in Omnipol. One hundred million."

Al-Waleed smiled. "I always thought that was wrong for you, a man who aspired to be a politician."

"I know. But the king thought it important that someone he could trust would know who was doing what." The secretary had been assigned a job. His funding of the largest independent manufacturer of plastic explosives in the world gave him the chance to see where it was going.

If it comes down to the last vote, they can use this against me, he thought. The Council was becoming divided. Those pro West would be concerned that the world's scrutiny would focus on a candidate who made money from selling explosives. But at the same time, he didn't want to give up access to the information. Al-Waleed was the perfect answer.

The manufacturer of explosives had his hand on the pulse.

"You will buy it, you will keep it, and you will make more money."

The secretary was right. Al-Waleed had the gift of good fortune. If he bought it for one hundred million, it would soon be worth two hundred million.

"Yes, it is done."

"Thank you, Al-Waleed. As always, my good brother, you are an asset."

CHAPTER 27

London

The tube continued beneath London until the last few stops. When it emerged aboveground, the late-fall fog was penetrated only by the glow of city lights. Parker stared at the beads of water streaking across the moisture on the windows. The wind pushed the droplets across the glass in streams. He leaned back on the subway seat, closing his eyes to the rhythm of the tracks. He looked down at his watch. It had only been a few hours. The fighter jet was cramped, but at forty-six thousand feet, using the jet stream, it took less time than a movie on the transatlantic flights for his return from New York. The oxygen in the face mask gave him a sense of euphoria as he looked down on the slower 747s and 767s below. But he hadn't slept now for more than twenty-four hours. He didn't want to waste one moment with Clark on something as unimportant as sleep.

Good God. This line of thought was a grave mistake. He couldn't afford to have Clark on his mind now.

The subway train's brakes squealed like fingernails on a chalkboard. A jolt brought the train to a stop.

Parker pulled up the collar to his Barbour jacket as he stepped into the fog.

The man waited there, out of view, in the corner of the station.

Parker sensed his presence. A hunter always knew when he was being hunted.

The glow of the streetlight barely made it to the sidewalk below. Parker saw the shape of a police officer near the entrance to the pub, in the opposite direction of the stranger. The officer stood below the overhang of a building, giving him some shelter from the drizzle as it came down. He waved his hand to the officer as he did whenever he passed. It didn't hurt for the police officer to know him. Parker knew the officer had registered him in the policeman's mind. The first time Parker had passed through the station, the officer stared at him. He could see in the moment of a glance that his look, his height, his frame were all being registered for future reference.

The street was pitch-dark, like spilled ink, in the spaces between the streetlights. Parker kept his pace, moving along the sidewalk, careful to keep the shadows at a distance. A dog knocked over a trash can in an alley, causing a loud metallic racket. He stayed on his side of the street. Lights came on with the noise, curtains moved; people looked out toward the sound.

Parker noticed the faces in the windows. The men had beards; the women were dark-skinned with black hair. The neighborhood was consistent. It was as it had been described. Walthamstow was the East End in the sense that here the newest immigrants attracted each other like magnets. In this decade, it was the home to Muslims from Pakistan, Iraq, Iran, and Saudi Arabia.

In the light, on the far side of the street, Parker saw a movement. It was his shadow. Trying to keep up with Parker's pace. He moved faster.

Mossad?

Could be, if Scott were to be believed.

It doesn't feel like Mossad.

Parker cut across the street, walking directly below the lamp, making sure that the man would see his direction. The sign below the light marked Forest Street. The flats were all stacked together like bricks lined up, row after row, with the doors barely separated by a window or two. Many of the flats were dark as it neared midnight.

One light was on.

She didn't have to do that. Parker sensed from the small things that Mrs. Zabara had had enough of death in her young life and just wanted to do the simple things. Leave a light on for the man who she was supposed to call her husband.

Their flat was across from a small park that everyone used as their vegetable garden. It was started in the Great War. In this case, the space for two of the flats was left open to serve as a public park. Each of the tenants had a small plot, some no bigger than the size of a throw rug in a small room, with barely enough space to turn around in, but still a place of earth that was tilled and cultivated and produced a summer's variety of tomatoes, squash, beans, and even corn. The plots were elevated and framed by large timbers stacked in long boxes. In the back, a compost pile came up to a man's chest. In the summer, the gardens were lush and full.

Now, as winter came on, the farm looked empty and dark. In fact, it was pitch-black, as it had no lighting.

That's where I would be. A small-caliber shot, with a can, through the back of the head. The silencer, with the right bullet, loaded with less than a full load of powder, would make no noise. It would speed through the moist air, leaving a streak for just a split second. But even with the light load of powder, the well-aimed shot would puncture the back of the head and tear through the brain.

Parker stepped into the alcove that protected the door. Inside, it didn't have a trace of light, but the space was no larger than a telephone booth. He unlocked the door with a key that she left in a crack in the brick to the far right of the door. He had to do it by mostly the feel of the small key. In the low light he could see it was bright, as it had been cut just for the new tenants.

Parker stepped in, quickly pulled the door closed, and locked it. As he did so, he put his foot behind the door the moment it closed to brace for any attack. He slid to one side of the door. It was a perfect opportunity for an attack.

But this time the assailant had failed to make his move.

Parker climbed the stairs to the second floor. Zdravo stood there at the top of the stairs in her nightgown, like a Praetorian guard protecting the emperor. Here, the emperor was her dead sister's baby.

"*Smracuje se.*"

"*Jes.*"

He pointed his finger to his mouth.

"I need you to go to the front with me."

He led her to the front room, to the desk near the

window, and there sat down at the desk. She stood next to him. Parker opened the notebook computer that the newspaper had given him. The room was dark except for the glow of the screen. He turned it to the side and, with him in the shadows, he pulled her over into the seat. Parker slid up against the wall, in the darkness, and moved toward the back hall.

"Where you go?"

"I will be back. Stay there. Don't move." He put his finger to his lips.

"*Jes*." She understood danger.

The hallway cut through the center of the flat; in the rear a short, steep stairway led downstairs. Parker had struck his head on the overhang the first time he'd tried to descend the stairs.

Tonight he instead turned the knob to the back bedroom and quietly swung the door open. He closed it behind him, listening to a child's deep breathing in her bed. His eyes were adapting to the darkness and, as he moved across the room, Parker passed the child's small bed. Beyond, a small window was slightly cracked, letting in the cool, damp air. Again in a slow and deliberate movement, he used the fulcrum of his arms to curl the window open, sliding it upward just enough for a man to pass through.

On the roof, Parker immediately felt his feet slipping on the slate shingles; remembering his skiing days, he turned his foot across the drop and carefully put only the right amount of pressure to keep the hold. It felt much colder outside now, as he was moving without his jacket. Already he found his skin damp—his shirt neared the point of being soaked.

Parker got to the edge of one roof and slipped again

across the edge to another roof. He repeated this several times until he came to an alleyway that cut in between the row of flats. Here, he worked his way, slowly, down the roofline to the corner, where he muscled his body around, holding on to the drainpipes only by his fingers. The copper pipes cut, but he knew how to concentrate and breathe, ignoring the pain, as he walked himself down, end over end, hand over hand, on the pipeline until he came to the descending drainpipe. It was still a long drop down to the stone pathway between the buildings.

In the alleyway, Parker didn't make the mistake of coming to the front to see if the man was still there. He knew a murderer would remain there if it took all night. A skilled murderer would wait until just before dawn to strike, and then only do so if everything were judged to be just so.

Parker turned instead to the right and headed back into the alleyway. At the end he stopped for a moment, put his back to the wall, and slid down into a crouch. The wall was wet with moisture, which soaked through his shirt, but he took the time to steady himself for what was to come. Parker visualized the path he would take, cutting up through the buildings to the street on the far side. Once there, he would cut up a block, well beyond his street, double back to the alleyway on the far side, and come in from behind the park.

He moved slowly, controlling his breathing, stopping in the dark corners to sense any movement. Parker crouched down for a second time, looking around. He knew that he would need a weapon. He was near the corner of the building where the trash was stacked in boxes. A carton of beer bottles balanced on top. Parker silently slipped one from the case. It was an amber-colored beer bottle made of thick glass. It had the perfect swing weight to it and was heavy on the end with the thick glass on the bottom.

Again, Parker moved forward slowly. His movement reminded him of a combat patrol. Move deliberately, stay low, be silent. Move too quickly and you were dead. He slid down the back of the building, staying in the dark, adjusting his eyes, as he slowly moved along. In the dark, away from the corner light, he cut across the street and followed the apartment building from the other side. He extended his hand in front of his face, moving at a snail's pace, feeling his way until eventually he touched the leaf of a large brown hydrangea that stood much taller than him. He remembered the plant. It was near the rear of the garden across the street. Parker continued to move slowly, patiently, around the corner of the plant, but stopped when he caught a faint whiff of cigarette. His heartbeat increased when he realized that he was close, very close. The stranger was within reach. Parker froze in place, watching, waiting.

The man was standing next to an oak, a small one that was beginning to lose its leaves for the winter. The tree's tall branches above, shorn of their leaves, let through a fragmented pattern of light. Enough for Parker to see the man's face.

Knez.

The man leaned against the tree, watching the house. Across the street, and above them, the glow of a computer illuminated a figure in the apartment. Suddenly the person behind the computer moved, and as she did, the man in the dark recognized that she was not who he thought she was. His body language immediately read agitated.

What will he do?

Parker watched as the man looked first down the street, then behind himself, and finally turned, seemingly directly at Parker. He stared into the darkness where Parker hid. Parker froze, not daring even to breathe. The man continued to stare for what seemed an eternity. He displayed a puzzled face, being unable to recognize something he should have known. Then he reached. He reached deep into the pocket of his long black raincoat and pulled out a pistol that looked like a Russian automatic. From another pocket he pulled out a long tube, black and metallic. He slid the tube onto the pistol, causing it to be well beyond the frame of the gun itself. Knez pulled the movement of the automatic pistol back, chambering a round, and then slowly slid it forward.

His intentions were clear.

Parker waited until Knez turned back toward the house with the woman and the child, innocents whom the Black Swan would surely not spare.

There would be only one opportunity, one step, one movement, and it had to be decisive.

The man intended to move to a car parked in the center of the street. It was a well-used minicar, painted a horrific orange-brown. He stopped at the edge of the car, sliding down for a second below its horizon as he scanned the street. Just as he was beginning to take his next step, a cat in an alley far away screamed out, causing the man to pause and look around again, up the street, down the street, and back to Zdravo in the house behind the computer.

Parker feared for her. She was now within range. A bullet could tear through the glass, slam into the side of her head, and she would be on the floor dead before Parker could even stop it.

For the moment he waited, only moving slightly when his opponent did, each step carefully placed. He placed each foot gingerly, one step at a time, so no dried limb or leaf would crackle.

It seemed the man had finally reached a decision. He moved toward the front door, more quickly now. He stood in the shadow, grabbed the doorknob with his right hand, turned the knob as far as he could, and then brought his full body to bear on the door. The frame was old and quietly cracked under the pressure.

Parker knew the time to act was fleeting. If he let Knez upstairs, it would be too late.

From upstairs came Zdravo's voice. "Sadik? Sadik, is that you?"

With those words, Knez would know he was in a trap. The woman should not be calling to her husband at the front door—not when Knez had watched the man walk inside only minutes before.

Knez turned and fired randomly into the dark. The silenced bullets whizzed by Parker, who leaned to the side of the door. One round tore through the front of Parker's shirt, but Knez immediately turned to fire in the other direction, covering all bases. As soon as Parker detected Knez's turn, he tore through the doorway.

Knez reacted and got off one more round, which shattered the beer bottle, but the glass was thick and the broken end transformed into a lethal razor.

In the instant between the time a man could fire one

round and then another, Parker shoved the broken glass deep under Knez's chin. Its shard cut deep into the throat, sliced the arteries, and caused blood to project out like water from a sudden cut in a hose. Parker gripped Knez's gun hand, turning the barrel away, but the man's strength was already gone.

He gasped, then mumbled a string words, scarcely intelligible except for one:

"Sadik?"

The sticky blood quickly covered Parker's hands as he dragged the limp body out into the street. It was all done in near silence. A man lost his life while others slept nearby.

Parker looked around and pulled the body across the street to the lot. It was fortunate that it was the beginning of winter, as not even the children played in the gardens in the late fall. A body could remain hidden there for several days, possibly a week. Parker didn't need nearly that much time. He pulled the dead weight into a hole next to the compost pile. In preparation for winter the gardener had dug it so deep that a man could stand in it up to one's knees. The trench had been dug so as to aerate the plot. It became the perfect grave. He quickly covered the man with the remaining leaves and dirt, leaving the pistol lying on his chest. When discovered with the Russian pistol, the first assumption would be a bad drug deal with the Russian mafia. As no one would miss Knez, the investigation would take much more time than Parker needed.

He cut back across the street, seeing no sign of life anywhere. The front door was not damaged to the degree he thought. It could easily be repaired in the morning.

"I need a bucket."

Zdravo was already at the top of the stairs with a pail of water. It was as if she had done this before. "Use this and I will get more."

He poured the water across the entranceway, diluting the blood, and then down the walk. He handed her the bucket and again she brought another. They repeated the effort until the last remnants of Knez had been washed away.

Parker pulled the door shut and was able to jam the lock partially closed. They didn't need much time. In a day, they would be gone.

Zdravo was still waiting, sitting on the top stair. Her face had that same ashen look of fear.

"Who was he?"

"Knez." Parker spoke quietly. Despite the death of a man nearby, they tried not to wake the baby.

"Why did he try to kill us?"

"He knew I was not Sadik."

"Oh. But why now? Why try to kill you now?"

"How did he know I was not Sadik?" Parker asked her, as she slid down into a chair, limp with fear.

"I don't know. I did not even know that he knew my husband."

"He knew Sadik." Parker answered the question. More important, he answered the other question. "And he knew I was not Sadik."

"So why was a member of the Black Swans looking here, now?" She would ask innocent questions because she was innocent.

And then Parker remembered. There was a connection.

"I was being checked out. And I know who wanted me checked out. And I think it was stopped."

If Knez told others of his suspicions it was not stopped and once Parker stepped into Pakistan he was dead.

There was a connection between this dead man and the Chechen.

CHAPTER 28

Walter Reed National Military Medical Center

Billie Cook waddled down the hallway with one hand holding a medical chart and the other her morning Starbucks. The waddle came from an old herniated disc, exacerbated years ago when she tried to stop a patient who fell out of bed without the bed rails up. He'd landed on her, and the rest was history. Like it or not, the odd walk had become her trademark. Fortunately, Billie wasn't the type to care about that sort of thing. From a small town in Texas just outside Lubbock, she had gone straight into the Navy's nursing program after graduating from Texas Tech. Her cropped gray hair, with a little trace of the black hair from years ago, framed her square face and blue eyes. She was from the plains of Texas, spoke directly, and remained a standout intensive-care nurse at Bethesda Naval Hospital.

"Has Reynolds come through yet?" She was talking to the night shift nurse about Dr. Anne Reynolds. The clock showed 6:45 A.M., and Billie was getting ready to go onto the day shift.

"No, not yet."

"I could have killed that little bitch yesterday."

"Don't get your blood pressure up. It isn't worth it." The desk nurse on the night shift was even older than Billie and had tolerated any number of neurosurgeons during her career at Bethesda.

"She made that young Marine's mother wait two hours. Told her later she was tied up."

"Yeah?"

"She was at lunch."

"Billie, that's not so bad."

"She's a good surgeon, but I am still trying to get her broken in right."

Billie took a sip of her hot coffee as she opened up the chart.

"I swear, if she doesn't wake up, I'll make life miserable for her." Reynolds was brilliant in the operating room, but she still needed compassion. Billie was determined to teach her that which was not in a text book. Billie Cook didn't tolerate a physician who didn't take to her training. Not on her floor. Wolfforth, Texas, produced two things: Billie Cook and rattlesnakes. The snakes were more famous, but anyone who knew Billie could attest as to which had the sharper bite.

"How's our gal doing?"

Billie was talking about only one patient. Maggie O'Donald hadn't been there long but had already won Billie over. The two had nothing in common. Maggie was from California and exceptionally beautiful. Billie Cook was exceptional only in one thing, being a nurse. But Billie knew Maggie's world had changed, permanently.

"Not much better."

"Are the NICoE people going to do their testing today?" Cook was referring to the new traumatic brain-injury team. With the invention of the IED and nearly a decade of traumatic head injuries, the military had little choice but to accelerate its research into the treatment of head injuries. Now that it existed, the National Intrepid Center for Excellence, like the military's burn center, would quickly become *the* place to go for head-injury patients.

"Yeah."

"You know, I think she's gonna make it." Billie rarely said that about a severely injured patient, but she had a certain pride in her ability to call it. Most of the time, the call was that the young man would not make it through the night, or the week, or even the month. But when she gave the gold seal that someone was "going to make it," she never had been wrong.

"Let me go check on her." Billie took another sip of her Starbucks and tucked the chart underneath her arm. Her stethoscope bounced around her neck as she waddled down the hallway.

The curtains nearly blacked out the room. Billie pulled them back, letting the bright light of a fall day wake up her patient. Maggie was in a ball, sleeping on her side; where her lower legs should have been the bed's blanket lay flat.

"Robert, is that you?"

"No, honey, it's Billie. How are you doing?"

"Okay, Billie." The inflection of her voice did not indicate that she recognized who Billie was.

"Good."

"I can't meet him at the London flat."

"It's okay." Billie really didn't want Maggie to say more. "Just rest."

"Tell Robert it's down to five."

"Sure, sure, I'll tell him."

"The prince needs only five votes. Salman and Mutaib will oppose him."

Billie checked her pulse. Much slower than normal.

"Five votes, I understand."

"It's important, Billie. Salman and Mutaib need to be removed."

Maggie's pupils were sluggish as Billie flashed a light toward them. It was as if Maggie were falling into a deep stupor.

"Yes, very important." Billie didn't want to agitate her too much.

"No, you have to tell him. The secretary needs only five votes. Time is running out. If he doesn't get the five votes . . ." Maggie's voice trailed away as she spoke.

"I'll tell him. Get some more rest for now." Billie pulled the curtains closed and checked the bed rails to make sure that they were locked in place. The IV had just been changed at the turn of the shift. "I'll check on you a little later."

"Billie, you will tell him. Five votes? The secretary needs only five."

"Sure."

Billie walked out of the room, tossing the last of the Starbucks into the trash can. The chart was clear on what she needed to do next, and Billie knew it.

"Hey, guys, cover me for a few minutes."

"Sure." The day clerk looked up from the computer screen at Billie, who continued to walk by.

"I need a cigarette." Billie Cook thought she had broken the habit several times. And then she had another day like today. She had only been on shift a total of twenty minutes and already she needed a cigarette.

As she walked down the hall to the stairs, Billie looked at the chart again. She reread the words typed and highlighted in bright, bold yellow. It made her sick. Billie Cook was on that floor for one reason beyond being an excellent nurse. She had an eidetic memory. She could repeat anything that anyone said once, exactly. She was a combat veteran, having made two trips to Iraq, and had a top-secret clearance. As the daughter of an Army command sergeant major, she'd known since childhood how to follow orders. And she knew perfectly well what the chart's words meant.

All conversations reported immediately. Maggie's chart listed a telephone number below.

It wasn't later than 7:45 that morning before the transcribed conversation reached Robert Tranthan's office. His young communications assistant was waiting the moment Tranthan arrived at work.

"What do you have?" Tranthan sensed the communications officer hadn't been at the Agency long. He appeared to be some young kid, probably just out of Penn State or Michigan, exceptionally smart but exceptionally poor. The days of the nation's young elite signing up for the CIA were long gone.

"Sir, you were to get any of these communications as

soon as they came in." The clerk held up a red-jacketed folder, sealed on the end with a TS/SCI sticker and the signature of the communications chief across it.

"Okay, thanks."

Tranthan didn't bother to ask what was in the folder. The messenger would not have known. He signed for the envelope and carried it past his secretary.

"Morning."

"You have a videoconference at eleven."

Laura did her job well. Years ago, Tranthan had interviewed several experienced assistants from the pool before selecting her. She had one asset that he had picked up on immediately, and which he'd appreciated ever since: She could keep her mouth shut.

"Thanks, Laura Lou." He had given her that nickname.

Tranthan closed the door behind him, thanking his lucky stars again for Laura. Not only could she keep a secret, but she also made sure that a cup of coffee and pack of Marlboros were both waiting for him each morning. He lit a cigarette and took a sip of the coffee. Black as tar. The only way he would drink it. Several years in the Pentagon's operation centers on the night shift had gotten him into the bad habit of drinking straight caffeine from glass pots coated with evaporated coffee residue. As he took another sip, he turned the communication over and saw its source. It caused him to stop.

Damn.

He broke the seal and pulled out a single sheet of paper. He read it and then reread it again.

"What the hell?"

It was deadly on several fronts.

Tranthan picked up his telephone and buzzed Laura.

"Who is working on the computer that was Maggie's?" He had given up a long time ago in trying to disguise his relationship with O'Donald from Laura. It would have been impossible. Nor did he question her loyalty or discretion. But just in case, he'd made it very clear that if he went down, Laura would be back in the secretary pool, and most likely to be assigned to the communications staff that came on at midnight. Laura had a young family and a child in day care. She liked her day job and her boss's flexibility with her schedule. She had agreed to protect him, knowing that they were in this together.

"It's that computer tech," she said. "Ah . . . George. I think that's his last name."

"Can you get George up here?"

"Yes, sir."

Now that he had a clue, maybe Tranthan could finally get somewhere. For one thing had not changed in the days since the bombing in Doha: Robert Tranthan needed to know everything that Maggie knew.

CHAPTER 29

Walthamstow Central Station, London

Enrico Hernandez looked at his watch and tried to do the math.

3:32 A.M. What do I add?

It was still set on Atlanta time.

He was starting to feel it. But he wasn't to stop anywhere. Not until he had finished his mission. The Suburban took him straight from the CDC to Hartsfield and the British Airways flight. At Heathrow, he took the express directly to Paddington Station, where a sizable crowd of people seemed to be headed for work. Most who passed looked different from what Hernandez had thought of as being British. A majority were south Asians, many women wearing brightly colored cottons that stuck out at the hems of their fall overcoats. Lots of the women walked together in groups of two and three, chatting in a language that he didn't understand.

He looked at his watch again.

8:33 A.M. GMT. Yeah, that's right.

Hernandez was early, which wasn't bad considering

how far he had come. He reached into his pocket and felt a package of spearmint gum that looked perfectly harmless. The early November chill caused him to pull up on the collar of his jacket.

A train slowed as it pulled into the station half full.

He watched as the doors opened and a few women came off. Their body language expressed a sense of fatigue that could only have come from working the night shift somewhere in greater London; now they were headed home.

As the train readied for departure, a voice called out.

"Why don't you get on?"

Hernandez smiled. The tall, lanky, bearded man who stood behind him was the reason he had flown several thousand miles.

"Hey, boss."

"Let's grab this one." William Parker talked and moved as if he were only engaging in brief pleasantries with a stranger.

They boarded the last car, destination King's Cross. Hernandez took the seat near the end of the car, while Parker stood nearby, casually looking around. The train passed through Blackhorse Road and then Seven Sisters. They didn't speak. At Finsbury Park station, William waited a moment after the doors opened and then walked out. Enrico hesitated a second and then followed the lead several paces behind. They cut across to another line, taking the train to Holloway Road. Again, Parker exited the train, and again Hernandez waited and then followed.

They worked their way across several trains heading back into the heart of London. Finally, at Green Park,

Parker left the station, cut across the street, and entered the park. Once he entered the park, he stopped for Hernandez.

"You didn't need to do this."

Parker was referring to Hernandez's new baby, only a few months old.

"Hell, sir, that baby cries too much. I needed to get out of there."

Parker could only smile. "I'm trying to picture you, a staff sergeant, raising a girl."

Hernandez grinned again. "My wife wasn't too crazy about naming her William."

"You know what's going to happen about sixteen years from now?"

"Yeah, it won't be pretty." Hernandez had already considered the thought. "Guess it's my karma."

"I hope not."

"You look good with the beard."

"Thanks. You got something for me?"

"Yes, sir." He handed Parker the sealed package of gum. A blue pack that held eight pieces in two rows of four blister packs. The package bore both Arabic and English writing, Mamoun Sharawi spearmint. "The third one on the second row."

"Nice touch on the package."

"Mr. Scott wanted you to know that was his idea."

Parker shook his head. "Message received."

"Oh, and Dr. Stewart wanted me to tell you to not touch it until you were sure you were in the window."

William slid out the pack to view the perfectly sealed, separate pieces of gum. He pushed one through the seal and stuck it in his mouth.

Hernandez was taken aback by the action.

"Damn!"

"A perfectly sealed pack wouldn't look right." Parker chewed the gum as they spoke. "Are you going to get your little girl something while you're here?"

"Yes, sir. At the airport they had some teddy bears that look like they're cops."

"You mean the bear that looks like a bobby?"

"Yes, sir, that's it. The kind with the hat."

Hernandez smiled sheepishly, knowing how funny it must sound. Twenty years ago, he wouldn't have dreamed of giving his child anything bearing the image of a cop. Enrico himself had been delivered into this world at California Hospital on South Grand, which made him a homegrown product of south Los Angeles. California Hospital was also where his older brother had died of gunshot wounds. The Marines, and in particular, one Marine colonel, had changed Enrico Hernandez's world. For the first time in his life, someone had put faith into his world. Not just a pat on the back, a life-and-death faith. The type of faith you didn't let down no matter what. This was how William Parker's team was built.

"All right, you have a flight back today?"

"Yes, sir. It leaves in a couple of hours."

"Wait a couple of minutes and then take a taxi to Paddington. It's not far."

"Yes, sir. And watch your flanks, sir. This Scott was the same guy we had on North Korea."

"I know, Staff."

"And Marine, Semper Fi."

Parker smiled. "In this case, *Fortius Quo Fidelius*."

Hernandez gave him a puzzled look.

"Look it up, Staff." Parker put his fist to his chest.

Hernandez squeezed the collar of his coat tight. The chill cut deep.

And the freakin' mountains of Pakistan? Shit!

He watched as William walked away, hoping that he would see the man again.

Hernandez checked his watch.

5:05

He hadn't bothered to reset the time.

Bet the baby's up already. My wife's probably walking into her room right now.

This was their first. His wife had never said anything about what he did before, but now with a child she had a different look on her face when he told her he was going.

Maybe a quick beer at a pub.

Hernandez started walking briskly north, toward Piccadilly Arcade, never for a moment noticing the man following him.

CHAPTER 30

Building One, Central Intelligence Agency, Langley

The lunch at the executive dining room was a buffet. Tranthan didn't like the dining room because of its nonsmoking rule. As a consequence, he would always eat quickly and leave. A man of habit, he took tuna on whole wheat toast, lettuce, and no mayonnaise. He had a Diet Coke without ice. And he always ate alone at a table against the wall in the back of the room.

Tranthan could be social if he had to be. For years, he had played the social game. Now he didn't want to be bothered. There was no one in the room who he cared about. Besides, he could tell from their looks that many knew what was going on with Maggie.

Hell, it's an intelligence agency. Surely they would know when their executives were having affairs.

But his wife wasn't just anyone. Her father, the senator, could bring Tranthan down with a phone call.

For her part, Maggie had kept their secret. She was smart—brilliant, in fact—and knew the likely consequences. Now, though, she was out of control—her own control. And there wasn't a hole deep enough to put her in.

An orderly changing her bedpan could hear something. *One misspoken word.*

Suddenly, he didn't feel hungry anymore.

He reached for a cigarette as he walked down the hallway to his office.

"Hey, Mr. Tranthan."

"Laura?"

"Mr. George is waiting to see you."

"George?"

"Yes, sir, the IT fellow on Ms. O'Donald's computer."

Robert turned and stepped into his inner office.

"Sir, I'm Todd George." The man wore a tie that looked more like an afterthought. His plaid shirt and plaid tie were a perfect mismatch.

"You've got the computer from our agent in Doha?"

"Yes, sir."

"What's on it?"

"Nothing. At least nothing retrievable."

"That's not much help, Mr. George."

"Yes, sir."

"You were the one who pulled the photo off our security officer's cell?'

"Yes, sir, what was left of it."

"Bad?"

"Yes, sir, very bad."

"I need you to do the same on her computer. It is important."

"Yes, sir."

"Okay, if you find out anything let me know. Let me know directly. Do you understand?"

"Yes, sir." The startled look on George's face told Tranthan that the young man had never had been ordered to deliver information to only one person.

Tranthan repeated his order. "You understand?"

"Absolutely, yes, sir."

"Thanks." Tranthan absentmindedly pointed toward the door. It was rude for even him, but this had been a particularly bad week.

"Oh, Mr. Tranthan, I can say one thing."

"Yeah?"

"The computer downloaded the contents of a flash drive just before it was destroyed. It was one of the new ones from EMC^2."

EMC^2 didn't mean anything to Tranthan. He assumed it was some sort of cutting-edge IT company.

"Was the flash drive found?"

"No, sir, I checked the inventory. No flash drives. But even if we find it, we will also need the password. This equipment is made to be pretty much bulletproof if someone wants to flush something."

"I imagine it would be." Again, Tranthan looked to the door, putting the cigarette to his mouth. "Thanks again, Mr. George."

CHAPTER 31

King Street, West London

"You're going to the BBC?" The editor of *Al-Quds Al-Arabi* was standing at Sadik Zabara's door.

William Parker looked up from his computer in the cubbyhole that was his office. It was an old building, and its windows tended to let the wintery London air seep in. On mornings like this, Parker typed his stories while wearing a sweater and a coat.

"Yes."

"What's the meeting about?" Atwan was more than just the editor of *Arab Jerusalem*, the English translation of the newspaper's name. He was the soul of the newspaper. Born in a refugee camp in Gaza, Atwan had survived the worst of Deir al-Balah. He and his little paper were unknown until a man named bin Laden granted the newspaper and its editor one of the first interviews.

"A tomato factory." Parker was tossing a jab at his boss. He knew that Atwan spent much of his youth working slave labor in a tomato factory. It was Zabara's way of saying leave me alone and read it when it's done.

"Well, who are you meeting with?"

"BBC's chief producer for *Five Live,*" Parker said, not wishing to make an enemy for no reason. *Five Live* broadcasted the news live for the BBC around the world. "I want to discuss with him the House of Saud's influence on the media."

"Oh. Excellent!"

Atwan's paper only had a circulation of around fifty thousand, but it thrived on cutting-edge stories from the Arab world. Online, it was read by more than two million unique users every day. Some questioned the stories' accuracies, but the stories certainly attracted attention. It had been a rub with *Al-Arabi* and many in the Arab world that the West never told a story that criticized the royal family and the House of Saud. If the king of Saudi Arabia didn't like what was being said, he would affect advertising. And if the king were truly angered, he would affect the price of oil sold to Great Britain.

"Your article on America's support of the upper class in its idea of democracy in the Arab world was excellent. Washington didn't like it." Atwan paused. "Which is always a definition of a good article for our paper."

Parker nodded pleasantly, then checked his watch. "Oh, I must go. The meeting is at White City. *As sala'amu alaikum,* brother." William Parker smiled and clasped Atwan's hand.

"Yes, *walaikum as sala'am!*"

Atwan and *Al-Arabi* were not far from White City. A short ride on the Hammersmith & City line would take

Parker to the BBC's Broadcast Centre, a complex of buildings from which the BBC broadcast its television, radio, and Internet shows. But it was a long walk to the Hammersmith station.

Parker flew through the walkers strolling down King Street. He looked at the time on his PDA as he grabbed the next tube on the pink Hammersmith & City line. The commute was only twenty minutes as the train passed by Goldhawk Road and Shepherd's Bush Market. At Wood Lane, he switched to another subway that took him the short distance to White City.

The BBC's headquarters were a complex of buildings directly across from the train station. The glass, steel, and gray brick structures covered several blocks. In the center, a doughnut-shaped modern structure reflected the glint off its glass of the early winter's bright sun.

The security guard gave Parker a glance of doubt. His beard was now several days old, his sweater worn, and his gray cotton pants well used. He looked suspect.

"Can I help you, sir?"

"I have an appointment with Daniel Suthby."

"Do you have some identification?"

Parker thought for a second.

"No, I don't." Parker hadn't really thought about it, but any identification may not have been much help. He had his Serbian passport back at the flat, which would have probably caused more trouble than not having any identification.

"But please call Mr. Suthby and tell him Sadik Zabara is here."

The guard's face showed doubt, but he went to the telephone on the far side of the desk. As he passed the other guard, he whispered to him. Both guards kept a watchful eye on Zabara while he called. But the guard's face changed again when he spoke to the person on the other end of the line.

"Mr. Zabara, here's your pass. Please come with me."

The guard led the way through the security detectors, leaving his partner to handle the front desk alone. He led Parker down the hallway to a bank of elevators. On the fifth floor, which seemed near the top, he led Parker to a conference room at the far end of a hallway.

"Mr. Suthby will be with you in a moment." The guard opened the door to a wood-paneled conference room with no windows and left him there.

Parker took off his coat and pulled up the chair at the end of the table.

"Hello, Mr. Zabara, I'm David Suthby. I think this is what you need." A man in a dark gray pinstriped suit walked through the door on the far end of the conference room. He handed Parker a sheet, written by hand, that had several quotes and some background information on Suthby. Parker glanced at it. Suthby had graduated from Oxford and worked his way up within the news agency. Several quotes reflected a denial of any influence by the House of Saud but also showed dates and times of visits from officials from Saudi Arabia. It was incriminating, but not dangerously so.

"Thank you."

Suthby nodded and left, closing the door behind him. A short moment later, James Scott walked through the same door with another man.

* * *

"I'm impressed," said Parker, referring to the idea of the BBC interview as a cover for their meeting. They could meet for whatever time it would take, and the BBC complex was so large and so secure that no one would see anything other than his appearing at the front door.

"Why, thank you," said Scott. "It means an awful lot, coming from you."

"But we can only do this once."

"Once is all we need. Colonel Parker, this is the man who is going to keep you alive." Scott stepped to the side as the man stuck out his hand.

Scott's companion was clearly an active military officer. His close-cropped hair went down to the skin at the hairline, but, oddly, he wore a full, brown beard.

"Sir, I'm Captain Furlong. Mark Furlong."

Army Captain Mark Furlong's reddish-brown beard was full of curls, which seemed to make his thin face fuller than it actually was. Dark hazel eyes framed by a scar that extended through the eyebrow over his left eye and a sunburned face gave him the look of a man who had spent most of a hard life in the outdoors.

"Where are you from, Captain?"

"Colorado, sir."

"What did your father do?" Parker had learned long ago that what one's father did said much about the man, even in this day and age. More important, how the son described the father often said more.

"He ran a hunting service."

"Elk?"

"And bear."

"You know the outdoors."

"Born there."

A hunter made the best soldier. He knew patience, he weathered the hot and the cold, he knew movement, and he knew the significance of small, seemingly insignificant signs. A broken branch, a rub of bark, a bedding down in brush could tell whether the animal was sick or healthy, old or young.

"How many tours?"

"One in Iraq and three in Afghanistan."

"I can save you some time." Scott interrupted the conversation. "He and his team are the best, the very best. I have worked with him bcforc, and their OP team has never let me down."

"OP?" Parker asked the question.

"Sir, it's Oscar Papa. Just a name for our team."

Furlong was dead serious, and Parker liked that. He needed a team of intense alpha males where he was going. He didn't want anyone who knew anything less than success.

"You've heard 'an army led by lions'? This is my army of lions led by lions." Scott smiled but seemed sincere.

"What's your army consist of?"

"Sir, our team has five in it. Two sniper teams each with spotters. And me."

"How about medical?"

"We are all capable. You name it. Push an IV, triage, stop bleeding, whatever it takes. We carry two full med kit bags. Everyone in the team has the training of a four-year ER trauma nurse."

"Language?"

"Two are fluent in Pashto and Dari. I can understand

it but can't speak it." What Furlong was really saying was that he couldn't speak it fluently. He understood both, like all of his team.

Parker was impressed with Scott's backup team. "Okay, Scott, what are your thoughts?"

Scott pulled out a laptop that had at least a seventeen-inch screen and rugged green casing. The machine was obviously meant to function in a combat environment. It had a mobile card that was much bigger than most, with a black, tubular-shaped extension that seemed like an oversized antenna. He spun the computer up and turned it around. A live satellite image of western Pakistan filled the screen.

"Your invitation will be to Peshawar. After pickup, they will take you into the mountains of western Pakistan somewhere north of the Khyber Pass."

Scott ran the cursor across the terrain. It was an instant, up-to-date satellite view of the mountains of eastern Afghanistan and western Pakistan. The mountains were topped with snow, and it was starting to extend down into the valleys. Parker could see vehicles moving slowly over twisting roads. The earth was barren. It was a cold, bare, brown, rocky world. A moonscape looked more inviting.

"Why would he take me into the mountains? Why not just meet in Peshawar?"

"He wants to show off. He is a god with some of these tribes."

Parker nodded.

"We think he will take you to one of two valleys. Both are well above fifteen thousand feet, so I hope you're still in shape."

Parker would have just completed his tenth marathon

if he hadn't been sitting in this room. For a moment, it made him think of his running mate several thousand miles away.

"I'm good."

"Sir, as soon as we get a sense of what direction you are going to, we will insert our team." Furlong pointed to a mountain range close to the Afghan border but still well within Pakistan.

"You'll be in Pakistan."

"Yes," Scott cut in, "and no one will know who they are. They are going full maverick on this one. Neither the Pakistan Army nor us. We won't risk any leak whatsoever."

Parker couldn't have agreed more.

"Once we know where you are going, we will get in, set up shop, and stand back. The plan is that there will be a well-camouflaged tent probably to the east of this valley here." Furlong pointed to a particular grid.

"What will be in the tent?"

"Just like what you said," said Scott. "An ice chest with two drips of Oritavancin and Rocephin."

The powerful antibiotics could stop a bad bug, but the key word was *could,* especially and only if the timing were absolutely correct.

"I need some other gear in the tent. An HK P30 .40 cal with an Evolution silencer." Parker began reciting a list he'd created in his mind.

"Yes, sir, good choice." Furlong leaned back in his chair. "What else?"

"A Windrunner, set up with a .338 barrel and a Titan can."

"Again, good choice. . . ." He was hesitant.

"Bad idea?" Parker asked.

"I did my tour at the sniper school and the marksmanship unit, but . . ."

Parker read Furlong's face. "But why not a Hellfire from thirty thousand feet? Right? Or even a cruise missile if the target is important enough? Is that your question, Captain?"

"Yes, sir, exactly."

"It's because we miss," said Scott. "He moves to a different hut to sleep, he changes caves, the randomness of combat, explosives, fate. And worse of all, we don't know we didn't get him. You see?"

Parker watched Furlong, who nodded. It was a compelling argument: Someone had to make the kill personally, on the ground.

"A Windrunner, then?" said Furlong. "With a .338 Lapua Magnum barrel?"

"Yeah. The M96."

"One thousand two hundred and thirty-six yards, sir."

"What?" Scott asked.

"Exactly, Captain." Parker smiled. "Mr. Scott, one day the captain and I will tell you all about it."

Furlong smiled. They had a secret.

"It will work."

"You have Moncrief with you." Parker didn't pose it as a question.

"Yes, sir, he's already at Lakenheath."

Parker nodded, heartened by the news. So Gunny had already arrived at the RAF air base in eastern England.

"How will I know the tent's location?"

"When we sight you and know you're in range, we'll flash a light for two seconds."

"Won't they see it?" Scott asked the question.

"Well, they may see it," Parker answered for Furlong, "but they won't register it. The difference is that I'll be looking for it. They won't."

"We just need to make sure you're looking in the right direction when we flash it." Furlong's look was deadly serious.

"If I'm not, your Windrunners need to take everyone out." Parker said, equally grave.

"Yes, sir."

"That's not a request, Captain."

"No, sir, I didn't think it was."

"Give me your hand, Captain." William Parker reached for a handshake, and Furlong took it. "The next time we shake hands, this will be over."

Furlong met his eyes and offered his first smile of the meeting. "Yes, *sir*!"

CHAPTER 32

Walter Reed National Military Medical Center

The cold rain was beginning to wash the remaining leaves of autumn from the trees, leaving only the bare skeletons. It had started last night. With the wind, the temperature was starting to descend down into the thirties.

Under the reading light in the rear of his executive Yukon, Robert Tranthan scanned the short articles in the *Early Bird*. The e-mail was a cut-and-paste condensation of important stories from newspapers and magazines from around the world. Somewhere the Pentagon had a staff of people who spent their days reading the publications of the world, cutting them out, and copying the composition. Its daily message was delivered to Tranthan's laptop no later than 5:00 A.M., seven days a week. He scanned the laptop before he was picked up at exactly 5:15 A.M. every morning, seven days a week.

One article caught his attention.

COUP LEADER EXECUTED

> RIYADH—Major Ahmed Maiad Zahrani was reported to have been executed after a court-martial found him guilty of leading an attempted coup against the king of Saudi Arabia. Zahrani was beheaded in the desert outside of Riyadh. On September 3, 2008, Zahrani was arrested after authorities discovered the coup involving a crown prince and some 150 officers of the National Guard.

He saved the article.

Crown prince involved? He smiled at the thought. The Bay'ah Council had, for the first time, overtly allowed politics to enter the process for the selection of the next king. There were thirty-five votes up for grabs. And the losers would not go quietly into the night.

The Yukon stopped at the entrance to WRNMMC.

"I won't be long."

"Yes, sir."

He now knew the way to her room. Across the lobby, up the elevator to her floor, and third room on the left. She was still in the intensive-care unit. She was still isolated from others. And her visitors were still restricted to only one. It didn't matter, as Maggie had no surviving family.

"Hey, Maggie."

She smiled, the narcotics clearly still flowing. It was a dazed, sleepy smile. The heart monitor continued to beep in the background.

He squeezed her arm. It was cold.

"Mr. Tranthan?"

He turned to see the nurse standing at the door.

"Oh, hello."

Nurse Billie Cook.

He walked to the glass sliding door that separated the room from the hall. Tranthan stepped out into the hallway and pulled it closed behind him.

"You don't have to do that." Billie Cook's voice clearly told Tranthan that she didn't like what was going on.

"What do you mean?"

"She has substantial hearing loss from the bomb, and if she could hear you, she wouldn't be able to remember it five minutes later."

"Then why in the hell is she yapping about stuff that she needs to forget but not a damn thing about what she needs to remember?"

"It's just the way the brain works, Mr. Tranthan."

"Well, then tell me how it's going to work in a few weeks? Or months?" He paused. "Or years?"

"If she's really very lucky? Not much better." Billie set her jaw, obviously growing angry.

"Will she ever be able to keep her mouth shut?"

"No."

"Okay." He turned, slid the glass door open, and stepped into the room. "Starting today, she needs a private room. In some quiet spot."

Billie stared at him.

"You understand?" Tranthan issued the command in a low, flat voice, almost a growl.

"Yes, I understand." Tranthan never understood how

much he was underestimating the nurse from west Texas.

Tranthan stepped into Maggie's room, closed the glass door behind him, and sat next to Maggie on the bed.

"Maggie, do you remember the last e-mail?"

"Sure."

"What did it say?"

She had a blank, confused look on her face. Short-term memory loss was the term that the doctors had used. But Tranthan could tell that it wasn't a short-term memory problem. She had seemingly no memory. Then suddenly, she would remember conversations from years ago. Or weeks ago. It was like herding cattle that all wanted to go in their own direction. With this herd nothing seemed to work.

"I don't know."

"What was the password to your flash drive?" He tried to look directly into her eyes.

She looked toward the window, as if trying to remember.

"Which crown prince was behind the coup? Was it Salman or Mutaib? Or someone else?" He peppered her with questions in his frustration. All he drew in response was a blank stare. She was unpredictable. He would ask her a question and receive no answer, but then later she would tell her nurses everything. She would tell Billie too much.

His cell phone rang.

"Damn." He looked down at the number.

Maggie reacted to the cell phone with the look of a child who thought her parent was angry with her.

Tranthan walked out into the hallway, looking for a place where no one could hear the conversation. There was a door marked EXIT that led to a stairway. He glanced up a flight of stairs and down a flight, seeing no one.

"Yes?" Tranthan was as impatient on his cell phone as he was elsewhere.

It was his secretary, Laura. She only called him when absolutely necessary.

"They sent a box over."

Robert Tranthan stared at the pictures on the far wall of his office. In effect, they chronologically charted his career path. A younger man progressed up to the present one. He started with senators and occasionally cabinet members. At the end, an older Tranthan posed with the president in the White House, as he grew closer to the source of power. But now, Tranthan's world was closing in on him.

The computer tech George had laid out in front of him the remains of the CIA office in Doha. Burned-out shards of a computer, several cell phones, a broken pistol.

Tranthan put her in Doha for a reason. Purely personal. The affair was getting too much attention. And he knew she would not go away quietly. She wanted an important post. He wanted a safe place to store his secret. He sighed, spun, and looked at the small bar behind his desk. Laura restocked it weekly with a new fifth of Grays Peak. He kept the credenza equipped with the vodka, olives, extra-dry vermouth, and an ice maker. Today, he didn't fool around with the vermouth. Just two cubes of ice and vodka.

He took a large sip and hit his intercom.

"What do you have, Laura?"

She came in quickly, carrying a box. "The investigating team said they could release this to you." She put it on the center of his desk directly in front of him. It had been sealed with a red plastic tape marked "Secret."

"Thanks."

Laura left equally swiftly, knowing he wanted to be alone.

As soon as he opened the box, the room filled with the odor of burned plastic and rubber from the explosion in Doha.

Amazing.

The one type of injury that Maggie hadn't suffered was burns. Apparently, the fire occurred sometime after she was evacuated from the rubble. Nevertheless, the items in the box had been singed. They included several loose reports, a small recorder broken open and empty, the keys to a Ford, and a blackened ladies' wallet atop them all. He opened the wallet and pulled out a driver's license from D.C. It showed the face that he had fallen for.

A small Glock pistol, missing its clip, lay in a pile of ash and cinders at the bottom of the box. He tilted the box and then set it back down on the desk.

As the ash and cinders shifted and settled, Tranthan caught a glimpse of a metallic, gold object at the bottom. He pulled it out from under the debris, finding a small tarnished gold photo frame no bigger than a man's wallet. It held no photograph. He weighed it in his hand. It had been bent and blackened by the heat.

He knew the missing picture well, a photograph that could have never been developed. The empty frame stood for their entire relationship, a symbol of pure impossibility.

"Fuck!" He threw it across the room. The frame struck the wall and fell to the carpeted floor. The room echoed the crash, then went silent.

This is stupid.

Sighing, he got on his knees and looked for the frame. It had fallen behind a table next to the wall. In the small space he could smell the alcohol. It reminded him of a father he was born to hate.

There it was. Tranthan grabbed the frame and backed out into the light of the room. Its glass was shattered. But the back of the frame seemed to be missing, maybe somewhere still under his desk? He looked underneath and then he saw it.

Tranthan backed out again into the light, now holding in his hand a small flash drive, black, no bigger than his thumb. It was scorched, blackened by the heat and slightly deformed, bent like the frame it had been in. He reached over to the telephone and placed a call to the IT section.

"This is the deputy director. I need something checked out, and I need it checked out now. Call Mr. George." A pause. "Yes, tonight."

CHAPTER 33

London

The double-decker bus blew past William Parker as he started to cross over King Street to the newspaper. He stepped back, between a parked Mercedes and a small Fiat, as the gust of wind blew past him. Another van followed right behind the bus. As he waited for a third van, Parker noticed a *London Times* newspaper box in front of the Hammersmith city hall.

MURDER IN WALTHAMSTOW
Gangs Out of Control

He shook his head. He'd known it was a mistake leaving Knez's body so close to his flat as soon as he saw the blue lights earlier that morning. The police cars had lined up on his street when he left for the newspaper. He was stopped twice, but the investigators had already made several assumptions, all of them wrong.

Apparently, this was the third death in the neighborhood in the last several weeks. A gang war had been raging for some time. It didn't matter, as Parker only needed a few days.

"Hello. It's Sadik." He held down the button on the intercom for several seconds.

The buzzer to the door was slow.

He bounced up the stairs.

"*As sala'amu alaikum*, sister."

"*Walaikum as sala'am*." The woman behind the desk always smiled when Parker came in. "Did you see the *Times* this morning?"

"Just the front page in the box."

"A man was murdered where you live."

"Yes, the police cars were at my front door." The word traveled very fast in London. It would be pointless for him to try to avoid the topic.

"Your poor wife must be horrified."

"Yes."

He had learned that the best way out of a conversation was not to have one. She meant well, but in the short time he had gotten to know her, Parker recognized why she had remained as a receptionist. She had the job because she was the editor's wife's cousin.

"There was a picture of the man."

"Oh?" The British newspapers were not known to hold back the gory details.

"He looked like the man who was here the other day. The one who was looking for you."

"Do you have it?"

"Sure." She pulled out the newspaper. It was folded around the photograph. Knez's half-open eyes stared out into space. "Isn't that him?"

"I don't know. I never saw him. Did you say he looks similar?"

"Yes, and the man who came to see you, he was from Bosnia, wasn't he?"

"That's what the message said. But I have no idea who he is."

Events were compressing the time available to him. Parker needed to get out of London soon.

"Oh." She seemed satisfied. "By the way, Mr. Atwan asked to see you once you came in."

"Is he in with anyone?"

"No. I know he wanted to see you. Something must be up."

Parker didn't like it. Atwan generally left him alone.

The editor's office was in the very rear of the building. One of the coworkers had accused him of wanting to be as far away from the street as possible. Parker knocked on the door frame.

"Hello, Sadik! Comc in."

"Did you hear of the murder?" Parker thought he would preempt the conversation.

"Yes, and the girls said the man may have been here just yesterday. Did you know him?"

"No."

"They are probably wrong. If you haven't noticed yet, they have a vivid imagination." Atwan had this habit of pulling up his sleeves when he talked. He would do it repeatedly. "But, more importantly, I liked your draft on the BBC."

"Yeah?"

"It will have the boys in White City boiling." Atwan had several grudges against the BBC. He knew that they would ignore it, but with a few calls Al Jazeera would run the story as well. It would keep his little paper in the minds of the Muslim world for another day. It would help sales.

"How did you get those quotes and details?"

"I had a very good source."

Atwan smiled. "You wouldn't consider sharing that source?"

Parker smiled but said nothing.

"I have something for you."

Atwan handed a manila envelope across the desk. He didn't have a chair on the other side of his desk so that no one could stay long in conversations. The paper was too small and the budget too little.

"What is this?"

Atwan nodded his head as if to say *go ahead and open it.*

The envelope was not sealed. He looked inside, seeing a Lufthansa ticket jacket.

"You are expected in Peshawar in two days."

"This is from Yousef?"

Atwan, beaming, nodded. "The interview of a lifetime."

Parker stared at the ticket in his hand for a moment, trying to look properly overwhelmed in the moment.

"I have something else for you." Atwan reached down to the bottom drawer of his desk.

"Here is a shawl that my father gave me as a young man." He handed Parker a black-and-white checkered shawl. "May it protect you in your travels."

CHAPTER 34

Bannu Road, Sarai Naurang, Pakistan

"The map."

Samullah handed Yousef a roll of paper longer than his arm.

"This is possible." Yousef spoke to the third man in the room on the second floor of the mud-brick house in the small western Pakistani village of Sarai Naurang.

Yousef was even more exhausted than before, if that was possible. The trip from Danish Abad had taken hours, but it was necessary if he were to stay alive. The most basic rule was always to keep on the move. Now the Pakistan Army was pushing across much of western Pakistan looking for the man he had come to meet.

Samullah Ullah had traveled with Yousef in the small Toyota pickup truck. It had an extended cab, but Yousef was lanky and long-legged. Samullah was, like Yousef, a tall man. So both were cramped up in the back of the truck for hours with the driver, the guard, and several AK-47s in both the front and back. But

Yousef needed Samullah with him for this meeting for a very important reason.

"You are suggesting what?" The other man had also come a long way. Zulfiqar Mehsud had walked for most of a day, hiking down from the mountains above Sarai Naurang and then riding on the back of a dirt bike for well over a hundred miles.

"Something that will be remembered." Yousef knew his reputation with the Pakistani Tehrik-i-Taliban would carry much weight; however, Zulfiqar Mehsud didn't commit his men to missions lightly. The jihad soldier was not an unlimited resource. And failure directly affected recruiting.

Zulfiqar Mehsud had survived several wars only by his cunning and skill. He was like a wolf. When possible, he would attack in a pack. If necessary, though, he would strike as the lone animal. A retreat was not dishonorable; rather, it was a strategy. Prisoners had their throats slit only because logistics required it. A retreating patrol could not spend time dragging a prisoner along.

The man had a well-wrinkled face, with skin that had been weathered by a life in the Hindu Kush. A twist of gray cut through the center of his black, curly beard. He had a large mole between his eye and the ridge of his nose. His hands were tough and leathery, small and stubby, with years of dirt under the nails. Like a pit bull, his tolerance for pain was high, his interest in comfort nonexistent.

Repeatedly, the United States reported Mehsud had been killed in an air strike. And repeatedly, a few weeks later, a video would surface with him laughing at the world. No one had collected the multimillion-dollar bounty on his head.

Yousef stood an even chance of not being recognized by the Pakistanis. He had bluffed his way through more than one checkpoint, but Mehsud had orchestrated too many bombings of important Pakistani officers. One recent bombing tore through a central mosque. It was well within the security ring of a military's base. The suicide bomber wore a vest full of explosives, climbed through a drainage ditch, under a fence, and walked into the mosque when it was full of officers, their wives, and little children. His pants, dripping wet, were noticed only at the last second.

Every officer knew who sent the bomber. The leader of Tehrik-i-Taliban, or TTP as it was called, was wanted, badly wanted, by the Pakistan Army.

Zulfiqar risked being recognized whenever he came down out of the mountains of western Pakistan. It had to be important for him to make the trip.

"There!" Yousef pointed to a paved road in the center of the satellite map. The detail was amazing. The road didn't look like a typical road, however, as it was much wider than any highway. It had several markings down the center and sides. Large dashes ran down the middle of the cement pavement.

While they were talking, an old woman brought a basin of water into the room.

Yousef dipped both hands into the cold water and rubbed his face. As in most of western Pakistan, a thin, powderlike dust seemed to hang in the air here. Traveling in the back of the truck with the windows open for hours had covered Yousef from head to toe.

Yousef passed the basin to Zulfiqar, who then passed it on to Samullah.

"What do you think of this plan?" Zulfiqar asked Samullah.

Samullah paused before he spoke. Despite his fame, these men had spent most of their lives killing others who wanted to kill them. Tribal wars were vicious. The Russians were known for gut shots aiming to kill with pain.

The Americans killed in another way entirely. They used Hellfire missiles from well above the clouds.

"It is a good plan," Samullah said at last. He was not known for overstating his thoughts. "*Allah Akbar*."

"We need a squad of warriors." As Yousef spoke, he pointed to the center of the satellite photograph. It had markings on it of a military base with a central runway.

Zulfiqar, never one to shy away from even the most impossible missions, took one look at the photograph and comprehended the full extent of the mission.

"You are a brave one."

"The reward is great," Yousef said softly. "Allah would be pleased."

The airstrip had the numbers on it of 12 and 30, signifying both the ends of the runways and the compass heading of the runway, 120 degrees to 300 degrees. But this runway was different. At the far end beyond the 30 were taxiways that led through gates, down a long pathway, to several bunkers.

"Indeed," said Zulfiqar.

For the Air Weapon Complex at Kamra was where the Pakistani military kept their nuclear weapons.

"It will be difficult. Very difficult." Zulfiqar would know. "It will require money."

Yousef nodded. "That is all true, but we have the money we need. What we lack is your warriors, men true to the jihad who can help us. We will make two attacks. A diversion will come directly through the lead gate. But the heart of the attack will come from across here, the Ghazi Brotha." Yousef pointed to what appeared to be a river on the south end of the base. "I will pay each warrior a hundred thousand U.S. dollars."

Zulfiqar's face showed astonishment.

Yousef held his gaze steadily. The truth was, the price of Zulfiqar's men was a small part of the overall expense.

"But even if you get the warheads, they say the components are separated."

"I do not need all of the components. All I want is the HEU."

Zulfiqar's face showed confusion.

"The enriched uranium. The core. They call it the *pit*. They will look like small shiny metallic balls no bigger than your fist."

Actually, Yousef wanted two cores. One would be used abroad, the other kept close.

Zulfiqar shrugged, apparently satisfied. "If that's what you need, brother, then you shall have it."

Yousef smiled. "Thank you, brother. Soon, you will have all of the information you need."

Though Zulfiqar didn't let it show, Yousef knew that the old man was already deeply committed to this mission. An attack on one of the main air bases of the Pakistani Air Force was enough of an achievement to last

Zulfiqar for years. A successful direct attack alone against the Pakistani Air Force's Air Weapons Complex would shake the very government to its foundation. But the capturing of two cores . . . that would shift the dynamics of the world—Zulfiqar's and everyone else's.

CHAPTER 35

Walter Reed National Military Medical Center

The fluorescent lights flashed on in the pitch-black room, darkened, then flashed again before bathing the space in blue bright light.

"Maggie, look at this." Robert held the small black flash drive directly in front of her.

Maggie's face showed a brief flash of recognition upon seeing the small object. But she covered her eyes with her pillow, acting—as she had been more and more prone to do—like a small child.

"Do you remember this?"

"God, what time is it?"

"Maggie, do you remember this flash drive?"

"Where is Billie?" She sounded like a child. "Tell Billie I need her."

"What? The pain?" Tranthan spoke the words more like a technician than a lover or a person who held some semblance of passion for the woman laying here in the bed. "Give her something."

Another nurse stood in the shadows. It was the

figure of a man, tall and dark, but dressed in white operation-room scrubs.

"Maggie, this is important."

Tranthan hovered over her, tired and angry and drunk. Some men would become happy or relaxed or joyful after several drinks. Tranthan became impetuous and gruff.

"What is that?" Maggie asked.

"It's the flash drive that came from your office in Doha. Do you recognize it?"

"Where was it?"

"In this." Tranthan held out the small gold photo frame. "Do you remember it?"

"I know that."

"Yes."

"I know that." She repeated the words.

"Give her something to help." Robert spoke to the man at the edge of the darkness in the far corner of the room.

"Where's Billie?" Maggie said, suddenly agitated. "I really need to talk to Billie."

She winced as the chemicals flowed into her IV. Almost immediately her eyelids became visibly heavy.

"What was the password, Maggie?"

Suddenly, Maggie O'Donald's face showed fear. "Where's my buzzer?" She ran her hand down, as far as she could reach, along the bed rail, looking for the feel of the buzzer.

"Maggie, I need you to concentrate."

"Okay."

"Was the password a word?"

"No."

"Maggie, lives depend upon what is on this flash drive. The Gulf could blow up without this. We need it!"

"The park," she said without warning.

"What park?"

"The park is important." Her face was full of confusion.

Tranthan signaled with his hand. The figure in the dark handed him a small laptop, which he opened and turned on. Tranthan didn't say anything. After what seemed an eternity, he connected the flash drive to the computer.

"Maggie, help me on this."

The password box came up.

"Try *Battery Kemble,*" she said.

The park where they used to meet . . . Hidden deep in Washington's northwestern corner, on a side street, the park's small entrance was known only to the few homeowners whose houses backed up to it. Well over a hundred and fifty years ago, the steep hill that formed the far northern end of the park was a battery emplacement to protect Lincoln and the city from the advancing Confederates.

The beep of the computer signaled a failed password.

"Maggie, it says we only have two tries left." Tranthan felt his anger building into recklessness. "Try harder." He looked to the man with him. He injected her again; again, it wasn't the morphine that Maggie would be used to.

"I don't know. I need to sleep."

"Maggie, help me on this and we'll let you sleep."

"Oh, God," she said. "I don't look good." She began to sob. "I will never look good again."

"Maggie, you won't. I can't lie. But you are a professional. Lives depend upon your being a professional. Can you do it?"

She tried to stop the tears, but they continued to pour down her face.

"Try BKP06," said Maggie, her voice nearly a whisper.

"Battery Kemble Park." He hesitated. "Oh-six?" He paused as he thought of the number. "June?"

"Yes."

"Our first meeting."

He punched the numbers into the password. Again, the computer refused the attempt.

"Damn it, Maggie . . ."

Tranthan didn't say anything for a moment. Finally, he shook his head sadly.

"Maggie, with what's going on now, I may not get a chance to see you again."

"What?" She began to sob again.

"We need that password."

Tranthan continued to look at the computer screen, seeming to ignore her.

"Concentrate, Maggie," he chanted softly. "Concentrate."

Her expression changed, becoming more distant as her voice faded. "Please get me Billie."

"Come on, Maggie."

She closed her eyes, concentrating, then mumbled something.

Tranthan couldn't hear what she was saying. He leaned over.

"What?"

She seemed to be struggling to repeat what she'd said. No sound came out. She was fading faster.

He watched her lips, reading the words as she tried once more. *There!* He had it. Without trying the password, he knew with certainty that he had the correct one. He closed the computer and walked out of the room.

Robert Tranthan made several decisions at that moment. The renegade operation to find and stop the man that caused all of this would be shut down.

Shut down. With prejudice.

Tranthan considered the odds. If Scott's plan succeeded it risked exposing his link with Maggie. It risked exposing her source.

"I think I know who it is." He spoke the words to himself as he walked down the hall.

And Maggie was simply too much of a risk.

CHAPTER 36

King Street, London

Parker stopped at the bottom of the stairs before stepping out into the cold, wet wind. The inner pocket of the coat held the airplane tickets and visa pressed against his chest. A lower side pocket bulged with the scarf that Atwan had just given him. Parker pulled the zipper up; only a sweater cap protected his head.

Parker glanced at his bearded, somewhat wild-looking reflection in the storefront's glass window. *God, what a sight. She would laugh at me.*

As he moved out of the doorway a double-decker bus stopped directly in front of the building. Parker stopped again, waiting for it to move on. It pulled away to reveal a man standing across the street under the cover of the overhang of the extended roofline of a government building. It was someone that he did not recognize.

The stranger, dressed in a dark ski coat, looked not

at the traffic or the pedestrians or the storefronts, but above Parker, to the second floor and the *Al-Quds* office.

Parker sensed trouble. His stare met the stranger's for a moment, but a passing lorry broke their eye contact. Once the truck cleared, the man was gone.

Oh, shit.

Parker wheeled around, back to the newspaper building, pulled the door open, breaking the lock as he did, and headed up the stairs two steps at a time. After the first two steps, a flash picked him up and threw him back down the stairs and through the closing glass door. The heat, plaster, and wood hit him like a shotgun blast.

Parker reached to his face. In the stunned moment, he felt his own, unfamiliar beard, along with a new, sticky substance. As he tried to sit, his head began to swirl. Little stars flashed across his vision as a woman bent down beside him. Another man came out of nowhere and grabbed Parker under the arms and was pulling him down the sidewalk, away from the blaze. The woman's mouth was moving, but Parker could only hear a ringing in his ears. He sensed the wet sidewalk, though, and his pants being drenched in the rain puddles.

Slowly, the ringing started to quiet.

"You're bleeding." The woman was shouting the words, looking at the top of his head.

Parker reached up and pulled his hand away, seeing blood—his blood.

"I'm all right." He mumbled the words in English, then realized he needed to slip back into the Bosnian dialect. He closed his eyes momentarily. When he opened them again, he was looking at the second floor of the building, which was ablaze.

"The people." He pointed to the second floor.

The man who had pulled him out of the debris was shouting the words as well.

An ambulance technician leaned over. Parker saw him before registering the wail of sirens in the background. The technician dabbed his forehead with a large gauze bandage while another felt Parker's legs and arms.

"Not bad, lad." The technician cleaned the head wound. "Anything else, George?"

"I don't think so. Bloody lucky he was standing where he was. One step to the left or right and he would have gotten a chest load of glass fragments."

"Thank you," Parker mumbled in accented English.

"We need to take you in."

"I'm okay."

"Still, we need to take you in."

Sadik's wife. The thought struck Parker harder than the explosion. *If, by chance,* I *was the target, Zdravo and her niece could be next.*

"Check on the others. I'll be all right here. Just let me sit here for a moment."

"Let's pull him up under this doorway. I'm hearing we have badly burned victims behind the building."

The two techs pulled Parker to a nearby foyer, retrieved their bags, and headed to the back of the building.

Parker watched them disappear, then rolled over on his forearms, waiting a second for the vertigo to abate, and did a push-up to his knees, finally standing up. He leaned against the doorway, trying to get his balance back. The rain drenched his face as he crossed over King Street, heading south to the tube.

He removed the bandage and trashed it quickly.

Good God. His head was still swimming, causing him to stop again in the doorway of a café. Parker looked back at the raging fire that was consuming what was left of the newspaper. King Street had now been blockaded by the fire trucks and police vans.

On a nearby light pole Parker noticed for the first time a pair of security cameras covering the street. As he made his way down the street, he pulled out his PDA and checked the time. He had two minutes until the next train on the Victoria line. It was a straight shot to Walthamstow. He started to run across the tube's entrance, past the stores, reaching into his pants pocket for the rail pass, and once through the gate ran down the escalator, running past the Londoners standing on the steps.

The clock was ticking.

He heard the train and felt the warm wind blow through the connecting tunnel. It was still a long walk to the train heading north, but the express would be faster than even what Scott could do. Parker ran through the walkways, down another escalator, and reached the train just as its doors started to close.

He took a seat.

The woman sitting across from him had a young girl, perhaps four or five, who was staring at him. Her eyes were like saucers, big and brown, looking frightened.

Parker saw why when he glanced up at his reflection in the glass of the train's window. Blood still streaked his face. He pulled the sweater hat off only to find a shard of glass caught in the fold. The hat was soaked from the rain, and he used it as a rag to clean up his face. He smiled at the child, who smiled back now that the blood was gone. The entire time her mother never looked up, talking intently on her cell phone.

Parker looked at the PDA again. The train had another ten minutes until the last station. He put in the password and texted Scott.

Explosion ws Al Q

It didn't take more than a second for the reply.

We know

Parker began typing another reply.

Check street sec cam

Again, the response was immediate.

Got it

Parker thought a moment and looked at the time again. The train was still five minutes out of the station. He thought of Zdravo and the child.

The police officer who patrolled the station. He would be the closest source of help.

Parker starting texting Scott again.

Woman n child at rsk . . . gt wrd to p at W.Sta . . . he is close

This time there was a delay. Scott was reading the text and then, Parker hoped, he was talking to his man at Scotland Yard.

Come on, come on. The train was still two minutes out from the station. There was no text reply. Parker sent another.

Status?

Still no reply. Perhaps being in the tunnel had interrupted the signal.

The train pulled in to the station. It seemed an eternity for the doors to open. Walthamstow was aboveground and open. Parker stepped through the doors as soon as they started to pull apart. The station was empty. He sprinted across to the entranceway, looking for the police officer who always stood in the corner. The policeman was missing.

A good sign. The policeman was never missing. *He must have gotten the word.*

Parker began to run. The street was just ahead. Ahead he saw an object lying across the curb and sidewalk. As he moved closer, he saw the limp shape of a body dressed in a blue shirt and dark pants. The shirt was stained in a circle of blood that went down the side to a puddle below. It was the station officer. Scott had gotten the word. Parker stopped, checked for a pulse, and looked down the one-lane street. It was empty. He could hear the sirens in the distance. Parker felt around the officer's waist, looking for a weapon. There was none.

He started walking down the street. It remained quiet and empty. No one was moving. He saw no one. The sirens were getting louder. He was alone. Only him and the man.

Parker kept walking down the street, keeping a car to his back as he moved, expecting anything. Just as he got to the flat, he looked up at the window where she would sit with the baby. It was vacant. He moved up to the front door. It was ajar, opened only the width of a man's fist, but the opening caused him to shudder.

She would never leave that open.

He slid the door open with his foot, staying behind

the protection of the wall and staying in the alcove, just out of sight from anyone on the street. Parker paused, planning his next move. The sirens were getting closer.

They're on the street.

In moments, an armed team would be charging through this doorway. He—

The second explosion of the day ripped through the brick building around him.

CHAPTER 37

A village south of Quetta

Yousef rolled off the rug just before the first break of light. The trip from Sarai Naurang had taken most of the night, with their two-vehicle convoy cutting far to the east several times to avoid Pakistani patrols. The cramped quarters of the truck were more of a problem than the lack of sleep. The cold had started to harden the muscles in his back. His knees popped and creaked as he tried to stand.

A true soldier needs no more than two hours' sleep. Napoleon Bonaparte. When in combat, Yousef taught himself to go days without sleep. Exhaustion was simply a frame of mind that he told his younger jihadis "allowed the stronger warrior to survive on the battlefield." It was another weapon over the weak.

Yousef's bed consisted of a prayer rug that he'd been given by his grandfather, the gardener. It came from his great-grandmother's village in northern Iran, where craftsmen had woven such rugs for more than five hundred years. Yousef's oldest son would inherit the rug. It was no less a part of his family than his sons, his daughters, or his wife.

As the first light started to break through the window of the small mud-brick house, Yousef carried his rug out into the garden, laid it out pointing to the west, and prepared for his morning prayer. The others, his guards and Umarov, joined him for the dawn ritual.

Mecca. Just to the west of that peak.

The wall of purple mountains to his west was rising out of the darkness.

Yousef looked at the others as he thought of the home of his religion. An imaginary compass line pointed to Mecca from his valley. It followed a point just south of the largest peak on the western wall of rocks. He checked it once on Google Earth and was surprised to see that the computer's extended line crossed the path he had envisioned—from the valley, west, over the tall peak, and then continued on for fifteen hundred miles to Mecca.

They will never see it. The thought struck him as he looked at the men bent, on knees, next to him. They would never see the white pillars of Mecca or touch al-Hajar al-Aswad, the Black Stone.

Yousef al-Qadi had traveled regularly to the city during his youth. His family drove through the desert, across much of Saudi Arabia, to the hajj every year. Yousef's memory as a child was the crush of people. Strange people from different lands with mixtures of languages and strange looks, most he could not understand. His stepsister would hold his hand tightly, cutting off the circulation, and scold him when he would wander off. His stepmother would yell at him at the first signs of a runny nose or cough. The crush of people carried the risk of illness, and the stepmother would always blame the child of the gardener's daughter as the reason her other children became ill.

But the hajj also gave him an early sense of the power of his faith. Millions would travel to Mecca, but hundreds of millions believed. Most would never be able to travel to the center and source of their religion, but still they believed. Many would give their lives because it was Allah's will, because they believed.

A true Muslim state. This was Yousef's dream for his people.

Saudi Arabia was not the true Muslim state. Its leaders were false prophets.

He looked up to the mountains that formed the little valley that surrounded his small apple orchard. The Americans waited on the other side of the mountain range. Those same mountains went to the south as far as he could see and, for over a thousand miles, to the north as well. The mountains to the north had been given silly Western names by the infidels: K2, Everest, and others.

As Pakistan had torn itself away from India, it was now his mission to pull these people away from Pakistan. Yousef carried with him a small map of his dream. It had a black outline that went well beyond Afghanistan, east into the Waziristans, both north and south, and the tribal areas north of the Khyber Pass. It extended down to the south, beyond Quetta. It went west into Iran. The West had created many of the countries of this world. Certain tribes that held the power had created many. But it was the original land that he sought.

A state that would be a harbor for true believers.

Yousef smiled at the thought.

Hasbun Allah wa ni'am al-wakil. He will be my guardian. The challenge will not be the Americans. They will go away. The challenge will be the tribes. Yousef knew that only a bold warrior could unite the people. It would take an evangelical fervor. It would take credibility. He had to be known. The name Yousef would be carried on the lips of both the young and the old. He would be the one.

"How is the plan?" Umarov asked.

Yousef looked around for a moment and then, deciding it was safe, pulled Umarov close to him, watching carefully for the others.

"The Chicago cell is in place and is just waiting to be activated. The Canadian cell is activated. They just need the nuclear core. And our little pilot is on her way." Yousef smiled.

And then he laughed out loud.

"The little girl." Yousef spoke the words as he looked to the mountains beyond. He had seen her trying to play soccer in Danish Abad with a ball made of socks and plastic bags. He knew she was perfect after her brother had introduced her. No one had connected her to Samullah. She was driven. She would not fail. She would go to Canada. She would tell them she was there for help with her leg. She would pass through customs without question. The limp would distract. But she now she had been trained. She was a quick learner. Despite her leg, a frozen knee torn apart by a fall from a bridge in Danish Abad to the rocks below, she was a natural athlete with perfect hand-and-eye coordination. She was the perfect pilot. They never would have suspected that she could fly anything.

"How about the technician?"

"He will help us build our own bombs."

"We are ready." Umarov stood above Yousef.

"Yes." Yousef stayed on his knees, rolling up his rug. Despite its journey with him, the rug still seemed to hold its bright reds and blacks and blues. "All we need are the nuclear pits."

The fifteen kilograms of highly enriched uranium would look like a shiny, metallic tennis ball. It would be the core in a larger ball of gelignite explosive. The end product would look like an oversized basketball wrapped in rolls of tape with small wires coming out from under the tape. The explosion would compress the neutrons of the nuclear tennis ball with such force that a most brilliant flash would follow. Even if it didn't reach the level of a chain reaction, the debris would be deadly for a hundred years.

"We need to move." Umarov did his job well. Survival meant never staying too long, never stopping in the same place twice. That had been bin Laden's mistake.

"The newspaper man will be coming soon." Yousef looked at the mountain range as he spoke.

Umarov's scowl telegraphed his thoughts. He feared bringing in a stranger. A stranger always bore risks. Yousef understood this.

"The trucks are ready?"

Umarov nodded. "I will get them."

Yousef knew that his wife and sons would be ready. She obeyed well. He stepped into the mud-brick house, its thick walls keeping the night chill inside. During the blistering heat of the summer, it provided relief. But at this hour the rooms were frigid.

"Come, now."

"We have something to eat." She handed him a wheat pancake.

"You are a good woman." He didn't compliment her often. He never said it in front of others.

She also had the two boys with their backpacks and rugs rolled up. Both were chewing on their pancakes. The little girl was sound asleep.

"You will travel in the second truck."

"*Inna lillahi wa inna ilayhi raji'um.*" She praised Allah during this difficult time.

Yousef's wife had never been a particularly attractive woman. He had picked her out of the group of sisters because she had the reputation of being the most obedient. But, more important, she had brought him two healthy boys and a daughter. As a consequence, he took no other wives. It gave her a special status. She was the only wife of Yousef, the warrior, and she believed in his dream of an Islamic state.

I will take more wives when this war is over, Yousef told himself. Like his brothers, who each had three or four. But no matter, she would remain Yousef al-Qadi's first wife and the mother of his oldest son.

"We are traveling well to the north."

Yousef had been to the valley before. It was well protected, with a deep cave on the far southern end. The road to Peshawar was just over the mountain. The Konar River passed nearby. It was well within the Pakistani border, but that seemed to matter less and less as the Americans became more aggressive. Most important of all, the valley was well protected by the Pakistani Taliban. The TTP had a network of villages that surrounded the southern end of the valley. It was one place that the Pakistan Army would not venture into.

"Patoo can ride in the truck with me."

The small boy showed a wide, toothy grin, brown eyes saucer-wide.

I hope he remembers. Yousef knew that the child would have a great responsibility one day. This would be the last trip with his father for some time. The family would be moving to Yemen soon. He'd had his brother buy a house near the beach, in Al Hudaydah. It looked out on the Red Sea. There, the boys would be protected and she would be respected.

But Yousef would survive and they would be together again. He constantly reminded his brothers and sisters that they had endured the worst that Russia and America had to offer without harm. The Islamic Emirate of Afghanistan would have new borders extending well into western Pakistan, sharia would rule the land, history would know its founder as Yousef al-Qadi, and it would be protected by nuclear weapons. And the family of Yousef al-Qadi would be strong and live long.

CHAPTER 38

A helicopter above London

"Easy."

The rhythm of the blades' rotation could be felt through the stretcher as William Parker started to come out of the fog.

"Take it easy." A medic was taping an IV feed to his left arm. The medic wore a bright orange flight suit with a white flight helmet that concealed his face, but he was a sturdy, short, and well-built man. Parker tried to move, realizing suddenly that straps held him firmly to the stretcher.

"Don't try to move. We're less than two minutes out from the hospital." The medic was shouting his words over the sounds of the jet engine.

"Where?"

"We are diverting to RLH."

"What?" Parker voiced the words but could barely hear his own voice. A familiar smell emanated from the medic leaning over him. *What was the smell*?

"Royal London Hospital."

Parker stared at the ceiling of the helicopter with its padded insulation. *God, get these straps off. What did he mean by "diverted?" What the hell happened?* His memory started to come back, like a computer warming up after being rebooted.

"What about the woman? The child?"

"I don't know. Just got you."

Parker knew that he had to force himself to relax. If Navy SEAL training had taught him anything, it was to not resist that which was impossible to resist. A fight against an ocean or a flooding compartment was a waste of energy. He was the only Marine Recon officer in the class, and the senior chief petty officer made it clear on day one that Parker would not make it. Being a Marine and wearing the silver bar of a first lieutenant put two targets on Parker's back. But Parker's 13:58 three-mile had swayed the chief.

It was the dive chamber that pushed the limit. They were sealed in this massive chamber that quickly filled with frigid water. The water rose to the point that the only remaining pocket of air was no more than a small box of matches in width, a very small box of matches. The chamber was totally dark. And the airspace was so small, the only way to breathe was to place the end of the tube into the airspace, remaining submerged the entire time. Claustrophobia quickly set in. Many candidates were dragged screaming out of the chamber just before drowning, washed out of the program. Parker had learned an invaluable lesson when the chief advised him not to fight it.

He felt the helicopter's skids settle on the ground; the gurney started to move, but Parker's head remained braced in a fixed position. He could tell that they hadn't given him anything for pain, since he now felt the sting of the straps on the cut on his forehead.

Good, he thought. *Treating me for a concussion means no narcotics. I'll be clearheaded, at least.*

Another man had joined the medic, pushing the gurney from behind Parker's head. He sensed this new person was not a part of the medical staff. They passed through several hallways. The fluorescent lights went by, one after another. And then he felt the wheels of the gurney bounce.

"Thanks, lads, we've got it from here."

Parker recognized the voice.

An elevator.

One man was cutting the tape that held his head in the frame. Another was loosening the body straps.

"Well, Parker, that was a close one." James Scott pulled the last strap from Parker's chest.

"Two in one day is pushing it." Kevin Moncrief, now with the medic's flight helmet removed, came around to the foot end of the gurney, loosening the rest of the straps.

"Who did it?" Parker started to lean up on his elbows when a ringing started in his ears.

"Hold on a minute." Scott put his hand on Parker's shoulder, pushing him back down into the stretcher.

The elevator doors opened behind his head to a hallway with little lighting. They rolled the gurney down the short hallway with Scott on one side and Moncrief on the other. Parker heard a click of a door behind his head and felt the wheels roll over another divider. He slid up on his side to see a solid metal door swing back, closing behind them as they went into another hallway deep below the hospital above. Scott turned the gurney down another hallway and then into a well-lit hospital room.

"Where are we?"

The room had all of the equipment necessary for any medical procedure. A doctor in his white coat was waiting for the new patient.

"This is our own private little hospital, Parker." Scott was cutting the remainder of the tape holding him down.

The doctor started to flash a light in Parker's eyes and began examining him.

"How do you feel?" The physician was starting his own mental checklist.

"Fine. How about Sadik's wife and her child?"

"Not now," Scott said. "This is someone we trust, but no one needs to be in any conversation beyond his own responsibility."

The doctor moved Parker's head and neck.

"Any wounds other than that cut on your head?"

"No."

"Your man is good to go. A slight concussion, probably a pretty good headache tomorrow, and maybe a stitch or two in that laceration. Otherwise, nothing."

"Can you use some of this on the laceration?" Scott handed the doctor a small tube. "We don't need evidence of a lot of medical care."

"Yes." The doctor understood. "It is just inside of his hairline. In twenty-four hours no one will know the better."

"Thanks, Doctor."

Parker could feel the cold, sticky substance on his forehead and the pressure as the doctor pushed on the wound.

"There you go."

The doctor left the room without saying more.

Scott waited for the door at the end of the hallway to click and then swing closed.

"What about the woman and child?" Parker repeated the question again.

"Dead."

The word was simple, unemotional, and to the point. Scott said it in a matter-of-fact manner.

Parker wasn't feeling so calm. "She saved my life."

He remembered her holding the child, shielding him from the blast, whether purposefully or not. Parker looked down at his hands.

"We saved your jacket." Scott held up the raincoat. "More importantly, what was in it." Scott handed him the envelope with the tickets. "And this." The small blue pack of chewing gum.

Parker was sitting on the side of the gurney as Scott laid both the envelope and packet next to him. He didn't touch either.

"I know how you feel." Scott's voice changed. For the first time his tone expressed the faint hint of concern. Moncrief stood quietly in the background.

"Who? It doesn't make sense that Yousef would do this."

"It wasn't Yousef." Scott leaned against the wall as he spoke. "Someone wanted this mission stopped."

"From the inside?"

"Bloody well." Scott paused. "But not in the usual way. Not just sending a message saying stop."

"Well, if the inside, why not cancel the flights? Cancel the operation."

"No, it's like they want it to fail, not just stop."

“I don’t know about this.” Parker grabbed the side of the bed. Things were becoming too unpredictable, unacceptable.

“It’s understandable to feel confused after a—”

“No,” said Parker. “I mean about the mission. Going forward with it.”

“If Yousef wins, there will be a lot more dead women and children.” Scott’s voice sounded like it had gained some grit.

The ticket in the envelope lying next to William Parker would have him in the air in mere hours. Of course he wanted to stop Yousef. But could the mission succeed now? Could Parker himself carry it forward successfully?

“What was the child’s name?” Parker looked directly at James Scott.

“What?”

“Their child. The child that Sadik and Zdravo Zabara adopted.”

Scott had no response.

“Amirah was her name. The daughter of Zdravo’s sister, who died at eighteen.”

“Amirah.”

“Yeah.” The name reminded him as to why he was here. He lifted the envelope with the airplane ticket in it. A decision had been made.

“There is something else.” Scott said the words slowly.

“What?”

“Hernandez never made his flight.” Scott paused. “And we have picked up on a conversation. Something is going on in Canada.”

“So stop it.”

"We don't know enough yet. We can guess it is connected, but don't know more than that."

Parker stared at Scott, then looked to Moncrief, who nodded.

The ringing had begun in Parker's ears again.

"Enrico would never miss that flight." Moncrief said what Parker was thinking.

"I didn't need him to even be here." Parker had asked Hernandez to carry the meningitis package to London because he trusted Enrico. But anyone could have done that. Now a little girl was at risk of being without a father. Meanwhile, a father had already lost his wife and child.

"We have to play out these cards. Our best chance to find E. is by you making that flight." Moncrief always said what William Parker had already thought.

Parker looked up to his gunny.

"Heraclitus?" Moncrief asked the question. "Remember Heraclitus."

"Yeah." Parker had quoted the ancient Greek often to his men. Now, he was being quoted back to him. Since Heraclitus of Ephesus said it over twenty-five hundred years ago, Parker lived it.

"Will," said his old friend. "You were not made for defeat."

CHAPTER 39

Langley

Robert Tranthan sucked on his Marlboro as he scrolled down on the computer screen reading the daily news summaries.

Bombings in London kill six. Key witness missing.

It went on to say that the husband and father, a Sadik Zabara, was missing. Tranthan smiled.

The cell phone in his pocket vibrated. He looked at the screen. It was a secure cell phone, nevertheless, little would be said.

"Yes?"

"Step one requires payment."

"Payment is keeping me happy." Tranthan wasn't very tolerant with a loose operative.

"Payment." The voice repeated the words.

"What about Scott?"

Even with a secure line, it was bold to mention names.

He next heard a click.

The Agency knew of certain freelance operatives. In

fact, the age of terror had encouraged their use. The bombing at the Boston Marathon only renewed certain officials' authority to seek help elsewhere, away from all scrutiny. And Tranthan knew who to use. They came cheap for someone at the highest level of the CIA. And they were well beyond the subpoena power of Congress.

Not too quickly, though.

It had to be done incrementally, and with the mission still on.

CHAPTER 40

South of Atlanta

Clark stopped to stretch just short of the opening in the woods to their mountain trail. The temperature had dropped into the twenties and was expected to last like that for several days. The muddy puddles on the road froze during the night, but the sun would warm them up during the day, turning the ice back into liquid. And when the sun set, the puddles would then turn, again, into solid ice. The first sign of winter.

Clark still was riding the high from the marathon, but her muscles felt like boards, inflexible and unbendable. Especially after nearly four hours of running on pavement. Even with the months of training, the pounding had taken its toll. She could barely get out of bed for a day or two after the race. But the run had hooked her.

"Look at that sky." As she spoke, the steam from her breath clouded the perfectly clear, cobalt-blue sky. The northwestern front from Canada had cleared out all of the clouds. The sun sparkled in the chilled air.

I think I'll do ten.

A ten-miler would mean two laps of their mountain trail. With the bright sun, it wouldn't take long for the body to produce enough heat to overcome the chill. She looked at her watch, trying to gauge the time. It was a new Nike Triax Mia with several functions that she knew she would never learn, but it kept her pace and time. Plus, it was cute. It was her reward for running more than twenty-six miles.

He should be home soon. The run next week would be the same, but she would be doing it with him. She smiled at the thought.

Clark heard the rumble of a car on the gravel road. She and Parker lived alone here on their small mountain. Visitors who started on the road usually gave up after several miles. If they got far enough, the NO TRESPASSING signs turned the stubborn ones around.

"Hey!" Clark saw the Stewart County Sheriff's patrol car and the driver who pulled up in front of the lodge.

"Hey, Ms. Clark. How's it going?" Deputy Mack Dennson had a round, happy face and looked perpetually younger than his years. He'd been with the Sheriff's office for more than ten now.

"What are you doing this far out in the middle of nowhere?"

"You know Will told me to check on you, right?" Mack smiled. "And you know how we follow the colonel's orders."

She laughed, but Mack was half-serious. He'd served a short tour in the Marine Corps, so a favor to another Marine was not a problem.

"I'm fine, but I appreciate your checking in."

"You have my cell?"

"Yep." She recited it from memory.

"Exactly. How about some protection?"

Mack was asking whether she had her own firearm.

"I have the pistol he gave me." She had never felt comfortable with the small Glock. She didn't even know the caliber, but it fit easily in her hand. The *pop, pop* of the bullets made her hand sore between the thumb and forefinger. But Will had insisted on her learning to not only shoot the pistol but also reload the clip and chamber the rounds. William was insistent that once a month they go out to the stump behind and below the lodge for target practice. Afterward, he would clean it with the same rag and a solvent that would stink up her kitchen. And then he would put it in the drawer near their bed, with the two clips full of the tiny rounds. One clip was kept in the pistol and the other next to it.

"Good. Going out for a run?"

"Yeah. Want to go?"

She knew that Mack thought she was crazy. And given Mack's waistline, she knew he'd take it as a joke.

"No, ma'am. But thanks."

"*Unit twenty-six, status?*" The patrol car radio chirped up with a call.

"No rest for the weary." Mack grabbed the mike.

"Twenty-six, I'm out at the Parker farm."

"Twenty-six, ten-four."

"Let me go check on some of my bad boys. You would think this cold weather would slow some people down."

"Yeah." As a veteran court reporter, she knew exactly who the bad boys were. And she knew that cold weather didn't matter a whit to any of them. "Well, thanks again." She waved as he turned the patrol car around.

Clark would never see Mack alive again.

CHAPTER 41

North Terminal, Gatwick International Airport, London

This is one of those turning points.

William Parker looked at the ticket in his hand for Flight QR076. Qatar Air's Flight 76 departed Gatwick's north terminal gate 26 at 9:30 A.M. He sat on a bench seat just across from the gate, watching the different passengers standing in line to board the Airbus A340 wide-body aircraft. A man and his wife were the first to board.

The woman walked behind the man, dressed in her black embroidered *abaya* with a black shawl that together covered her from head to toe. The man with her, however, wore Western clothes, a perfectly tailored charcoal pinstriped suit with black shoes that shined like freshly minted silver coins.

Parker continued to study the two first-class passengers. He wore a white shirt with a black-and-white striped tie. His beard was well trimmed and the eyebrows were as thick and black as the beard. The edge of a large gold Rolex watch showed just beyond the white cuff of the shirt, and a gold ring with a large emerald was on the small finger of the same hand as the watch. The gold complemented the brown tone of the man's skin. Parker noticed a pen in the left front pocket and from that realized the man was right-handed. The man was a distant cousin of a royal family, not directly in the tree of hierarchy, as he was leaving Gatwick on Qatar Air and not a Gulfstream.

Their final destination will be Doha.

The man, Parker guessed, was in London as a representative of the royal family negotiating cable television rights or franchisees for a new Pizza Hut or something similar. The wife, now back in her sari, would go shopping at Harrods, spending thousands of pounds sterling on colorful dresses, in sharp contrast to the simple, silk black robe she was now wearing. She wouldn't be able to wear them in Qatar, but they would wait in her closet for the next trip to New York or Aspen or Paris. At night she would stay in the room, receiving room service while he and his driver would go to the lounges. The ones that were forbidden in Qatar.

Once back in Qatar, a Bentley would pick them both up at the airport, taking them directly to their home, probably somewhere near Suhaim Bin Hamad on the C-ring outside the capital, where he would immediately change into his white silk *dishdasha thobe* and *shimagh* scarf.

God, and me?

Parker ran a hand over the scraggly beard on his face and the itch of the fast-healing cut on his forehead. Parker was still sore from being thrown back by two separate concussion waves. He felt as if he had just gotten out of the ring after a ten-round bout. Being so worn and sore probably helped him play the part of Zabara at the airport. Certainly, he was dressed perfectly for the role—that is to say, poorly. He would not be sitting in first class or business. He noticed the eyes watching him as he passed through security, following him like radar. With just a small, worn Nike bag over his shoulder, Parker passed through the security gate, where British security took everything out of the bag. He was searched twice, in detail. As he walked down the long concourse, Parker noticed a security tail that followed him to the gate. It shouldn't have been any surprise. He perfectly matched the profile. Sadik Zabara's passport noted the religion was Muslim, he was from another country, Bosnia and Herzegovina, and he was traveling alone. He looked the part—like a man who had little to lose.

It's a miracle they let me on this plane. William leaned forward with his elbows on his legs. *That is, if I get on.*

Parker rubbed his face again and thought of the several deaths. Zdravo and the child, Amirah, were dead. And probably Hernandez.

"This is the final boarding announcement: All passengers for Qatar Air's Flight 76 to Doha, please board at this time." The attendant making the call stood behind her desk dressed in the fancy crimson uniform. Qatar Air was a five-star airline that served Dom Pérignon in the front with chilled caviar in first class. In the back, the travelers with worn Nike bags sat shoulder to shoulder.

How can this possibly help Hernandez? Parker asked himself as watched the last of the passengers show their boarding passes and leave the lounge. With Moncrief, he could stay in London, follow the trail, and have a chance to locate Enrico.

He slid his hand into his pocket until he touched the PDA.

One message to Scott would shut it down.

Even if Scott didn't want to help in the search for Hernandez, both Parker and Moncrief had plenty of contacts from which to rebuild the trail.

"Thinking about it, aren't you?"

Parker turned to see Scott sitting down next to him. For a moment, he was disappointed in himself that he hadn't seen this coming.

"Yousef probably has somebody watching us," Parker said quietly, unhappy at the risk Scott had chosen to take.

"Yes, I thought of that. I didn't want to say anything until the last one got on. We know everyone else here. Did you see the *Times*?"

"Yes. They aren't looking for Sadik Zabara very hard, are they?"

The lead headline was the two bombings and deaths of six. Sadik Zabara, a radical journalist, was missing.

"No, you will slip through their fingers," Scott said.

"And the rest here are all friendly."

"Yes."

William looked around the gate. There were only a few remaining. In a quick glance, he knew Scott was right. The few remaining were dressed like businessmen, tourists, and airline staff, but they were all shaped like linebackers.

"It doesn't help that they're all dead."

"I didn't plan that." Scott's voice had a trace of regret. "But I've got it covered."

"How?"

"It has been leaked that Mossad did it trying to get Sadik Zabara. They freaked out because of a feared plot to take down an El Al."

Parker had to hand it to Scott. Once the word *Mossad* filtered through to Yousef, he wouldn't hear anything beyond that.

"Who was really behind it?"

"I'm not sure you would believe me."

"Since it is my life, go ahead."

"We think it's someone from the home team."

This is what Scott had suggested immediately post-explosions. Parker had been groggy at the time, though, and afterward had hoped it wasn't true. Now he looked straight ahead as Scott talked, waiting for him to elaborate.

"NSA picked up a garbled conversation. It mentioned what sounded like a cell in Canada."

"Wait. What about the home team? What are we dealing with here?"

"Honestly, I don't know. All we can do is forge ahead. I'll let you know if I find anything to back my hunch. But meanwhile, remember the Canada item."

"Why is that?" Parker asked, irritated.

"I'm just saying, if you get the chance, if the subject comes up with Yousef, look for any reaction he might have about Canada. Okay?"

Parker nodded. "What about Hernandez?" Parker's hand stayed in the pocket of his jacket. He could feel both the PDA and the pack of chewing gum.

"Listen, I know you don't trust me. I doubt that you even like me."

Parker's face didn't disagree.

"But I do know this. The guy you are going to see . . ." Scott paused, "can be traced all the way back to Pan Am. And if Hernandez were sitting here, he would tell you to go. Someday Hernandez's little girl will be getting on an airplane, or walking through a train station, or visiting New York."

"I hear you. But I'm still asking: What are you going to do about Hernandez?"

"Mr. Parker, if he is alive, I will find him."

William Parker looked deep into Scott's eyes and, for the first time, believed him.

CHAPTER 42

The village of Durba Khel,
north of Peshawar, Pakistan

"Wait here." Yousef pointed to a side road behind the mud hut on the single-lane road that passed through the small village of Durba Khel. The road cut north, around a small jut of rocks, to another village called Nahakki. At a fork in the road on the north side of Durba Khel, the right road went toward Nahakki and the left road crossed into a small valley, short of the mountain range, and beyond the mountain range, the Afghan border.

To the south, the road headed to Warsak, and farther south, Peshawar.

They had stopped using cell phones. They were well into the Predator killing zone now, and one misspoken word would result in a strike. Short, quick meetings at times and places picked at random were the only safe routes. Despite the CIA's repeated efforts, no one had ever broken into the network. No one had ever become admitted to the inner sanctuary of the leadership that hadn't been back-checked and back-checked and known thoroughly. Many had tried, but at any hint of betrayal, the problem was easily solved.

"Here?" Umarov pointed to the side road that cut through the two mud-brick shacks.

"Yes." Yousef liked the fact that Umarov said very little. They could travel for hours in the Toyota truck without a word being said.

"*Soecu!*" Umarov screamed as the little truck swerved to avoid the collision with the Nissan Diesel that cut across their path on the main road, using a curse word he often said in Serbia. A cloud of dust swirled around the two trucks.

Yousef cursed at the freight truck that passed by, nearly missing the smaller one by inches. The Nissan's horn blared as the driver stuck out his arm and hand from the cab. Called a "jingle truck," it was covered with brightly painted pictures of horns and yaks and the shapes of naked women, and it had racks of bells and ornate rings welded above the cab's windows. Rows of chains were welded to the front bumper. The truck was one of thousands upon thousands that had been customized by its owners to serve as a proclamation of the driver's identity. They were even considered the driver's bride, many said.

"They always own the road," Umarov muttered.

"They think they do." Both Yousef and Umarov's AK-47s were knocked down to the floorboard up against Umarov's leg and the gearshift. Yousef picked them up one at a time, rubbing the dust off the assault rifles. Everything was covered with a layer of dust, but the Kalashnikov always functioned. It could be buried in a mud hole for months and still fire. The rifle was made in a knockoff shop in Quetta for less than thirty bucks, but it always fired without fail. He pulled the slide to his rifle to make sure that the weapon had a shell in its chamber.

Another jingle truck passed, this one green and yellow with fringe along the windows. It was much larger than the last, a Mercedes tractor trailer, with more chains. It was covered with bright murals of lakes and mountains and green fields. And the chains, rattling with the movement of the truck, made a sound like hundreds of small bells. The constant ringing was intended to keep evil away.

"Ha!" Yousef let out a loud roar of a laugh. The first truck had missed them by inches. The second truck, with its much larger proportions, would have crushed their small pickup truck. It had been overloaded with cinder blocks stacked well above the cab. Yousef watched it recede down the road, swaying with the weight of the cement whenever the driver steered even slightly from the center of the road.

An absurd but chilling thought struck him.

The new Muslim state could have been stopped by a mere jingle-truck collision. Allah must be protecting us for a reason. . . .

The thought caused Yousef to reach into his pocket to check on the cell phones. He had two, one in each pocket of his coat. The one on the left didn't concern him. It was a disposable one that he used, only now if needed, to talk to others in Pakistan and Afghanistan. It would be destroyed and replaced every two weeks. The other, in his right pocket, had never been used. A piece of electrical tape was wrapped around the flip phone so that neither he nor anyone else would casually open it. He made sure it was charged every night. There was only one number in the phone's memory, a long-distance call to Frankfurt. More than enough money was kept in the telephone's account for the one simple call. No other calls would be made from it so as to ensure that it would never be traced. From Frankfurt, one cell would be activated, which would call two. Two would call four. One ring was all that was necessary. And then the phones would be destroyed.

"There he is." Another truck, this one a Mazda, beaten up and with no chains for evil spirits, pulled off the road. It had come up from the south. It stopped just short of their Toyota.

"*As sala'amu alaikum!*" Yousef stood taller than the little man and reached over to give him a bear hug.

"*Walaikum as sala'am.*" Zulfiqar never smiled, a fact Yousef had quickly gotten used to.

"I have what you have asked for." Yousef took a plastic bag from Umarov, who had reached behind the driver's seat. It was full to its limit.

Zulfiqar opened the bag. Wads of hundred-dollar bills were stuffed inside. The United States currency remained the unofficial currency of terror.

"You will find over a hundred thousand."

Zulfiqar looked around as if worried that another clan or gang would appear. People died for far less than this plastic bag.

"Don't worry, brother." Yousef put his hand on Zulfiqar's shoulder. As he did so, another strange thought came to Yousef's mind. His older brother was so similar to Zulfiqar in both looks and mannerisms. Both held their right hand back, using it in true Muslim mannerisms rarely, only to eat their meals in the bare-handed fashion. Both men were seemingly taller, but now seemed almost childlike in that they were so much shorter. And both had a broken tooth in their smiles. Yousef's brother's tooth had been repaired years ago with the money that his brother had inherited from their father. Zulfiqar's tooth, however, remained broken, but it reminded Yousef as to how his older brother's tooth was cracked. A rock thrown, out of frustration and hate, after a ferocious beating, which only led to another beating. Both the brother and Zulfiqar had one other characteristic in common. Both were hateful men, fully capable of tormenting the weaker or smaller or less resistant. Yousef would use Zulfiqar as needed, but he reminded himself always to remain aware.

"I will have the men ready in two days." Zulfiqar took a small step back from Yousef as he spoke. He would never remain too close to another for long. The Predators always put a thought in the backs of the minds of those in western tribal provinces.

"Excellent."

"And you do have the man?"

Yousef knew exactly what Zulfiqar was talking about.

"Yes."

"And the plans, you have the plans to Kamra?"

"I do." He turned to Umarov again. "Give them to me."

Umarov gave him a look. Yousef knew what he meant. The release of plans too early always risked the deadliest threat to an operation: a leak.

"Get them."

Umarov reached into the truck again. He pulled out a manila envelope and handed it directly to Zulfiqar.

"Midnight in two days. The man in Kamra will be ready when I call. Not sooner, not later."

"Brother, we will be ready."

"I will be in the *plar*." The cave was a protected site.

"Yes." Zulfiqar put his hand up to his mouth. He had the habit of rubbing his lips when he was hesitating to say something.

"What is it, brother?"

"This man, is it wise?"

Yousef didn't think anything was a secret in the mountains of the northwest frontier province, but he had made the point of only a very few knowing about the planned visit of the journalist from London.

"It is important, brother, that we earn more bags like this one." Yousef poked the bag of money with his finger. "The journalist will help us do that. A movement must have a face. It must have an identity."

"I understand."

Yousef knew that Zulfiqar was lying. A man like Zulfiqar could not see beyond the limits of his tribe. He could never have envisioned a plan like Yousef's, never could have raised the funds or created the cells that were needed to implement such a plan.

"I do need your help with security. I may need the TTP to be available in the next few days."

"We will have a company of men within easy reach."

"Brother, the next two days. We will be like clouds dropping much rain." Yousef's quote of Muhammad from the Koran was more than just a metaphor.

"Yes." Still no smile, but Zulfiqar had a spark in his eyes that Yousef recognized. The old man had become a believer in him.

The meeting ended, the vehicles leaving in two different directions, with Yousef's heading up the valley, to the west.

"Stop here." Again, Yousef pointed to the side of the road, just short of the riverbed, at the mouth to the valley. "You know what you need to do with the other one."

"Yes."

The second bag of money was going to Peshawar. It was stuffed with another hundred thousand dollars. It was to be handed to just one person, a woman. She was the badly ill mother of a young man and a much younger daughter. Both the woman and her daughter had developed chills some months ago. They continued to lose weight. The daughter was only a child of twelve, already painfully thin. The mother and her daughter were infected with tubercle bacillus. It was as Yousef had promised that both the mother and daughter would have the money to move to London and receive the treatment needed. The bag also had identification cards and passports that would allow the two ill people to be treated as if they had lived their entire lives in the East End. With some luck, Yousef promised, the two would survive. In return for this gift, the woman's son, a technician at Kamra, needed only to do one favor.

"I will walk the remainder of the way."

"Here!" Umarov threw a water bag across the cab. Dehydration remained a constant threat, particularly at this altitude. The valley's floor was well over ten thousand feet.

"Brother!" Yousef drank from the bag. It would be well below freezing soon. He wore an army coat layered over his *salwar kameez*, a pajama-like, thick cotton outfit.

"Keep it."

Yousef slung the water bag over his shoulder, then the rifle.

The cave lay several miles up in the mountains. "I will see you in a day after you pick up our new friend."

Yousef turned and headed to the northwest. He reveled in this opportunity to be alone. He would follow the riverbed for several miles and then cut up into the mountain ridge. As far as the eye could see, the landscape offered an endless stretch of frigid boulder-strewn rubble. In the cloudless sky, the white-capped peaks of the Himalayas could be seen well to the north. He followed the potholed, twisting, pencil-thin road toward the mountain range.

He also knew that he would be at his safest while he walked alone. The Americans would never take notice of a man walking alone toward the Afghan border region. The tribe of the valley knew who he was and that he must be protected. The man with two cell phones would be an easy target walking alone. A single bullet would prevent the birth of Yousef's new nation. He smiled. No one would notice. And no one would stop him.

CHAPTER 43

RAF Lakenheath Air Base, north of London

"The pond is over there."

James Scott could barely hear what the crew chief was saying over the roar of the Pave Hawk helicopter's turbine engine, but he could tell from the chief's motion, pointing out the open door, what was being said.

"There's the village and the pond is just there." The chief was yelling the words. Scott leaned forward in the canvas seat. The harness tugged at his waist as he looked out over the snow-covered landscape. Property lines were marked in odd-shaped rectangles and squares of tree lines that surrounded the village. The air should have been chilling, but the jet engine warmed the blast coming through the open door. The helicopter tilted hard to the right, pulling Scott back into the seat, as he looked down directly to the ground below.

A blue pickup truck with a snow shovel on the front end was directly below the helicopter, pushing snow along streaks in front of a thick, rectangular bunker that was a part of a network of buildings. Each of the buildings were linked by a black-striped taxiway in a chain. The helicopter tilted again, sharply to the right, pushing Scott's shoulder into the tubular frame of the seat.

"I've read about the pond," Scott yelled back to the airman. "It's the reason the Roman Legion was here."

Lakenheath's Pond existed thousands of years before the first Roman soldier set foot on the island, but the freshwater supported the establishment of the first garrison. Scott saw in his mind the encampment of the Legion in the clearing next to the pond, a perfect quadrangle, holding more than twenty thousand Romans. In the center of the encampment was the praetorian's, or general's, tent, the lines of the streets and tenting perfectly straight, like the geometry of the Coliseum. The small tent city was surrounded by a rampart, more than a dozen feet high, followed by a ditch twelve feet wide and twelve feet deep. The Roman measurements were exact. They had built the perfect killing machine.

But it was here in the center, the praetorian's tent, that Caesar stayed during his visit to the frontier.

Here, in Lakenheath. Julius Caesar.

Julius Caesar had been a success because he became an emperor after being a great field general. The empire lasted a thousand years not because of emperors like Nero and Claudius, but because of the Legion. The Legion, under command of men like Agricola, refused defeat. An engine of warfare, the machine took forty years to march through this island, but eventually it crushed the tribes of Britain as it did with all of its enemies.

Almost every day, Scott found that some lesson from Gibbon's *The History of the Decline and Fall of the Roman Empire* came to mind, often in a relevant way. He'd studied Gibbon at Eton and Oxford.

Scott glanced down at his Submariner Rolex. He twisted it the several hours to mark the time in western Pakistan.

Parker is well over the Mediterranean by now.

The Pave Hawk helicopter's skids settled to the ground as Scott uncoupled his belt and stepped out on the tarmac.

"Thank you!"

The crew chief saluted his passenger.

Scott turned to see the concrete bunker with a pair of F/A-18F Super Hornet fighter jets sitting inside. RAF Lakenheath's row of hangars paralleled both sides of the runway.

The modern engine of warfare. Scott looked across the airfield to see the U.S. Air Force's front line of strike fighters.

Lakenheath was the home of the Americans' 48th Operations Group. On the other end of the row of hangars, one stood out. A massive, high-winged cargo aircraft stood parked in front of the last hangar on the far end of the runway. The T-tail stood well above the roof of the nearby hangar. Clouds of hot mist floated up from the ramp, which was extended below the towering tail of the aircraft. Scott noticed the shapes of several figures near the nose of the aircraft. Armed guards with M-16 rifles surrounded the C-17.

"Will it take off in this?" Scott pointed to the sky through the windshield as he spoke to the driver of the

Air Force truck waiting to pick him up. The snowstorm had shifted into a driving, blinding wall of white.

"Sir, those guys roll in zero visibility. They had us drive the runway in the last fog bank. I could barely keep this on the asphalt." The driver was talkative. "As soon as we called in that we were clear of the strip, all you could hear was the spin of their engines. You never even saw it." The airman first class stared directly ahead as she drove across the airfield. Her knuckles were a blanched white as she squeezed the steering wheel.

Scott needed a C-17 crew like that.

"Are we going directly to the WOC?"

"Yes, sir."

The operation center controlled everything on the field.

The pickup truck's driver had the heater on high. The snowflakes hit the warm glass and turned instantly into drops of water. Despite the approach of midday, the temperature seemed to be dropping quickly. The new snow stuck to the already plowed taxiways. The driver drove the truck like an ambulance, flying across the airfield with a red flashing light on her cab's roof, stopping only briefly as she crossed the main runway.

The truck stopped in front of a low, one-story block structure with a dark metal roof that was covered largely in white with drifts of snow. The building was missing any windows. A sign directly in front said WING OPERATIONS CENTER.

Scott ran into the building. He didn't even bother to take the time to thank the driver.

"Mr. Scott, your pass." Another airman handed him the magnetic card. It wasn't as if Scott hadn't been here before. He walked down the hallway, past several airmen armed with short-barreled M4 rifles with their vest jackets. He scanned his pass and entered the vault marked *SCIF*. The Sensitive Compartmented Information Facility had walls nearly a foot thick, covered with copper mesh that foreclosed any eavesdropping from an outside source.

The room was no larger than an oversized cubicle crammed with computers and LCD screens covering the three walls remaining beyond the vault door entrance. A table in the center was covered with satellite photographs and pictures of bearded, turban-dressed men. Several men, also with beards, sat at the desk studying the pictures.

"Well, gentlemen, he has crossed the Rubicon." Scott took off his coat, knocking the snowflakes from it. One of the bearded men, in a plaid shirt and blue jeans, stood up to take it.

"Do you have the pictures of the ridgeline?" asked Scott.

"Yes, sir." The man, Captain Mark Furlong, hung the coat and handed a packet of satellite photos across the table. They were marked up with black tracings showing the major gradients and pitch of the land.

Scott pulled his chair up to the table. "The ridgeline goes from the northwest down to the southeast. The riverbed is on the south side, and intelligence tells us that the caves are in the mountains on the far side of the bed."

"Any water in the riverbed?" A blue-eyed, black-bearded soldier asked the question from a chair that was leaned back against a filing cabinet. A wad of snuff tucked into his cheek made him look like a man with a bad toothache. He held a plastic cup, which he would occasionally spit into.

"Sergeant Frix." Furlong mentioned the name as a way of introducing the shooter to Scott.

"It's dry and rocky. It looks like a gravel truck dumped a pile of crap into a ravine and called it a riverbed."

Frix nodded his head.

Scott had a sense of the team's structure. Frix sat next to another lanky soldier with brownish-blond hair and a short brown beard. His name was Don Burgey, and he too had a cheek swollen with a pinch of snuff. Scott knew that those two, like the other team, Sergeants Vaatofu Fury and Nel Villegas, had spent years working together. In-country, they communicated with a look or, in the pitch-black darkness of a rocky outcrop of rocks, a squeeze of a shoulder or arm, a spotter and shooter, setting up kills in perfect sync.

Parker's requested man, Kevin Moncrief, also sat at the table. Though he didn't have a beard to match the other operators and he was at least a decade older than the most senior man, Furlong, the ex–gunnery sergeant, looked comfortable enough with the team, and they with him.

"We'll drop in on the northwest of this mountainous finger in the other valley." Furlong pointed to the ridge that paralleled the dead riverbed. "And we'll move up to the front of this point. Several valleys should be visible from somewhere in here." He continued to point as the others looked over his shoulder.

"Pull up the bird and let's see what activity there is." Scott directed the briefing.

Sergeant Burgey turned to a keyboard, bringing an

image up on the largest of the several LCD boards. As he focused in, the sprawl of Peshawar could be seen to the southeast. Soon Peshawar disappeared as the view shifted farther to the north. A river twisted across the screen, from upper left to lower right. A scattered row of clouds to the south gave the picture a sense of depth. Burgey continued to focus in and, as he did, a twisting dirt trail could be seen at the base of the mountain range. At several points, the dirt road turned toward the mountain and then suddenly stopped.

"There's one of the caves."

"What's that?" Scott stood up, crossed over, and circled an object on the ground.

Burgey focused in, and with each click the image of a man, walking alone across the rocky desert, became obvious. He left a moving shadow that was much longer than his height. The sun was setting, distorting the proportions.

"Take it all the way in."

The spy satellite had the sensitivity of a microscope. The form of a man changed to a clearer image that showed his outline, then his manner of dress, and then the beard on his face. Even though darkness was approaching on the desert plain as he moved quickly across the rocky landscape, his rifle was slung over one shadow.

"What do you think the chances are?" Scott smiled. If he wasn't who they hoped he would be, he certainly was a bad guy. He was heading in the wrong direction to be a good guy. Now, if he only stayed there.

"It can't be that easy," said Frix.

"Let me call Langley." Scott reached for the secure phone.

"This is Scott."

The others watched the one-sided conversation.

"Yes, indeed."

Scott looked up at the digital clock on the wall with the several time zones.

"Yes, departure is in six hours."

The tension in the room was thick. They had all done this before, but there was always the risk of the random bullet, the pin-sized fragment of shrapnel, or the ricochet splinter of shell casing. But the team would not go in without one or the other.

"I hope not."

No, the mission wasn't being canceled by weather or storm or sleet or rain.

Scott picked up the pen from the desk, grabbed a piece of paper, and wrote *weather*.

"Yes, got it."

This time he wrote in big, bold, block letters: *TALIO*.

"Yes, Operation Talio."

Langley had assigned the mission its official name.

Only Scott knew the word's meaning in Latin.

Retribution.

CHAPTER 44

Qatar Air Flight QR 076, Doha

"Please fasten your seat belts."

The flight attendant was standing just behind William Parker when she said it. The airplane had flown across the Mediterranean through the night. Most in the cabin had tried to sleep in the small economy seats, either sitting up or twisted on their sides. Parker had been leaning against the back of his neighbor's chair, lying on his side. He only slept for short pcriods of time, but it was a deep, hard sleep.

God, I feel like shit.

He didn't need another explosion, even one he walked away from. It was like too many hits in the NFL.

Parker winced, thinking of Zabara's wife and their adopted child. He had thought about them all night. Them and Enrico.

And Hernandez's wife and baby.

He pulled open the shade to see a cloudless sky and

a brown, tanned, rock-strewn surface below. In the short distance, several high-rises rose up near the aqua-blue water that marked the far end of Doha City and the edge of the Persian Gulf. Passing inland, Parker saw boulevards that were wide, broad spokes of a large wheel with two separate and distinct multilane highways that circled the city like the inner and outer rings of a doughnut. The airplane banked again, to the east, and as it did an unusual sight just on the horizon caught Parker's eye. A burned-out shell of a building in the northwest of the city. A massive hole stood in the center of the large compound that surrounded it. The dark hole appeared to be full of chocolate-brown water. Burned piping from the building rose up in an odd pattern similar to children's twisted sticks.

"The American embassy." These were the first spoken words from Parker's seatmate. He was a young man with a long, curly black beard and a short crew cut. His clothes were thick but simple wraps of heavy linen cloth cut in loose trousers with a large vest. A yellow-tinted white, wrinkled collared shirt finished out the outfit.

"A bombing?"

"Praise Allah. Several dead."

Parker noticed the young man's hands. Black dirt was caked underneath the man's nails. The tops of his hands were already brown and cracked by a lifetime of being exposed to the sun. His hands looked like the hands of a man much older. His shoes were plastic slip-ons, similar to shower shoes bought at a dollar store. These were a cheap form of footwear that provided little warmth but plenty of durability. The man's bare feet were like his hands. They had been exposed to the elements for most of his life and looked tougher than his hands. He had a broad smile of large, stained teeth, as if he'd had a pack-a-day habit since he was a young teenager.

Parker looked again at the wreckage below.

So this is where it all started. Less than a week ago, he had been living in another world. The bombing here started the chain of events that resulted in his sitting in the seat on the airplane, leaving Clark on the other side of the planet. It had also left innocents dead and missing, and Kevin Moncrief stuck in some RAF air base preparing to leave.

Parker felt a surge of anger rise inside him. He thought of Sadik Zabara, sitting in some safe house, and he wondered if Scott had had the guts to tell Zabara that he was a widower and now childless.

The man sitting next to him seemed to sense the sadness.

"I am sorry, brother."

"Oh?" Parker acted ignorant. But the neighbor seemed to know more.

"We all have our losses."

It was then that Parker realized his seatmate knew of Sadik's losses—thought he was, in fact, Sadik Zabara. Which meant that Yousef also thought so.

"Yes. It is Allah's will." Parker spoke the words softly.

At that moment the PDA in his pocket buzzed.

Parker pulled it out, noticing the display on the front screen. He looked around, seeing several with their BlackBerrys activated as the airplane prepared to touch down. Even the man next to him had a cell phone and was using it. Parker turned in such a way to ensure that his seatmate could not see the screen of his phone, then opened his e-mail program.

Times reports Mossad linked to bombing. PM outraged.

Now Parker too could be outraged. The message went on.

Crew launch 0600

Long/Lat marked

He knew the last part meant that the landing zone of the team was marked in the classified Google Earth map he had in the cell phone. He would take a quick look at it and then flush the information. The cell phone pulled up what looked like Google Earth, but this one had a much sharper, clearer image. As he focused in on the ground, Parker could see several moving objects.

Cars. Damn! The cell phone was pulling a direct satellite link in real time with the details of every car and truck on the roadways.

The area was marked to the north of Peshawar in a valley along the Afghan border. The small map could be focused in to the smallest detail. In testing the system, he pulled it down on one individual, a woman sitting on a curb on a street near a mud-walled hut that looked like the village's small store.

Amazing.

He was sitting in an airplane using a cell phone looking at a woman captured by a satellite several thousand miles in space, relayed several thousand miles back to Parker's phone, and shown in crisp, living color.

Parker zoomed the image out. The woman sat next to a road in a small village marked *Durba Khel.* He pulled out the image even farther. To the west of Durba Khel the mountains rose up out of the valley. Snow-capped mountains stretched both south and north. A finger of peaks stuck out to the east of the range and down into the valley. These mountains were lower and did not have the tracing of snow that capped the larger mountains to the west. A map line cut through the center of the mountains marking the Afghan and Pakistani border. Just to the north and west of the end of the finger the map was marked with *LZ-1*.

Parker understood the plan. The team would occupy the high ground at the end of the finger. It would give them a clear view of the entire valley. The tent would be just to the north of the finger tucked into the rocks and cliffs.

He could tell from the movement of the clouds and the snow that the ground would be brutally cold and windy. The advantage point of the finger location would give the team access to all of the potential hiding places north of Peshawar, but their roost would be both freezing and dangerous. Also, while the high spot might allow the team to see the valley, any visible movement in their camp would enable the valley residents to see the team.

Parker sent his own message in reply:

Status of Sgt.?

It would be some time before he got his response.

CHAPTER 45

Walter Reed National Military Medical Center

"Is that you, Billie?"

The room was pitch-dark, even though it was still light outside. Like a bottle of black ink spilled onto a desk, the darkness filled the room.

Maggie couldn't tolerate the light. The head injury was seemingly becoming the worst of her several injuries. It had robbed her of her appetite, her taste, and her hearing. There was a constant ringing in her right ear. Maggie was becoming painfully thin, with little desire for the food trays that they brought. The food technicians had tried to increase the calorie count by bringing several meals, which she hardly touched.

"No."

The figure in the room was dressed in white scrubs.

"Okay. I'm going to just take a short nap."

The figure had the shape of a man. The voice, even in the single word, was masculine, but many nurses seemed to come and go in Maggie's room.

In the low light, a syringe was barely visible in the

visitor's hand. The nurse stuck the needle into the IV bag and squeezed the yellow-tinted liquid into the saline solution. He had on surgical gloves.

Maggie heard the glass door slide shut.

Her IV needle started to burn with increased intensity. The pain woke her from the drowsiness of her sleep as it increased, like a wave, pushing her down.

"Oh, God, oh, God. It burns. Please stop."

She reached for the nurse button, trying to find it in the blanket that was wrapped up in a wad near her chest. Her hand searched frantically for the cord.

"Oh, God."

Nausea surged through her body. Her stomach churned, causing her muscles to contract. Then it became difficult to breathe. Her lips started to turn black as her skin became a pale white.

"Daddy, please help me."

"Good God!" Billie Cook put her hand to the pulse in Maggie's neck. The beat was pounding like a MRI machine at full force. "Hold on, kid."

"I can't breathe, I can't breathe."

The pain was now ripping her chest apart. Unspeakable pain stunned her like a child being electrified by a live wire.

"Code blue!" Billie shouted at the top of her lungs. She wrapped the plastic oxygen hose under Maggie's nose and turned the pure oxygen up. "Hold on, help is coming."

"I can't breathe."

"What's going on?" The resident for the afternoon shift was standing behind Billie.

"Three fifty-two over one sixty-six." She looked at the monitor, which was beeping constantly now.

"Someone shut that beeper off. I'm giving her epi!"

The young doctor pulled out a syringe from the crash cart. It had a long needle that extended the length of his hand.

Billie Cook held on to Maggie's hand. The squeeze was cutting the circulation off in Billie's hand.

"No!"

The doctor gave her a look.

"No! No!" Billie repeated what she was saying. "She needs nitro, not epi." Maggie's heart was already racing at a high rpm, like a race car at Daytona. The veins were already constricted, forcing blood through the pump at an increased speed. Nitroglycerin would relax the heart muscles. The nitric oxide would slow the beat down.

"Okay, *Doctor,* then give her nitro." The resident's order was dripping with sarcasm. He knew after looking at the monitor, however, that it was the right thing to do.

Billie slipped a nitro pill into Maggie's mouth.

"Okay, honey, just let this melt."

"Thank you, Billie." Maggie's voice was barely audible. She had her eyes closed, locked in a grimace.

Billie watched the monitor, holding her hand, waiting for the numbers to start coming down.

"Come on." Billie was waiting for the nitric oxide to reach the muscles.

Suddenly, the monitor alarm went off. A steady scream of a beep.

"Shit!" The monitor had gone flat. Maggie's grip became like a vise, and then it relaxed.

"Clear out," the resident yelled as he tore Maggie's hospital gown open. He put the paddles to her chest. "*Clear!*" The limp body jumped. The line remained flat. "*Clear!*" Again, the limp body jumped. The line remained flat.

"Let's declare it." The doctor looked up at the clock. "Four-oh-six."

Billie stood back in shock. She had never lost one like this. Death was no stranger to the combat nurse. But not like this one.

"She probably threw a clot. With all of this." He looked down at her wracked body.

Billie knew was he was thinking: Maggie was a double amputee with a head injury and multiple wounds. The only surprise was that she had lived this long.

"No." Billie said it in a quiet voice. She pulled the saline bag off the hook, cut the tube, and then tied it off.

"What are you doing?"

By now the room was crowded with the resident and several of the floor nurses.

"I'll be right back."

Billie Cook went down the several floors to the basement and the hospital's lab.

"Is Tommy here?"

The lab clerk looked up from her computer.

"Sure, Billie. Are you okay?"

"Yeah. I appreciate your getting Tommy." She held the saline bag close to her chest.

It didn't take the lab technician long. The lab was ending the day shift and Tommy was heading out the door when the clerk stopped him.

"Hey, Nurse Cook. What's up?"

Tommy and Billie had this formal thing where they called each other "Nurse Cook" and "Mr. Carota." A doctor had harassed them several months ago about being not professional enough for his liking, but as a team they always seemed to get things done. It had irritated the surgeon because, again, Billie's guess was right. He had refused to run a CBC, which, when Tommy ran it, showed sepsis and saved a young Marine's life.

"I need you to run this." She held out the saline bag.

"Billie, it's after sixteen-hundred and that's saline. Can't it wait?"

"No."

Tommy's expression changed. For a nurse to insist that a test be run on a saline bag and stay to do it after a shift change told the rest of the story. She was hugging the bag up against her chest. Her body language said that no one was touching this.

"Okay. Let's go." He ran his card on the magnetic strip, unlocking the door to the lab. He paused just inside the lab. "Has it occurred to you that if we find anything that it may not be a good idea to do it this way?"

She shook her head. "I already know what's in it."

CHAPTER 46

Georgetown Pike, near CIA headquarters, Langley

Robert Tranthan reached into his coat pocket, pulling out the vibrating Sectéra cell phone. He looked up at the driver to ensure that his eyes remained focused on the highway. The cell phone was a top-secret SME PED. The screen had multiple choices, in color, to include one that was labeled *Sensa Secure Mail*. He opened the secret mailbox. The e-mail was simple.

Call office.

The e-mail wasn't from Tranthan's office. The visitor to Maggie's room was telling him to expect a call.

"We need to go back."

The driver had driven the deputy director since Tranthan was appointed to the office and authorized to receive the special security of an armored Yukon. He never asked questions.

"CIA?" The driver said, more as confirmation of an order than a question.

Tranthan paused, looking out of the window at the leafless winter trees, seeing glimpses of the Potomac

River. A bundled-up runner was running on the path that paralleled the highway for a short distance, her breath visible and frigid.

"Yes."

The trip didn't take long; the morning traffic had already thinned out. Fifteen minutes later Tranthan was picking up his messages at Laura's desk.

Laura looked up.

"Mr. Tranthan?"

"Yeah." He had to act as if he didn't know.

"Nurse Cook at Bethesda called." She handed him a telephone message.

"It's over, isn't it?"

"Yes."

He showed what he thought was an appropriately solemn and sad expression to his secretary. "Hold my calls."

Tranthan pulled the door closed and picked up his telephone. He held the receiver in the crook of his neck as he pulled out a cigarette and lit it up. At the same time, he opened his e-mail on his computer. Cook's cell phone only rang once.

"What happened?" It was Billie Cook who opened the conversation. Her voice was brooding and angry.

"What the hell do you mean?" Tranthan knew anything was possible now, including telephone conversations being recorded.

"She just didn't throw a clot."

"What time did she die?" He made sure to modulate his voice, fainter, sadder.

"Thirty-five minutes ago." Cook still seethed.

Tranthan followed suit, speaking with heat. "Listen,

you little shithead: Don't forget who you work for. Period."

"You're not stopping an autopsy."

Tranthan didn't respond but slammed the telephone down.

Hell yes, I will stop an autopsy.

He inhaled the cigarette, blowing the swirling smoke up into the air, as he leaned back in the chair. He looked at his hands, noting their softness. They didn't look like the hands that dug ditches in his little Chicago suburb of Burr Ridge. Throughout high school, Tranthan worked for the street and road department, digging ditches and throwing asphalt. He remembered coming home to the small house on Hamilton Avenue from a day of shoveling dirt to the sharp, antiseptic smell of vodka that hit him as soon as he stepped through the back door. The old man's voice always followed.

"Boy? Get in here!"

Robert Tranthan's father spent every extra cent he had ever earned in the glass factory on a stop he made every day coming home from work. The old man worked the night shift, getting off at seven. His breakfast was picked up around eight when the liquor store opened. A cheap fifth of vodka slowly worked its way through his father's liver.

A scholarship to a small college on the Susquehanna River deep in central Pennsylvania proved Tranthan's way out of that hell. He hadn't cared where he went. He left the old man at home and never looked back.

Tranthan knew the girl on sight when they met in class. The only daughter of the rookie senator from

Pennsylvania. Robert could see the insecurity in her eyes. She carried the pain of never coming anywhere near the bra sizes or glamour of her sorority sisters, but she was the senator's daughter, so most people had enough sense to leave her alone. Tranthan talked her into eloping six months after their first date. He used the excuse of love, but it took two years before she ever traveled to the broken-down house on Hamilton Avenue in Burr Ridge. A new owner was gutting the small ranch. He explained that it was a different world, back when the nearby highway was Route 66, not the truck-clogged Interstate 55. Back when it was a house in the woods of suburban Chicago. She never met his father or his poor, pathetic mother, who had taken the old man's beatings in silence.

Tranthan picked up the telephone again.

"Laura, can you get me a sandwich and coffee?"

"Sure."

He looked at his watch and waited for five minutes. The canteen was on the other side of the CIA campus. It would take her at least thirty minutes. He didn't need nearly half that time. He opened his side desk drawer, unlocked a metal lock box, and pulled a pad out from within. It had a series of numbers on one sheet of paper.

Tranthan walked out to Laura's desk, pausing to look down the hallway. Few people ventured into this floor and this end of the hallway. Most employees treated this part of headquarters as holy turf to be avoided.

Tranthan sat down at Laura's computer and went directly to the SMTP mail server. He had an idea as to what e-mail address to use and pulled out the sheet of paper, putting in the IP address:

2001.0db8.69d3.1212.8a2e.0404.liz1

He then opened up the computer's day, date, and time and wound it back.

Others would do the work, but James Scott and William Parker would soon be dead.

Tranthan's counterfeit e-mail was read on a BlackBerry just east of London. The recipient forwarded it to another BlackBerry at a train station near Madrid.

The first recipient handled the BlackBerry only with a glove and then placed it under the tire of his car parked at a meter on the street. The wheel crushed it as the car drove away.

The other BlackBerry rested on a train track seconds before the commuter train entered the station.

Another target was added to the list that Tranthan had originally sent: this one British.

As Tranthan sat behind her desk, he looked up to see a man standing there.

"Shit!" Tranthan yelled out.

No one ever came to his end of the hall.

"Yes?" He yelled it out loud.

"Sir, I'm sorry." The computer technician, George, stood there sheepishly. "I didn't mean to surprise you."

"Yes, what do you need?"

"I was able to save the flash drive."

"It wasn't too damaged?"

"No, sir, and your password worked. I have the flash drive decoded."

CHAPTER 47

Prince Salman Heart Center, King Fahd Medical City

Several white Hummers with mounted machine guns, blue lights, and screaming sirens led the secretary's Rolls-Royce through the city. The convoy raced across Riyadh at breakneck speed, with a helicopter escort traveling above in a parallel course.

The prince knew that all was not right as his car sped into the entrance to the Prince Salman Heart Center. The medical campus appeared to be under siege, with armed military troops stationed everywhere in sight. Large armored troop carriers with .50-caliber machine guns on top sat across the streets, causing the allowed traffic to run an obstacle course of weaving between the various stop points.

The secretary recognized the king's personal assistant, the young Prince Al-Bin, waiting at the entrance.

"What is his status?" The secretary didn't hesitate.

"Serious." Prince Al-Bin looked around as he spoke.

"It's too early, too soon." The secretary knew that this would only throw the Bay'ah Council into confusion. "The Council could end up being more destructive than positive."

"I agree. It was meant to facilitate the transition, not be a vehicle to confuse it." Prince Al-Bin looked too young for the job he was in. The prince was a thirty-year-old who appeared to be just out of high school. It didn't help that he was a small man who had to look up to most of his royal cousins. "He wants to see you."

Al-Bin followed the secretary in through the glass doors, to the lobby of the heart center. The hospital was so new that it was still recruiting physicians. Painters were still putting coats of paint on the walls in the hallways. The staff was as fresh as the paint. The nurses and physicians mostly came from the West as a result of the generous pay and a ransom of benefits. The center was a part of the larger King Fahd Medical City, which was home to well over two thousand medical staff members. But it was still far from the standards and capabilities of Western hospitals. Most of the royal family was treated in London, New York, or Houston. But the patient had to be stable enough to make the journey. Sloan-Kettering, Mayo, and MD Anderson were options if there was enough time for the patient to make it to his operating room.

"Your Majesty." The secretary bowed as he entered the room. The patient had a pasty white appearance, as if much of his blood had been drained from his body. The king's ink-black mustache and goatee seemed painted on the chalky white face.

"You have always been the first one by my side." The king's voice was weak, almost like a whisper.

"You took care of me as a young boy. When the others were bullies, you stopped them."

"I did, didn't I? Even then, I told Mutaib I would order his head off if he picked on you." The king chuckled until he started gasping for air. "Even at twelve, I was ready to lead."

"Indeed."

"You are aware of Yousef's plans?"

The secretary didn't say anything. The king always knew more.

"The dynamics of the Council could become unpredictable."

"Yes, sire."

"I do not wish to be the last leader of my nation." The king paused. "And I understand that your friend is meeting with a journalist from London?"

The secretary winced at *your friend*.

"A particularly troublesome journalist—one bent on fanning the fire."

"And what will he tell the journalist? That Saudi Arabia is run by a corrupt king? That the Muslim world needs a new leader? That his followers need to empower a new kingdom?" The old man started to cough, a deep hacking cough, gasping for air between breaths. "We do not need a confrontation," the king said. "You do not need a confrontation. Not now."

The secretary understood what was being said. The fragile illusion that he had maintained was at risk. Those who believed that the secretary, as the new king, would keep the country on the same course were placated by the current king's support of him. Likewise, those who pushed for a new course, away from America, away from the path of the last several decades, were placated by the secretary's known support of Yousef.

"I understand."

"And to think . . ." The king gasped for air. "He funds his acts with oil from here!"

The secretary remained silent.

"El-Haba . . ." The king referred to the oil field that fed money to Yousef and his family.

The secretary nodded.

"Perhaps it needs to go dry."

CHAPTER 48

RAF Lakenheath, north of London

"Scott."

James Scott turned around to see Moncrief standing in the hallway. Moncrief had stayed behind after the others on the team headed out in the raging snowstorm to board the white, ice-covered Air Force cargo van that would take them to the waiting C-17 transport jet.

"You don't need to say it." Scott knew what was on Gunny Moncrief's mind. Both men stood just inside the entranceway to the building looking out at the waiting van. Scott also knew that Moncrief would say it anyway.

"Listen."

"One second." Scott stepped outside into the frigid air. The building's cover provided some small protection, but the wind was pushing the snow at an angle into their faces. Scott had stepped outside, away from the two guards who stood just inside. Moncrief followed him.

"You understand about Hernandez." The gunny's back was to the wind, but his face was close to Scott's.

"Yes, I understand. If he is alive, I will find him. Now get going, old boy," Scott said.

Moncrief's mouth came even closer to Scott's ear. "Don't fuck with us."

"They're spraying down the bird," Furlong yelled from the van with the open door. "We need to roll." The transport jet was visible just beyond the corner of the building. Several large cranes were hosing down the aircraft with a green liquid as plumes of condensation were billowing up from the engines.

"Just find him."

"I will," Scott yelled as Moncrief ran for the van.

Scott looked at his watch. The forces were all in play now. He pulled out his cell phone and dialed a number.

"I need to see you for a moment."

"I haven't heard from you in over a year." The voice had a slight accent. It sounded as if the person were more comfortable speaking in another language.

"I need a favor."

"My friend, when don't you need a favor?"

Scott smiled. He didn't like asking Reuven Zaslani for any favors. In fact, Scott didn't even know Reuven's real name. It mattered little. They both had known each other for years. Scott had no children but had known each of Reuven's three sons since birth.

"How are your boys?"

"Fine. Two are pilots. They fly helicopters. And the youngest is a sergeant with the Sayeret Tzanhanim."

"Ah . . . like his father." Scott knew that Reuven had served with the elite Sayeret Tzanhanim commando unit of the Israel Defense Forces. Many believed that they were the best-trained commandos Israel had.

"I hope not. I hope he is smarter. What do you need?"

"I can be in London in an hour."

"Then I will see you at the Rotti in two."

Rotti was a small restaurant on Shepherd's Street several blocks behind the Park Lane, and Zaslani was known for keeping a room at the nearby Park Lane Hotel. The restaurant was an Italian café with only three tables and was barely larger than a closet, but at this time of day, in the winter, it would be empty. The owner was a friend of Israel, which was why Zaslani trusted it.

Scott's black Range Rover pulled up and parked in an open space just across from the Rotti. It had been a rush. The Air Force Pave Hawk had to fly below the storm in nearly zero visibility, but it had gotten him closer into the city of London. The helicopter landed at RAF Northolt just to the northwest of London, and from there he spun his Range Rover at full speed along the A40 in order to get into the center of the city.

Shepherd Street was more of an alleyway that opened up into a small square. Only one street intersected into the square at a straight line. Shepherd Street was straight for several blocks. The other two streets twisted around several buildings as they entered the square. Scott parked his new Range Rover in a spot just across from the pizzeria. He liked to hear the solid *thud* when he closed the door to the jet-black SUV. It was a special-order vehicle, one he was very proud of.

Despite working for the Americans, Scott still maintained a flat in London's Earl's Court. After his mother's death, Scott sold the cottage in east Milton Keynes. And as in many London suburbs, her eighty-two acres became more valuable as urban sprawl spread out into the country. When the modern self-contained town of Milton Keynes was built several decades ago, her property suddenly was worth more than anything the little woman could have imagined.

There was another benefit to Scott's chosen field. The tax service gave him a bye. It was in the security interests of the United Kingdom to not know everything about Scott's finances, and MI6 had the power to ensure such. The list, as Scott's compatriots at MI6 liked to call it, was a fairly short, highly classified list of names that was carried to Her Majesty's Revenue and Customs service every year. The fact that Scott didn't have to worry about the annual April 5 deadline meant that he had his millions.

Scott had met Zaslani before at the small cubbyhole of a restaurant. It was unmistakable and in the same physical state as when Scott had seen it several years earlier. The exterior walls were whitewashed and the door was framed with two planters that still had some withered flowers from the fall. The front doors were long plates of glass, and on each side of the doors large windows opened up the view of the several tables inside. Everyone on the small cobbled side street could see who was meeting at Rotti on any particular day. More important, those in the restaurant could see everyone on the street.

Scott would not have preferred Rotti. It was not his style. It was too open and too visible. But time was running out and he had to see Zaslani before catching his own military flight to Afghanistan. A Gulfstream crew was fueling the aircraft right now. The flight plan had been filed and it would be waiting for its last passenger, its only passenger, at RAF Northolt.

"My friend."

Zaslani was standing next to the front door. He wore a heavy black cashmere overcoat that was open. A Savile Row–vested charcoal-striped suit showed underneath with a crisp, starched white pinpoint shirt and a burgundy-and-black striped tie.

"I haven't much time."

"Then let's go in." Zaslani opened the door and put his hand on Scott's shoulder to lead him in.

A table up against the back wall in a small nook had a bottle of wine and glasses on a white, heavy linen tablecloth. Zaslani had called ahead. They would be left alone. The waitress would stay downstairs in the kitchen.

Zaslani pulled off the heavy overcoat and threw it onto the other chair.

The table was small, causing Scott to be close to his companion. As always, Scott noticed the pockmark scars on Zaslani's cheeks. He guessed that as a young child Zaslani had been scarred by a slow-healing bout of chicken pox.

"What can I do for you, my friend?"

"You saw the *Times*?"

The London paper had already run with the story that Scotland Yard was looking to a Mossad link with the bombings, a direct result of Scott's attempt to provide Zabara more credibility with Yousef.

Zaslani nodded soberly.

"Who will be the lamb?" asked Scott.

They needed the story to take on more. It had to have substance.

Zaslani smiled. “A young radical Jew from Russia. He has been a pain in the ass for some time.”

The Mossad was capable of throwing another Jew under the bus if it was required for the greater good. Someone had to be blamed for the bombings that killed Zabara’s wife and the baby. Documents tying the alleged bomber to the Mossad would be found in his flat. The Mossad would be damaged in the local press, but in Israel it would be described as a necessary act to stop the missile attack on an El Al jet departing Heathrow. Zaslani would charge Scott an expensive fee of future favors for this one.

“Tell me something, James. You are aware of a cell in Canada?”

Scott tried not to react but quickly changed his mind. He knew that Zaslani could see a lie a mile away. “Yes.”

“There is a young woman with a limp.”

God, they are good.

“We know very little beyond that,” Zaslani went on, no doubt telling him all of this for a reason. The Canadian cell must have caused the Mossad serious worry.

“I may find out more soon.” Scott stared into Zaslani’s eyes. “If I do, I will share it with you.”

“Yes, my friend, it may be best for all.”

“I have another request.”

Zaslani made a gentle *tut-tut* sound. “Your credit is being used up . . .”

Scott pulled out a photo of a young Marine sergeant in his alpha uniform. The khaki tie and shirt were in a perfectly straight line underneath the dark green uniform. The Marine’s brown eyes looked directly into the camera.

"This is some years old." Scott implied that he was looking for the man.

Zaslani didn't even look at the photo. "I am told that he is dead."

Scott didn't show any emotion. "When?"

"Within the last forty-eight hours, I'd say."

Zaslani's information seemed to be confirmed by the timing.

"Who?"

"I am not sure. Would you like me to find out?"

Scott hesitated. He didn't want to be indebted to the Mossad agent again. Not for a dead man. Even if he did promise Parker. Scotland Yard would find the body eventually.

"No."

"I am sorry, my friend."

"I must go."

"I will walk you out."

Zaslani threw a fifty-pound note on the table as he pulled on the overcoat. He always overtipped and overpaid. But he had one of the largest networks of sources in London. He knew how to play the game.

Scott stepped out onto Shepherd Street, stopping to stare at his gleaming, chrome-detailed Range Rover.

Shame to leave it . . . especially for Afghanistan.

"Nice Range Rover." Zaslani patted him on the shoulder again.

"Thank you, Reuven."

"If I hear further on your missing Marine, I will let you know." He hesitated. "No obligation."

Scott nodded and crossed the one-lane street, unlocking the Rover as he stepped up to the door. As he swung open the door, his cell phone began to vibrate.

Scott sat down in the gray leather seat and turned the seat warmer on as he spoke into the cell phone.

"Yes." He closed the car door, which locked automatically. Zaslani was still standing in front of the restaurant, smiling and waving.

"Hello," Scott spoke again into the phone. The connection was poor.

Whack!

The bullet slapped the driver's window with such force that it caused the Range Rover to rock to the side. The sniper's silencer had suppressed any noise from the rifle. Scott looked up in time to see Zaslani up against the wall, in the nook of the doors, reaching into his coat. In a flash, he was aiming a small pistol up toward Shepherd Street. His pistol was pointing upward as if the shooter had fired from the top of a building.

An older couple was frozen across the alleyway, staring at the scene with the look of absolute fear on their faces.

Scott was frozen in place as well. Once he caught his breath, he felt his face and right arm searching for blood. The bullet had struck the center of the window, on the driver's side, inches from his head.

James Scott should have been dead.

"James!"

Zaslani was shouting at him from outside his door now. In a daze, Scott opened the car door a crack.

"James, are you all right?" Zaslani looked at Scott, then alternatively quickly back up the street, pistol still in hand.

No matter how many times, no matter when or where, Scott was still stunned by a shooting. He slowly laid the phone down on the center console and opened the door fully. He kept his face and body behind the glass of the door as he pulled his own pistol out.

"I'm fine, it seems."

His eyes swept the rooftops. He knew, however, that the shooter would be long gone by now. Only in the movies did a professional remain behind to fire more bullets. The trained killer would wait for another day, another opportunity.

Zaslani couldn't help but to smile. "That's some vehicle."

Scott managed a wan smile in return. "Bulletproof glass. It's a custom Rover."

"Whatever it cost, that accessory was worth the price."

Scott nodded. The glass had stopped the rifle round, which remained embedded in the center of the window.

"Two twenty-three, I reckon," said Scott.

"You are doubly fortunate, my friend. A larger caliber and that glass may not have held."

"Indeed."

"And it tumbles on impact."

Scott knew the ballistics of the .223. It was nearly identical to the 5.56 NATO round in the M-16. He had seen what a tumbling 5.56 did to a man's neck. A chainsaw did less damage.

"Did you see him?"

"Just a glimpse." Zaslani nodded over his shoulder toward Shepherd Street. He still had his Jericho 9 millimeter pistol in his hand. The Israeli-made black steel handgun, nicknamed the Desert Eagle, seemed small in Zaslani's grip, but it was deadly.

"Who was he?"

Zaslani shrugged, his face grim. "I wish I knew."

CHAPTER 49

New Doha International Airport
Doha, Qatar

"Odd."

Parker heard Scott say hello and then the line went dead. He looked up at the clock and calculated the time zones in his head.

It couldn't be too late. He had a sense of when Scott was leaving London. It should not have been for at least an hour.

Parker stood up and stretched. As he did, he noticed several Qatari soldiers staring at him from the far end of the new terminal. The airport guards were carrying M4 automatic rifles and dressed in the uniforms of the Qatari Army. A man dressed in a suit was standing with the other soldiers, staring at him.

A Mubahathat.

Parker knew that the secret police had unlimited authority. He made a point of not making eye contact with the security officer. He walked over to the window to look out over the sparkling new silver-and-gold metallic-themed airport. The roofs were all shaped in waves in a modern series of structures. Rows of palm trees in blocks broke up the sharp lines of the metal-like buildings. Qatar's wealth was well reflected by its new airport. The crescent-shaped control tower reflected the bright sun flashing off the green-tinted, glazed glass control room that was perched at the top of the structure.

The airport had one other characteristic. It all seemed to be built oversized with wider taxiways and higher gate structures. There was a purpose for the difference. The airport was built for the Airbus 380. The jet, which was twice the size of a 747, with its double decks of seats, could easily taxi and park at the new airport. Qatar Air was building its fleet around the new mega-jumbo jet.

Parker stared out at the cloudless sky. He calculated another time zone in his head.

She's asleep.

There would be no telephone calls.

It may have been a mistake to go to New York.

He needed to put thoughts of Clark out of his head. But if it wasn't her he was thinking about, it was Hernandez or Zabara's wife and child.

No. He needed to be Sadik.

As he stood, looking at the sky, a mammoth Airbus landed. The sun was setting behind the airfield, causing the shadow of the terminal to paint a dark shape across the cement tarmac. The Airbus's landing lights pointed directly toward Parker as he stood there. It was painted white. The weight of the aircraft caused the wings to twist and flex. As it floated into its final touchdown, Parker thought of another reason for his being there: The Pan Am flight had never had the chance to land.

"Brother, it is time for prayers."

Parker turned around to see his seatmate from the previous flight. In an instant, it occurred to him what he had to do next. An image of Zdravo and her baby girl—blown to bits—flashed in his mind. He didn't have to manufacture the rage.

"Bastards!" He clenched his fists, and made as if to spit on the ground, then restrained himself, bringing a fist to his mouth instead.

The man watched him, eyes cautious but sympathetic.

"Those fucking Jews. I want to kill every one of them." Parker turned away, looking out the window toward the airplanes. Now he put both hands to his face.

"Yes, I know. I have heard. Allah does all for a reason. You will have your chance."

Parker rubbed his eyes, gritting his teeth, the muscles in his jaw flexing.

"Come, brother, let's go pray."

"Yes. Where is the mosque?"

It was a stupid and dangerous question on Parker's part. The prayer hall in a Muslim airport was always clearly marked.

"Of course. You are distraught, my friend." The seatmate acted as if he knew of everything, including the death of Zabara's wife and niece. But he didn't say any more.

For his part, Parker didn't say anything either. He simply followed. Then he stopped.

The man turned, looked back at Parker, saw that he was staring down the terminal at the *Mubahathat* officer.

"*Mubahathat?*" The man asked. He knew what Parker was thinking. "You do not need to worry. As long as you do not place one foot outside, he will leave you alone."

Parker nodded. As long as the traveler kept on going, he would be watched, observed, but left alone.

"I forgot." The man turned to Parker and faced him. "*As sala'amu alaikum*."

The man squeezed Parker's upper arms as he touched his cheek to the left and then the right.

"Walaikum as sala'am."

"I am Liaquat Anis."

"I am Sadik Zabara."

Liaquat nodded as if that fact were obvious.

"Where are you traveling to, Sadik?"

"Peshawar."

"Yes, good. I am too. The flight tonight at nine thirty?"

"I believe so. Three forty-six?"

"Let's go to prayer and then get something to eat."

"I am not hungry." But Parker followed the man. He got a better sense of Liaquat Anis as he trailed behind him. Liaquat couldn't have weighed more than a hundred and thirty pounds and stood no taller than Parker's upper chest.

Rows of shoes were lined up outside the prayer hall. It was a simple room with a cold linoleum floor. Several lines of men bent over in prayer. Some had prayer rugs, but all faced the *Qibla*. The men recited the *Salaat* in a quiet, peaceful tone, chanting the name of Allah and the plea for forgiveness. At the end, each man looked over his right shoulder, telling the angel of his good deeds, and then over his shoulder to his left, telling the angel of his bad deeds.

Parker thought the *Salaat* reflected the best of the

Muslim faith. It was a brief moment of quiet, peaceful reflection.

"I prayed for you, brother."

"Thank you." Parker knew the man was a messenger of Yousef's, but he was still trying to gauge him. "Maybe I can eat a little."

Parker's self-anointed travel companion slipped his shoes on.

"Good. You must keep up your strength."

"Yes."

"They have a Pizza Hut here in the food court. I love the Pizza Hut." Liaquat pointed to the far end of the food court.

The two stood in line for only a few moments and bought small pizzas. Parker watched as Liaquat pulled out a small pouch from under his well-worn *dishdasha thobe*. The pouch had several dollars, U.S. currency, wrapped tightly together with a rubber band.

Interesting. American currency. . . .

Parker watched the man inhale a pizza as he sipped a Diet Pepsi.

"Why are you going to Peshawar?"

"I am a writer for a Muslim newspaper in London." Parker tried to say as little as possible.

"Really?"

"Yes."

"Which one?"

"*Al-Quds Al-Arabi.*"

"Yes, I know it well. It is a very good newspaper. It tells the truth."

While sitting at the table, Parker noticed the *Mubahathat* agent walk by several times. Liaquat Anis was serving an important purpose. The lone traveler stood out. Two men traveling together seemed to be normal. He needed Liaquat, but he didn't need Liaquat to know any more about Sadik Zabara than he already knew.

"And you. Are you from Peshawar?" Parker asked.

"Not originally, no."

Liaquat struck Parker as a shy man. Even with all of the conversation, he seemed to have a hard time looking him in the eyes.

"I'm from Lahore." Liaquat said.

"I know of Lahore. Akbar the Great."

"Yes, indeed. Akbar, the king of the Mughal Empire. A true leader of the faith."

Lahore was on the far eastern border of Pakistan. Akbar ruled a nation of over a hundred million Muslims.

"What do you do in Lahore?"

"I don't live in Lahore anymore. I was a physician."

Parker tried to suppress the surprise.

"Where did you go to medical school?"

"Punjab Medical College."

"Why aren't you practicing medicine anymore? Surely there is a need."

"It isn't as simple as that. I came from a poor family. My father cleaned an office building. We lived together in one room and shared everything, nine of us. After I got my degree, we ran out of money. Without a further degree in some specialty, I wasn't able to get a job. It was meant to be. I was nothing, and Allah wanted me to remember that." He looked down at his hands on the table.

Not guilt, but shame. Parker thought of the comparison in the Arab mind. A man could feel guilt in the desert, alone, but not shame. Shame required the judgment of others. A poor man whose family scraped together everything so he could attend medical school and who then could not find a job in medicine was shamed.

"Be patient in tribulation and adversity." Parker quoted the Koran.

"Yes, indeed, *Allahu Akbar*." Liaquat looked up. "Our world is poor and miserable. The infidels have corrupted the government. They help the Americans kill our brothers and sisters. They help the Americans rape our women."

Parker remained silent.

"It is nothing to be a doctor. At LGH, the patients come by the hundreds and wait from before dawn to well past dark to see a doctor who is paid less than a hundred dollars a month. And then he tells them to take antibiotics that they cannot buy."

"LGH?"

"Lahore General Hospital." Liaquat became more animated as his anger grew. "Now, I am known. Now, my people respect me. I and my brothers against my cousin; I and my cousins against the stranger!"

By venting in this way, Liaquat had let it be obvious for the first time: This otherwise unassuming man, this doctor, was the enemy. An emissary of Yousef, here to escort Parker to his chief.

And that's when reality finally sunk in, striking Parker with the force of a sledgehammer:

The mission had begun.

CHAPTER 50

A cabin in remote Canada

"You didn't bring much?"

"No." The pilot didn't feel much like talking. She had slept for nearly twenty-four hours after they reached the cabin. It had been a brutal trip across the Pacific and then, in the small van, across much of Canada.

"It is . . ." she paused looking for the words. "Different?"

Her mind was trying to comprehend the vast, almost shockingly different colors of the changing fall forest. The burned reds and bright oranges overwhelmed. Her world different, a palette of browns and blacks, dust and dirt, mud and rocks.

"Yeah." Her Canadian counterpart spoke almost as little as she did.

This isolated cabin was a way station on her mission, and he the guide. He was to get her across Canada and then drop her off. Each part of the cell remained isolated, none knowing the role of the other.

The stop would be brief. Soon they would move on again.

"It is time for prayers."

"Yes."

He pulled out his prayer rug and pointed it toward a mountain range to the east. She had given up her rug as a part of this journey. Even in New Zealand, she had only dared pray with the curtains tightly closed.

It was a dispensation that the Chechen had given her.

"Muhammad would approve of such. It is a time of battle."

They would pray and then sleep. And then, as before, head east.

"I have a dream," she said. "Now, it is every time I close my eyes."

It would not be long now before she reached her destination. And then she would embark on her final flight.

CHAPTER 51

A cave west of Durba Khel, Pakistan

Yousef was awake well before the eastern sunlight started to illuminate the cave entrance, cut by the hand of nature into a crack at the base of a cliff. It was bone-chillingly cold. The cave lay on the far end of the valley, below the steep mountain range to the west. Yousef moved slowly as he stepped past the bodies asleep on their prayer rugs back-to-back on the dirt floor. As he shook off the sleep, he looked toward the entrance, where dim gray light marked the early beginnings of the day.

The cave faced the east. Several mud huts, directly in front of the entranceway, had been built on rock-stacked foundations that had supported other huts from the past, which had occupied the site for centuries. The cave had provided protection since the army of Alexander the Great first crossed the mountains to the south. And as during time of Alexander, today the people of the valley resisted the invaders. Time was irrelevant; resistance lived on.

The sun first lit up the peaks well above the cave; the end of the valley remained in a dull light.

At the opening to the cave, an old woman poured a cup of steaming liquid from a black pot kept in the glowing coals of the fire pit. The pit was tucked into the entranceway, under the overhang of a lip of granite and out of sight of the sky. The smoke drafted back into the cave, which saturated the clothes that they wore, but the overhang kept the heat of the fire from registering on the satellites that constantly combed the mountains.

The liquid burned as he put the cup to his lips.

Yousef wrapped the end of his shawl around the metal cup. He blew on the chai. Steam floated up in the chilling morning air from the mixture of hot milk and tea.

"Give me the cell."

Umarov, squatting next to the remnants of the fire, handed him a cell phone. It was one of several that would be used only once. Umarov never slept.

"And the card?"

"Mahmud had the bag."

"That worthless dog." Yousef threw the cup of chai against the wall of one of the mud huts. It clanked as it bounced off the yellow dirt wall. "Why did you give it to Mahmud?"

Umarov shrugged.

Yousef's patience with Malik Mahmud had been wearing thin. Mahmud was the son of the senior Malik Mahmud, who led what had started out as the Free

Aceh movement of Indonesia. When Yousef had insisted that Mahmud stay and fight with him before receiving money for his father's group, he hadn't realized the sad truth: Mahmud was not like his father. He was a whiner who could not abide the cold winter climate of Pakistan. It wasn't only the weather, though: Mahmud always expected more than he would be given.

"Wake up, you flea-ridden carcass!"

Yousef kicked the small man sleeping at the edge of the group. It pushed Mahmud into another sleeping man less than an arm's length away. The only thing that separated the two was the AK-47 machine gun that each kept close.

The twenty-odd fighters looked like geese sleeping in a large, dense flock. And like geese, as one awoke, the others awoke. Like dominoes, one turned over and, in turn, another one started to wake. They slept together in a tight roost, sharing their body heat in the frigid cave.

Umarov had taught those on guard duty to sleep on the outside of the circle. The guards would wake up their reliefs in two-hour shifts.

"You stupid fool. Where are the cards?" Yousef barked at the little man huddled on the edge of the circle near the wall of the cave.

"What? I'm sleeping." Mahmud rolled over, ignoring Yousef, despite all the others starting to stir and shake off the sleep.

Yousef grabbed a rock from a pile stacked up at the entrance and slammed it into the back of Mahmud's skull.

"*Tuhan baik!*" Mahmud yelled like a scalded cat, "Good God!" in his Indonesian language.

Yousef knew better than to seriously injure the man, but he drew blood nevertheless.

Sullenly, Mahmud threw the bag of phone cards at Yousef and pulled up against the wall of the cave holding the back of his head with blood dripping through his fingers. He looked like an abused pet huddled in the corner of his pen, his eyes locked on Yousef's.

Yousef reached inside the small cloth bag and pulled out one of the NobelCom cards. It provided twenty minutes of international time, but, like the cell phone, it would only be used once and then tossed into the fire.

"Umarov, do you have the number?"

"Yes."

"What time is it in New York?"

"Eight thirty-seven." He stared at the cell phone in his hand. "Eight thirty-seven last night."

Yousef looked at his own cell phone. It was just past 6:37 in the morning. He dialed the number on the phone card, entered another number, and then dialed New York.

Yousef stood at the very edge of the cave, trying to hold the signal. He didn't dare venture too far into the open. The cell towers were to the southeast, down the valley toward Peshawar, but the Predators were never far to the west, roaming above.

The cell phone rang only twice before being answered.

"Yes." Masood had expected the telephone call.

"Brother, Allah sends his thunderbolt!"

"Yes, Allah be praised!"

"All planning is Allah's!"

"Indeed, Allah be praised!"

Yousef heard a click. The Americans' eavesdropping satellite was also stationed above the eastern frontier of the Afghan border. Conversations had to be short. But each man knew what was being said.

The plot began.

Masood would receive an international Federal Express letter from Frankfurt with an unmarked key in it. The number had been filed off. It opened a mailbox in Brooklyn. In the mailbox was a slip to a package; small, but too large for the single box. The package had been held by the post office for several weeks.

The instructions were simple.

The verses of the Koran spoke to Al Rad: *He sends thunderbolts*.

Masood would write the number 13. It was the thirteenth verse.

"And all planning is Allah's."

The phrase spoke to the forty-second verse.

P.O. box number 1342.

Masood would open the package and take out a Federal Express overnight inside. His job was to deliver the package to the nearby Federal Express box. The Federal Express package contained a flash drive. It would go to an address in Chicago on North LaSalle Street. The secretary to the director of Chicago's OEMC operations center would open the package to see a letter from the director of DNCO with the accompanying flash drive. She wouldn't have the slightest hesitation when she saw the stationery and signature of Homeland Security's director of Domestic Nuclear Detection Office.

She or her boss would slip the flash drive into an office computer and open it up. It would appear to be another briefing on foreign threats. In this one, the flash drive would *be* the threat.

The programmer who'd built the flash drive had a special reputation. His online handle was simply Plato. The Chinese government had allowed him to freelance for several years as long as it was the right project. And as long as Plato kept his superiors informed. He was considered a *fen qing,* another brilliant computer genius who was angry, very angry, at the Americans' attitude and very angry at the imperialists. He and several in the Ministry of Defense made a profit from these jobs. Usually it was in the tens of thousands. This one was in the millions. He was a safecracker who got the thrill of hearing the tumblers click, but this job had to be his last. He and everyone along the line of payment would need to disappear after this final job.

Plato's malware program created a back door deep inside the computers they were sent to. It would throw a switch when activated by a cell phone in a mountain cave in western Pakistan, which would drop the guard of the most sophisticated computers in the world.

"Tell that dog to go back to sleep!" Yousef joked with Umarov as he tossed the cell phone into the fire pit. He smiled broadly. "Our special guest will be the first to report on Titan Rain!"

Yes, Sadik Zabara would get the journalistic opportunity of a lifetime. An early tip on the story of the century. *Titan Rain* was a code word for the computer virus, so named by the Department of Defense when, shortly after 10:23 P.M. Pacific time on November 1, 2004, it opened a hole in the computers at NASA, Redstone Arsenal, and several other military-related computer sites across the United States. Many thought it was a Chinese effort to probe the military and intelligence computers of the United States. Unlike Titan Rain, Yousef's malware would cause another set of equally important computers to go blank at exactly the same second.

"Are the other cells ready?" Umarov warmed his hands over the fire as he spoke.

"What?" Yousef squatted down by the fire pit and picked up a stick, then poked at the melting cell phone.

"The delivery cells?"

Umarov was asking too many questions. His words were a problem. It was the voice of doubt.

"Yes. They are all ready. All we need are the HEU cores."

The plan had been mapped out for months, four interlinked but independent cells in an operation that would circle the globe. The PIA cell in Islamabad consisted of two men, well paid, who would receive the small wooden crate marked as containing picking levers for a Sulzer G6200 weaving machine. Pakistan was known for building some of the best industrial weaving machines in the world. Picking levers were small metal parts no bigger or more unusual than staplers on a desk. Buried inside, under the stack of levers, would be a small lead box. It would emit no radiation, and only a well-trained customs agent looking for something unusual would find it.

The crate would be shipped by air express on the PIA cargo liner directly to its pickup in Toronto, Canada. The second cell would pick up the shipment in a small cargo van rented from Ryder Trucks. They wouldn't try to cross the border but, instead, would drive north to a small village on Georgian Bay. The drive would take most of the night, heading north to a small harbor where a boat would be waiting. The boat would head north, following the shoreline, until it crossed over to a small, isolated place named Lonely Island.

The girl with the limp would meet them on the road on Georgian Bay. She had been trained as a pilot in New Zealand for a reason. The same training in the States would have put her on a list.

Piloting the seaplane, she would leave Lonely Island on a direct course, south by southwest, never climbing more than fifty feet above the surface of Lake Huron and well below radar detection. The pilot would follow a path over the water into Saginaw Bay, where just south of Grand Rapids it would enter the United States. The aircraft's fuel capacity would allow her to cross over the land without stopping, still on the south-by-southwest course, passing just south of South Haven Lighthouse as it again headed out over the water of Lake Michigan. From the lighthouse, it would be unstoppable, too low to detect as it crossed the water, heading toward the center of the city of Chicago.

At precisely noon, the software virus, buried deep in the Office of Emergency Management, would shut down both the OEMC operations center and Chicago's Operation Virtual Shield, a network of security cameras that covered the metro region. The city's disaster-response capability would be paralyzed.

Also at noon, the seaplane would cross the bay on the final leg of its trip. While the technicians were frantically working on the downed emergency system, she would near the buildings of Chicago and reach for the trigger on the yoke.

The seaplane would deliver a solid, twenty-kiloton

nuclear explosion, its fallout intensified to perhaps twice its magnitude if there happened to be any early November snowfall.

Umarov nodded his head in agreement. “I only wondered . . . separate cells? All at the same time? All must work perfectly, yes?”

“Umarov, my friend, are you in doubt?” Yousef moved next to his leader while holding his palms out, facing the warmth of the fire. “Have you ever heard of the doomsday principle?”

Yousef knew the answer. The man could barely read.

“No.”

“There is a probability that mankind will become extinct. That only a finite number of humans will ever exist.”

“Yes?”

“It is our duty, we must . . .” Yousef poked the fire as though putting a blade under the ribcage of his enemy. “We must make sure that the last man standing be a true Muslim. That is our duty.” He paused as he continued to push the stick into the glowing embers of the pit. “This American giant must suffer a deep and severe wound. Only this will bring him down.”

CHAPTER 52

CIA headquarters, Langley

Tranthan stared at the print of the photograph. The technician had blown it up to a full eight by eleven, a color photo of Maggie O'Donald. The only item on the flash drive had been this single photograph.

"A fucking photo?"

Was this her idea of a joke?

Many thoughts entered his mind as he sat in the dark of his office. Only the brass and crystal table lamp lit the room. Tranthan held the photo directly under the lamp.

There she is, standing, smiling, as if her world would never fall in.

She stood beside her desk in Qatar, in front of the library shelves crowding her space, only a short reach from her chair.

A dead end.

Tranthan lit a cigarette and leaned backward in his chair, watching the smoke drift upward.

What's the downside?

He reached for the telephone on his desk. He squeezed the receiver in the notch of his shoulder, holding the cigarette in his hand as he used the other to pull open the main drawer and start searching through business cards. He went through several before coming to the right one.

Tranthan shifted the telephone to his left and, while ashes fell from the cigarette in his hand, he dialed the number on the card.

The phone rang only once.

"Federal Bureau of Investigation."

"This is Robert Tranthan at the CIA. I need to talk to Agent Tom Pope."

"Sir, can I take a message?" The young female voice sounded inexperienced.

"No."

"Sir?"

"Just tell Agent Pope it's Robert Tranthan."

The voice hesitated for only a second.

"Yes, sir."

"Agent Pope?"

"Yes, Mr. Tranthan."

After a painful quiet, Tranthan spoke. "I have something for you."

"What?'

"I'm scanning it now—check your e-mail."

A minute later Tom Pope was looking at a photograph of Maggie O'Donald. His first impression was how exceptional she looked. In addition to her striking beauty, she had a slight smile on her face, a devilish smirk.

"Maggie O'Donald."

Tom Pope knew who she was. In another stack on his desk, Pope had surveillance photos of several of

Robert Tranthan's visits to Bethesda. The Bureau's report on her death also lay somewhere on Pope's desk.

Pope grunted affirmatively into the phone.

"You know she died yesterday."

"I do."

"She was our field agent in Qatar."

"I know all this, Mr. Tranthan. Is there a reason you're sharing a picture of her?"

"She had this photo stored in a highly encrypted flash drive. Just the photo. Nothing else."

"All right." Pope pulled a pad of paper close to him and started to sketch on it. He wrote the word *Doha* in the center and drew a circle around it. In another circle he wrote *Op Officer* and drew a line to the circle in the center.

"It means something."

"Mm-hmm. What are you thinking that might be?"

"It may be a message to me, or to someone else."

"Really? What kind of message?"

"I—I don't know."

For some reason, Tom Pope got the impression that Tranthan intended this telephone call to accomplish more than a simple exchange of information. It seemed more like a stab at getting a "get out of jail free" card, as in being able to tell a grand jury, *Hey, I did my best to cooperate with the investigation*.

"Thanks, Mr. Tranthan. I'll ponder this, and you do the same. If you get any more ideas, please let me know."

"I will."

Tom Pope wrote *RT* in another circle and drew a line to the center.

"Let me know what?" Garland Sebeck entered his

office as Pope hung up. He was holding a bright red folder.

"What's up, smart-ass?"

"*Nada*. Who was that?"

"Tranthan."

Sebeck raised his eyebrows. "What did he want?"

"Sent me this photo." Pope turned the monitor to Sebeck.

"Wow."

"Yeah. Maggie O'Donald," Pope said. He explained how Tranthan believed that the photo was more than a portrait—that it held some sort of personal or professional message. "What do you think?"

"I think she's beautiful . . ." Sebeck studied the enlarged photo for another minute. Soon Pope joined him in staring at the image.

"I wonder if the flash drive this came off of had anything else on it?"

"Is that what Tranthan claimed—it had only this picture?"

Pope nodded.

"I doubt it."

Another nod from Pope.

"Truth is, Tom, I don't trust those spooks any farther than I could throw them. Especially Robert Tranthan."

CHAPTER 53

A C-17 cargo jet, forty-one thousand feet above the eastern border of Afghanistan

"Sergeant?"

Gunnery Sergeant Moncrief was asleep, but still grabbed the airman's wrist when he felt the nudge. It was a combat reaction. If he hadn't stopped, the next move would have been to the throat.

"It's Gunny." In the Marines, there was a substantial difference between a sergeant and a gunnery sergeant. One ran a squad; the other was someone you stayed out of the way of.

The C-17's cargo bay was barely lit by a red light glow. Moncrief peered out of one of the windows to see a moonless night. Down below, a solid bank of clouds extended as far as the horizon. In the far distance, the snowcapped peaks broke up the shape of the seemingly flat tabletop of clouds. They looked like ships in the low light, crossing a white-foamed sea. A thin, white, transparent coat of ice covered the aircraft's large wing. A wispy vapor of superheated water molecules struck the frozen air behind the jet, causing a white streak to trail each of the engines. Moncrief knew that a cold front cleared the air above the mountains.

A perfect night.

The cloud cover below would give them a chance at dropping into the valley sight unseen. The clouds provided protection unless the altimeter failed.

An altimeter off by one digit and we will be toast.

Moncrief looked in a trance at the quarter moon above and the gray clouds below.

The team would be slicing through the air at well over a hundred miles an hour toward the rocky cliff face of the eastern edge of the Hindu Kush. If one were very lucky and his parachute opened late, he would only break his legs and fracture his hips. The fentanyl lollipop would barely deaden the pain of being carried by the team across the mountains. If he were even luckier, he would be off course by only several hundred feet and, falling totally blind in the high clouds, would slam into a rocky riverbed. The force of the impact would leave a crater, death instantaneous and painless.

The gunny made out the outlines of several team members sitting in the seats against the wall of the aircraft, eating what looked like hamburger patties out of clear plastic Tupperware containers.

"Here, this is yours."

Army captain Mark Furlong took a seat next to Moncrief, handing him another plastic container.

"What's this?"

"*Chapli* kabab."

"Chappy the fuck what?"

Moncrief took a bite of the spicy kabab. It was

shaped like a hamburger but heavily spiced with garlic, salt, chili powder, and coriander. Sliced tomatoes, cucumbers, and lemons surrounded the patties in the little plastic container. Moncrief had the image in his mind of some local Afghan café in Lakenheath carrying the food out to a waiting driver.

"Eat as much as you can."

Moncrief complied, though the coriander didn't help much.

"It's the food of the Pashtun."

"I got it." Moncrief understood the purpose behind it. His body would absorb the spices, then ooze the scent back out through the pores of his skin. A sniper lying motionless, camouflaged in wait, eating the same food as his target, would have no distinguishing smell from the man who was walking by. A small advantage, but nevertheless an advantage.

"It may be the last time you get anything to eat for a while."

"Yeah." The gunny could go a long way without eating a meal. A recon, like a Ranger, knew that pleasures such as meals and sleep became secondary once one stepped out of the door of the airplane.

"You cut out the other scents?" Furlong asked.

"Please. I knew that much." Moncrief had tossed the aftershave and deodorant out several days ago. He had been a hunter all his life. Scent was a weapon no less important than the rifle he carried, or sight or sound.

"Here's some *kawa*."

Moncrief tasted the lukewarm green tea. It had leaves floating on top.

"Not bad." He hesitated. "Not freakin' good, either. Jack Black would be preferred."

"Speaking of which, I don't know if you want these or not." Furlong handed him a small, unmarked packet containing several tablets.

"What is it?"

"CAP go pills. Something new from DARPA. The next generation, they say."

"What the hell does that mean?"

"It's Red Bull on nuclear steroids. You won't sleep for several days; you won't be too hot or too cold. You will hear a fucking flea fly pass by and count how many times he flapped his wings."

Moncrief opened up the unlabeled container and swallowed two of the small pink tablets. He swallowed some more of the green tea to wash the pills down. It was the new age. The age of the pharmacological warrior. Who was he to stand in the way of progress?

"Here's another pack. You shouldn't need it."

In a short time the gunny started to feel a euphoria coming on. As he looked around the cargo bay of the jet, Moncrief felt sure he was hearing sounds in the jet bay that he hadn't noticed before. Far forward in the bay, the crew chief was telling one of the crewmembers that an engine would go out soon. It would be number four. And Vaatofu Fury was telling Vaas to finish packing something called the FireFly. No doubt about it: Moncrief could hear more, see more.

What the fuck is this stuff?

"You don't know us, Gunny." Furlong sat next to Moncrief. "I'm not thrilled about you being here. We can't carry a man with a broken leg or a bad back. You get hurt and you're on your own." The implication was also that Moncrief was older and, therefore, slower.

"Captain, you don't have to worry."

"If you get any one of my men hurt, you won't have to worry either."

Moncrief wasn't offended by the speech. He had given speeches like this before to others. He nodded, watching the men go about their work. Furlong's men had finished their meals and were in the process of unpacking large, black, sealed containers. Some of the packs contained clothing. Moncrief recognized the brown-linen kurtas and the wool *pakols*. The short kurta shirt and the round chocolate-colored *pakol* hat would be typical wardrobe items for Yousef and his mujahideen.

Vass and Villegas had also laid out two Windrunner sniper rifles with scopes. The XM107 Windrunner was a simple machine, a black, lightweight, stainless-steel rifle. Both rifles were resting on their bipods on the floor of the aircraft. One scope was much larger than the others. The weapons should be relatively easy to carry in the high-altitude Hindu Kush.

Burgey was unpacking several black jet-pilot-styled helmets connected to small black tanks. The gunny recognized the HALO gear used in high-altitude jumps. Burgey's job was to ensure that no piece was missing, no strap was loose.

Villegas went to each piece of gear, checking for anything that could create noise, and picked the gear up and shook it. Occasionally, a small, metallic *click* could be heard as he shook the gear. Once he found something loose, Villegas used an enormous roll of electrical tape to wrap it tight. They all knew that just one metallic strap slapping against a magazine or the stock of a rifle could send out a telegraph to the enemy.

Frix continued to load magazines with bright brass

rounds that had odd black tips. The cargo bay seemed to be a surgical suite, with the skilled operating-room nurses preparing their instruments, laying each out and counting each one, leaving nothing to chance.

"You need this as well." Furlong handed him a curled-up plastic tube in a sealed, clear plastic bag.

"What's this?" Moncrief didn't want to appear stupid later on. He had not seen something like this before. It looked like an IV apparatus.

"You remember asking about this being the Oscar Papa team?"

"Yeah."

"Everyone on this team is OP—blood type O positive. We let you come with us because you are Parker's man, but also because you are O negative."

"Damn. You're saying that each team member is the other man's potential blood supply?"

"Yes and no."

"Okay?"

"After seven combat operations, each of these rangers have shared their blood with the other. Every one here had his life saved by a teammate." Furlong pointed to the lanky sergeant loading the magazines.

"Frix is our best doctor. He dropped out of med school in his second year. He had worked four or five years as an EMT before that in Brainerd, Minnesota."

"I know Brainerd. Camp Ripley?"

"Yeah, you've been to Ripley?"

The National Guard camp had been used by the military for cold-weather training for years. The Mississippi River cut through the camp, but that far north it was a stream no larger than the width of a two-lane highway.

"Two winters."

"Good. Frix is good, very good. He is the guy we need to get to your man first. He's been spun up on meningitis."

Moncrief was reminded abruptly that soon his "man" would be both contagious and very ill.

"Frix is going to give each of us a booster shot. It's mixed just for this bug."

"Ten-four."

"Frix and Burgey are one team. Burgey is our best shot, and Frix isn't a bad spotter. I'm putting you with them."

"What about the others?"

"Fury and Villegas are our best speed shooters. They can take out twenty guys in less than twenty seconds. All with head shots. All of us were raised on hunting. Frix and Burgey hunted in the north. Burgey's from the Upper Peninsula. They can track anything over ice and snow. Vee and Villegas are both from south Texas. South of San Antonio."

"Vee?"

"Yeah, that's what we call him. He works the radios. He can take a solar sheet in a sandstorm and give you enough power to call in."

The solar panel could provide electricity for days.

"So where'd they all come from?"

"Seventy-fifth Rangers. All of them did a tour as instructors at the Sniper School. Two of them could have been Olympians. The Army didn't want their faces plastered on posters, so they were ordered to take a pass. Burgey could split a dime at a hundred meters. A dime held between your fingers—sideways."

"Shit."

"No one's married. Only two have any living parents. No distractions."

"Any vices?"

"Yeah." Furlong laughed at the question. "They all have bikes."

"Motorcycles?"

"Harleys. Don't get them started on the difference between a panhandle and a flathead. Frix has a V-Rod. Burgey's into Sportsters. It's the one thing that will get 'em spun up."

Moncrief's own Harley had been a Super Glide until he put it through a fence on a wet night. He understood the magic of a Harley. After running on special ops in combat for three or four months, peacetime could drive a man crazy. One minute you're setting an ambush in some mountain valley, ripping apart killers with your M4, and then forty-eight hours later you're ordering a Big Mac in small-town North Carolina. The transitions were abrupt and highly disjunctive. Adrenaline jolts stateside were always at a premium.

"We are doing a HAHO in from about twenty-five thousand. You've done high-altitude jumps before?"

"A few. I went to the MFF School at Bragg and Yuma."

The free fall school was the only one of its kind in the military.

"Damn, Gunny, you've been around." Furlong stopped for a second. He looked out the portal between his seat and Moncrief. Several seconds passed before he spoke. "My old man was a Marine. He fought in Grenada."

Moncrief let out a loud laugh, which almost caused him to gag.

"What's the problem, Gunny?" Furlong wasn't amused.

"My father was a Ranger. He fought on hill two-oh-five."

"In the Korean War?"

"Yeah." Moncrief looked away. "You know the difference between us, Captain? If someone asked me what I was, I would say a Marine. If they asked you, you would say a Ranger. But we'd both die to protect our teams. In that regard, not much difference at all."

Furlong nodded. It was a concept that most of the three hundred million people that called themselves Americans would not fully understand. Yet it kept the wolf away from the door.

"What about your man? Parker? Why are you here?"

"Parker. He can shoot like Burgey. Language savant. Marathon runner." Moncrief paused. "Aw, hell. That doesn't really describe him . . . who he is." He paused again. "The reason I'm here is he asked me to help, and . . ." Moncrief shrugged. "He saved my life."

"In country?"

Moncrief nodded. "Iraq. Recon went wrong. I took some grenade shrapnel in the gut. Parker taped me up and got me out."

"Duct tape?"

"Yup. How in the hell did you know? Good old, cheap-ass duct tape." In all of the years that had passed, Moncrief never got the image out of his head: looking down at the duct tape holding his gut in, blood everywhere.

Just a nick, Parker had said, smiling at him.

Moncrief had seen the smile and for some reason simply stopped worrying.

"Tonight's jump is gonna be brutal. You know that, right?" Furlong brought Moncrief back to the moment.

"How bad's bad?"

"We're dropping in on the east side of the Himalayas. The wind currents will be rough."

"What altitude we pulling the chutes?"

"Fifteen thousand. The aircraft is going to report an engine failure on number four in about fifteen minutes. He will swing out to the east, wandering over Pakistan, so that he can turn back toward Afghanistan."

"Then the HAHO?"

Furlong nodded.

A HAHO was high-altitude, high-opening jump. A HAHO's greatest risk was the jumper being seen. But it also had benefits: The jumper could use the ram air wing of the parachute to act like a glider and carry him quietly for miles. If the winds were played right, the team could jump many miles away from their landing zone. The high opening also allowed the *pop-pop* sound of the deploying parachute to occur well above and far away from the enemy's hearing. The drop at night, in cloud cover, gave them the protection of not being seen, but it exposed them to the crosscurrents of high winds for a much longer time.

"It's our best shot," said Furlong, "particularly with the FireFly."

"That's what you use to get the gear in?"

Marine special ops had used something like a FireFly. A parachute with a box of supplies, radios, some LFP40 sling packs, and most important, extra ammo, would fly by itself, remotely guided in by the lead parachutists. The sling packs were the portable solar panels that would provide them the juice to power their radios. The FireFly lightened the load that the jumpers would have to carry and, ideally, it would land in the right place.

"Yeah. And I'll lead you in. All you have to do is follow the red bouncing ball."

By way of explanation, Furlong picked up one of the helmets.

"Heads-up display. Something else from DARPA. A computer integrated with GPS, the winds, everything."

"How do you make sure the altimeter's right?"

"We'll drop a reader that will relay the true barometric readings and its altitude back to my headset."

"Damn, Skip, you might have a future in this business."

Furlong smiled. "Skip, eh?"

"In the Marines that's what we call our captains. It's a compliment." Moncrief grinned. "And you can call me Gunny Ndee."

"Ndee? What's that, some nom de guerre?"

"Exactly."

"All right. We go on pure oxygen in fifteen minutes. We'll breathe it until the jump, when we switch onto our own tanks."

"Good, got it. I have to go up to the top deck and see if I can make a call or two. I want to check in with Scott about my other man."

The C-17's communications deck was outfitted for special operations. A telephone call could be made to anywhere in the world. Moncrief's first call, to Scott, went unanswered. It rang, and rang, and then switched over to a voice mail with no special message.

Moncrief looked at his own cell phone for the second number.

It only rang once.

"Hello?" Moncrief was making one final call to his source.

"Is that you, Gunny? I thought you'd be calling sooner." The voice sounded as if he was alone.

"You know why I'm calling?"

"Yes. Is this a secure line?"

Moncrief looked down at the communications-deck airman he was standing over.

"Is this secure?" he whispered to the young airman.

"Yes."

"Yeah, we're secure on my end."

The voice paused.

"Call me back at 023 336 718 3446. Do I need to repeat it?"

"No, got it." Moncrief wrote the numbers down on the airman's pad across a form that looked like a communications logbook. He could see the airman's frown. The kid's writing was near perfect, with times and dates and numbers in each separate box.

He should be an airman, Moncrief thought, as he looked at the perfect handwriting.

"Don't worry. This is important. Get me that number on a secure net," Moncrief barked at the communications airman.

The airman was good at his job. The Globemaster was specially outfitted with a separate communications desk. Through his headset, the gunny heard the phone ring, and again, it only rang once. The voice didn't waste any time on the small talk.

"I don't know what you've been told, but your man is still alive."

Moncrief felt relief and confusion at the same time. Paris was always right. Even on the secure net, he knew better than to get into the details. "Ludwig, what do I need to do?"

"Don't listen to Zaslani. He is full of bullshit and is just playing an angle to help out the Saudis."

Gunny Moncrief didn't even know who Zaslani was or what he was talking about; however, it was an easy assumption that Zaslani was Mossad and was probably in London.

"I'll ask again: What do I need to do?"

"Nothing, just your mission. Parker's success will do the rest."

So my source already knows where I am and why I'm here?

Shit, who else *knows?*

CHAPTER 54

Qatar Air Flight 346

Parker had made a point of getting a window seat on this final flight. It was dark, but the cloud cover had an opening just below the aircraft. His seat was intentionally on the pilot's side of the jumbo jet, which would have allowed him to look to the north. It was a small gamble, as the final leg in to Peshawar didn't necessarily have to be directly out of the west. On this night, it was. Parker was lucky.

The clouds to the north are solid.

He could see the mountain range extend to the north and the thick clouds north of Peshawar. The snow-capped mountains were mystifying in their enormity. They grew larger and higher as he looked to the north. Eventually, their tops disappeared into the clouds. Even at the altitude the airplane was traveling, Parker could tell that the mountain peaks went well above them.

It has to be to the north.

Their gamble had always been that Yousef's encampment was to the north of Peshawar. It was a rational, logical assumption. In the past, what little they knew of the man had him being somewhere north of Peshawar and under the protection of a local Taliban chief called Zulfiqar.

They have to be getting close.

Parker knew that Moncrief and Furlong's team would need to be on the ground, in position, well before Sadik Zabara was to meet Yousef. In his mind, he computed the time forward from when they should have left England.

It has to be about now.

Parker imagined the military cargo aircraft, radioing in to Afghanistan that it was having an engine problem. The Pakistani Air Force would be listening in and the engine's failure would account for why the American's C-17 was much lower, dangerously lower, to the twenty-thousand-foot peaks. It would also allow the Globemaster to swing out, across the border to the east, before it turned back into Afghanistan to land at Jalalabad Airfield.

It'll be a rough ride.

Parker's experience as a pilot put him in that pilot's seat. The updrafts and downdrafts would shake every bolt, rivet, and weld. The pilot would be slammed into his seat and then pulled up into the straps. It would be one wild roller-coaster ride.

Parker looked down, however, at the ground below.

The only lights on the ground came from a twisting convoy of cars and trucks. Unlike the United States or Great Britain or much of the world, this world was stark, empty, seemingly lifeless and dark.

He looked down for a certain twisting path of lights.

There it is. It has to be.

A path of truck lights turned and twisted in the dark through what must have been tortuous hairpin turns and perilous, high-altitude switchbacks.

The Khyber Pass.

The sword cut through the mountains.

Parker watched the traffic even though it was nearly three in the morning. The Americans' demand for goods caused the trucks to continue to roll through the night. The Khyber was the only route this far north.

It was Fontane who spoke of the slaughter of the British Army in 1842 when he wrote: "With thirteen thousand their trail began. Only one man returned from Afghanistan." Parker remembered Butler's painting of the sole survivor, a Dr. Brydon, barely alive, drapped over his horse, as it wandered through the pass.

For several thousand years, the Khyber had been the only route in or out.

Every stone soaked in blood.

There may not have been another place on earth where more men had breathed their last breath.

Alexander the Great had traveled this path. And countless others through time immemorial, many of them coming to grief.

Now it was Parker's turn.

The wheels of the jumbo jet screeched once, and then the airplane floated for a second. As the weight of the aircraft settled down, the wheels screeched again.

"Oh, my friend, we are here." Liaquat Anis awoke from his sleep in the tight seat next to him.

The aircraft suddenly shook again, violently, as it slowed down.

Parker glanced at his seatmate.

"Don't worry." Liaquat smiled. "That's the railroad."

"Railroad?" Parker spoke the word in broken Pashto. The conversation was now in the language of Peshawar, the city where they'd just landed. The words came easily to Parker's mind, but he feigned a struggle with the language so that Liaquat wouldn't find his Bosnian companion too fluent.

"Oh, you speak a little Pashto? Good, yes, very good."

Parker smiled.

"Yes, the Khyber railroad track cuts across the airstrip. It may be the only place in the world where an airplane has to stop for a train." Liaquat laughed. "I'm just kidding, my friend. The railroad stopped many years ago, but its track does cross the runway."

"I understand." Although he spoke and understood, Sadik would not being saying much. He didn't want to press the issue.

"Where are you staying?"

"The Rose Hotel. It's near the Khyber bazaar."

"No. You will stay with me tonight. I am also near the market."

"You are kind, but others are expecting me at the Rose Hotel."

"No, my friend, they are not. They are expecting to see you at my house."

Parker smiled an uncomfortable smile, imagining how the real Zabara would react to this preplanned manipulation. He shrugged and nodded. When Liaquat, satisfied, looked away, Parker reached into his pocket and felt the PDA and sealed packet of chewing gum.

Soon the cell phone needs to be gone.

He would send one last message. If anything happened, if he suddenly disappeared, if he left no other trace, it would at least give them a lead.

Contact made: seatmate.

After that, it would be too dangerous to send more.

CHAPTER 55

London

The pillow was damp, cold, and musty, and smelled like it had been boxed up in the lightless, dark room for years. The room was a cave.

"Oh, Madre de Dios. Me duele la cabeza . . ."

Enrico Hernandez's head was pounding. His eyelids seemed to be weighed down to the point that he had to concentrate just to open them. The blanket only came up to his shoulder blades, and the chill of the room above the wool was painful to his neck and upper shoulders.

"Oh, God." He tried to move his hand up to his face. The handcuff cut into his wrist and wouldn't move. Hernandez's mouth was dry, but his head hurt more. He lifted his head away from the pillow, realizing that the dampness was from his drool. The drug suppressed everything except the pressure on his bladder.

"Help, help." Enrico heard his voice. It seemed as if it was coming from someone else. "Help me." It was barely stronger than a mumble.

Two men were talking in some other language. He could hear their voices coming through a thin wall.

"Help, please. *Por favor!* Help me."

Again, Enrico lifted his head so his voice carried beyond the pillow. The voices in the other room stopped. Footsteps seemed to be crossing a wooden floor. And then the door opened.

"Oh, Jesus. The light!"

The bright light blinded him.

The man closed the door part of the way; however, the light still came through the partial opening like a searchlight. Enrico focused on the wall.

Plain, simply plain and green.

Enrico was struck by how the wall had no pictures, nothing hanging on it, and it was painted in a pale green.

Where have I seen that color?

He tried to focus his mind. It was a watered-down green.

Easter.

It was that pale green that he remembered seeing in the Walmart aisle under Easter decorations. It reminded him of his daughter.

"My friend, are you okay?"

The man was young. His voice carried an accent. He was clearly Arab, with a well-trimmed moustache that extended just beyond the limits of his mouth. He had white teeth, one of them crooked, distorting his smile. The man's shirt seemed to have been doused in cologne. He was so close that the smell nauseated Hernandez.

"I'm thirsty."

"Of course you are."

Enrico's captor held a cold bottle of water to his lips.

Hernandez downed the water in one desperate gulp.

"Easy, my friend. There is more."

He drained the bottle.

"Another, please."

The man reached across the room. Hernandez heard the chatter of ice as the man pulled another bottle from a bucket of some sort.

"Here, try this."

Hernandez drank half of it before coming up for air.

"Easy."

"I need to use the head."

"The head?"

Hernandez's brain felt like he had been hit with a sledgehammer between the eyes.

"The bathroom."

"My friend, can you focus?"

The man used the term *friend* too often for his taste.

"Yeah," he lied. It didn't matter. He needed to use the head or the bed was getting ready to get soaked.

"Listen to me, Mr. Hernandez." The man pulled out two photographs from the pocket of the brown coat he was wearing. "You see these?"

Enrico focused in the dim light.

He knows my name. And my goddamn family!

"Listen, you son of a bitch—"

"No, you listen! I'm going to uncuff you. The loo is through that door." He pointed over his shoulder.

"Okay." Hernandez would have to reach deep, but with some luck he would have his hand on the man's throat as soon as the key slid the lock open on the cuffs.

"Understand this, friend. You can no doubt kill me in a matter of seconds and be on the street in a bloody instant. But if you do, the two people in those photographs will never see tomorrow's sunrise."

CHAPTER 56

The Secretary's Palace, Riyadh

"He is here."

The secretary looked up from his reading. He folded the *London Times,* laying it on the Tufft pier table next to his chair in the library. The hour was late, near midnight.

"Has he passed through security?"

"Yes, Your Highness, he has been checked twice."

The secretary didn't want the meeting, at least not directly. The man was born in Saudi Arabia but had spent the last several years in Yemen. He had been wanted for some time. His reputation was, like many others, of being someone who believed what the Yousefs of the world were saying. Muslims were being abused and the faith was in jeopardy.

"His name is Abdullah Hassan, Your Highness. He wishes to surrender to you directly and has a message from Yousef."

"And why does Yousef need to use a messenger?"

"He says Yousef can't leave his current position. He

carries a cell phone that Yousef will call into at midnight precisely. He says that Yousef has an urgent update for you."

The secretary wasn't sure that he wanted to talk to Yousef again. It had only been a few days since their last meeting. The last thing he needed now was anyone talking about him conducting ongoing communications with Yousef. Now that the news of the *Al-Quds* correspondent's planned visit to Yousef had spread, many on the Council were nervous about what would happen next. The secretary tried to act confident, but inside he felt frantic.

What will you do to me next, Yousef?

He sighed. *Time to find out.*

"Well, bring him in."

It was well past Ramadan, but the man had pled for a visit. The secretary was a member of the House of Saud and a Sayyid. It was his duty to give an audience to any believer who asked for a meeting. The tradition went back thousands of years, to the times of the first Bedouin. As a Sayyid, he was a direct descendant of the prophet Muhammad; a descendant of Muhammad's daughter, Fatimah, who some believed was the Islamic prophet's only daughter. And as a member of the House of Saud, he had his responsibility to his tribe. Visits such as this were usually granted during Ramadan, but the messenger had an important message to deliver.

"*As sala'amu alaikum.*" The secretary rose to greet the visitor.

"*Walaikum as sala'am.*" The man looked pitiful standing before the secretary in simple sandals and broadcloth robes tied at the waist. His feet were cracked, dry, and the brunneous sort of dark brown that one would expect from a life lived without shoes or socks. His hands were small, but the secretary noticed the black dirt under the long, broken nails. He was weasel-faced, with eyes that darted back and forth across the room but never made contact.

"And why are you here?" The secretary didn't offer the man a chair or tea or any other courtesy. It may have been a violation of the Koran, but the man was suspect. The secretary wouldn't allow this meeting to last one minute beyond what was necessary.

"I come here as a humble man doing the will of Allah."

He seemed nervous. Something was not right. The secretary looked beyond the man to his assistant. His eyes telegraphed the message: *Are you sure this man is safe*?

The thin, dirty man was sweating visibly.

"Are you all right, brother?"

"Yes, I have Yousef." The man reached into the pocket of his coat and pulled out a cell phone. The others in the room stood back as he reached for the cell phone. Everyone in the room was dubious of his intent, but the security force had always done a good job. And he had cleared security twice. The man dialed a number on the phone.

"Yes, yes, I am here." The visitor spoke into the cell.

The secretary could barely make out the conversation, but with the few words he heard he recognized Yousef's voice.

"Yes, I am here with the secretary. I just greeted him. He is here, now."

An odd comment.

"Yousef would like to speak with you. It is his wish to make amends."

The secretary took the cell phone and lifted it to his ear. It felt sticky and warm.

"Hello, is this my cousin?"

"Muhammad has taught us that we must do everything in our power to stop the infidels, even if it means the loss of our lives. *Dam butlub dam*. Blood demands blood. Did you really think the spy woman in Qatar would stop me? Did you really think that cutting the oil out of my inheritance would deter me?"

"Is that why you wanted to speak with me, Yousef?" The secretary's anger was building.

Loudly, the clock chimed midnight.

In that same moment, the secretary looked down at the cell phone and saw what had caused it to feel sticky: Bloody fingerprints.

"Allah!"

At precisely the same time, a text message arrived on the phone: *Dam butlub dam*.

"Praise Allah!" the man cried as he stepped toward the secretary. A white wisp of smoke suddenly started to come from below the man's shirt, from his side.

A flash of light hit the secretary at the same moment the blast struck him in the center of his chest. Despite his being a man of good weight, the bomb lifted him off his feet and threw him back into the pier table, which his body weight crushed.

The visitor's upper torso disappeared from view, but his legs remained there, standing, the shaped charge in his abdominal cavity having blasted forward, not downward.

As the secretary lay on the floor, struggling to breathe,

the security guards and medical personnel rushed in, surrounding him. He lifted up his hands to see blood everywhere. Mostly the visitor's blood, it appeared, although the secretary's eyes were out of focus, as his glasses had been blown away in the blast. He saw—and felt—that he'd taken a great gash across his palm. Apparently, as he raised it to protect himself from the blow, the bomb had cut it deeply.

But the secretary, third from the throne, a leading candidate to become the next king of the House of Saud, was still alive.

CHAPTER 57

Above the Hindu Kush

The jumbo cargo jet dropped several hundred feet at once, leaving Moncrief feeling much as if the cables suspending an elevator had been suddenly cut. Kevin Moncrief grabbed on to one of the rails, holding on as the loose cargo rose up in the air, suspended for a moment in a zero-gravity state. It seemed to hit bottom, and as it did the airplane jerked up just as quickly.

Moncrief sucked down the pure oxygen from his mask. He could hear his own deep, rapid breathing as he looked out through the face mask.

Calm down.

He didn't need to hyperventilate. Between the pure, cool oxygen and the go pills, Moncrief smiled in his mask.

"Hey, Gunny!"

Moncrief could hear the entire team through the helmet's headset.

"Who's that?"

"It's Villegas."

One of the men, fully suited up, raised his thumb up to signal he was Villegas.

"You going to make it, old man?"

Moncrief smiled again.

"Who the fuck do you think you are, *kemosabe*? You look like a big, black sack of high-grade shit."

"Oh, shit, we got a Lee Ermey."

"We are jolly green giants walking the earth with guns." The voice was different, in an intentional low, booming tone.

"Now you got Frix going. He's gonna go with *Full Metal Jacket* for the rest of this operation."

"Stand by to break off." Furlong's stern voice interrupted the conversation.

The Globemaster continued to jump up and down like a roller-coaster ride at the beach. The only problem was that Moncrief was riding it standing up—and with a hundred pounds of gear strapped on.

"Break off in ten!"

Each of the team members gave the thumbs-up signal.

"Five, four, three, two, one . . . *break*."

Moncrief twisted the air hose and disconnected from the Globemaster's oxygen supply. He immediately switched to his own tank, causing colder air to flow into the mask.

The aircraft's loadmaster started to drop the C-17's ramp, causing a roar of noise to overwhelm the cargo bay. Even with the helmet, Moncrief felt like he was standing next to the vortex of a tornado. His face mask lit up into a heads-up display of red and green.

"Is everyone up?" Furlong's voice overrode the background noise.

"Yes." Moncrief chimed in with the others. He could feel the cold sweat on the palms of his hands in the gloves. The jet was well above the solid cloud cover, but still passed through a broken cloud as it bounced back and forth across the mountain range.

"Gunny, you got the heads-up guide?"

Moncrief saw a small triangle in a box in his face mask's display. As he looked out to the rear of the jet, a map overlay showed the hills and valleys behind their path. He held up his thumb. The Plexiglas visor was a computer screen full of information.

"Out the door in ten." Furlong turned and shuttled up to the edge. The loadmaster walked by the line and pushed the FireFly up to the edge. The team split in half, with some on the left and others on the right of the cargo.

"Five, four, three, two, one, out the door."

The team shuffled to the edge of the ramp.

Moncrief stepped over the edge.

"Boogity, boogity, boogity!" Villegas yelled into the mike. "Let's rip it!"

His use of the NASCAR announcer Darrell Waltrip's phrase seemed appropriate. They were going from a dead stop to over a hundred miles an hour in one step.

Moncrief saw the shape of Villegas to his right, and then he was gone. And then Moncrief was alone in this wind tunnel of mist.

God, I hope I'm sealed up.

Flying at more than a hundred miles an hour in temps approaching thirty degrees below zero, the frigid air would be like a blowtorch, burning any exposed skin in an instant. It didn't matter now.

"Gunny, you got me?"

"Yeah."

"All team, winds are cutting at sixty knots out of the northwest. I'll lead the way!"

Moncrief hit the wall of clouds. The display showed airspeed of 122 knots. The altimeter was spinning down, the numbers dropping.

"Deploying in five, four, three, two, one . . . *mark!*"

Moncrief pulled the ripcord as twenty-four thousand feet showed on the altimeter in his heads-up display. He saw the triangle jump on the display as Furlong's parachute caused the captain suddenly to slow.

The clouds and darkness completely blinded the gunny's visibility. He looked down toward his feet and could see nothing beyond his waist. Looking up, his parachute lines went above his head into the dark mist. The parachute was not visible. Moncrief held his hand up to his face. He could barely make out its shape.

In the darkness and cloud cover, the heads-up display was comforting. He continued to follow the track as Furlong headed north for a short distance, into the wind, and then cut back to the south.

The map showed them passing through a valley opening. Moncrief looked to his left, where a mountaintop was supposed to be. He could see nothing in the dark, but sensed the pelting of his face mask with water and snow droplets. He felt the continued flow of oxygen in his mask.

Somewhere out there, I just passed between two enormous peaks.

Suddenly, they broke through the bottom of the clouds. Moncrief started, pulling on his toggle that controlled the steering line, as he realized how close he was to the rock wall on his right.

Shit!

The ram chute slipped hard to the left and then settled down. Moncrief pulled on the opposite toggle, causing him to settle in like a glider, behind the red triangle.

The team said nothing as it continued to glide down to the valley's floor. The gunny imagined the convoy of parachutes, led by the FireFly, trailing one another to the ground.

Moncrief looked to the east, down the valley, seeing the light of a vehicle off several miles. The map on the heads-up display showed a name of Durba Khel. A highway was marked, extending from the far right to the far left.

"Down!"

Moncrief felt the last-minute surge of panic as the ground suddenly started to rise up toward him. The altimeter was sinking fast. He pulled on the toggles, following the triangle that now seemed fixed just to the south.

"Come on, baby." He didn't need a broken leg or torn-up knee. Moncrief pulled hard on both toggles, bending his legs, feeling the wing of the parachute as it started to break.

"Come on, come on."

He was lucky. The impact was on soft dirt and sand, perhaps the bottom of some creek bed. His boots hit, and as they did, he felt the rush of blood in his feet. Just as suddenly, the gunny felt his weight as he stood up. The parachute lost its wind and collapsed behind him.

"Hell, another one!" Kevin Moncrief counted every successful jump as *another one.*

Furlong was standing beside him, already out of the jumpsuit and dressed in the brown kurta and *pakol*. He had baggy, thick brown linen pants. The only part of the garb that stood out was his sandy-brown pair of Danner boots and an M4 rifle with a silencer on its barrel. It was wrapped with a brown camouflage tape to break up its black metallic outline.

The captain grabbed Moncrief's parachute and helped gather it up in a tight ball as the gunny pulled off his suit and quickly changed into similar clothes. Moncrief quietly chambered a round in his .45-caliber pistol after tightening the silencer on its end. He carried it in a shoulder holster, which he covered with a cotton jacket, also brown, that he wore over his kurta. The gunny then went through the same process, chambering a round in the silenced M4.

"The FireFly is just beyond that outcrop of rocks." Furlong pointed farther up the valley. As he spoke, the remaining members of the team passed by, silently checking in and then spreading out in a 360-degree pattern. They now spoke only in the hand signals, their private language, silent as they moved, like actors in a well-rehearsed play, each knowing his role.

"We will put your man's tent there, just above the first rocks." Furlong pointed to the base of the ridgeline due south of their position. "And then we will move well back up the ridgeline and into the mountains."

The mention of the tent and "your man" brought Kevin Moncrief's thoughts back to the reason why they were there. The FireFly had more than ammo and solar panels. It also had carried in a small, specially modified Hilleberg Atlas tent. Like a chameleon, the high-tech tent would match the surrounding shades of sand and rock, becoming effectively invisible. The FireFly also carried a cooler that Frix had iced down with several plasma bags loaded with antibiotics. The tent was also armed, per Will Parker's instructions, with a Windrunner and an automatic pistol.

"If he makes it to the entrance of the valley, he should easily see the flash of the light."

The tent would be next to a large rock. The rock would serve as a reference point.

"Did you see them coming in?" Furlong was whispering in Moncrief's ear.

"No."

Furlong pointed to the other side of the ridgeline. "Three trucks, parked up the other valley, near some mud huts."

"So we guessed right?"

"I hope."

CHAPTER 58

The other valley

"Did you hear that?"

Malik Mahmud looked to the top of the ridge-line above the cave.

"What did you hear?" Mohagher Iqbal asked. They were speaking in English, as Mahmud's Bahasa Indonesian and Iqbal's Filipino Tagalog didn't mesh well.

Iqbal pointed his AK-47 to the north and threw his cigarette to the ground beside the Toyota pickup truck. The three trucks were parked pointed down the valley between the separate mud huts. The walls of the huts hid the vehicles well, except from someone looking above.

They both looked into the dark.

Mahmud put his finger to his lips, signaling for his fellow guard to be silent.

The mountains were silent. The cloud cover blocked any shape of the higher mountains to the west.

Finally, after several minutes of silence, Mahmud spoke.

"These bastards always have us on guard duty."

"Your complaining only pisses him off." Iqbal had had enough of Mahmud, as had the others.

"What time is it?"

"I thought you wanted us to be quiet."

"It was nothing." Mahmud hesitated. "Maybe it was a wild goat?"

"That would be meat!" Iqbal's hunger could be heard in his words. "I miss meat. I don't think they would know what to do with meat."

The rations had been short since they had moved to the cave.

"Do you think we should see if we can hunt it?"

"If you want your throat cut by Yousef. Fool!"

Mahmud hung his head.

Suddenly Iqbal noticed Yousef standing next to them.

"Oh, Yousef!" Mahmud turned around.

"Are you on guard, brothers?"

"Yes, of course. It will be dawn soon." Mahmud looked to the east. The first color of dawn was beginning to turn the clouds to a pink tint.

"Our brother should be in Peshawar picking up our guest. It is important that we be like Bu Zaid and treat our guest with hospitality. It is our supreme duty."

Iqbar nodded enthusiastically. In his mind he couldn't help but imagine a plateful of roast goat. He sneaked a glance at Mahmud, who clearly had the same thought.

CHAPTER 59

CIA headquarters, Langley

Robert Tranthan had hoped that Pope would be of more help with the photo. So far, he had heard nothing. The picture still lay on the desk in front of him.

Maggie.

The locket around her neck had turned out to be a dead end. After he noticed it in the picture, it had been checked and rechecked.

The books could have been another clue. They looked typical for an agency's embassy office. *Jane's* books on ships and weapons of war were the bibles of the observers. Nothing unusual there. Another seeming dead end.

But she made too much effort to save this photo for any other reason.

A thought suddenly occurred to him. He took out a ruler from his drawer and held it over the photograph. His eyes ran across the line of the ruler, looking at every detail.

Read it backward.

The old editorial trick caused one to see things in a different light. Misspelled words stood out if you read a paragraph backward. But nothing in the picture called attention to itself.

He sighed and took out a magnifying glass. *One last try*. He pored over the magnified photo, looking at the details. *Hmmm*. Maggie's books were disorganized, much as her desk had always been. Volumes were out of order. But that was all.

Again, nothing.

The cigarette burned through to the filter.

"Damn it!" Tranthan stubbed it out and leaned back in the chair, his mind wandering to Billie Cook.

I hope she likes Guam.

Cook had only three years to retirement. It would be a miserable three years. But she would keep her mouth shut.

She's not stupid.

If necessary, it would have also been easy to frame her with some drug-abuse charge. She would be accused of having access to the cart that was missing morphine, or Percs, or Oxy. Her drug test would come back positive. At the very least her retirement would be screwed up so long that she would be cold before the first check could be cashed.

Tranthan pulled open the drawer and put the photograph in it, then picked up the telephone.

"I need the car."

It was late. The house would be dark, and his wife would be in bed. She had stopped sleeping with him years ago. Her bedroom was on the other end of the house.

Tranthan pulled on his overcoat.

This has been a long, cold winter.

He turned off the lamp and cut across the room in the dark. The hallway was well lit. Tranthan knew that once he reached the door and opened it there would be plenty of light.

He swung the door open.

The hallway had photographs of different sizes hung on the wall, black-and-white pictures of locations from around the world. Tranthan glanced at the pictures, many different sizes but in perfect order.

He stared at the framed photos, some small, some large, but in a row.

No, that can't be it.

Robert Tranthan turned and raced back into the office. He turned on the lamp without taking off his overcoat and took out the photo again.

Oh, my God. It showed Maggie's hand on one of the shelves.

Tranthan pulled out a pen and pad of paper.

If the volumes on that particular bookshelf had been arranged in any order, it seemed to be by size. No, that wasn't it. But here was something: Each of the books was a volume from a different series, all showing their volume number on the spine. He started with the book just above her hand and followed the row. The first book was volume ten, but it was upside down. Likewise, the sixth book was volume ten upside down.

Ingenious!

011 966 01 435 9456

That can't be correct.

He double-checked it. Each number was correct. If he weren't mistaken, Maggie had been quite clear with her message.

A phone number in Riyadh.

CHAPTER 60

Khyber Bazaar, Peshawar, Pakistan

The auto-rickshaw slammed on its brakes, causing the tail end to jump up off the street, throwing its passengers into the driver. The mule cart ahead ignored them.

William Parker awoke from a light doze and shook off the sleep. Liaquat was wedged tightly next to him on the bench seat in the back of the small taxi.

It was nearing dawn. The sky was still dark; the clouds were a griseous blue-gray. But the lights of the Khyber bazaar lit up the street with lurid red-yellows and white and fluorescent tubes of artificial light.

The taxi driver passed the mule cart with only an inch or two to spare between it and a green three-wheeled taxi heading in the opposite direction. Parker pulled his arms in as the two carts passed by close enough that he felt the draft caused by the two moving objects.

The bazaar was full of men of all sizes and shapes, but virtually all were dressed in long white shawls that went down to their knees. Most wore small white caps on top of long, stringy heads of black hair. Occasionally, one would pass with a black-and-white turban.

Parker studied Liaquat's face as they moved through the traffic. Liaquat was dozing off again in a contorted, odd position, with one hand holding on to the bar in front of him and the other holding up his head. He had a chiseled nose. In an exotic way, Liaquat and his people were quite handsome-looking, with noses and eyes and chins all in balance with the shapes of their faces.

Above the street, odd-looking signs were stacked, one above the other, with oversized paintings of red-and-white dentures marking a dentist's office. Legal scales with Arabic script underneath marked a lawyer's office. The main street of the Khyber bazaar was the main street for the professionals of the city. Poles with wires lined up one on top of the other, string after string, paralleled the main road.

What's that smell?

Peshawar exuded an ever-changing combination of smells and scents. Some were typical of a city. The charcoal-burned smell of barbecued meat stood out. But there was another . . .

Not meat on a spit. Something else.

Parker's mind was wondering.

Sharp. Like ginger, but different.

He rubbed his face with his one free hand. The other held tightly onto the edge of the roof of the scooter.

Cardamom, that's it. The Arabic name?

"*Hayl?*" Parker meant to ask the question of only himself, but he spoke it aloud.

"Yes, I think so. It gives coffee a special taste." Liaquat also apparently slept extremely lightly. He tapped the driver on his shoulder. "Over there." He pointed to an alleyway. It was a tiny, dark side passage with barely any light. On the corner next to it was a shop crammed and stuffed with blankets and shawls like the ones on the old man's cart. The blankets were hung from the ceiling. The shop was brightly lit, but the alleyway beyond looked like an entrance to a cave.

The Qingqi scooter stopped just short of the alleyway.

"Thank you, brother. May Allah be with you." Liaquat handed the driver ten rupees. "You see that over there?"

Parker looked across the street. The windows were boarded up. The face of the building was burned, and twisted rebar stuck out from torn cement.

"Yes."

"Our brother sent a message to this government. Over forty were killed." The bomb had been ignited in the middle of the busy street just as a bus passed by. Well over a hundred were seriously injured.

"Why?" Parker regretted the question as soon as he said it.

Liaquat looked at him oddly. "A true soldier. The government had killed a leader of the Taliban the week before."

"Who was he?"

"The Taliban leader?"

"No. The bomber."

"I don't know, an orphan, a street worker. Does it matter?"

Parker looked at him with confusion.

"He is now respected. He has regained his *karam*."

His self-respect, his dignity. It depended upon the respect given to a man by others. It was what the others thought. But what good did it do him now?

"Allahu Akbar." Parker repeated the phrase. "Give us victory over the unbelievers!"

"Indeed!" Liaquat led him up the alleyway in the dark.

Parker could barely see. As he followed Liaquat, he noticed a shape in the dark corner of a building from its movement.

"Hello, brother!"

A man dressed in the long white shawl, with the same painter's cap, stepped out of the darkness. Parker could see the shape of an AK-47 automatic rifle.

"Welcome back."

Liaquat turned into a smaller alleyway. A dim lightbulb marked a stairway at the end. The stairs went up the side of a two-story building. Liaquat climbed the steps two at a time. It seemed that he had gained energy from being back.

At the top of the stairs a door was open to an apartment. Liaquat disappeared inside. Parker followed.

Inside, several men grabbed Parker and threw him against the wall. One stood in front of him.

"So, is this Sadik Zabara?" The man with a rough red beard stood in front of Parker. He had a deep, long scar that crossed the upper part of his cheek down to his neck.

"I am Abu Umarov."

* * *

It was black, but Parker sensed daylight beyond the rough linen hood that was over his head. As he turned, the ropes cut into his wrists. There were men talking in another room.

"Are you sure?"

"Yes, I followed him like we planned. I have no doubts."

The last voice was Liaquat's.

Footsteps. The hands of a strong man grabbed him by the shirt and pulled him up.

Umarov yanked the hood from his head. The sunlight blinded him. The room looked plain, barren, and small. A simple green wooden table was in one corner. Two windows marked the southern wall. The sunlight came, unrestricted, in the room.

Umarov pulled a knife from his side. It reminded Parker of the Marine KA-BAR knife, a sharp tongue of black steel the length of a man's hand from the wrist up. He sliced the rope around Parker's wrists.

The knife didn't cause him to jump. Something did, however. Parker noticed the small tattoo on the inside of Umarov's wrist. It was a sign of the *Crni Labudovi*.

"So, my Brother Sadik, you must forgive me." Umarov's voice didn't sound very apologetic. "Your belongings." Umarov walked over to the table.

"Yes, brother?"

"A passport. Some pounds, a few rupees." Umarov seemed to be conducting an inventory. "What's this?"

He held up the PDA.

"For the newspaper."

"You must show me how it works." Umarov tossed the cell phone to him.

"It gets e-mails. And I can record on it. For interviews."

Parker turned on the phone, logged in the password. In the millisecond he had time to glance at it, he saw an e-mail from the team. It was a satellite map. It marked a location in a valley for the tent. It also marked the location of a Taliban encampment in the joining valley. He quickly deleted it with his thumb and logged out.

"Ah, here, see? An e-mail from the newspaper. They are waiting for the first story on your boss." Parker held up the ordinary e-mail for Umarov to see.

"Even the bastards have not stopped our paper!"

In fact, the bomb hadn't. *Al Quds* had moved further down King Street and already set up shop. It didn't take much in this electronic world.

"Daily, political and independent!" Parker smiled as he quoted the paper's saying.

"They will have to wait for some time." Umarov took the cell phone from Parker and crushed it with his boot.

"And what is this?"

"The gum?"

Again, Umarov tossed the object to Parker.

"I haven't had anything to eat in some time." Parker took the third piece from the second row of the packet and placed it into his mouth. The one that he slipped into his mouth had a small black dot on the edge of the foil. It had a strange saccharine-like taste.

The clock began ticking.

He smiled.

"Would you like one?"

CHAPTER 61

The cave

"I don't know. He hasn't gotten better."

Yousef put his hand on his child's forehead. Patoo was hot, very hot, and sweating through his pajama shirt. He had held a temperature for two days.

"Has he eaten anything?"

"No. I put some sugar on his pancake. It didn't help." The child's mother looked worried.

"Allah will take care of the child."

She gave him a look.

"Umarov is in Peshawar and coming soon. I will call him and get some medicine." Yousef didn't want to make the call.

Two calls back-to-back. I don't know.

It worried him.

"I will walk across the valley to the other side and call."

Perhaps I can use two cell phones.

"Malik, give me the cell phones."

Malik Mahmud had gone back to sleep after guard

duty. He was rolled up in a ball on a small prayer rug at the edge of the cave. Yousef didn't care if he was asleep.

Without saying anything, Mahmud rolled over and handed him the bag that held a dozen cell phones. Yousef took two and a calling card for New York.

"Let me see the child again."

Yousef ran his hand around the child's neck. Both glands were swollen to the size of small walnuts.

"I will have Liaquat get him some antibiotics."

She looked relieved.

He picked up the AK-47 and slung it over his shoulder.

"I will be back in several hours."

A man alone would always attract less attention. He was probably safer walking across the valley alone than staying at the cave with the others. But the trucks were well hidden and they stayed inside, out of sight, if the sky was clear.

Perhaps I will cross over the ridgeline.

Yousef started out in the morning light. The ridgeline behind and above the cave was nearly a cliff, so he headed east, down the valley toward the dried riverbed. There was a rough road that seemed more for a mule-pulled cart than a four-wheel vehicle, which paralleled the riverbed. In a mile it crossed over the deep ditch that at that point formed the riverbed and started to circle around the end of the finger of the ridgeline. After crossing the ditch, he cut up the boulder-strewn ridgeline and climbed up the rocky grade for more than a hundred yards. There, at the peak, he pulled up on one large rock.

I can't lose Patoo. Not Patoo.

Yousef pulled out the first cell phone. He knew Umarov's cell phone number. The phone was not to be used except in an emergency. Yousef knew the look he would get from Umarov. Umarov, who had given up his entire family for the fight, would never try to understand.

"Hey, brother, I need to speak to Liaquat."

Yousef hated to use a name. Liaquat's voice came on the call.

"The child of mine is sick. His glands are swollen."

"I will get him some amoxicillin."

No more needed to be said. Yousef closed the cell phone and mouthed a quick prayer of thanks.

The second cell phone required the use of the card. Again, it would be a short conversation. Even though it was late in New York, Masood would answer.

"Yes."

"Brother, how are you?"

"I am fine, very fine. And my family?"

"We are all fine."

"Is it cold in New York?"

"It is frigid."

"How is our cousin in Chicago?"

"He left for home today."

"Good, very good. I will give your love to your mother."

They traveled under the assumption that every conversation was taped, every word analyzed, every thought considered dangerous. But Yousef knew that the flash drive had made it to its destination. Chicago's emergency-response system would be paralyzed.

Yousef put both cell phones on a rock and crushed them with the butt of the AK-47. Those cells were turned on, like a light switch, and were now unstoppable.

I don't know why I bother. Another person probably will not cross this way again for another hundred years.

Yousef looked out across the valley to the east and then turned to the one to the west. The road etched in the rocks at the base of the ridgeline circled around the point of the finger and then headed up the other valley.

What was that?

He thought that he saw something move for just a moment, a flash of a movement, just enough to make the mind curious. Yousef had a feeling, a sense, and a premonition that someone was watching.

He pulled back the bolt of the AK-47, chambering a round. The metallic sound of the bolt running the round home, into the chamber, seemed to echo in the silence.

Yousef studied the road and the valley. He held his hand over his forehead and followed the ridgeline with his eyes. The sun was starting to bear down, and even though it was deep into the winter, the day was becoming warm.

Nothing.

Yousef leaned on a large boulder that came up to just above his waist. He waited several minutes, constantly scanning the ridgeline, the rocks, and the twisted path of a road.

Finally, he turned, heading down the rocky slope.

She will be happy. She has been a good wife.

* * *

The satellite assigned to support the team had picked up both conversations. Scott was relieved that they had selected the right valley.

At the same time Moncrief watched through the optic sight on his M4 as the man turned and walked away. Moncrief focused back on the boulder where the Arab had just rested his machine gun.

After a few minutes he saw movement at the base of the rock. Moncrief wasn't surprised at the movement. He watched as Sgt. Vaatofu Fury, virtually impossible to see and covered in sand and rock, pulled back away. The sniper had been within an arm's reach of the stranger the entire time.

I guess that meal worked.

Fury's smell hadn't alarmed the man at all. Moncrief smiled.

I don't know who that Arab is, but he is living on borrowed time.

CHAPTER 62

The FBI's Strategic Operations Center, Pennsylvania Avenue, Washington, D.C.

"Look at this e-mail that just came across the wire." Tom Pope turned the laptop to the side so Garland Sebeck could lean over from his seat to see the screen. The taller man put a hand on Pope's desk and read the message.

"What does he want?"

The e-mail was from Robert Tranthan. It asked Pope to call as soon as he received the communication no matter what time.

"I guess we need to find out."

Pope walked up to the communications deck with Sebeck following behind. The on-duty communications clerk was doodling on a pad. Tom Pope nudged the young clerk.

"Yes, sir?"

"I need to place a secure call to Langley."

"No problem. Do you have the number?"

Instead of writing it down, Pope picked up his laptop and brought it back to the communications deck. The clerk wrote the number down on his pad and circled it seemingly to add emphasis.

"Just one minute. You can take it on one of the phones."

"Can Agent Sebeck listen in?"

"Yes, sir. He can just pick up another one across from you."

In a matter of just a few minutes, Tom Pope saw the light flashing on the receiver, picked it up, and heard a voice.

"Agent Pope?"

Pope sensed that Tranthan was on his own cell phone. The line, however, would be secure.

"Yes, sir."

"I have discovered something that may be of help to you. The photograph of Ms. O'Donald."

Tom hand signaled Sebeck to have the communications clerk bring him his laptop. He opened the attachment that was labeled *Tranthan Investigation.*

"And what is that?"

"What she was trying to tell us is a telephone number. A number in Saudi Arabia."

Pope looked at the photo. His MacBook Pro screen enlarged its contents with a touch. He doubled the photo's size, squared out the area near her hand, and doubled it again. Now that he was focusing on a numerical clue, he saw it almost immediately.

"I see it. Whose number is that?"

"I don't know." Tranthan paused. "I am having our people find that out right now."

Tom Pope closed the photo and opened up an e-mail to his IT specialist at Chantilly. The topic was marked *urgent*. Tom held his hand over the telephone. "Get Chantilly on the line." Then, to Tranthan, "I imagine that she wanted you to know that number."

"Yes, I would guess that."

Tom Pope heard Robert Tranthan's voice change as he said it.

"I would also guess that whoever that number belongs to would be expecting your call."

"Yes." In fact, Tranthan's voice changed dramatically. "I agree."

"Mr. Tranthan, we need to listen in when you make that call."

Tranthan paused for a long moment before responding. "There's someone else who needs to hear it as well."

"Well, that's up to you. Can we set it up for, say, an hour or so? The time is right for Saudi Arabia."

James Scott's chin rested on his hands as he waited for Robert Tranthan to make the conferenced phone call to Saudi Arabia.

"Do I have everyone?"

Scott sighed. "Hold on a bloody moment." The sudden invitation to listen in to this impromptu call was the last thing Scott needed tonight. But he was in no position to refuse.

He opened the bottom drawer in his desk in this godforsaken office he'd been given in an old hangar on Bagram Airfield. The operations center here ran the war in the northeastern provinces of Afghanistan, and that was why James Scott had set up shop in this location. It was the operation center that could best keep an eye on his team and the Pakistan border.

From the drawer he withdrew a small flask of single-malt Scotch that he'd brought along to get him through the more stressful moments of this operation.

"Scott, are you still there?" Robert Tranthan again.

Scott took a quick slug from the flask, and then returned it to its drawer.

"I can hear you."

"Okay, I have you and Agent Tom Pope of the FBI on this line." Tranthan was quiet for a moment, giving Pope the opportunity to speak up.

"Yes, this is Pope."

Scott had been woken for the telephone call. He had spent the last twenty hours flying through the night from London, trying to catch up to his operation. He had been shot at and his new Range Rover had a bullet hole in its window. Worse yet, he wasn't sure who had pulled the trigger and why. He didn't care for this distraction at all; but at least, he supposed, it had awakened him. It wasn't like he could afford to be sleeping, either.

He already had known about Maggie O'Donald and her relationship with Tranthan. But he had no idea why someone from the FBI was also on the line. It violated the unspoken rule. Furthermore, he wasn't sure that someone on the line wasn't responsible for that bullet hole in his Rover. The only thing that he knew for sure was that for now, he was in the safest place he could possibly be. What had the world come to when he was safer on a military base in northern Afghanistan than in London or Washington?

"Let's do it," said Scott.

"Yes, you may lose me if we don't. I'm in transit." Pope's voice crackled. Scott guessed that he must have been on an aircraft somewhere.

"All right, I'm dialing. Just listen in."

The telephone rang once, then twice, and then a third time.

"*As sala'amu alaikum.*" The voice was that of a man.

"This is Robert Tranthan of the CIA. Maggie O'Donald gave me this number."

The line was silent. The voice seemed to be absorbing the words. "Yes."

"I was to call this number. She wanted me to call this number."

"Wait a moment."

Scott could hear the man talking with another in Arabic. Again, silence.

"I am to say . . ." The voice paused as if making sure what he said was exactly right. It was clear that another in the room was giving directions. Scott had every idea as to who that other one was.

"He is putting a very bold operation into play. Your city is not safe . . ."

Again, the voice stopped. This time, however, it seemed as if there was some hesitation. And again, they heard the voice speak with another in the room.

"Look for a woman with a limp to your north."

"What?"

"She's a pilot."

The world *pilot* made Scott sit bolt upright.

Finally, after several seconds of silence the voice

came back on. "He is trying to obtain a device." The voice hesitated. "Do not call again."

It didn't matter as to that number. It would be a cell phone, and the device would be destroyed within moments of the telephone call. It, and the number it had used, would both prove untraceable.

One thing was certain, though, thought Scott: The word *device* could mean only one thing. Put it together with *pilot* and. . . . The possibility seemed every bit as unthinkable as it was real.

Robert Tranthan smiled as he rocked back in his car, finishing his cigarette. He swallowed a large gulp of vodka. It had been a bold move, to bring Scott in on the call. It would prevent anyone from linking him with the attempt on Scott's life. The deck of cards was changing. It had been reshuffled.

I may come out of this fine after all.

CHAPTER 63

The other valley

"Do you want your Hoo-Ah bar?" Fury whispered to Moncrief.

Moncrief smiled at the dig.

"You know its proper name."

The two were wedged in between a pair of boulders that formed a small shelter at the top of the ridgeline. Villegas was farther to the south, protecting their flank. The energy bar came with the first-strike ration. The portable meal carried several thousand calories under the rubric of one of a wildly mixed menu item, from pound cakes and barbecue pocket sandwiches to cheese tortillas. The FSRs were meant to fix a problem. The old combat meals were heavier. And when packing over a hundred pounds of water and ammunition, the Ranger would toss out that which he didn't like and didn't want to carry over a mountain range. Often he only kept what he wanted to eat and often what he kept didn't have many calories. So the FSR lightened the load and did its best to taste good.

The altitude carried a chill. They were well above any tree line, and the calories helped generate some warmth.

Each meal pack contained a nutrition bar. The bar was dual-labeled with the Marine yell of *Ooh-Rah* and the Army yell of *Hoo-Ah*.

"How about your Zapplesauce? Come on, Gunny, you don't need the calories!" Fury pointed to Moncrief's waist. Moncrief wasn't any heavier than Fury, but it didn't stop the harassment.

"Hell, this Zapplesauce?"

Moncrief opened the pouch without any intent of sharing it.

"I could hear you guys in Texas." Villegas pulled in behind the rock. He leaned his Heckler & Koch 416 rifle up against the rock. The German manufacturer had especially made the black-steel weapon for Delta Force. This one had a can on the end to silence the SOST round, a special bullet that could rip through a car door like a laser beam. The 416 with the SOST round could punch through a window or a door or a mud wall and still pack the power to rip through a man's chest.

"Here." The go pills had cut his appetite anyway. Moncrief handed Villegas the energy-boosted applesauce.

"Damn, Gunny, you are the man." Villegas started sucking the plastic bag. "I worked my way over to the cliff just above their cave. It's about a mile away."

"The captain's gonna cut your freakin' ding off," said Fury. "He told you to stay put."

"What did you see?" Moncrief asked.

"They have about fifteen in the cave. We could dust them, easy."

"Yeah, you do realize just how fuckin' far away you are from anyone who would even look your way when they are cutting your throat?" Fury's anger was becoming more visible. He was right, however, as the closest friendly troop was on the other side of the mountain range. It would take most of an hour for a Blackhawk with reinforcements to cross over the Hindu Kush.

"I got something in my eye with all of this crap." Villegas's right eye was tearing up and swollen.

"How are you going to shoot the Windrunner with only one headlight?" Fury kept pushing his partner. "Did you bring the olive oil?"

"What?" Moncrief hadn't heard of this one.

"Yeah. Hold on a second." Fury starting searching through the small pack he had the night-vision optics in. "Here it is."

He pulled out a small, clear plastic dropper with a green liquid inside.

"It's great for sewage work. If you have to wade through a slime pond, you put drops in your eyes and ears and it keeps the crap out."

"Thanks, man." Villegas put some drops in his eye.

Moncrief looked at the two Rangers huddled up below the rocks. They now had gone for most of twenty-four hours without sleep, but the two didn't seem fazed. Rather, they seemed in the game, focused, intent. Kevin Moncrief felt a familiar sense of being, of belonging. They had accepted him.

"It'll be dark soon." Moncrief slowly lifted himself off the ground and peered over the rock. They were several hundred feet above the valley floor and had a view for several miles down both valleys. He scanned the skyline for several miles.

"Well, I think it's time to get to work."

On the skyline several miles away, a dust cloud hovered over the desert road.

William Parker woke up from his drug-induced sleep in the backseat of the Toyota and stared out the SUV's window off to the mountain range in the distance. It was hot and the truck smelled. The cloth seats were torn, with the yellow foam bulging out. His sense of smell seemed to have changed. It was different. The truck had a sharp, sickening smell, like someone had become ill. More important, he realized that he was feeling the beginnings of a fever.

I feel like shit.

The checkered black-and-white shawl that the editor at *Al-Quds* had given him was damp with sweat. It wasn't the full illness. His throat tasted like sand. The chill of a low-grade fever made him shiver in the warm morning sun, but the worst had yet to come. When the disease started to cross over the blood barrier, then the headaches would come, the photophobia, and the rash. He was nearing the window when he would be contagious.

Fuck! Not too soon, not too late.

Initially, he would not be contagious.

He said when the headaches come.

When the pounding came he would be a danger to touch. And then the full-blown disease. Thereafter, without the specific antibiotic, there would be the brain swelling that would lead to a coma and, after the coma, a slow, horrific, painful death. In twenty-four hours it wouldn't matter what they gave him.

"Our passenger is awake."

Liaquat Anis leaned back over the front passenger seat.

"I am sorry about the drug." Liaquat, the physician, was speaking. "You can imagine that we must make sure, for your own safety, that you don't know where we are."

"I understand. It makes sense." Silently, Parker thanked the doctor for the drugging. It would help account—in their minds—for his pale skin and cold, clammy appearance.

"You don't look good, my friend."

"I said I understand. I'll be fine." Parker continued staring out the window. Between Umarov, who was driving, and Parker sat Liaquat. In the back cargo space, two mujahideens were crammed with their AK-47s. One slept in a contorted ball with the rifle between his legs.

The Toyota passed a sign, rusted and hanging on a tilt, near several mud huts. The Arabic writing said DURBA KHEL. Shortly after passing it, the Toyota turned west, heading for the mountains.

Remarkable.

The peaks were dressed in a white coat, but the valley looked starkly different, a moonscape painted in khaki browns and rust and dotted with rocks everywhere. The land seemed a place that no one could live in nor should want to. The road led west toward the left side of a massive finger of rock.

This is it.

Parker remembered the glimpse of the satellite picture.

Moncrief is on top of that ridge. The highest point. If he's doing his job, he's looking at me right now.

"You didn't tell me," Umarov growled at Liaquat while he drove.

"What?"

"You were supposed to meet up with my brother in London."

"He didn't show up. I tried the hotel in the East End where you told me to go. They said he was still checked in. But he never came to our meeting place."

Parker listened quietly, thirsting for a drink, any drink.

"That's not at all like Knez."

Liaquat nodded, his remorse evident. For his part, Parker tried to appear impassive, disinterested. Fortunately, Umarov said nothing more, staring ahead while he drove, never realizing that the man who'd cut his brother's throat sat inches away.

CHAPTER 64

The cave

The man standing in front of the mud hut didn't seem capable of being the mass killer he had spent his lifetime becoming. Youṣef al-Qadi smiled, watching Parker get out of the truck, but behind him stood a group of bearded, gaunt men with distrustful eyes. Some appeared old and some very young versions of the older ones, but all wore the same expression in their eyes.

"*As sala'amu alaikum,* good brother!"

Parker consciously forced himself to smile at the killer as he responded to the greeting.

"Walaikum as sala'am."

The two men touched each other's cheek from one side to another. Parker felt the man's much smaller frame in his hands, caught the beginnings of gray in Yousef's beard. He squeezed the terrorist tightly, thinking, *This is one of the killers of my mother and father.*

"I have known about you for some time," Yousef said.

"And I about you."

"I am sorry for your loss."

Parker stood motionless for a moment. He allowed the thought of Zabara's dead wife and adopted daughter to sink in fully, which in turn enabled his eyes to convey an honest, emotional reaction.

"Yes, yes." He paused. "Yes."

"The Jew-bastard Mossad."

Parker nodded and looked away, hoping his body language relayed the proper reaction to Yousef's statement.

"They will pay, my friend. They and their sponsors will pay heavily. For your family and mine." He took Parker's arm. "Come meet my brothers and my family. Come meet the warriors who will avenge you."

Yousef led Parker around as if he were a child, going from man to man, introducing each by name and explaining in detail the man's family and his heroics on the battlefield.

"This is Muhammad Kundi. He has served since the Russians. He is a true jihadist, once wounded by an American Hellfire missile. But he survived."

The nearly toothless man smiled and nodded.

"And this is Amir Parvez." No smile here.

Yousef continued down the line, coming to a young teen with pimples on his face. "In his village he is useless, unemployed. He is an embarrassment to his family. He brings shame on his house. But here, he fights to protect the two holy places. Here, he fights for Riyad al-Jannah. Here, the world listens when he speaks!"

The teenager's eyes shone with pride.

Yousef repeated the same message in different ways,

accusing the Americans of occupying the land of the two holy places, stealing the oil of Saudi Arabia, and slaughtering the children of Palestine.

"There is another warrior I want you to meet."

Yousef led Parker into the dim light of the cave.

"Get up, Patoo."

A small boy struggled to stand up. Like Parker's, his face was red and flushed. But unlike Parker, Patoo had a more advanced fever, his small, frail body soaked in sweat.

"This is my son, Patoo."

"*As sala'amu alaikum.*" The boy's voice was barely a whisper.

"Walaikum as sala'am."

Parker hesitated.

Hugging the boy would guarantee his death.

Parker kept some distance away from the boy. He didn't bend down to kiss the child's cheeks.

"I hope he feels well soon." Despite having the boy's illness as an excuse for keeping his distance, Parker saw in Yousef's eyes disappointment at the less-than-warm greeting.

"Come this way for some chai." Yousef led him to a fire pit in the shell of a mud house ringed by red-and-black and yellow prayer rugs.

"Have a seat, my brother." Yousef crossed his legs and sat next to a smoldering fire. "Bring us some chai. Peshawar's best! Have you had some?"

An old woman, permanently bent over with a round hump of a back, turned away and went back into the cave.

"You have fought a long and successful fight. You are our Sa'd Ibn Abi Waqqaas." Parker used the name of one of the earliest companions of Muhammad. Abi Waqqaas had been the first to shed blood for the new faith. At the time other nonbelievers were setting upon Muhammad, but Abi Waqqaas stopped them with the jawbone of a camel. He beat one nonbeliever to a bloody pulp. And with this fight, violence became a remedy for all time.

"Have some."

Yousef poured a cup of the tea and mixed sugar into it. It was a large metal cup shared by many in this dusty, dry mud hut. He gave the cup first to Parker, who drank from it.

Parker found that it had an odd lemon-ginger taste, but he welcomed any liquid in his quickly weakening state. He sipped the drink and then sipped it again, slightly turning the cup in his hand. His lips touched the cup again.

"This is good."

Parker handed the cup back to Yousef, who held it on his lap.

Yousef didn't drink, shifting the cup to one hand, using the other to stroke his beard.

"I have something for you."

Yousef pointed to one of the younger ones. The boy brought their leader a brown manila envelope, which Yousef handed to Parker. Parker could feel a thick packet of paper inside.

"This is my fatwa."

Parker showed surprise.

"You are giving it to me?"

"Of course. I have chosen you to begin it all."

"And *Al-Quds Al-Arabi*?"

"Yes, I think it is fitting. Don't you?"

Less than two decades earlier, the same newspaper had published the fatwa of another terrorist. The world had not heard of Osama bin Laden in August of 1996, when he wrote "Declaration of War against the Americans Occupying the Land of the Two Holy Places."

"Yes, indeed I do. Excuse me, but last night they took my PDA."

"Yes?"

"I record my interviews on my cell phone, but it was lost." Parker was playing the part of journalist as best he could. "I have nothing even to write with."

"Oh, yes." Yousef signaled to Liaquat Anis to come over to the fire pit. "We have been rude to our guest."

Liaquat frowned at the comment.

"Our journalist has nothing to write with. Bring him some paper and a pencil." Yousef paused. "Tell me, brother, it is most important, but will you return to London?"

Parker hadn't even given the idea any thought. Scott's cover story had the newspapers of London quoting Scotland Yard as looking for the missing suspect.

"Given what has happened, I don't know."

Yousef looked at him strangely. The man had just been given his declaration of war.

"I do know this," said Parker. "I will continue to write until I die. And *Al-Quds* will gladly print this story."

Yousef smiled, then turned to shout at his men. "Where is his paper? Where is his pencil? Get it now!"

Liaquat scrambled back to the truck, yelling at others as they searched through the cab.

"And your fatwa?" Parker turned the conversation back to Yousef.

"Bin Laden became a house cat. He no longer knew how to hunt the rats. He became an easy kill."

"And you do know how to hunt the rats?"

Yousef frowned at the comment.

"Yes, brother, I do." Yousef paused. "In ways far greater than bin Laden."

Liaquat brought back a pen with a small yellow pad with the edges rolled up in the corners.

"Yes, this will do." Parker started to write. "So how *do* you begin to 'hunt the rats' in this day and age?"

Umarov sat down next to Yousef with his AK-47 lying on his lap.

"I will create a new Islamic state out of this desert. And like Abi Waqqaas, from this we will wage war on the Zionist-Crusader alliance. I have an army of youths who love death more than the Americans love life." Yousef's eyes burned and his voice rose as he gestured wildly with his free hand.

Parker continued to write. "You began this years ago, correct? Some say as far back as Pan Am Flight 103?" Parker couldn't help it. He wanted to hear the words directly from the man's mouth.

"You are a good reporter, Zabara!" It was as if someone had asked Jonas Salk whether he had cured polio. "Yes, I was a young lieutenant in the ANO. Nidal was like a father to me."

Nidal was known for his recruitment of the best and the brightest. Parker decided to provoke Yousef subtly once more. "Some say he was paranoid."

"You have heard the stories?"

"Yes."

"They are lies. He was strong; it was others who were afraid."

"You attended Harvard in America."

"It was there that I learned to truly hate the Zionists. I remember one professor said I could only attend the school because of oil. The police?" Yousef hissed angrily. "They harassed anyone of color. What was it that Du Bois said? 'I was in Harvard, but not of it.' But I *did* learn how to make money. As I saw the increasing bloodshed in Palestine, I was ashamed for having done so little in my life."

"What was Flight 103 meant to achieve?"

"It achieved what it was supposed to achieve."

"I don't understand."

Yousef warmed a hand over the fire, still holding the teacup with the other.

"The Muslim nations are all controlled by governments that do not allow a voice to be heard. In Saudi Arabia, the *Al Hayat* and *Al Jazeera* write only what the king wishes them to write. In the UAE, the *Al Bayan* does the same. So how do we get the message out? Pan Am Flight 103 showed the world that the Americans could suffer. The Beirut bombing of the Marines caused the Americans to leave Aden in less than twenty-four hours. In Somalia, when a dozen soldiers were killed in a minor battle and a pilot was dragged through the streets, the Americans left. And these victories were all on CNN, and then they eventually had to be on the front page of *Al Jazeera* and *Al Bayan.* It encouraged a thousand other young warriors to join."

"I can see the short-term effects," said Parker. "What do such acts do for the mills that grind slowly?"

"Ah, yes. Longfellow. 'Though the mills of God grind slowly, yet they grind exceedingly small'?" Yousef knew the verse. "The long-term message is that retribution is not solely for the Americans."

Parker kept scribbling and nodded. Then he looked up. "The tea?" Parker pointed to the cup.

"Yes." Yousef took a sip and then handed him the cup.

"I am sorry. It is the travel. I have a headache coming on."

"The tea helps." Yousef smiled. "Drink some more."

Parker smiled as he took the cup and another sip.

CHAPTER 65

Joint Operations Center, Regional Component (East), Bagram Airfield, Afghanistan

James Scott hurried back to a second desk that he'd staked out in the operations center—this one in the rear of the bridge near the AO cell. The air operations cell controlled the air in the northeastern quarter of Afghanistan, where Scott's team perched on their hilltop.

Five large flat screens covered the one wall of the bridge and, like other operations centers, the desks and computers rose like stadium seats on platforms facing the displays. A large air-ground map shone in the center flat screen. Scott could see on the map Kabul to the south, down the valley, and the several mountain ranges that encircled Bagram. The airfield's single runway was at just less than five thousand feet above sea level, but the mountains to the north, east, and west all climbed up to fifteen thousand feet in less than a few miles. It made for an elevator-like descent when landing.

"What's the weather looking like for the next twenty-four hours?" Scott asked one of the staffers. He had just returned from his conference call with Tranthan.

The young, freckle-faced man, a Kansas native, Scott had learned, frowned. "Frankly, sir, not good. There's a sandstorm blowing in from the northwest."

"How soon before it arrives?"

"Hold on, sir." The airman turned to his computer terminal to pull up the weather report. The picture of a dark-haired girl in a bright white-and-red cheerleader's uniform was taped to the terminal. "Here it is. Winds expected up to sixty miles an hour in the next six to twelve."

"What will that do to air?"

"It will shut down the Blackhawks."

Just as Scott had feared. Exfiltrating Parker and his team had just become immeasurably more complicated and uncertain.

"Can you raise the team?"

"Yes, sir."

Scott had tried to keep the communications down to a minimum, but Furlong needed to know his options.

Scott took the headset.

"Slashing talon six, this is checkmate six, over."

The *six* meant that the commanding officer was talking to another commanding officer. five would be the second in command and one through four might be the different platoon commanders.

"Checkmate six, this is slashing talon six."

"Severe weather expected your position from twenty-one-hundred zulu to oh-three-hundred zulu. No air. Do you copy?"

"I copy, twenty-one-hundred zulu to oh-three-hundred zulu."

Zulu time provided a uniform reference point—

Greenwich Mean Time. Translated, a storm was going to hit at three in the morning and stay there until well after sunrise.

The conversation with Furlong didn't last much longer than a few seconds. Scott imagined the captain tucked in behind a pile of rocks looking out over the valley with his thermal night-vision binoculars. The optics would pick up anything with a heartbeat or a body temperature above the cold rocks. Furlong would be lying in the dirt, camouflaged, marking the locations of his men and feeling the tickle of an occasional scorpion crawling up his sleeve.

"What are they doing down there?"

A group of servicemen had grown quickly below them, at the lowest level of the bridge.

"Sir, if you don't mind, I might check this out. I've been wondering myself."

"Yeah, please do."

Scott watched the five screens as he sat in his chair, sipping a cup of black coffee that had a stale taste to it. He looked into the cup, seeing the stain on the ceramic above the liquid lines from past cups. The mug was borrowed from the mess and well used.

The airman came climbing back up the steps quickly, a stunned look on his face.

"What is it?"

"Sir, they're watching CNN International on the terminal."

"And?"

"They're reporting that the Pakistani weapons complex at Kamra was attacked an hour ago. Two nuke cores are gone."

CHAPTER 66

The cave

His temperature was rising.

Parker leaned back on the prayer rug and touched his hand to his forehead, then ran it through his hair. The skin was cold and wet, and the hair was matted with sweat from the fever. Parker's neck felt stiff, almost as if welded in place; as he tried to turn it, pain shot through his shoulders. His head was starting to pound. Even staying still, he felt as if a large wooden mallet had struck him in the rear of his skull.

Parker squeezed his fist, once, twice, and then a third time, suppressing the pain and trying to focus. "It is time for prayers."

Umarov and Liaquat, who were still by the fire, looked over at him lethargically. The disease was now in its sixth hour. They were probably starting to feel the initial effects, their eyes glowing eerily in the twilight.

A wind was rising out of the northwest.

Parker looked up in the sky and could see bright

twinkling stars, despite his sense that there was a coming change of weather.

This could change everything.

The cave was well above ten thousand feet and, being closer to the heavens, the stars seemed more pronounced, much brighter than home. But Parker had seen it happen before, a sky full of stars and then a sandstorm. You could go from unlimited visibility, spotting mountaintops a hundred miles away, to being blinded, unable to see even one's hand.

"We must pray."

Umarov grunted, stood.

Parker rose on his knees and then pushed up with his hands. His head swam as he tried to stand erect.

Yousef had left the cave some time ago. Parker could hear his voice, seemingly on a cell phone, at the edge of the encampment. He sounded excited.

Parker took a prayer rug to an opening on the far side of the huts and the first of three trucks parked between the remaining walls. The trucks were covered with dry, brown tarps that started to flap in the rising breeze. He faced west, toward Mecca, and removed his shoes.

"Do you have water?"

Liaquat had laid his prayer rug down, behind Parker's, as if to keep an eye on the stranger. Liaquat looked somewhat unsteady himself.

"Yes, of course." Liaquat yelled to one of the women in the cave. "Bring us some water for Al-Wudu." The ritual of the prayer required a cleansing.

The old woman from the cave brought a pitcher.

"I noticed on the flight you made your fist." Liaquat,

the physician, was talking. His suspicions seemed to be building. "Did you hurt your arm?"

"Yes, years ago." Parker knew that attempting to evade the question would cause more curiosity. "It is nothing."

The woman handed Parker a small metal cup. *Odd.* Parker looked at the woman in detail as she held the brandished pitcher up to pour. She had short, stump-like fingers, fat and rounded at their tips. The woman would die soon. Parker had seen it before. She was sick. Her lung disease was cutting off the oxygen to her body, causing her fingers to club. When hit by the meningitis she would be one of the first to die.

Liaquat washed his hands, three times, and then his face, and then the back of his neck. As the woman came to Parker, he looked into her eyes. Her head was covered, but her eyes in the glow of the fire seemed to be large and tired. She and her people lived in the worst of a stark, barren, cold, hopeless world. Parker washed his hands three times, and then his face and neck. The water was bitterly cold. For Parker and his rising temperature, it felt good.

"So, Umarov is from Grozny?"

"Yes." Liaquat laid his prayer rug down next to Parker's.

Parker noticed Umarov's accent, when he spoke, had the hint of something other than Arabic. Chechen had similar consonants and sounds to Arabic but sounded quite different.

"He has the mark of the *Crni Labudovi*?"

"Yeah."

Parker decided to play journalist.

"So Umarov was originally from Grozny, raised a Muslim."

"Yes."

"But the Black Swans are Bosnian?"

Liaquat looked around. No one else was within range of listening.

"All you need to know is that he's a killer." Liaquat said the words in a near whisper. "His family was killed in the first Russian purge of Grozny. He joined the Committee of Revolutionary Justice with Nidal. He blew up a Russian train back in the late eighties. It killed a lot of Russian children on a holiday."

"And that's how he got to know Yousef?"

"Yes. They were with Nidal together, but the Russians were giving Nidal help with explosives against the Americans."

Flight 103.

"So Nidal cut him loose. He disappeared for a while and then showed up in Bosnia. He did such a good job that they made him a brother of the *Crni Labudovi*."

Meaning, he killed more children.

"And then back in Grozny against the Russians in 1996. And finally he came here to Yousef."

The Maghrib prayer began at sunset. And Parker followed the Salah, or prayer, through its separate steps. But Yousef was nowhere in sight.

At the end, he turned to the right and spoke to evil and then to the left and spoke to good. And then Parker thought the last of the Longfellow poem.

Though with patience he stands waiting, with exactness grinds He all.

They all stood at the completion of the prayer and hugged each other, kissing each other on the cheek.

Yousef came across to them, looking like a child at Christmas. "My friend, get your pencil and paper. I have news. Very special news."

"What is it?"

"We have our weapons. They are being moved as we speak!"

Umarov gave Yousef a look. Parker noticed the look as well. It said, *You're talking too much.*

Thank God Umarov never heard from Knez, Parker thought. It was clear that Parker would be lying in a pool of blood by now if Knez had ever communicated to anyone any suspicions.

"Weapons?"

"Yes, Pakistan's nuclear weapons. Zulfiqar did well. They will be here by midnight. Praise Allah!"

"Praise Allah!" Parker managed to beam a smile. "But they must be used in the right way, yes?"

The trap had been baited.

"One will go to our cell on the lake—"

"We speak too much." Umarov interrupted Yousef.

"Perhaps, perhaps." Yousef hesitated. "My friend, you will be the first to know, but let's wait a little more."

"I understand." *Near Canada,* Parker recalled, and believed he had what he needed.

Umarov continued to frown.

"No, brother," Yousef told Umarov. "It's okay. This is why we wanted Sadik here now. When the time is right he will tell the world! With this, the world will listen to my fatwa!"

"This will make you formidable, formidable indeed!" Parker came over and hugged Yousef again, placing a kiss on first his left cheek and then his right. "You must tell me everything."

"Soon, indeed." Yousef continued to smile like a child. "Please. Let us go in by the fire. The women will bring us some food."

Parker followed, looking briefly up into the mountains. Somewhere up there the team was probably learning of the change in the game. *If they thought the weapons were here, the team would be on top of us by now.*

Inside, everyone huddled by the fire, in all, more than a dozen men, sharing a common plate of *chapli* kabab and chai. Again, Parker sipped the tea, savoring the moisture. And again, he passed the cup to Yousef. Again, Yousef sipped the tea from the same cup. The comment about the headache passed his ears.

Her last drink would probably have been tea.

He imagined his mother, sitting in her airplane seat, the flight attendant bringing her a cup of tea with cream and sugar.

Parker looked at the AK-47s stacked next to the entrance to the cave.

Parker thought of his grabbing one of the machine guns and spraying the huddle next to the fire. He wouldn't survive the attack, but that didn't matter.

But we wouldn't know where the nukes were. The highly enriched uranium cores would disappear into a place like Danish Abad.

Yousef was obviously intoxicated by his achievement. He continued to smile and babble on. "You see this, my friend." He held up a cell phone to Parker. This one, unlike the others, had a short stub of a cigar-shaped antenna. "This is a Mobal."

"Mobal?" Parker thought he mispronounced *mobile*.

"Yes, an Iridium. A satellite phone."

"I see."

"It has one number in it. You see it here, my friend." Yousef showed a single number in the phone's directory. "With this, a simple touch, I can activate the cells that will deliver this blow to the heart!"

"I don't understand."

"A nuclear weapon is being delivered to the heart."

"The heart?" Parker was playing the journalist, writing on his pad. But to himself he thought, *Chicago*.

"Yes, my friend. But I cannot say more, not now. But you will be the first to report it. And the name of Yousef al-Qadi. You will report on the rise of a new Islamic nation."

The wind started to howl through the encampment.

Parker was slowly slipping away. Fortunately, the interview with Yousef was long over. The headaches were becoming horrific now. He had begun to shake uncontrollably from the fever.

"You don't look good, my friend." Liaquat pulled next to Parker at the fire. "Do you have a fever?"

"I may."

Liaquat turned to Umarov. "Oh, I spoke with London." Liaquat had been gone for some time. This explained it.

"Yes?"

"Knez is dead."

"What?" Umarov leaned up. As he did, he grabbed his head. The quick change seemed to have caused his head to pound. "Not Knez. Not Knez."

"I'm sorry. He was found murdered."

"In London? Who would have hurt my brother there? He knew no one."

Liaquat glanced toward Parker at that moment. Liaquat knew more than he was saying.

"You had a brother?" Parker asked.

"Yeah." Umarov's face glistened with the sweat. "Not by kin, but by blood."

"What?"

"I was a mujahideen with the *muslimanska oslobodilačka brigada*. He was my blood brother. We fought together. On more than one occasion, he saved my life."

Parker had heard of the Gestapo mujahideen. A corps was formed of Muslim fighters from other countries. The best, or the best in killing, were then taken into the *Crni Labudovi*.

Umarov continued to mutter while Liaquat kept watching Parker.

Parker turned away, pulling his rug up against the remnants of the mud wall that once was a hut near the opening to the cave. The wind continued to blow. The stars were now gone. A sandstorm was just beyond the opening in the wall, causing the canvas covering the trucks to begin to flap. He would have to move quietly and quickly. He would have to find the trail that followed the ridgeline down and then around into the next valley.

God, I am sick.

Time was running out, but the mission had changed. Now he had two nuclear weapons to find.

* * *

Parker was thinking that the fierce sandstorm might provide a clean escape when the victorious raiding party arrived back at camp. He'd had only fitful bouts of sleep, and his temperature had risen through the night. He steadied himself against the wall as he stood, then wiped his drenched forehead with the shawl that his editor had given him.

God, it has to be now.

It was painful simply to move, to breathe. Nausea swept through his body.

Clark.

He thought of her running through her first marathon. The pain she had to endure. Not letting the idea of stopping even enter her head. Now he couldn't let the idea of stopping enter his head.

Parker quietly stumbled across the roofless room, watching Yousef and Umarov for any sign of movement. At the door's edge, he wrapped the shawl tightly around his head and across his face, leaving only a small slit for his eyes. He felt the windblown grit strike his face as he stepped out of the doorway.

Visibility was rapidly going to nothing. He turned his head away from the wind and used his hand, running along the mud wall, to guide him. The sand stung his hands. With one on the wall and the other holding his shawl as tightly as possible, he was working his way through the maze when he stopped.

Are those lights?

In the rapidly decreasing visibility, headlights bounced up and down as they headed toward the compound.

"*Allah Akbar! Allah Akbar*!" A guard was shouting

behind him. In a second, Yousef and Umarov were standing nearby.

"My friend, have you ever seen a core?"

"I'm sorry?" Parker managed.

Not just escape, then. Escape with Yousef's stolen nuclear device.

Yousef turned away and smiled as the Toyota SUV pulled up in front of them. The passengers and driver, all armed with their AK-47s slung over their shoulders, dismounted their trucks and hugged Yousef.

"Where is Zulfiqar?"

"He is with a convoy of warriors behind us. They ran into a Pakistani patrol. With the bombs missing, the army is everywhere. They will be here around dawn."

"And where is it?"

The driver opened up the latch door on the rear of the SUV. There, in the low light of the Toyota's lamp, was a box marked with the radioactivity warning logo.

Yousef pulled the small metal box toward him and unlocked the latches. He hesitated.

"Is it radioactive?"

A young man, a passenger from the second vehicle, spoke. He wore black-framed glasses and appeared to be more than a mujahideen. Probably a young scientist or technician.

"It is, but as long as you don't touch it, you should be okay."

Yousef swung the lid up. Inside, surrounded by a black, foam-like material, a bright, metallic gold ball no bigger than an oversized softball glowed in the dim light. It had lines that bisected it, giving it the appearance of having come in several parts.

"Like Allah, this can level their cities." Yousef turned and spoke the words directly to Parker.

"Isn't there more to it than this?" said Parker.

The young technician answered. "This is the enriched U-235 core. We surround it with a plastic explosive that must be triggered instantly and perfectly."

It was then—in Yousef's moment of triumph—that Parker first noticed his face, which, despite the gathering wind and dropping temperature, was bathed in sweat.

The bastard isn't far behind me.

Parker's initial mission had been accomplished.

Again Parker had to wait. It took another hour, but finally the camp had started to quiet down. The wind was howling now. A torn tarp near the entrance to the cave flapped wildly.

As he sat by the fire, Parker rehearsed how he would make his way to the small pickup truck at the far edge of the row of mud huts. It now had an armed guard along with its most valuable cargo inside.

Parker slid up past the little Toyota pickup truck wedged in between the walls of the mud huts. The guard seemed half asleep, on his feet, with his scarf pulled up tightly around his face and head. Parker reached to the ground and picked up a rock the size of a grapefruit but with a sharp, pointed edge. He moved slowly, very slowly, placing each step carefully. The guard didn't move. It would take one stroke at the base of the skull. There could be no mistake. It had to collapse the man instantly.

Thump!

Only someone this close would have heard the crush of bone as the point struck the skull, breaking it like an eggshell. Parker grabbed the man as he slumped to the ground, pulling the body to a nearby wall and placing it just out of sight on the other side. He slipped into the seat and closed the door very slowly, tugging it with all of his strength so as to close it without making a sound.

The truck was a late-eighties Toyota 4Runner with torn cloth seats and the smell of oil, gunpowder, sweat, and some type of spice, either ginger or cumin. The cab was filled with the haze of dust from the sandstorm, like a fine talcum powder.

He looked back to the cargo bay where the device, in its box, lay like a piece of forgotten luggage.

The keys. Where are the keys?

He felt around the cab in the darkness. The keys were still in the ignition. Between the seats, next to the stick shift, he felt the warm wood and cold metal of an AK-47.

"Okay, here we go."

Parker began to turn over the key. He knew that as soon as the first sound of an engine began the guards would start the chase and then Umarov and Yousef would follow. But the truck had been separated from the other vehicles, turned around, and was aimed in the right direction, facing downvalley and toward the edge of the finger. They had planned for an escape with their important cargo if necessary.

The key caused the engine to sputter and then start. Parker shifted into gear. The truck rolled forward, into pitch darkness. After several yards, he reluctantly gave into the reality of his surroundings and turned the headlights on. As the light illuminated the blowing sand in front of the truck, it felt as if a red-hot iron had been pressed against his forehead.

Oh, God.

Severe meningitis meant severe photosensitivity. The disease had started to infect the sac around the brain and spinal cord. The pain was a stark reminder that soon it would be too late for the antibiotic to save him.

The truck started bouncing along the trail. The lights jumped up and down as he tried to focus on the cart path.

Pow, pow, pow.

A rifle started to fire behind him. The person was aiming high. They would be wary of hitting the nuclear cargo with a stray bullet, an advantage that Parker hadn't anticipated.

Trying to keep his focus in the dark, in the wind, and with the disease making him more and more ill by the second, Parker followed his sense of direction. He sensed the mass of rock just to his left and no mountain face to his right. It would guide him.

Another set of headlights started to follow.

Thwack, thwack.

Rounds began to strike the vehicle. Parker ducked and increased the speed, trying to keep it on the path. Occasionally, a boulder appeared out of the darkness in the center of the path. Parker slammed into one, knocking it off the trail. The jolt made his head feel as if it would split in two. A bullet struck the roof and ricocheted off into the dark, making a brief green-and-yellow glow as it spun into the darkness. Parker tucked lower in the seat, trying to get as much protection as the frame of the truck would provide him.

God, I hope I can make it.

The trail kept going, refusing to bend around the rocky finger. He knew that once he made that turn he would be crossing over into the adjacent valley. Once he made that turn, he'd be provided a few minutes of shelter from the gunfire. But the trail kept pulling him to the right, away from the ridge.

A third set of truck lights started to bounce its reflections off the rocks. This one had an extra set of lights. Parker suspected the last one would have Yousef and Umarov in it—Yousef's Toyota SUV. The truck in the middle of the chase was a pickup. Looking back, he could see the flash of rifle fire coming from the back of the pickup truck over the front cab.

The second truck seemed to gain on him, coming closer. As when skiing, it was easier in a race to follow the path of someone in front. The one behind could cut the curves shorter. The few extra seconds it took Parker to pick the path were seconds that the following truck didn't need to waste. All the truck driver had to do was follow the rear lights.

I'm not going to make it.

Scott watched the action, helpless.

"How long can the Predator hold this?"

"In these winds?"

The airman kept the Predator's thermal sensor focus on the three moving objects. Occasionally short streaks of lights shot out from the second truck to the first one. Only with the thermal sensor was the Predator able to see anything in the gathering sandstorm.

"She's flying into the wind, and at this headwind she is almost standing still on full power." The operator seemed to strain with his ship, even though it flew on the other side of a mountain range.

Scott imagined the pilotless aircraft holding itself against the current of the winds above. The engine would be spinning at full speed trying to hold the grade.

"Sir, we need to do something. We only have one missile."

"What do you suggest?"

The airman lined up the sight on the first vehicle. The Fire button for the Hellfire missile was less than an inch away.

"No. Not that one. That has to be Parker."

A hand reached over the airman's shoulder and moved the sight to the middle vehicle. The man's wrist showed the scars of a bad burn. Scott turned around to see the senior air officer on duty moving the crosshairs of the sight for the younger man.

"This is the one you want. It will give your man more time and block the last vehicle."

Scott had met Colonel Danny Prevatt briefly. He said he'd only been on duty here for a week, but as a veteran of hundreds of combat missions he was clearly at home in this environment and a good man to have in command. Prevatt seemed to sense the appropriate target as he moved a stub of cigar from one side of his mouth to the other.

"Go." Scott sensed it was now or never. Parker wouldn't be there much longer.

Prevatt squeezed the missile trigger.

"Help me keep it on track." Prevatt continued to press the control against the wind. "It won't help if the wind pushes us into the first one."

Scott nervously folded his arms.

"Come on, come on." It seemed that the missile took minutes to travel to its target; but it only could have lasted seconds. A silent flash of light lit the screen.

"Did you see that?" Prevatt let out a whoop. A ball of flames engulfed what was once a pickup truck. "Hit 'em right in the ass."

CHAPTER 67

The valley

The explosion lifted the rear of Parker's SUV for a second, but it did more than that to the truck in his rearview mirror. The gunmen who had been firing were gone, turned into dust, as if a vengeful god had struck them down from above. The blast pushed Parker into the steering wheel briefly and then threw him back into the seat. The concussion wave shut off the engine.

The detonation lit a fireball that momentarily blinded him. The pain in his head and eyes felt equally blinding.

"Come on, come on."

Parker blindly found the key and turned it on, but the engine was dead. Keeping the truck coasting straight, he pulled the AK-47 from the passenger seat, then swung the truck off the road and into a scattering of boulders. He slipped out the door, gun in hand, and retrieved the bomb case from the rear of the truck.

Looking back, he heard another rifle shot and saw the shape of Umarov behind the wreckage, cutting around the wreckage efficiently while firing at him. Or, rather, his vehicle. The bullets chunked into the chassis as Parker slipped into the boulder field, turning into the wind, cutting through the rocks.

Thank God for adrenaline.

Now I need to keep my bearings.

The light of the explosion had illuminated the rocks for a millisecond, and with the light he realized that he had almost reached the point of the finger of rocks. On foot, he cut across where the road couldn't go. He moved over a slight hill and into the next valley, heading back up into the darkness.

The headaches, the headaches.

Now he had a ringing in his ears, and his neck felt as stiff as a board. Parker continued to move, placing one foot in front of another, heading up the valley, shivering with the chill of a fever. It was as if he were in the final miles of a marathon, requiring to survive on will more than desire.

Looking back, Parker saw the lights of Yousef's trucks start moving around the point, about to make the turn up into the second valley.

Parker turned back again, looking up into the valley.

Where are you?

He stood out in the open on what little he could make of a goat path that cut through the rocks. It was important that he stood exposed. He needed Furlong and his team to see the thermal outline of a single man. Parker kept moving uphill, up valley.

The truck's lights started to follow.

I need to see that tent.

Parker feared that when the tent's signal flashed, Umarov would see it as well.

He kept moving forward but still no tent. Finally, he turned, looking back downvalley, and fired several rounds from the AK-47 toward the headlights.

He glanced back upvalley into the darkness.

And suddenly he saw it.

They must have seen my rounds.

Furlong, with his heat scope, could have seen the bullets coming from his rifle, then realized where Parker must be on foot.

The tent flashed for one second, but in the darkness it was a clear beacon.

"Did you see that?" Yousef pointed up into the darkness. "There are others."

Umarov looked toward the flash of light. "More than just one man on the run, eh?" He reached for some extra clips of ammunition for his AK-47, checked his pistol, and chambered a round.

Liaquat Anis, sitting in the back of the truck, leaned forward and spoke to Umarov in the front. "He must have been the man they saw with Knez in London."

Abu Umarov stared forward through the windshield, in silence, absorbing what was said. This man was the killer of his Knez. It was a pledge of the *Crni Labudovi* to avenge the death of a Black Swan.

"Why was Knez in London?" Yousef turned to Liaquat.

"I didn't want to say anything before because I knew how important Zabara was to you, but . . ."

"Speak!"

"The Bosnians had said that Zabara had changed.

They suspected he had become a traitor. The *Crni Labudovi* had sent Knez to check out the rumors."

Yousef turned and struck Liaquat with the full force of his hand.

"Why did you not tell me? Why didn't you say anything?"

"I was going to, but when we flew together, when I talked to him, I thought it was a lie. I knew how important this was." Liaquat slumped down with his head in his hands.

"Anis, can you reach Zulfiqar?"

"I'll try."

"Tell him that we may have an American special-operations group in this valley and we need his warriors. Tell him to muster everyone!"

Yousef looked flushed and was sweating in the cold wind. "Are you well, brother?"

Yousef waved off the doctor's concern. "It must be my son's sickness. I have a fever. It doesn't matter. I will hunt this infidel and cut his throat. Now, you go! Tell him where we are!"

"I will get Zulfiqar here."

"Guide him through this storm!"

They briefly stopped the truck, and Liaquat jumped out.

"We will follow the trail. Hurry!"

The fourth passenger in the truck was the young warrior from Indonesia, Malik Mahmud. Useless now, still in shock from seeing his friends blown into pieces and onto the windshield of the SUV that had followed theirs.

"I go from here on foot." Abu Umarov opened the

door to the truck and also jumped out. "You keep following the trail with your lights on."

Umarov disappeared into the darkness and blinding wind.

Yousef saw Liaquat running, in the glow of the brake lights of the truck, back toward the cave and help.

"Mahmud, come up front here and make sure you have enough ammunition."

"Yes, Yousef."

"We need to find Sadik Zabara—and kill him."

CHAPTER 68

The tent

Parker had been mentally prepared to take a bearing as soon as he saw the light. It was an advantage that he had. He expected the light. They didn't. The tent was to the west, up the valley, in the face of the rocks, ten degrees to his left. As a pilot, he knew how to take a bearing. More important, it was near a dark chocolate-colored rock that stood above a man's height. But it was a chocolate-colored rock in a field of rocks in the dark.

Where is it?

And the sky was now gone. The stars had disappeared from sight. The wind had increased, now blowing directly at him.

If I had a star.

Parker's mouth was dry, his fever relentless. The headaches continued to pound his skull.

If I had Venus.

As a child, Parker's father would point out to him the brightest star in the early sky. It was called Anahita for over a thousand years. And then the Greeks called it Lucifer.

The plan has changed.

Parker's original plan was to enter the camp, infect Yousef, and then try to escape. Simple. The disease would hit Yousef and spread to the leadership. Few would survive. And the propaganda would be that Allah had punished these wayward mujahideen. As the children of the local villages became ill, America would bring the antibiotics. America would become the hero. The villagers would turn against the visiting mujahideen, who only brought death.

But now nuclear weapons were involved. The plan needed to change.

I know how to find the second one.

Parker tried to concentrate. It was now critical that he made it to the team. He had to make it to their radio. He looked back at what was once the sky.

Abu Ali Sina.

Parker's mind started to wander, between the fever and the progression of the disease. He recalled his father telling him of Abu Ali Sina, the astronomer from Afghanistan, within a hundred miles of where he stood, who first discovered the transit of Venus.

The transit of Venus. The planet's passing across the face of the sun.

As Parker moved through the dark, he knew he'd drift to the right without thinking. It was what a right-handed person did. Only a matter of inches, each step would be slightly to the right. In a hundred yards, he would be ten yards to the right. Unless he corrected for the unconscious step.

He intentionally made every step slightly farther to the left.

If I had Venus.

They could light up the tent again, but if they did it would draw the hounds to him. In the original plan, the team was to stay away. Parker was to disappear in the night. There was a chance that Yousef might not even follow. In the original plan, Yousef wouldn't have known what path Parker would have taken. And shortly, Yousef would be distracted by the illness, with others becoming sick rapidly. But the plan had changed; his team would now be improvising, just as Parker had been.

He stopped. Nausea took his breath away. It had now been more than twelve hours since he'd chewed the gum. He was close to the point of no return.

He walked another ten paces and stopped. The weight of his gun and the case were becoming impossible burdens. He moved a step to the left and walked another ten paces forward.

God, I can't find it.

He leaned against a boulder. His thirst was overwhelming. He looked west toward what was once the mountain range. Visibility had reduced further. Suddenly, headlights lit up the rocks behind him. Yousef's truck had to be no more than a hundred yards away. He slid in behind the boulder, putting it between himself and Yousef and the wind. Parker put his hand on the rock. It was sharp and pocked with jagged edges across its face.

Volcanic.

Eons ago, this rock had been liquid.

He felt for the next rock, for new and better cover from the approaching vehicles.

But what Parker touched next didn't feel volcanic. It felt like the smooth, man-made fabric of a tent.

The lights from the truck suddenly went dark.

Thank God!

Parker felt for the tent's zipper, found it, and slid inside. Darkness, complete. Parker moved his hands in the darkness along the inside edge of the tent. The wind continued to buffet the shelter, causing it to rock slightly back and forth. He came to the cold steel of the Windrunner rifle with a scope on top. Parker pulled the bolt back and used his finger to feel the brass cartridge in the chamber. It was ready to fire. He slid his hand down the length of the weapon, feeling the round cylinder of a silencer at the end. He put the AK-47 to the side, going with the better weapon, and left the device box on the far side of the tent.

Parker kept moving his hands along the base of the tent.

"There it is."

A small plastic ice chest tucked in the corner.

"I don't have much time," he whispered to himself as he opened the chest and felt inside. A plastic ziplock bag held a tube and a long needle. He put his hand back into the chest full of the liquid and ice and felt a second plastic bag.

"All right, let's get this going."

Parker turned around, putting his feet to the opening of the tent. As he did, he sat on a small metal object. His hand felt a .45-caliber automatic pistol with a long silencer attached to the barrel. He quietly chambered a round and cocked the hammer.

He pulled off his shawl and pulled up the sleeve to his shirt. Every second mattered. He hung the IV bag, hooked up the tube, and took the needle. He had discussed this with Dr. Stewart at the CDC. It was best to put it in a vein on the back of his hand.

Parker stuck his hand back into the ice chest and halfheartedly washed it off. It wasn't sterile, but would have to do. He felt for that small bulge just to the outside of the back of his hand. He tied a rubber strip that came with the bag and made a fist. A distended vein stuck out on the back of his hand.

He stuck the needle in the vein and then slid it slowly deeper. He released the valve to the IV bag and almost instantly felt the cold liquid enter his body.

The wind rocked the tent, moving it back and forth as the gusts changed directions.

Parker leaned back with his hand on his chest, in the dark, holding the pistol in the other.

All he needed now was time.

A shadow crossed over the tent.

Parker tried to focus his eyes in the dark.

A shadow?

A shadow meant a source of light. It had to have been from the headlights of Yousef's truck.

God, I'm thirsty.

Parker's mouth felt as if it had been stuffed with cotton. His tongue seemed welded in place. He felt the IV bag. Still half full. But at least the vancomycin cocktail was passing into his body.

The shadow passed again over the tent.

Parker pulled the pistol up to his chest. The wind kept rocking the tent. He listened for a sound other than the howl of sand blasting against the rocks and tent.

Finally his thirst became overwhelming. Parker reached for the small cooler and stuck his hand back into the icy water. It became irresistible. He pulled the cooler over, putting his hand into the cold liquid and bringing a handful up to his mouth. He swallowed the water with a small piece of ice. *So good.* He lifted the cooler and drank the cold water.

More time; just need a little more time.

He reclined again with the pistol on his chest.

Lights flickered above, bouncing up and down, in silhouette against the roof of the tent. And then a shadow passed over again.

"Allah!"

Umarov's blade sliced through the tent, narrowly missing Parker's head. Parker grabbed Umarov's wrist as it came through the opening in the fabric; as he did so, the IV ripped out of his hand. Umarov's body fell on Parker's other arm, with his weight on the pistol, but as it did a silenced round fired from the gun.

Whish.

The silent bullet tore through the tent and ricocheted off the larger boulder nearby.

"*Srati!*" Umarov growled at Parker. He swung again with the knife.

Parker caught his hand again, holding the knife just above his head.

"*Srati!*" Umarov screamed, shifting his weight to his right arm and the knife. The blade was just above Parker's throat, the steel point pressing into his flesh.

Parker pushed up with his body and, as he did, for a flash of a moment his other hand came free.

Whish.

An animal cry as a second silenced bullet from Parker's pistol tore through the flesh of Umarov's right forearm. He pulled the knife away from Parker's throat but then came back down, sticking the blade into the upper part of Parker's right arm.

Umarov kicked the pistol away into the rocks. The tent was now shredded around the two men as they struggled.

Umarov pulled back up against the rocks, lifted the IV bag, and looked at its label, recognizing not only what it was but also what it was for. He used the knife to cut the tube from the needle.

Parker crouched, looking for an opening. But he had no gun he could reach and no knife to match Umarov's.

"Yousef!" Umarov yelled out.

"Umarov?" A voice came from well behind the rocks.

"They have infected us."

"Umarov! Where are you?"

The sand came in gusts, stopping for a second and then bearing down again.

"Here! I am here! I have their medicine." Umarov stood up, holding his side with the one hand and the IV bag with the other. He looked at Parker, a growing pool of blood at his feet, and smiled.

"Maybe you should die like this."

Umarov turned and then stopped, seeing the pistol lying nearby.

"And then, maybe not."

He reached down to the .45-caliber automatic and picked it up, with the intent of putting a final round into Parker's face.

Just as he turned, Parker hefted a large stone that he'd managed to palm and struck.

Umarov fell in a heap.

"Maybe not." William Parker, on his knees, cradled his injured arm across his chest, panting for breath, and realized that he had survived.

CHAPTER 69

Just beyond the tent

"Umarov? Umarov?"

No answer. Yousef assumed the worst and fired his AK-47 blindly into the howling wind, aiming toward what he thought was the last echo of a sound.

In the past Yousef had seen the Chechen kill, be severely wounded, and then kill again. It was an impossible thought that any man could put out the life of this *Crni Labudovi*.

"Umarov?"

Yousef yelled the name once more as he scrambled to the passenger side of the SUV and knelt down between the open door and the body of his truck. The SUV's lights still shined up the valley.

"I need more ammunition."

Mahmud also crouched outside the truck, in the back, behind the second door.

"Mahmud, ammunition. Now!"

Mahmud stood up briefly to hand Yousef a loaded clip over the open door.

Whack!

The sniper's bullet passed through the glass of the window, striking Mahmud in the forehead. He collapsed like a rag doll dropped to the floor.

Yousef sprayed the darkness with another magazine, firing from under the side door. He had never been on the battlefield alone before. He could feel his heart pounding as he hugged the rocks and dirt. The wind was mercilessly howling in gusts, surging up and then down. One moment it would scream and then the next it would be silent. Like a turbine engine being turned on and off, it would spin up to a roar and then spin down to a stillness before it rose again.

I need Zulfiqar!

Yousef fumbled with his cell phone. It was the wrong one. This one was the international one with the number of the American cells. He reached in again, in the truck, keeping low, searching for the second cell phone.

"Allah, please, Allah."

He found the second cell phone and hit the Call button. It rang and rang.

"Zulfiqar, come now, come now!"

"Let it go."

Vaatofu Fury whispered the words as his sniper partner squeezed the trigger. It was the spotter's signal to the sniper to fire the bullet. Villegas's Windrunner .338 Lapua made a muffled *thump* as the silenced round left the barrel.

Fury kept the thermal bi-oculars on the target. The wind-blown sand was blinding, but they could keep track of the target from the warm red shape of a head above the cold blue of the truck body.

The bullet tore through the glass and knocked the terrorist back a foot. The unknown and unnamed red shape disappeared behind the cold blue outline of the SUV.

"We have one more out there," Fury whispered to his sniper and Kevin Moncrief.

"What about Parker?" asked Moncrief. "Can you see him?"

"He hasn't moved. Not since that last shot."

"Any other movement?"

"There's one more out there. I think he's behind that front door, but I don't have the angle." Fury kept scanning the area around the truck with his AN/PAS-28 thermal bi-oculars. The letters AN/PAS were the military designators used to signify that it was a government-bought device and hence the designator *Army/Navy*. Using the invisible infrared light, the bi-oculars amplified the vibrating photons through sensitive optics that made dark objects visible.

"I'm going to get my Marine."

"Don't you want to wait a minute, Gunny?" asked Villegas. "You can't help much if that last one gets you."

Gunny Ndee had a smile, more of a smirk, on his face.

"If you could see me, you would be reading my lips right now, Villegas." The gunny pulled the .45-caliber automatic out of his shoulder holster and pulled the slide back, checking the round in the chamber. He twisted the Titan silencer to make sure it was tight.

"Got it?" Villegas asked.

"Yeah."

"Here's an extra one." Villegas handed him another clip of ammunition. "Keep your head down."

"Hold on a minute, Gunny." Fury held his hand out. "We've got company." Fury scanned down the valley with his thermals. The lights of several trucks were shining on the rocks down the valley and behind Yousef's truck.

"Shit. One, two, three, four." Fury stopped counting. The trucks looked like a convoy. He switched to his throat mike and radio. "Slashing talon six, this is slashing talon one, over."

"One, this is six." Furlong was keeping the conversation to as little as possible.

"One-zero-zero plus coming up the valley." Its meaning was clear to Furlong. A force of more than a hundred was making its way toward them.

"Got them; pull out to alternate bravo."

"Six, this is one. We copy." They were to pull out from their forward position and move back up the valley to a preplanned, alternate meeting site under the protective fire of the second sniper team.

"You fellows go ahead," said Moncrief. "I'm gonna go get my man."

"You sure, Gunny?"

"Hell, yeah, I'm sure."

"Then we ain't going anywhere. We'll cover you."

"We don't have time to debate this." Moncrief pulled out a small pill packet, ripped it open, and swallowed two more super-pills.

"Shit, Gunny, I almost feel bad for the army coming up the hill."

"You got that right." Moncrief flashed a smile, then

dashed down the rocky slope, navigating as best he could at speed through the lunar landscape. The truck still had its lights on, which marked its spot for Zulfiqar's men, but also helped Moncrief keep a bearing on the rock where the tent was. He could hear the trucks coming up the valley and see the beams jumping up and down on the rocks. As he neared the tent, the lights of the others suddenly turned upvalley, toward him, and started to reflect light off the rocks that surrounded him.

"Will?"

Moncrief ducked as a pistol round passed over his head. It wouldn't help to be shot by his own man.

"William? Parker? William?"

Moncrief heard a weak voice on the other side of the rock.

Moncrief saw the figure in between the rocks drop the pointed pistol.

"Damn, William, you look like shit." Moncrief bent over Parker, who was bleeding from a laceration to his arm. Clearly, though, the real problem was the meningitis, which had weakened him severely. He was white, ashen white, even visible in the low light.

"We need to get out of here." Moncrief pulled out a compression bandage and a small glue-like tube of hemostat wound repair from his hip pocket. He pulled up Parker, leaning him against the rock. "This will stop the bleeding."

"Okay. I'm fine."

"Yeah, right."

"There's something we have to take. Here. Carry this." Parker handed him a small but heavy box.

Moncrief raised his eyebrows inquiringly.

"It's one of the missing nuke cores."

"Holy shit." Moncrief looked at the box and then over the rocks toward the lights. "They're coming up here fast. Yousef got himself reinforcements."

"Just get out of here," said Parker. "Take that box to Furlong."

"Marine, I didn't come this far to leave you."

"Okay, then wait two minutes and then fire a round into that truck." Parker handed him the Windrunner and then picked up the pistol lying near Umarov's body.

"Are you sure?"

Parker managed a no-shit smirk, much like the one Moncrief had given Fury.

"All right, then," said Moncrief. "But hurry up."

CHAPTER 70

Yousef's truck

"Praise Allah," breathed Yousef as he saw the convoy moving up the valley.

Now in the truck, Yousef stayed low behind the front wheel, waiting for the others to arrive as the wind whipped over his truck. He checked his rifle again to make sure that the magazine was seated. He had another full clip. He left on the vehicle's lights, knowing that it made him a target, but equally sure that Zulfiqar's men wouldn't find him quickly enough without a lighted beacon to follow.

Whap!

A round struck the front hood of the truck.

Yousef felt the vehicle move, rocked by the force of the round. His fear began to take over again.

Whap!

Another round struck the radiator. Again, the truck rocked back and forth. Liquid started to gurgle out the bottom of the engine.

Yousef rubbed his forehead, feeling extremely feverish. In fact, despite the cold he was dripping in sweat. Muscles shaking.

The lights of the trucks came closer.

Zulfiqar. Come on.

He became emboldened once more by the approaching lights.

Yousef stepped out of the truck and sprayed the rocks with a full clip of ammunition. Sparks popped up as the bullets careened off the harder rocks. He stooped down below the truck, ejected the empty magazine, and loaded another.

Just as Yousef turned to spray the rocks with another clip, he felt a metal cylinder pressed against the back of his head.

"Put the rifle down." The voice was in English.

Yousef didn't turn around. Without doubt, the man he knew as Sadik Zabara would squeeze the trigger. He heard not an inkling of hesitation in his voice. Yousef dropped the rifle.

"You will not escape this valley," said Yousef. "You will die here."

"Lie down on the ground."

Yousef lay spread-eagled with Parker's foot on his back. Parker slid his hand down the side of Yousef's coat, finding a cell phone. He tossed it into the rocks.

Yousef started to raise himself up, and Parker popped him on the side of the head with the pistol.

"Who are you?"

Parker didn't answer.

"I'll have them cut your throat with a dull blade."

Parker ignored the threat and searched through the

other side of Yousef's coat until he found what he wanted. The international cell phone.

"You have meningitis. You can feel it by now. The fever. Neck and head pain? At best, you have a few hours of consciousness left. Do you understand?"

Now Yousef lay in silence.

Parker turned the cell phone on, hunching below the truck and out of sight of the approaching trucks. The phone only had two numbers in it. He looked at them closely, memorizing the numbers carefully despite his head aching, nausea, and fever overwhelming his body.

312?

Chicago.

Parker crushed the second phone and tossed it far in to the darkness. He turned to Yousef.

"December twenty-first, 1988. You recognize the date?"

"No."

"How about Pan Am 103?"

Sullen silence.

Parker cracked Yousef on the back of his skull with the pistol butt. It was a good, solid hit, but only intended to stun him. Yousef would remain conscious, but the disease would continue its progress. The lining to his brain would continue to swell and the bleeding would start. Blood seeping out of the corners of his eyes and ears, his fingers and toes turning black, with the blackness progressing up his legs and arms. Shortly, his legs would not work. He would try to speak, but nothing would come out. Soon the smell of rotten flesh from gangrene would keep any human away. It would not be a fair death nor one that Yousef would want his young son to watch. It would only be fair to the many whose deaths Yousef had caused.

"With exactness grinds He all." Parker slipped into the darkness.

CHAPTER 71

Joint Operations Center, Bagram Airfield

"What the hell is going on?" Scott looked at the thermal sensor from the Predator floating over the valley. An armada of vehicles was coming up the valley, each vehicle loaded with small white thermal dots signifying an army of men.

"Sir, it's a pile."

The airman moved the thermal sensor on the aircraft. In the hillside above the valley two white dots were moving back up the valley. Farther up, three more white dots were on the ridgeline.

Scott could see two white dots next to the lead vehicle. The truck remained motionless. Its lights stood out in the thermal-registered darkness like the beacon of a lighthouse.

"We need some help."

Prevatt sat in the chair in front of the terminal. "I have a fully loaded Predator on station to the south. I can get it up there in thirty minutes."

"But can we get them out of there?"

Prevatt was silent for a moment.

"You had a mission of Blackhawks, but the wind and altitude killed it." Even in perfect weather, Blackhawk helicopters could, at best, climb to a ceiling of fifteen to twenty thousand feet, which barely puts them in the valleys of these ranges.

"Sir, we have another problem." The junior airman zoomed the view on another terminal out to a hundred-mile radius. It was the radar for the sector. Several objects were moving in from the south.

"Pakistani Air Force."

"A flight of helicopters." The airman spoke up. "On the other side of the front."

"Maybe they can help," said Scott.

"I don't think so, sir."

"What's wrong?"

"They will assume that no one is friendly up there," Prevatt cut in, "and if we tell them otherwise, they will probably take your men down just out of spite. Remember: They're missing a couple of freshly stolen nukes. They are royally pissed off. I expect they'll shoot at any moving target. Period."

"What are our options?"

"Your men could pull back into the mountains and wait a couple of weeks."

"That's not an option. One of them is very sick." Scott knew that Parker would never make it another day, let alone another week. Plus, he was contagious. "By now, more than one."

"We have a Marine special-ops team about an hour south of here," said the younger airman.

"If an Army team can't get in with Blackhawks, what are the Marines supposed to do to get there in time?"

"They—ah—have another way of getting there."

Scott looked at the convoy of trucks moving up the pass, then to Prevatt. "What do you think, Colonel?"

Prevatt shrugged. "It's our only choice."

CHAPTER 72

The valley

W*hap, whap.*

Bullets started to pop over Parker's head as he struggled to get back to Moncrief and the safety of the rocks.

Whap. Zing.

Jesus, how many of them are there?

Parker tried to zig and zag, but the disease seemed to have affected his sense of balance. Every step felt as if his foot were sinking into a bog. The wind did the rest, resisting every step he tried to make. He bounced off the boulders, trying to keep his balance.

A much larger caliber bullet flew over his head. This time the rifle was firing from the rocks ahead and shooting back toward the approaching convoy. Moncrief's Windrunner was tearing through the engine blocks of the vehicles in the chase. Occasionally, a man would drop as well. The .338 bullet needed only to strike a meaty portion of the target's body, for then the force of the blow would punch out the arm or the leg or the flank of the target. It was like being pummeled at close range with a shotgun loaded with ball bearings.

Whoosh.

Parker heard the small *crack* that followed as the round passed through the air at supersonic speed. But this time the rifle was coming from yet another direction. From behind Parker came a long, sickly moan.

Gut shot, he thought automatically. *Another sniper from our team, shooting to wound.*

Others in the army heard the man's moans and cries for help, and with those cries others began decelerating their trucks, lightening their attack. The *rat-tat-tat* of AK-47s slowed, like popcorn finishing in a microwave.

"William?"

Parker heard the voice from behind a rock that he just passed.

"Gunny?"

"Well, I hope you got what in the hell you wanted to get. Does the word *Alamo* mean anything to you?" Moncrief's wide smile could be seen in the flash of headlights from the trucks.

"I bet you tell jokes at your best friend's funeral too, don't you?"

"We need to head up to our alternate rendezvous site. It's about a click." Moncrief didn't even ask if Parker could make it. It didn't matter. He had to make it.

"Lead the way."

The gunny had slung over his shoulder a pair of bi-oculars like Furlong's. With bi-oculars, a single lens takes in the light, the thermal computer registers the heat, and the two eyepieces on the other end act like binoculars. The thermal AN/PAS-28 bi-oculars made night into day as Moncrief looked up the valley, and also had a built-in direction finder that pointed the way.

"Stop."

"What is it?"

"Listen." The rifle shots coming from up the valley were increasing, the big bullets volleying over their heads.

"Good, some cover."

"Yeah, and the wind's letting up a little." With the wind dying down, the others in the team were able to better locate their targets and make more kills.

"Come on!"

Moncrief headed north through the *whap*, *whap* of bullets flying past. The pursuing men's shots were not well aimed and flew by harmlessly. But that wasn't the case with Villegas's Windrunner. With each booming shot Parker knew that another man fell.

Six, seven, eight.

"Does that other team know to get out of there?" he whispered to Moncrief.

"They should, but hold on." Moncrief stopped to radio them.

"Slashing talon one, this is slashing talon alpha. Are you on the move?"

"Alpha, this is one. We are out of here."

It was a good thing, as the guns below had become silent.

They're reorganizing and making their plan.

Parker knew that if they were led by an experienced warrior, their leader would adapt to the situation, move his forces uphill, and try to get the high ground. From there, his men could fire rocket-propelled grenades down onto them.

A bright flash of yellow light suddenly lit up the darkness.

The ear-shattering sound of the Predator's strike followed the flash a millisecond later. Parker felt the rush of wind, dust, and chips of rock blow past as he was knocked to the ground by the concussion wave.

"What the hell was that?" Moncrief lay next to Parker, their ears ringing from the blast.

"Our guardian angel." Parker rubbed the dust from his face and eyes.

Just as suddenly, the lights of the remaining vehicles went dark. The ragtag army had learned a painful lesson. Headlights only guided drone bombs to their targets.

"They're gonna move above us," Parker whispered to Moncrief.

"Yeah, and they'll be spreading out so another missile will not catch them together."

"They know that this valley is a dead end. They were raised in these mountains, so they know every rock."

"Shit, yeah."

"Worse problem is that they know there's no way out."

Parker's team was in a box with one side being Zulfiqar and the other three being the twenty-five-thousand-foot Himalayan peaks.

Moncrief nodded. "And as long as they think we have this"—he patted the box that held the nuclear core—"they won't stop, no matter what."

CHAPTER 73

Alternate Site Bravo

"Your man's not looking good." Sergeant Frix leaned over Parker as he spoke to Moncrief. "I'm gonna give him a lollipop. It will at least make it easier."

Frix unwrapped the fentanyl-laced lollipop and stuck it in Parker's mouth. The morphine drug would release into Parker's bloodstream at an even pace.

"What can we do?" The climb had been brutal, taking Moncrief to his physical limits, and Parker beyond that. But the sniper fire had served to make their retreat possible, at least so long as their bodies held out.

"Clark, Clark." Parker was starting to mumble to himself, semiconscious and in obvious pain.

"We need to get him on the antibiotics as soon as we can. And even then, it's going to be close."

"I'm not sure how they are going to get us out of here." Furlong was on his knee, huddled nearby. "The winds are moving fast over the mountains, so they say helicopters are out."

"Do they know about the nuke?" Moncrief had placed the box on the ground in the center in front of them.

"Yeah. Believe me, they do."

"What about the other one?"

Moncrief stared. "There's two?"

"Yeah."

"That may be why he went back to the truck."

"Back to one of their trucks?"

"Yeah."

"How is he, doc?"

"It's going to be close."

Parker lay immobile and seemingly insensate on the ground.

Moncrief looked around in frustration. "There's got to be something else we can do until help comes."

"Did he use both of the IV bags?"

"Both? I don't know. I only saw what looked like one empty bag near the tent."

"There was another."

"In the cooler?"

"Yeah, there were two IV bags."

Furlong shook his head and whispered to Moncrief, "Without that second bag, he has a zero chance. He just didn't get enough antibiotic into him."

"Shit!" Moncrief cried. "All right. I'll go check and see."

"What?" Furlong stared at him. "Have you lost your mind? That tent is a thousand-plus yards from here and in the middle of a beehive."

"I'll go with him." Villegas spoke with his back facing the team as he looked down the valley.

"Like hell you will," said Furlong. "I don't need everyone scattered out all over this damn place."

"I'll be back in an hour," said Moncrief. "If anything happens during that time and I'm not back, go home without me."

"I can stop Villegas, but I can't stop you," said Furlong quietly. "But remember: He may already be dead."

Moncrief shrugged, his mind made up.

"Good luck, Gunny," said Furlong. "We're going to move to alternate site delta."

The move would push them farther up the valley. It would also buy them more time as the army below tried to outflank them.

"I'll keep him alive for an hour," said Frix, pulling out a plastic tube like the one that each of them carried.

"Who are you going to use?" asked Furlong.

"Mine," said Frix. "I know how much to give without burning me out."

Moncrief realized Frix was talking about transfusing his own blood into Parker's system.

He clasped hands with each of them in turn before turning to leave.

"Okay, Gunny," said Furlong. "You have one hour."

The thermal bi-oculars gave Moncrief a chance of making it. They also revealed his situation starkly:

Goddamn, they are every*where.*

He cut down, on the far left side of the valley, thinking that was the one place no one had been. But the small army's leader was also thinking that he didn't want anyone to escape by going downhill. So as Moncrief moved down a washed-out streambed, he saw with his bi-oculars five men moving in the opposite direction.

Shit.

Moncrief stopped, burying himself between two rocks by making himself into a small, tight ball. Even so, he sensed the body heat of the two men as they moved by. He could even smell the same cardamom scent from the tea he'd drunk in the aircraft. More important, they didn't smell him. He didn't stand out.

The two were whispering to each other, stopping within an arm's reach of Moncrief. Even in the foreign language, he could tell by their voices that the two were young, barely out of their teens, and bitching about the cold and the wind.

Bitching: The universal language of the soldier.

Moncrief smiled.

He counted to a hundred after they passed, waiting to be sure that it was safe. And then he climbed out of the rocks and scanned the horizon. The team of five had moved up the creek bed, stopping every so often, and then moving again. He scanned the valley to the different sides and counted the white shapes in the thermals.

Damn, there has got to be more than two hundred out here.

The white shapes appeared everywhere in his biocular's range of vision. Most were walking in line, following a trail on the top of the ridge.

It will be light soon, and they will be above us.

With daylight, the thermals would be neutralized as

an advantage. The high ground was what any force would want.

Moncrief followed the bed farther down the hill, and then cut across using the trail of the two. He felt his Apache blood taking over as he looked for the subtle markings left by both the two that had passed him and the others moving into the valley. At the base of the valley he took his bearings from Yousef's ruined truck and calculated that the tent stood less than a hundred yards away.

"How in the hell am I going to do this?"

Two of the enemy were posted by the site of the tent, seemingly in case Zabara decided to return.

Moncrief drew his pistol and tightened the silencer. But it would take more than the silencer to quiet the round. With the enemy army covering most of the mountainside, a bullet had to be perfectly silent. He sidled up to Yousef's truck, finding the body of a young fighter. Yousef was gone. Moncrief had to get close to the two guards without raising their suspicion.

The sky was starting to turn gray.

I'm running out of time.

He picked up the dead body that had taken the sniper round to the head and hauled it over his shoulder. Moncrief slid the pistol and silencer in between his own chest and the body. The dead man was small and weighed little, even in death.

"*As sala'amu alaikum,*" he called out to the two guards.

Both turned and, seeing a fellow soldier in the dark with a wounded warrior, lowered their rifles for a moment. It only took a moment. Moncrief's silenced rounds tore through each of the guards.

One fell onto the remains of the tent. Moncrief pulled the body away and as he did he struck the boot of another, larger man wedged between the rocks. A moan came from the body.

Moncrief pulled out his pistol and aimed a round at the head of the body on the ground and then, for some reason, paused.

"Shit, I don't have time to pop every damn body."

He turned and dug through the collapsed tent until he felt the outline of a small ice chest. He plunged his hand in and retrieved the full IV bag just as two other fighters marched toward him noisily from the direction of the truck. Moncrief slipped behind the boulder and quietly moved down toward the creek bed, carefully cradling the bag in between his shirt and warm body.

CHAPTER 74

Alternate Site Delta

"Do you see them up there?" Furlong pointed to the ridgeline to both the south and north. They were slowly being surrounded. Now the wind and storm had left, moving off to the east. It had become quiet. Quiet on the battlefield is never good. Like the eye of a hurricane, silence only ever signals the imminent return of the storm.

"They'll be above us if we don't move." Frix was huddled nearby in the rocks with Parker. As it was nearing dawn, the temperature was dropping. Frix's words had a wisp of visible vapor as his warm breath turned cold.

The stars were back, but with the increasingly graying light they were disappearing one by one.

"Can he be moved?"

"I can do it." Parker suddenly stirred, then leaned up from the rock. The transfusion of blood had bought him time and a false sense of security. The fentanyl lollipop hadn't hurt either.

"Captain, you have to make a call."

"What?"

"Now! I may not have much time."

Furlong reached for the radio. A broadcast at this point would let the world know who they were and where.

"Are you sure?"

"As sure as the four million in Chicago."

Parker spoke with Scott only briefly, giving him two cell phone numbers. One was in Chicago and the other, locked in Yousef's phone and Parker's memory, in New York.

The message was sent through the system by a plasma designator. Red hot. No higher designation. In a few minutes, teams from the FBI and Canadian Mounties were chasing the trail of every new transient that had arrived in Canada. The description was a young woman with a limp.

"It's a hump up to that plateau, but they can't get above us." Furlong was studying a laminated map in the gray dark. He was using a small pin light with a red filter and was hugging the bottom of a rock to stay out of sight. "Any chance of you making it, Colonel?"

"Yeah, I can make it."

"What about the gunny?" Frix asked.

"Where's Moncrief?" Parker's face looked chalky in the dark, all the more so framed by his black-and-white checkered shawl wrapped tightly around his neck and *pakol* hat pulled down as far as it would go.

"He went on an errand." Frix put his finger on Parker's neck to check the pulse.

Like the leader he'd been trained to be, Furlong didn't

hesitate with his decision. "Fury, you and Villegas get to LZ Echo on that plateau and lay down cover fire. If the Gunny gets back, Frix will give Parker the IV. We will gather up the rest and join you as soon as we can."

"We'll stay on this eastern face." Fury pointed out a path that cut up the ridge.

James Scott looked up at the digital clocks above the screens in the bridge.

"It's getting near dawn." Prevatt's face showed a look of frustration. The clock seemed to slow down as they waited. Both Scott and Prevatt stared at the thermal feed from the Predator on station above. The two watched the small white dots move in small lines across the terminal screen like ants moving across a sidewalk. The dots seemed to be surrounding a much smaller group of other dots in the center.

"You told them about the core?"

"Oh, yes."

Prevatt had made it clear to the Marine Special Operations Team that the stakes were very high, not merely combat-essential. The MSOT team would not turn around for any reason.

"Checkmate six, this is Dash One."

The radio transmission was being fed directly into the bridge. Everyone in the operations center had gotten a sense of what was going on. The tension was building as the transmissions were broadcast over the speakers.

"Dash One?" Scott questioned the call sign.

"It's a Marine squadron," said Prevatt. "VMM three-six-five. The Blue Knights. I've seen them in Iraq. They come back with their aircraft looking like Swiss cheese, no problem. Nothing stops them."

"How are they going to get through that front?" Scott held up a printout of the weather over the Hindu Kush. The lines of isobars indicated powerful winds when they were close together. Similar to the topography lines on a map, when the parallel lines were bunched together like the engravings on a dollar bill, they indicated one was heading toward a cliff on a map. On the weather map, one was flying through a cliff.

Prevatt looked at the weather map again and shook his head. Mountains that topped twenty-four thousand feet, flying on night vision and close isobars, meant one hell of a ride. In those mountains, there were no ground lights. At well over three hundred knots, a hiccup would mean eating a cliff face.

"Dash one, this is checkmate six."

"We are rocking and rolling up here. We are one zero miles out."

"Dash one, roger." Prevatt was handling the communications directly. "Slashing talon six, are you at LZ Echo?"

"Negative."

Prevatt shook his head. "God, I hope they make it."

Scott nodded. "You and several million fellow citizens."

CHAPTER 75

The evacuation attempt

Whap, whap, whap.

The bullets popped, ricocheting off the rocks that surrounded Furlong, Frix, and Parker. The enemy had now climbed above them, firing down in the morning light.

Seemingly from nowhere came a familiar voice: "Well, how long will this take?"

The trio turned in surprise to find an exhausted Gunny Moncrief crouching next to them, holding the antibiotic solution bag that he had retrieved from the tent.

"It takes what it takes." Frix sounded more like the physician who had finished medical school. "Hey, Gunny."

"What?"

"You did good!"

Whap, whap.

"There are two on that south ridge that have us

zeroed in." Furlong took a brief glimpse around the rock. "But several more are moving up."

"Colonel, how are you doing?" Frix felt Parker's pulse. It was rapid.

"Ready to get out of here." Parker's voice sounded slightly stronger.

"Okay. Just five more minutes." Frix laughed. "You look like shit!"

Parker had a twisted little grin on his face.

"We have to hump it up that hillside." Furlong peered over the rock and then ducked down again. "Now!"

"The way they're zeroing in on us, we don't have more than fifteen minutes. After that you won't have to worry about blood poisoning," Moncrief told Furlong. "You'll have lead poisoning."

Wham.

"There you go." Furlong liked the deeper sound of the .338 Lapua high-velocity round from Villegas. It meant a fair fight.

"Frix, can you carry Parker while Burgey and I do cover?" Furlong checked the magazines. One was empty. He threw it on the ground and put the two loaded magazines in his front pouches so that they could easily be reached.

"I've got it." Parker started to stand up. "Let's get the hell out of here."

"Fifty meters up this hill and then we can run this IV." Frix was being optimistic. "I'll save the rest of this in case you make it to the top."

"I'll lead," said Furlong, "and then Parker will follow. That way, if the pace gets out of whack, you others can help out." Furlong was suggesting that he knew the route but that Parker needed to be near the front or risk being left behind. "Gunny, you have the box."

"Great. So if a stray bullet hits my box, I'm the one that gets vaporized."

"You, us, and all of western Pakistan."

"No problem."

Parker was using his one arm and the pistol with the silencer.

Furlong waited for another *wham* from the Windrunner. It meant one less gun to worry about and the enemy would keep their heads down for a few seconds. He disappeared around the rock.

Parker inhaled, and started to move out. At first he felt the blood rush to his head. Then the adrenaline took over. He followed Furlong's moves, cutting up the goat path that crisscrossed the rocky hillside. Furlong stopped and then Parker stopped. He heard the *whap, whap* of bullets increase as the hostiles detected his team moving up the hill line.

God, I'm thirsty.

Parker felt like his tongue had been glued to the roof of his mouth. He tried to breathe through his nose, stopping only briefly, and then moving, trying to keep his pace irregular so a sniper's aim would be off. For what seemed an eternity, Parker moved up the hillside.

Come on, Clark. Run me into the ground.

The miles and miles they had run through the summer in the sweltering heat, up hills, exhausted, with the muscles in their legs burning—all of the miles were now keeping Parker alive. He actually moved closer to Furlong, using short, choppy steps like a long-distance runner to work his way up the steep hill.

I can do this.

The small object flashed across his vision in the dawn's light. The rocket-propelled grenade missed Furlong and him narrowly, detonating ten to fifteen meters away. Though Parker hunched and knelt instinctively, the blast knocked him to the ground. Matter-of-factly, he managed to stand and begin moving again. He heard Moncrief's rifle firing behind him, the silencer making a *thud, thud* sound with each round. Furlong, a few feet ahead, was down on his face, bleeding from the back and stunned but clearly alive.

A glance across the ridgeline and Parker saw two of the enemy stand with another RPG aimed at Furlong's position. Moncrief was busy reloading. Parker couldn't see Frix or Burgey. He lifted his pistol and took aim. The two-hundred-meter shot would be nearly impossible for a .45-caliber pistol. It took more than aim. It took a sense of the drop of the bullet, like a golf shot being cut around a tree. And the slope. Still, he had to try.

Pop, pop. Parker's silenced pistol fired. The two men with the RPG disappeared.

Parker grabbed Furlong by the belt under his *payraan tumbaan* shirt and lifted him to his feet. Furlong whipped his head around, stunned. Parker put Furlong's arm around his shoulder and both moved up the hill with one dragging the other.

"We need some help if we're going to make it." Parker spoke the words just before the flash.

The Predator's Hellfire struck the other ridgeline.

Another flash and boom echoed across the valley, more missiles dropping in rapid succession now, one after another.

Parker crossed over the edge of the plateau just as a powerful gush of warm wind nearly knocked Furlong and him back over the rocks. Moncrief braced them from behind, keeping them from falling as the air filled with the sulfur-tinged smell of cordite.

The sky before them wavered with heat vapor, then split as the Osprey aircraft rose above the ridge. Its blades, in full tilt, caused the hybrid aircraft to stop in midair and hover directly over Parker's head as the machine gun in its tail sprayed the hillside across the valley with bullets. The hot, small brass casings rained on their heads as they dropped to their knees.

Within what seemed like mere seconds, Parker was surrounded by the Marine Special Op Team setting up a perimeter. He heard their silenced rifles pick off targets rapidly, one by one, as well as the continued boom of the Windrunners firing as he collapsed in the cargo hold of the aircraft.

"Let's get that going again." Frix was already kneeling over Parker, pulling up his sleeve and starting an IV with the remaining bag of antibiotics.

"Don't lose this." Moncrief handed the nuclear-device box like a football to a fast-recovering Captain Mark Furlong.

Parker felt the aircraft become light as it began to rise. He looked out of the open ramp on the end, seeing rocks and smoke and then blue sky.

And then the exhaustion took over.

CHAPTER 76

A Gulfstream over North Africa

"Well, how are we doing, Mr. Jones?"

William Parker felt as if he was awakening from a long night's sleep. He tried to focus his eyes on the physician, in azure-blue hospital scrubs, sitting at his bedside.

"What the hell?"

"Thirsty?"

"Yes." Parker tried to lean up in the bed. The sheets were clean and perfectly bleached white with just a small amount of starch. Somehow, for the first time in days, Parker felt clean, like the sheets. And hungry. He looked at his hands. The dirt of Pakistan remained embedded under his nails.

"Try some orange juice."

"Dr. Paul Stewart."

"Very good. It always helps a survivor of meningitis to remember my name." The Buddy Holly clone from the CDC continued to check the pulse of his patient. "Of course, you survived NM-13. Amazing."

"How about Yousef al-Qadi?"

"He did not make it. Intelligence reported that he made it back to his cave, cold and miserable."

"Any others?"

"My guess would be one or two. If they had someone in their family tree that survived the black plague they had a chance." Stewart had on reading glasses and was looking at the chart that had recorded Parker's vital statistics.

"I remember your telling me about that. Any eastern Europeans with inherited super-immunity."

"That's it. Were there any Europeans there?" Stewart looked up over his glasses.

"I knew of only one." Parker pulled the pillow up under his head. "But he should be dead. Any others?"

"It seems that the people stayed in their cave. We should not see any kind of major outbreak."

"How about our team?"

"Well, you should not have been contagious after getting that first IV, so they should be uninfected. But we're treating them aggressively as a precaution."

Parker looked around the Gulfstream. He was apparently in a medical suite in the rear of the aircraft. The oval windows were all dark with closed shades.

"Do you want to get some more sleep?"

"How long have I been out?" Parker felt stiff, as if every muscle had been strained to its limit.

"You been down for about thirty-six hours." Stewart looked at his watch. "I didn't want to put you back up at altitude while your blood pressure was all over the place."

"Thanks." Parker didn't know how close he had come to lights-out.

"Besides, frankly, I didn't want you and your buddies back in the States until I knew we had this under control." Stewart's CDC side was taking over.

"You didn't want to unleash NM-13?" Parker sat up on the side of the bed, got his bearings. As he sat there, he realized what Stewart was saying. If the disease wasn't stopped for both him and his crew, they would have never left the country. "Okay."

"Where's Scott?"

Stewart shrugged. "A few are up front, but they're all down for the count."

Parker glanced forward and saw the several sofa-like chairs folded out flat with odd-shaped bundles under gray-and-blue blankets. Although daylight crept in through the window shades, the cabin looked like a dormitory after an all-nighter.

The orange juice had an odd taste, which was, for the first time in several days, sweet and rich. Parker tasted the pulp. Following the fever, his senses seemed to be returning to normal.

"Here, take these. I want you to stay on some extra antibiotics for a few days." Stewart handed him what looked like large white horse tablets.

"Okay." He swallowed the tablets with another gulp of the orange juice. "Thanks."

"No. I think I need to thank you, Colonel." Stewart's voice was sober. "They told me enough that I understand the nuclear weapon was recovered because of you."

"How about the one in Chicago?"

"They shut down half of Canada. All along the Lake

Huron area. It's all over CNN." Stewart held Parker's wrist as he spoke checking the pulse. "Some crazy young woman. You can see it up front."

Parker smiled, looking through the doorway to the television screen in the front cabin. The graphics told everything.

Terrorist Cell Seized by FBI and Canadian Mounties with Seaplane Bomb.

No mention of the true nature of the bomb.

Six cell members killed in shoot-out. Pilot was Pakistani Woman.

What the news didn't say—and what Parker would only learn later—was that the girl never made it to takeoff. The airplane was loaded and she had begun her taxi out into the lake for takeoff, but a bullet from the Canadian Mounty reaction team caught her in the chest. The airplane's wing dipped, and it taxied across the water into the shoreline. The team found her dead, surrounded by maps and photographs of the South Haven Lighthouse. The cabin was full of blocks of explosives and, in the center, there was a small nuclear core.

Her dream remained a dream.

She had a look on her face, with her eyes fixed, open, big, brown, as if she had made the final turn to the target. Next to her, on her lap, was a small, odd round bundle of socks tied tightly together by loops of plastic bags. The Canadians were, at first, not sure of it, and carefully removed it wary of what it contained. Later, it was determined that the small round ball was harmless. It closely resembled the homemade "footballs" used by children in rock-and-dirt soccer pitches near the ghetto of Danish Abad.

They stopped it.

"What about Hernandez?"

"Who?"

"Never mind. Where are we going?"

"London."

CHAPTER 77

The FBI's Strategic Operations Center, Washington, D.C.

"We have a new name that has surfaced," said a mid-level special agent who had arrived late for the meeting and just joined the group around the table.

"Who?" The director, like everyone in his operation center, now starting a third day without sleep.

"A Chechen."

That caught Tom Pope's attention. They'd had virtually no Chechens on their watch lists until Boston. The Chechens hated Russia, not America. Now, the world's lists were all being revised. For good reason.

"Abu Umarov." The agent went on to say that the Bureau's G-cell in the Strategic Information and Operation Center had picked up the name in randomly monitored cell traffic.

"I know that name. Wasn't he connected to Yousef?" Pope could afford to be direct. His stock had gone sky-high within the Bureau. CNN was running with the lead story that the two stolen nuclear weapons had been retrieved in a lightning raid in Pakistan, but the world never knew how close it came to Chicago being vaporized. "I thought they were all dead in that valley."

"Excuse me, sir." At that moment, Garland Sebeck stood at the door to the conference room. He looked much like someone who was holding on to a secret.

"Mr. Director, may I go talk to my assistant?" Tom Pope rolled his chair back.

"Sure, go ahead, but let me know what you find out."

Tom Pope walked out into the hallway. He still had his coffee mug in hand. He used the mug to point to a smaller secretary's office across the way, its occupant missing for the moment. Pope closed the door behind Sebeck.

"There's something." Sebeck had a red folder marked TOP SECRET. "This is from one of our field agents stationed in Guam."

As Pope read the report, he thought of something. "You remember Chantilly?"

"Sure, your IT buddy." Sebeck had jibed his boss on more than one occasion about Pope's "pet geek."

"Did you see that last report he e-mailed yesterday?"

"The traffic from that computer at Langley?"

"There was one e-mail to a BlackBerry in New York. It mentioned two names."

Sebeck smiled.

"Yeah, the names Scott and Parker."

"Scott was that Brit on the conference call."

"Yes, he was."

“Let’s get Chantilly to trace the BlackBerry. My guess is that it connects back to Langley.”

“That shouldn’t be a problem.”

“There were some independents. I saw an intel report several years ago. Killers for hire. The suspicion was that they were CIA-connected.”

“Let me guess?”

“Robert Tranthan.”

“Yes.”

“And we need to ask Mr. Scott how we can find Parker.” Tom Pope looked back at the red folder, flipping the sheet within. The report recorded a detailed interview. “I knew it.” As Pope continued to read, his face started turning red. “I goddamn knew it!”

CHAPTER 78

London

Parker slowly buttoned the shirt, sitting on the edge of the bed in the Gulfstream jet's medical suite. The shirt was too large, especially after his loss of nearly fifteen pounds from the last several days. His cheeks had a hollowed look and, although color was coming back to his face, he still saw shadows under his eyes. But for the first time in days his face was clean-shaven.

Parker squeezed his hand, testing his arm. The knife wound, fortunately, had been more of a glancing blow. It had been stitched and was already scabbing up.

"I have some good news." Scott was standing at the door as the Gulfstream taxied to a parking spot at Luton International Airport, about an hour's drive from London.

"What?" Suddenly Parker realized how low his batteries were. He wouldn't have a lot of energy for a long conversation.

"We're stopping here to pick up another passenger. You want to guess?"

Parker gave him a quizzical look.

"Apparently someone from Saudi Arabia thought they needed to keep one of us for safekeeping. It couldn't be me or you."

"Hernandez?"

"Yeah, you got it in one."

"Is he all right?"

"You can ask him in a moment."

Parker stood up, tucking the shirt in his pants that were—like the shirt—two sizes too big.

Scott indicated the door with a nod of his head.

Parker walked to the open hatch, looking out to a drizzly, rainy midday at Luton. A long black limo pulled around the hangar and stopped at the bottom of the aircraft's steps.

"What the hell?" Moncrief was standing behind Parker, looking down the steps. "I knew he'd do anything to get out of a mission, but this is ridiculous."

Hernandez climbed out of the limo with two others. One was a well-dressed Saudi wearing a white, open-collared shirt and a dark pinstriped suit. The cut of the suit was from Savile Row and had the shape of accented broad shoulders, tapered down to a thin waist. He seemed a man of royalty. The other was similarly dressed but was very different. He too had well-cut clothes, but his stomach bulged out from the suit and raincoat he had on.

"Hey, Colonel." Enrico Hernandez didn't look any worse for wear.

Parker grabbed Hernandez's arm in a shake, like the Roman warriors of yore, above the wrist, then hugged his teammate.

"Are you all right?"

"Yes, sir. At first it was kind of crazy, but Ali took care of me."

Ali stood next to Hernandez.

"Colonel, I have heard much of you. I am Prince Ali bin Saud. On behalf of my nation and my father, we wish to thank you. Yousef al-Qadi had become a danger to us all."

"Then why take Hernandez?"

"Both you and Hernandez had become targets. If we didn't take him in, the *Crni Labudovi* henchmen would surely have. Knez was on your trail, as you know, but there were more. One particular man was right on Enrico's tail when we stepped in."

Parker looked over Ali bin Saud's shoulder. Another man was standing back, looking around, seemingly uncomfortable, scanning the buildings around the runway.

"Colonel, this is Mr. Zaslani of Mossad." Scott stood at the bottom of the stairway. "So you were able to find Hernandez after all?"

Zaslani didn't say anything, but looked sheepishly away from Scott.

"The hunt for Yousef al-Qadi certainly made for some odd bedfellows."

Parker was reminded of the fable about the scorpion and the tortoise. Each needed each other to cross the river, but in the end both died.

"Colonel," said Ali, "my father wishes to show his appreciation for your help."

Parker just shook his head. "That's not necessary."

"We will do something."

"Just make it up to Hernandez."

"You don't have to worry about that, Colonel." Hernandez was beaming. "My little girl has a scholarship for college, for medical school, for any degree she wants."

"Good." Parker looked back to Scott and the airplane behind him. Parker did a double take.

"Your eyes do not deceive you," said Scott. "We have a transatlantic flight of our very own."

As their jet taxied onto the active runway, Parker leaned across the aisle. "Prince Ali bin Saud. Should I know who he is?"

"Yes, his father is the secretary of the Bay'ah Council. You have a very powerful friend."

CHAPTER 79

A safe house on the outskirts of Peshawar, Pakistan

"I need money."

The hulking Chechen leaned forward on the mattress, holding his head in his hands.

"You are lucky, my friend." The doctor, a friend to Liaquat Anis since medical school, sat in a chair across the small room. He was the lucky one, working with the sick at Lahore General Hospital. He had a job.

"A concussion and . . ." he leaned back in the straight back wooden stick of a chair. "A survivor of meningitis."

"Allah has a purpose." Umarov's eastern European village had survived another disease several forefathers ago. The black plague had given him an immunity unique to his survival.

"No one survives."

"I did."

"We found what you were looking for." Another man, much younger, with a long, curled black beard and a dirt-covered robe, came into the room. "A man we know had been hired to kill him in London."

Umarov looked up. His forehead still had a blood-damped bandage wrapped around it.

"Yes."

"The kill was canceled later."

"By who?"

"He wouldn't say."

"Well, who is this piece of shit?"

"He was an American by the name of William Parker. He was Zabara. He stopped the Canada cell."

Umarov stared at the man as he spoke the words.

"Parker?" Umarov stood up. "His name is Parker?"

"Yes. Here is what you need."

"Passport?"

"Everything."

"And money."

"Yes, everything. U.S. dollars. And he may still be in Afghanistan. Our people tell us he was sick when he came out of the mountains. You may have a day on him."

"I understand."

"Your airplane leaves in just a few hours. London and then Atlanta."

CHAPTER 80

Cusseta, Georgia

"Excuse me?"

The girl behind the counter of the Chevron gas station barely looked up. It was late, near closing, and her cash register was off. "Yeah?" Her southern accent stretched out the one-syllable word.

"I'm looking for Highway 39."

The Chevron stood near the back door of Fort Benning, one of the largest Army bases in the South. This particular back door, however, lay in the middle of nowhere. Except for the lights of the station, the highway was dark and lonesome. The only neighbors of the gas station were the miles of pine trees.

"It's just down twenty-seven, about ten miles south of here." Now she looked up at the person she had been speaking to . . . and tried not to stare. *God, he is big.* The clothes were off-brand. His upper arms stretched the sleeves of the plain polo shirt to the point that they almost seemed to cut off the blood. He wore a Braves baseball cap, but it was still full of color, fresh, new as if purchased that very day in the Atlanta airport. It covered up his forehead. His hair was an orange and red, cut short on the sides, almost like a military cut.

"Okay." The man was orienting his map. He wrote on it with a black marker.

The bell for the station's door rang as three men in camouflaged Army combat uniforms came inside. They all had the same tan berets and sand-colored combat boots.

"Hey, Melinda! My beautiful Melinda."

The girl smiled at the attention.

The man in front of her looked quickly away from the soldiers. *Odd,* she thought.

"What you boys want?"

"We're done for the day and need some cold ones." One soldier put a six-pack of Budweiser on the counter.

Another soldier nudged his buddy, looking to the man with the map. "Excuse us, sir. We didn't mean to step in front of you."

"No, I was just asking for directions."

His English was okay, but he had some sort of accent, which seemed more noticeablc now. The girl almost asked, but he was already gone.

"Hey."

In the one word said over a cell phone, Clark felt a sense of relief. Just one word. She looked at the clock. It was nearly midnight. But she knew he wouldn't call until it was over. That was the deal. Don't call until it is over. Period.

"Hey, you."

"I need a run, a good long run."

"Yeah, me too." It made for an odd date; but then again, there was nothing like a good ten-miler. "When do you want to do it?"

"How about at first light?"

"Sounds good."

"See you in six hours."

"Six hours."

She closed the cell phone, and as she did, Clark looked up from the kitchen window. A security light on a motion detector suddenly illuminated the trees near the lodge. The trees, mostly longleaf pines, had been planted by William away from the lodge and down the slope, so that the security light was illuminating the tops more than a dozen yards away. They moved in the casual breeze. The marsh pines were survivors that could withstand the random fires, bugs, and diseases of the hot, humid summers. They left a dark, nearly impenetrable space underneath their canopy that was thick with layers of pine straw. But the light was set at a high setting. It didn't randomly go off.

What the hell could that be?

Clark walked to the front hall, where a cavernous stone floor stayed cold all year long, especially during the winter. She could feel the cold pass through her running shoes as she stood next to the door and looked out through the glass of the tall French doors. The doors were stained a dark mahogany, thick, and were tall like the entranceway. The glass was intentionally thick. When one opened the door, it swung heavily on the hinges.

The security light in the front was also illuminated. A breeze pushed leaves from some live oaks up the road across the front of the lodge.

Clark went back to the kitchen. The lodge was isolated, alone, on top of its hill, but she hadn't felt unsafe. She looked at her cell phone. It was fully charged. She scanned the numbers, seeing the first number on the directory: Mack, the deputy sheriff. She looked up, again, out the kitchen window, only this time to see a face staring back at her.

Clark cried out in surprise, dropping her cell phone to the floor, her heart racing out of control. She heard the crack of glass as she scrambled to find her phone on the floor.

"Oh, my God."

She grabbed the cell phone as she heard another crack of the glass over her head. Clark ran to the rear of the lodge, holding on to the phone, glancing over her shoulder to see a man tear the door down in the kitchen with the thrust of his body.

Think!

She had discussed this with William several times.

Get to the bedroom.

It was the first line of defense. Go upstairs, lock the solid wood door, use the few seconds before he came through it to call and get to the shotgun. Not the pistol. It had to be a shotgun. William had said it numerous times. When scrambling for one's life, few could hold a straight shot. A shotgun left plenty of room for error.

Crack.

A bullet went just over her right shoulder. With the one shot, she realized that this wasn't a random burglary or robbery. This was a killing. He wasn't coming for her, either. First her and then William.

Clark slammed the door and threw the bolt. She tried to breathe.

Step away from the door.

He had told her that several times. As she did, a bullet cracked the wood.

Breathe and think.

Now Clark understood why he had wanted her to run, to run a marathon. It gave her the chance to breathe, to survive. Her heart seemed frantic, pounding in her chest.

Call.

Clark scanned through the cell phone directory, trying to get back to the first number.

"Goddamn it." Her hand was shaking. Finally, she hit the number. Another bullet cracked the wood, followed again by a second. It seemed to be more of a message. The number rang and then rang again. She hadn't even had the millisecond of time for the thought that it was actually well past midnight.

"Hello?"

"Mack, this is Clark. I have someone breaking in."

Mack was the closest one. There was no time for Stidham or anyone else. Mack would blue-light it, and he knew the country roads.

"Okay, I'm on my way."

Another bullet ripped through the door around the hinge, followed by a series of bullets fired at the different door hinges. Clark grabbed the twelve-gauge shotgun and fired the Dixie Tri-ball three-inch shell at the door. It was a mistake. The large steel balls, the size of marbles, ripped through the wood, fracturing the door, only helping to dismantle it.

Clark fired the second shot at the window. The shotgun slammed into her shoulder like a baseball bat. It also ripped the glass and frame of the window from the wall. She jumped through the opening at the same time that a figure broke through what was left of the bedroom door. A portion of the roofline extended out on the second floor. Clark landed on her shoulder on the cold, ribbed, vertical steel-paneled roof. Her momentum kept her going as she slid down the panels and then fell over the edge. A gutter hung up her fall for a brief second, and as it did a bullet hit her arm, cutting the flesh like a hot poker. Its force helped push her off the roof.

Clark landed in a thick line of azaleas that lined the edge of the house. It broke the force of her fall but didn't stop her from slamming into the ground. She gasped for air, trying to get up on her knees.

Stay within the edge of the house.

He had told her to use whatever protection possible. Clark knew that the shadow would be waiting at the window's opening for her to run to the woods. Her movement would activate the security lights, and the lights would then cause her death. It would be an easy shot.

She moved slowly, on the ground, only putting her weight on her left arm once. The pain shot through the arm, causing her to collapse like an umbrella. She suppressed a scream.

Clark worked her way down the edge of the house and then around the corner. She was directly below the security light and its sensor. All four corners of the lodge had lights with sensors. Clark reached to the ground and picked up two rocks. She threw one around the corner back toward where the bedroom was. The light on the back of the house suddenly came on, and with it a bullet zipped back toward a shadow near the tree line.

She threw the other rock directly upward to the light above, and when it lit up the front of the lodge, another bullet zipped past the edge.

Clark ran across the front of the house, staying close to the wall, and then at the far end of the lodge sprinted across the open space to the drop-off and the tree line below. She crashed through the limbs, tripping on the pine straw and falling flat on her face. The straw cushioned the blow. Clark tried to breathe, getting up to her knees and moving deeper into the darkness, away from the light.

Her cell phone still lay on the floor of her bedroom.

CHAPTER 81

The farm

Midnight brought a full moon and a bitter cold to south Georgia.

William Parker turned up the heat in the cab, looking at the digital clock on the dash display of the Sierra truck. It showed 5:46 A.M. The sun would be breaking through the darkness soon.

It surprised Parker how his body had regained its energy. Most of the trip had been spent sleeping, taking in calories, and building his strength. Stewart's magic combination of antibiotics had worked their miracle.

Only a buzz in my ear. Not bad.

The doctor told him the tinnitus might never go away. It was a small price to pay for surviving NM-13. He was getting stronger. The shoulder was sore, but it was only a flesh wound. He felt his adrenaline starting to kick in again as he neared his land.

My land.

There was something about it being his land. Without a survey, Parker knew exactly where the property line was. A large white oak marked it.

A shape moved in the shadow at the edge of the road.

Parker turned his headlights on high, only to see the large ears and green glowing eyes of a doe standing at the edge of a pine forest. She stared directly at his lights, frozen in fear, as he slowed down.

The doe was fat. The rains during the summer had provided a forest full of thick clover. Her coat was gaining a darker, grayer look, so as the days became shorter and the sunlight decreased, she could absorb more of the sun's energy. Soon she would be chased by the buck, pulling him out of the deep woods.

The yellow clay road forked away from the highway just a mile beyond the white oak. He hadn't improved the beginning of the road so as not to attract any visitors. It would be more than a hundred yards into the road before it turned into gravel and another hundred yards to the gate. From the gate it would turn into asphalt, where it would wind around the airfield and then start to climb up the ridgeline.

Odd.

Clark rarely left the gate open.

The dawn had broken through the night. Even in the valley, the light was starting to reach the ground.

Something isn't right.

The road turned past the airfield. The hangar was closed. There was no sign of life, no movement whatsoever. After the airfield, the single lane of asphalt cut a path up the hillside to the top of the finger of rock. Parker followed the road as it climbed up the grade where on top it was level all the way to the lodge.

Jesus, what is that?

A deputy sheriff's car straddled part of the road, with the nose of the car buried into the base of a pine tree. The white-and-black patrol car, with its gold lettering, still had the engine running. The driver's door was open, and the uniformed leg of its owner was outside, in an odd, twisted angle with the shiny Corfam shoe barely touching the ground.

Parker pulled up his truck to the side of the road behind the cruiser. He moved carefully, scanning the tree line, looking down the road to the lodge at the far end. A bullet hole was in the center of the driver's front windshield. The deputy sheriff might have seen the flash the instant before his death. Parker checked Mack's pulse just above his collar. The skin was slightly cool. His eyes were fixed, wide open. *Dead*.

Parker reached over only to find the deputy's holster empty. If he had a shotgun, it was missing as well. The radio mike's wire was cut just below the mike.

"Damn." Parker glanced toward the lodge again. "Clark."

He glanced at the truck. If he took off, it would be thirty miles to the nearest gas station. She may already be dead, but he wasn't leaving without finding out. The one thing he knew for sure was that the killer was looking at him at that very moment. Parker could feel the sights of a rifle pointed in his direction.

Why am I not already dead?

The shooter must not be sure of his target. This meant one of three things. Either Clark was dead, or she wasn't cooperating, or she had gotten away. If she had gotten away, he had a fairly good idea of where she was. It would be the one place the shooter wouldn't go to.

Parker looked to the tree line, walked back to his truck, and just before getting to the door he dropped to the ground. As he did, a silenced bullet ripped through the glass of his driver's door.

He dashed to the tree line, jumping over a downed limb, and as he did a second silenced bullet tore through his right leg, causing him to tumble into the bushes. Parker felt the warm blood gurgle through the blue jeans. The bullet had only grazed the flesh, but it was still bleeding like a knife wound. It did, however, give him a chance. He scrambled up to his feet, moving to a line of pine trees, following them across the slope. He cut down the hill, trying to get to the deeper brush, like the buck moving to cover.

Whap. Another bullet struck the tree just above his head.

Parker ducked, turned, and landed on his other leg. He glanced back, then rolled down the hill toward the brush.

A .223.

Parker glanced at the man who came toward him.

Who is this son of a bitch?

The worst of it was that the man's face showed no emotion. He was moving through the woods methodically. Parker only had one advantage. He knew the land.

"There's no point in running," Umarov yelled from above. "You're wounded. I can see your blood."

Parker moved along the side of the ridgeline, staying in the trees just above the deep brush. He tried to move toward the lodge, but the hunter kept the high ground, moving along in a parallel path, staying between Parker and the lodge.

The blood from the wound started to saturate the jeans. Parker cut farther down the hill, stopping behind a rock that was surrounded by the pines. He tore off a strip of his shirt and wrapped it several times around the wound, cinching it tightly until the bleeding stopped.

"I have plenty of time." The voice projected above the pine trees.

No weapon and the lodge were becoming unreachable with the wound. Parker's foot was tingling either from the blood loss or nerve damage of some sort. And time was running out. For him and possibly Clark.

How can I go on the offensive?

"Your girl is dead."

The killer was trying to get Parker to say something, anything. It would help locate his target. Parker hoped the bastard was bluffing, frustrated at losing both his targets.

Parker moved across the hillside, not climbing nor descending. He worked his way to the north of the lodge. The killer followed, sounding like a bull, through the brush and trees.

Whap, whap.

Two more rounds cracked just above Parker's head. He stopped, exposing himself in an opening, seeing the killer put the rifle up to his shoulder.

Whap.

The bullet knocked several small tree limbs to the ground.

That's it! He's in blue jeans.

Parker knew just what to do.

Blue jeans!

And it was getting light by the second.

Parker ran, favoring his hurt leg, down the path. His lungs started to burn, his mouth becoming dry.

Shock.

He put fingers to his neck, gauging his pulse. It was becoming rapid and weak. He was starting to see stars. Time was running out.

He hobbled into another opening on a ledge and fell to the ground. His head was swimming.

The man stood just above Parker on the path, rifle to his shoulder.

Parker tried to get up on his one knee, the wounded leg stretched out straight. His hand closed around a sizeable rock.

"Get up. It's over," said the big man, clearly relishing the words.

"Not hardly." The voice came from above and behind Parker's pursuer.

Parker moved only his eyes to gauge the new arrival. To his surprise, he recognized the man: the same Marine who'd been hunting illegally on the property. He had returned to the ledge to hunt the buck in the valley. In fact, he had the same Remington 700, trained squarely on a very different target.

"What?" Abu Umarov turned, pointing his weapon at the hunter. At the same moment, Parker's rock struck the Chechen again squarely on the temple where he had received the same blow just a few days before. The blow caused him to squeeze the trigger of his weapon prematurely, sending a round into the dirt. The young hunter also pulled the trigger, but his round didn't miss. The deer rifle lifted the Chechen off his feet, blowing him back against the rocks and leaving him lying in a growing pool of his own blood.

"You still with us?"

James Scott stood over Parker on a stretcher.

"Clark?"

"Yeah, we found her where you said she would be. On the running trail. She's lost some blood, but they're bringing her out now."

The airfield looked like a military encampment, with several Huey helicopters parked on the tarmac. All of the aircrafts were black, with *FBI* in large white letters on their sides.

"Colonel, I'm Tom Pope."

A man in a dark blue suit stood over the stretcher.

"He followed us home?" Parker tried to lean up on the stretcher.

"Yeah. Everyone has been wanting this guy for a very long time."

"I had another chance and thought he was dead."

"Well, this time you thought right." Pope smiled.

Parker did the same.

"Lucky about running into that friendly, eh?" said Pope. "In the middle of nowhere."

Parker took a swig from a bottle of water, trying to rehydrate himself. "Not entirely luck," he said.

Pope raised an eyebrow. "How's that?"

"Were you ever a deer hunter?"

"No."

"Deer hunters never wear blue jeans. The one color a deer can recognize is blue. Mike Hendley would have known that this guy was not a hunter and should not have been there. Period!"

"Damn."

"Are you a baseball fan, Mr. Pope?" Parker continued.

"Yeah," said Pope. "The Cubs," he added, almost apologetically.

"Imagine being offered a chance to throw out the first pitch on opening day at Wrigley."

"Okay?"

"Would you miss it?"

"No."

"It's deer hunting season and our young friend had a personal invitation from me to come here and try to get himself a trophy deer. There was no way he wasn't coming back."

CHAPTER 82

Room 131, Russell Senate Office Building, Washington, D.C.

"Thank you for coming, Robert."

The senator rarely used the conference room that was adjacent to his office in the old Senate office building. The old stained mahogany panels and the crystal chandelier set the tone of authority. The Russell Building's cornerstone had been laid only six years prior to the sinking of the *Titanic*. In fact, it was in the Russell's hearing room six years later that senators debated how the impossible had occurred. Later, Senator McCarthy had held his infamous hearings in the same location.

"Senator."

Robert Tranthan knew that the senator disliked being called "Dad" by his son-in-law. He had never liked Tranthan, particularly after learning the true story of Robert Tranthan's humble background. It was a relationship of tolerance. Each tolerated the other, barely.

The older man nodded, but not in a friendly way.

He won't do anything. He wouldn't even try.

"I have someone here to talk to us."

The senator had an unpleasant habit of phrasing matters in terms of "us."

The senator picked up the telephone and hit the intercom button.

"Send them in."

Tranthan wasn't surprised by Pope or Sebeck. It was the third one who caught him unawares.

"I understand you have met Agents Pope and Sebeck. And you also know Nurse Cook."

It wasn't a question.

"Mr. Tranthan, you are under arrest for the murder of Margaret O'Donald." Pope held out a set of handcuffs, signaling Robert Tranthan to turn around. "Also, the conspiracy to murder James Scott and William Parker."

"What?"

"You gave the names of both Scott and Parker to a contract killer. You knew what that meant."

"You will never prove any conspiracy to kill those two." Tranthan was wildly looking for his cigarettes as he spoke.

"Probably," said Pope. "But we can prove Margaret O'Donald's premeditated murder, which should be worth all the years remaining in your life."

"Think of the embarrassment this will cause you," Tranthan said, turning to the senator.

"I'll take it."

"What about your daughter?"

"She has already started divorce proceedings." The senator gave him a rare smile. "Oh, you didn't know?"

Robert Tranthan's face turned ashen white.

"She was always smarter than you, Robert." The senator chuckled as the FBI men led Tranthan out of the room. "She learned the lesson long ago. Sometimes you have to cut your losses."

CHAPTER 83

One month later, the cabin

Parker stood next to his truck, waiting for his visitors.

They're early.

The small King Air twin banked over the lodge on the other side of the airfield as it turned the base leg and then entered its final descent.

It was another cold, clear, cloudless day. The hardwoods had all lost their leaves, leaving only the pines to hold the emerald-green color on the hillsides. With the end of deer season, it had become safe again to walk in the woods.

Parker turned up his collar and pulled down the orange-and-blue baseball cap close to his ears. The hat's Day-Glo orange was a safety feature that helped hunters distinguish between a human and a deer moving through the trees. Even in the off-season, it paid to wear a little orange when walking in the woods.

The pilot stepped on the brakes as the airplane rolled up to Parker at the runway's edge. James Scott was the first one out the door, followed by Moncrief. Another man followed.

"Well, Colonel, you got your color back." Moncrief gave him a bear hug, which Parker happily returned.

"Welcome back," Parker said to Scott.

"Hello, Colonel. And you remember Prince Ali bin Saud."

"*As sala'amu alaikum.*" Parker shook the man's hand, and then touched his own heart. "Your father is now the king?"

"*Walaikum as sala'am,* Colonel Parker. Yes," said Prince Ali bin Saud, "my father wanted to express his thanks. And how are you?"

"I'm well, thanks. Recovering, anyway."

"What about you and Clark?" asked Moncrief, direct as always.

"It's none of your business." Parker smiled. "I'll tell you this much. We have another marathon scheduled."

"Oh, yeah? Which one?"

"Oahu."

The plan was for them to heal together, rebuild their strength, and then move on. Running was now in her blood, and she liked the idea. The Honolulu Marathon was now one of the largest races in the world. Given what Clark and Parker had survived, though, a marathon no longer seemed like much of a challenge.

"What about you, Gunny?" asked Parker. "Got some houses to paint, I imagine?"

Moncrief laughed out loud. "Like hell!" He cut his eyes to the prince, then back. "I have tickets for the Yankees!"

"I have something for you too," Scott said to Parker. He indicated the red file and pointed to the hangar.

"Gentlemen, if you don't mind, I need to borrow him for a second."

Parker wasn't sure what was going on, but followed Scott the few paces to the inside of the hangar.

"What is it?" Parker asked.

Scott's face darkened. "The man who put your mission together in the first place? Well, it turns out he didn't want to leave a trail. Exactly what he did is unnecessary—and illegal—for me to tell you. Suffice it to say that he murdered one of our people in Doha and then tried to take out both you and me."

"Where is he now?"

"Supermax. The Alcatraz of the Rockies. For life."

Parker shook his head. Death was a better option than Supermax. It was solitary until the day you breathed your last.

"This is for you, Colonel." Scott handed him the blood-red folder. "I promised you the rest of the story."

Parker opened the cover. The label inside was simple. Only one phrase in bold:

The Lockerbie Report
TOP SECRET
AUTHORIZED EYES ONLY

"Nothing held back or redacted," said Scott. "Are you sure you want to read it?"

Parker nodded. "Yes."

ACKNOWLEDGMENTS

It takes a village to make a story and I greatly appreciate each member of my village. A thriller such as this is meant to entertain, but also possibly to give one thought about our need, always, for heroes. For we are fortunate that such guard our nation. In my two tours with the USO, I have had the honor of meeting many. Some have served on the front lines, in combat patrols, and some have served in the scorching heat of an outpost literally in the middle of nowhere so that the supplies can get to the front or the airplanes can be loaded for their missions—or just so that the world can know that there is someone guarding the gate. All are greatly appreciated.

And the authors who have participated in the USO tours have faced risks for the first time in their lives just to say thank-you to the troops. More than fifteen well-known authors have now participated in Operation Thriller and have flown across half the world to say hello to a corporal serving from Fort Benning or Camp Lejeune or many of our country's other bases.

When a C-130 drops out of the sky in an effort to avoid ground gunfire to land in Mosul, one appreciates the sacrifice that the troops make by being there, but also that of the people who give of their time to the

USO, and of course, the USO itself. Jeremy Wilcox and Lonnie Cooper spend countless hours on the road, often in C-130s and C-17s, supporting the tours, and their work is also greatly appreciated.

I am sincerely grateful to Gary Goldstein for being dedicated to the craft of writing and serving as a most talented editor and advisor. Likewise, to Karen Auerbach, Arthur Maisel, Adeola Saul, and all the staff at Kensington Publishing, who are determined to produce the best story possible: I thank you. And John Talbot, my dedicated agent: I'm thankful for your taking on just one more.

David Morrell has provided much-appreciated counsel and advice. It is a privilege to know one of the masters. And Kathy Reichs has also been generous in both advice and insight. Paul, a fellow Marine, has been a great sounding board. To all of my good friends and fellow writers at Queens University of Charlotte, thank you for your insights and suggestions.

Tom Ragsdale has also been a much-appreciated advisor, and he is an exceptional fellow Marine.

Ed Stackler has been an editor who has weathered a barrage of ideas that just didn't work. I greatly appreciate the skill and insight he has provided. And a special thank-you to my friend and coauthor Andy Peterson, who fearlessly chaired Operation Thriller into Afghanistan.

Meryl Moss has been an invaluable advisor, as has M. J. Rose—for their insights and suggestions on the trade, a thank-you to both.

Rick Sheehan works too hard! And I am one of the ones who has been served so well by his advice and generosity. My alias is Andy Harp and his work is www.andyharp.com.

I greatly appreciate Dr. Cecil Whitaker for his medical insight and Kevin Harcourt for his aviation acumen. If there is a technical error in this story on either point, it is the author's fault for asking the wrong question. To George Scott, who has dedicated his life to giving people the thrill of meeting a new author and who created Books for Heroes, thank you, as well.

Michael Goldman, my good friend and fellow ATO, knows the Yankees, and his introspection concerning the team and its stars was of great benefit. I greatly appreciate the help of Greg Grasso for his creative thoughts, Thom Hendrick for his talented eye, and Leigh and Alan Jenkins, and Rich Ikin for their suggestions and advice.

The hunting scenes would not have captured reality without the help of the *Tiny Bell* crew: Jimmy, Skipper, Sonny, Bobby, Dick, Neil, Jerry, Tommy, James, Richard, Steve, Grayson, Johnny, David, Mike, Allen, Gary, Warner, Glenn, Harold, Butch, and all the rest of the gang!

And most important, to those who serve in harm's way, to the Marines of Marine Special Operations Force, the Army's 75th Ranger Regiment, the U.S. Army Sniper School, the 11th Marines, and to those whom I cannot mention other than to express my gratitude, to SFC J——, C——, Capt. A——, Gunnery Sgt. J——, and the many, many others: for what they do that you will never know about, thank you.